ERNEST LANGFORD

Necessities of Life

A N o v e l

Battle Street
B O O K S

BATTLE STREET BOOKS
175 Battle Street
Kamloops, BC
Canada V2C 2L1

Publisher's note: This book is a work of fiction. Characters, places and incidents are the product of the author's imagination, or are used fictitiously. Any resemblance to actual places or persons, living or dead, is coincidental.

Canadian Cataloguing in Publication Data

Langford, Ernest, (date)
    Necessities of life

    ISBN 0-9699324-6-4

    I. Title
PS8573.A555N42 1996   C813'.54   C96-910129-5
PR9199.3.L323N42 1996

Distributed by Gordon Soules Book Publishers Limited
1354-B Marine Drive
West Vancouver, BC
Canada V7T 1B5

Cover and book design by Warren Clark

Printed in Canada

For Caroline

Chapter 1

"Know something?" Jamie Powell, poet, said to Alice Morgan, chartered accountant. "My brain's hardly functioning."

"You're lucky to have a brain. All I've got is common sense," replied Alice.

"How clever of you to have something so rare," Jamie said.

"Don't be a smart ass," Alice said.

The day was Sunday, the time 3:12 p.m., the month April, the year 1977. They were lying on Alice's single bed, Jamie diagonally, with his head propped against Alice's stomach, Alice across the bed, head hanging over one side, legs over the other. All Jamie could see of Alice's face was her china-white jaw, which reminded him of the base of a dry cereal box. For inexplicable reasons, Jamie geometrized most things in his life; even his poems emerged in geometric shapes. He turned, sniffed the skin around Alice's navel and remarked that she smelled of cow-cudded clover. That comment caused Alice to raise her head and stare at Jamie with her intensely blue eyes set in a large, squarish face.

"For kerist sake!" she said. "What the hell d'you know about cows?"

"My sisters persist in resurrecting childhood detritus . . . like us walking together in fields where placid bovines peacefully lay, chewing cuds."

"Stop whining."

"I'm not. I'm trying to say that my sisters believe you can hold the present together with flimsy twine from the past."

"If you don't like your family, then stay clear of them. That's what I did with mine." Alice rolled over and straightened herself on the bed while Jamie adjusted himself to recline against her protuberant buttocks. (On first seeing Alice nude, Jamie had unsuccessfully sifted through his brain seeking the word which best described her. Later, when thumbing through his dictionary and chancing to see the word, he castigated himself for failing to remember it, for he believed a poet ought to be able to recall words effortlessly. The next time he saw Alice he told her "callipygian" was the word that described her best; and Alice, who had no idea what Jamie was talking about, responded that he was as nutty as a fruit cake. Of course, Jamie explained everything to her, but Alice, being certain she was one of the most unattractive women in Canada, could not believe that Jamie thought her ass and hips were beautiful. "You're full of crap," was how she had responded. Alice's conversations were spiked with coarse vernacular, and it had taken Jamie a while to realize, behind the verbal barrier she built around herself, there dwelt a shy, sensitive woman.)

"Guys like you complain and complain, and never realize how lucky you are," she told him.

"My life's been burdened with luck," Jamie said. "Consider how lucky I was to meet you." He kissed her smooth bottom.

"Can it," Alice said. She was afraid talking about their relationship would destroy it. "You should of had my parents. They didn't give a shit about me. All they cared about was their two-bit store. They shipped me off every summer to my uncle and aunt's farm."

"There must be worse things in life than spending summer on a farm," Jamie commented.

"Not when you're a nine-year-old kid living with an uncle who can't keep his hands off her."

"Oh my God!" Jamie winced.

"The bastard got me into the feed shed and —"

"Don't!" Jamie cried and covered his ears.

". . . shoved me onto a pile of hog feed, pulled down my shorts and panties and . . ." She turned to look at him. "Well, what d'you think of that?"

"I'm horrified." Jamie's voice trembled.

"You have nieces?"

"Several."

"You ever done anything like that with them?"

"For God's sake, Alice!" Jamie leaned over to look at her face. "What do you take me for?"

"I take you for a guy that gets a stiff cock, then looks for a convenient place to put it."

"I'd never dream of doing such a thing!" He moved away from her to sit on the side of the bed, looking at the chair on which his clothes lay piled.

Alice, thinking he was about to leave (and perhaps never return) crawled across the bed to put her arms around him. "I know you're not like that, Jamie. I'm sorry. You're the only guy I've ever told what happened. Honest."

"Didn't you tell your aunt? Or your parents?"

"My aunt was too busy telling me how generous she was, taking me in without charging to feed me, and my parents too busy working eighteen hours a day trying to keep their crummy store afloat."

"But surely they would've wanted to know?"

"Get smart, will you?" At thirty-seven, Alice was five years older than Jamie and thought their age difference gave her the right to lecture him. When she did this, Jamie thought she sounded like his eldest sister Liz.

"Didn't you do *anything* about it?"

"You bet I did. I stole money from the store until I had enough to buy a pair of tin shears." Jamie shuddered and covered his ears again. "But he never came after me again. Then one summer he took a heart attack and died."

"And you never told anybody until now?"

"I told my aunt. After my uncle died, she sold the farm and moved to Saskatoon. That's where I was living then, slaving away, having my ass pinched in a shitty office. This was after I'd graduated from high school. One day she came to visit, and she'd not been in my crummy room ten minutes before she started on about how kind she and my uncle'd been to me. That's when I told her the sort of payment he'd collected off me." Alice stopped.

"Go on," Jamie urged.

"She called me a liar. Then she went into the bathroom and threw up. After that she came out, picked up her things and left." She stopped again.

"Yes?" Jamie prompted.

"She went back to her place, wrote a letter leaving everything she had to me, then took a heap of pills and pegged out."

"My God! Poor woman!"

"Like hell, poor woman! She was a sanctimonious bitch. So I beat it from the bum-pincher's office and used the money she left me to get a commerce degree. And I've never looked back, except to swat some guy who thought he could goose me and get away with it. Now, tell me about your family."

"I can't," Jamie said.

"Why not?"

"Because I can't offer a comparison."

"You mean there's no lunatics, pedophiles or bank robbers in your family? Christ! What a boring collection!"

"They are."

Alice now held his shoulders, flopped back and pulled him down between her thighs. She sighed with pleasure when Jamie, after mouthing her big pink nipples, slipped into her.

They never said aloud that they cared for each other. For Alice, there were good reasons for exercising caution: Plenty of men before Jamie had been eager to get into bed with her, but no man had ever looked into her sapphire-blue eyes and said, "I love you, Alice." And so, when she and Jamie first started bedding together, she thought of their relationship as being "decent sex", and it took a while before she accepted the idea that more was going on between them than just sex. She expected Jamie to be self-centred and insensitive, like every other male she had known, and distrusted his negligent gentleness and easy virility. To Alice, men who were different from the common run were either gays or weirdos who maimed or killed women; but as she and Jamie spent more and more time together, she came to realize that his diffidence was as much a part of his personality as hard-edged assertiveness was of hers. But once they had agreed — their agreement being a silent one; nothing explicit was ever said — that they wouldn't allow any external matters to intrude into their relationship, each began to reveal, albeit slowly, how they felt about the other. Still, they hadn't yet used the word "love" to express their feelings: It was too dangerous.

They had met at an art exhibition of an up-and-coming local painter in Vancouver's Gastown, which Alice had been coerced into attending by her boss. She had felt totally alien among the small groups of people who held glasses of warm white wine and talked loudly about themselves while ignoring the assembled paintings. Her legs ached and she detested what she saw hanging on the walls, but being a dutiful employee, felt she must remain at least an hour. Finally, she sat beside a glum, youngish man who was resting on the only bench in the gallery. To make conversation, Alice asked his opinion of the paintings. When he remarked the yellows seemed a shade diarrhetic and the browns too excremental, Alice agreed that they were "a bunch of crap". He nodded, got up and left. But, strangely enough, she encountered him the following week at the entrance to the Hudson Bay department store on Georgia Street. When she inquired how things were going, he answered, "Fine, fine," and walked on. A couple of weeks passed, and she saw him again, this time at the seawall at English Bay. "For crissake! Do I have to run into you every place I go?" she cried.

"We could slip past each other without speaking, like souls drifting in infinity." That remark should have warned Alice to move on, but instead she said: "I came out to have coffee and a piece of cheesecake. Want some?"

He shrugged his shoulders and said, "Sure, sure."

They went to a café across from English Bay to sit at a table by the windows where they watched people walking, jogging or cycling along the seawall. Alice managed to drag out of him that his name was Jamie Powell and that he lived alone in a basement suite not far from Commercial Drive in East Vancouver. Alice wasn't sure why she'd invited him to have coffee, and Jamie wondered why he'd accepted the invitation from this oversized, rough-voiced, blonde-haired woman, because the longer they sat at the table trying to converse, the less they seemed to have in common. A week passed, then Alice, who had never done anything like this before, hunted through the *Powells* listed in the phone book, and after half a dozen wrong numbers, identified his voice on the other end of the line.

"Hey!" she yelled. "It's me, Alice. Remember, English Bay? Coffee and cheesecake? How about us having dinner some night?"

"Sure," Jamie mumbled, and agreed to meet Alice at her apartment near English Bay at seven o'clock the next Friday. He didn't mention that he travelled around Vancouver on a bicycle, even in wet November weather; so Alice, the epitome of punctuality, was thoroughly irritated when Jamie didn't show up at the agreed-upon time. When finally he did appear at eight-thirty, he was saturated.

"For crissake!" she shouted. "Why didn't you say you don't have a car? Kerist! Look at you! Haven't you got an ounce of brains in your head?"

"Half an ounce," Jamie said.

"We can't go out to eat with you looking like that. Jeez! How did I ever get involved with a retard?" She went into the bathroom and returned with a large pink terrycloth bathrobe. "Put this on," she ordered. Jamie stripped, watched by Alice, who noted that his body was thin and muscular and that his masculine equipment, though retracted by rain and cold, seemed to be in good working order. While grumbling away, like a castigating parent, she informed him, among other things, that he was a "dimwit" and a "dumbhead". Jamie agreed with everything Alice said. "What the hell are we going to do about dinner? If I'd known you were going to mess things up, I'd've got something in."

"Pizza is humanity's last refuge," Jamie suggested.

"Oh yeah?" Alice commented. "What kind?"

"Any kind." His apparent readiness to be agreeable didn't particularly please Alice, who was loaded with prejudices and preferences. "For crissake," she snarled, "don't be so bloody polite," then went off to phone in an order for one ham and pineapple and one vegetarian pizza from a local pizza parlour. They ate them, sitting at the table in Alice's tiny dining area, while drinking mugs of decaffeinated coffee.

"Not bad pizza," Alice said, and burped. "Pardon." Jamie then burped and asked to be pardoned too. "If you keep imitating every goddamn thing I do, I'll hit you over the head with the pizza box."

"Do you always insult people who agree with you?"

"Men, I do. It means they're out to get something off me."

"I'm not here to get anything off you," Jamie told her. "But I've no objection to sharing experience."

That was the beginning of their relationship. The next morning, when Alice left the bed to visit the bathroom, Jamie, after watching her walk across the room, had called out: "You know, Alice, you really are splendid. Truly splendid."

"Cut the crap," Alice said, and ran to the bathroom where she sat on the toilet, repeating to herself: "You know, you really are splendid. Truly splendid." From puberty on, Alice had suffered because of her jutting breasts, protuberant bottom, and melon-like belly and thighs. During this entire time no one had ever uttered a single complimentary word about her body. Never once. Her women friends were more likely to speak of the advantages of surgical reduction of breasts and buttocks, while the men she knew never wanted anything from her but one-night stands. She washed herself, dabbed cologne in appropriate spots, and after redampening Jamie's clothes returned to the bed to tell him he couldn't leave because his clothes were still wet. "Anyway, it's Saturday," she concluded, "so there's nothing important you need to do, is there?"

"Anything I intended doing can wait," Jamie said, "but you didn't have to wet my clothes. I was going to stay."

"Goddamn it! How'd you guess?"

"Intuition."

"I'll bet!" She used this exclamation frequently during the first weeks because she couldn't credit Jamie's apparent ability to anticipate her thoughts, even more amazing to her because he was not a talkative person, and sometimes seemed not "all there". One day, several weeks after that particular morning, as she was walking along a downtown street past a bookstore, she saw something in the window that caused her to halt abruptly. What she had seen was the name *Jamie Powell* on the cover of two books: *Poems 1* and *Poems 2*. She went into the shop and purchased the books, and while receiving change was told that Jamie Powell was "undoubtedly" one of Canada's leading younger poets. Jamie's failure to tell her he was a published poet deeply upset her and she hid the books away in a dresser drawer, though from time to time she took them out to look at and puzzle over their contents. She didn't tell Jamie she'd purchased the books, and waited for him to tell her he was a poet, but when he didn't say anything she went back to referring to him as a "dimwit" or "retard" whenever she disagreed with him, though she became uneasy if ever Jamie referred to himself as being stupid, because she couldn't understand how a person who people regarded as an important poet could *really* be dumb; but apart from that, words like "dumbhead" were so much a part and parcel of Alice's daily lingo it was impossible for her to refrain from using them. She noticed, however, that words uttered by Jamie had far more significant implications than when she used them. Moreover, he seldom said anything unless he meant it.

"Don't you ever get tired of listening to me gabbing away?" Alice once asked.

Jamie smiled and shook his head. "You're ample in every way," he said. "That's as it should be. It's right and proper for you to be voluble, while for a skinny guy like me it's fitting to be laconic. Our speech matches our physiques."

Alice continued to order in pizzas, except now they drank six-packs with them, three cans each. Jamie usually left late on Sunday afternoon (the possibility they might live together had not yet occurred to them). When Alice invariably said, "Call me during the week," Jamie always replied, "Sure thing," to which Alice, following him to the apartment door, added, "Don't forget," and Jamie reassured her with, "I won't."

But one weekend Jamie didn't show up. Alice repeatedly punched out his phone number and became more and more agitated each time he failed to answer. She drove to his neighbourhood, located the house, pounded on the basement door, then rousted out a trio of young men who lived in another part of the house. They yawned, raised shoulders and eyebrows and said they hadn't a clue, which left Alice with no alternative but to return to her apartment and bite her fingernails, a childhood habit she had never been able to break. She called the hospitals in case he'd been hit by a car while cycling around the city, and called the police, too, but got nowhere with them, and so was left with nothing to do except go to work each day, stare at her apartment walls in the evenings and afterwards cry herself to sleep. A week passed, then on Friday evening, her buzzer sounded and she heard Jamie's voice saying, "Hi."

Her immense anxiety was now transformed into rage, and she began yelling at him the moment he entered the apartment. "Where the hell've you been, you son of a bitch!"

"At Liz's," he said.

"Liz's!" she shrieked. "What fucking Liz?" She didn't allow him to reply, but continued shrieking: "Some goddamn whore you took up with? Liz! What Liz? Who gave you the right to treat me like this? Tell me, then get the hell out!"

Alice continued shrieking until her relief, rage and anxiety played themselves out. When she stopped, Jamie explained that Liz was his sister and that he'd been at her house, working on some poetry.

"Why the hell didn't you call me?" Alice whimpered. "I looked everywhere for you. I thought you were hurt, I thought you could be dead." She tore into the bedroom, pulled out the two volumes of poetry, ran back and waved them in his face. "Must I find out everything for myself?"

"I intended to tell you," Jamie apologetically said. "No opportunity."

Alice collapsed in the nearest chair, sobbing. "Why the hell did I get mixed up with you?" she moaned. "I should've known better."

Eventually she calmed down and was able to see that Jamie looked exhausted and thinner than usual. "You look like you've been slaving in the salt mines." (Alice had a stock of similar phrases: *Slaving in the salt mines* and *Getting on the ball* were favourites.) "Doesn't your sister feed you?" she asked, then ignored him when he said Liz would have been happy to stuff him with food, but he never felt like eating while sitting at the window of his old bedroom, waiting for the galactic jumble of star words to stream down from the heavens to his desk where he sat in front of Liz's old typewriter, waiting to trap them.

"I'll make scrambled eggs and coffee," Alice said. "Families are all the same when it comes to feeding people. Cheapskates! Know something?" Now that Jamie was once more sitting at her kitchen table, she could ramble on: "My parents'd give every kid that came into the store a sucker. But did they ever give me one? No sir. Not even one that'd been in the goddamn sucker jar for years, with an inch of mould growing on it. I don't want anything to do with families."

Slowly, very slowly, they came to know each other, though Alice was never able to understand why Jamie periodically went off to work at his sister's house, nor did she question him further about his puzzling reference to star words flowing from the heavens onto his desk. "Goddamn it, why d'you do this to me?" she would storm. "Why can't you write your poems here? I'll fix up a den for you." But Jamie continued to disappear for periods that ranged from a day to a week, and the only difference now was that Alice, knowing where Jamie was, could — and did, after much lip-biting — telephone and ask to speak to him, even though the snotty woman (so Alice thought) who answered the phone always said Jamie could not be disturbed "under any circumstance". She also drove to the house on a Saturday afternoon or early in the evening after work, parked her little red Honda across the street and sat there, hoping her presence would insert itself into Jamie's consciousness so that he would instantly rush from the house (which Alice loathed the minute she set eyes on it) and drive off with her. Since she regarded herself as the essence of practicality, she had always dismissed as nonsense the idea of psychic communication. But now, as she sat motionless in her little car, she not only wished she possessed telepathic skills, but occasionally convinced herself she was actually making contact with Jamie. "Jamie," she would whisper, "Jamie, I'm out here. Let's go home and have pizza and beer. Jamie, I miss you so much. Don't you miss me?" She would then intently watch the porte cochère, and when Jamie did not immediately dash from the house, Alice would sigh, sniff and drive back to her empty apartment.

But although Jamie did not respond to Alice's silent appeals, Alice's phone calls and little red car had not gone unnoticed. Jamie's sister had deduced that the woman who telephoned Jamie was the same woman she saw in the car parked across the street. She went upstairs to the third floor, brushed dust from a dormer window pane, focused her binoculars on the red car and, in the light of the spring evening, was able to examine Alice's glum, silhouetted face. "She has blonde hair," she reported to her sister Amanda over the phone. "Probably dyed."

"There are lots of natural blondes around," Amanda said. "I'm one. You couldn't see the rest of her?"

"I couldn't very well ask her to step out of the car, could I?"

"She must really be in love with Jamie to sit there like that," Amanda said. "You should go out and introduce yourself, Liz. Invite her into the house."

"I'll do nothing of the kind," Liz stated. "I've told her on the phone that Jamie's at work."

"Well, you could at least talk to her."

"If I'd known you were going to make such a stupid suggestion, Mandy, I wouldn't have told you about the car," Liz said and hung up.

Amanda was pathologically curious about the lives of other members of her family, especially about Jamie, her junior by three years. She had instructed Jamie in all the basic necessities of life, beginning in the nursery and continuing nonstop to the present; and while Liz, as Jamie's oldest sister, might feel she had the right to protect Jamie the poet, Amanda considered that she alone had the right, even the duty, to interfere in Jamie's personal life. She telephoned their cousin Natasha, who was married to Amanda's half-brother, David, and passed on Liz's news.

"Really? How exciting!" Natasha had spent the early years of her life as an only child, fascinated by her noisy Powell cousins. She had always been intimidated by Liz and secretly in love with David, who was the same age as Liz and had been adopted by Liz's parents after his mother's death. Now, married to David and the mother of four children, Natasha was still a little in awe of Liz. Like Amanda, Natasha loved gossiping about other members of the Powell-McLeod families, especially about their emotional lives and love affairs. There was never a lack of topics as, besides the five Powell siblings, Natasha's mother, Nanda Powell McLeod, had married Stuart McLeod after Natasha's father had died and had borne four more children.

"Liz says the woman phones or sits there every night Jamie's at the house doing his star poems."

"Ooh!" Natasha breathed. "She just sits in the car?"

"At least an hour! Listen, Tashie . . ." (Natasha was known in the family as Gorgeous Tashie, because of her beauty: long black hair, enormous dark eyes, almond-coloured skin, and heart-shaped face, inherited mostly from her part-Hindu father. She had been named Natasha because her mother happened to be reading Tolstoy's *War and Peace* at the time of her birth, and everyone thought the name fitted her perfectly.) Amanda whispered into the phone — Amanda's phone conversations tended to be conspiratorial in tone — ". . . listen, you don't live far from Liz, so why not walk around the block, have a look at the car and take down the licence plate number?"

"But would it be right to do that, Mandy? I mean . . ."

"I'd do it, except I'm stuck at my job." Amanda was a registered nurse who cared for private patients, which often meant working afternoon and evening shifts. (Nobody in the Powell family, except Jamie, had ever understood how Scatterbrain Amanda — as everyone called her — had managed to get through a nursing program and later acquire a Bachelor of Science degree.)

"I'll see."

"She must be desperately in love with Jamie," Amanda said.

"Or jealous," Natasha suggested. Natasha was extraordinarily jealous of her husband. Even *thinking* of David smiling at another woman filled her with hatred for the woman, and the fact that he frequently told her how much he loved her made no difference; and because she knew how devoted Liz was to David, and had been since childhood, the animosity

Natasha directed towards her was far greater than she felt for other women, though she expertly hid her true feelings about Liz behind a facade of lukewarm friendship.

After a few polite questions had been exchanged about each other's children, Natasha and Amanda ended the conversation. Amanda knew Natasha wouldn't be able to resist walking past Liz's house and the small red car in which the blonde woman sat, then peeping around the corner to look at and write down Alice's licence plate number.

The following afternoon, when she knew Amanda would be awake, Natasha telephoned with the licence plate number and the name of its owner.

"How clever of you, Tashie," Amanda cooed. "Alice Morgan."

"She lives near English Bay, in one of those ghastly apartment towers. Here's her address. A friend of David's got it for me."

"Tashie, you're wasted staying home and being a mother. You should be a detective." They laughed, thoroughly pleased with themselves.

"So what do we do now?" Natasha asked.

Amanda hesitated. "You could stroll by again, but this time speak to her."

"I couldn't do that, I mean, suppose Jamie found out?"

"Okay. I guess we'll have to leave things as they are."

"Oh, I think so, I really do. She could be sitting there for some entirely different reason than Jamie."

"You mean she might be a TV cameraman trying to get a picture of Liz?" (Elizabeth Powell had had a brief — 1972 to 1976 — but notorious career as a member of the provincial legislative assembly. Retired from politics now, she worked at a city college where she taught a woman's studies course called "Women in Canadian Politics: Is There a Future?") "I don't mind doing it. After tomorrow, I'm finished my night job."

"But do be careful, Mandy."

"Of course."

The next evening the children's regular night sitter arrived early. Amanda drove to the neighbourhood where Liz lived, parked her Volvo and walked to Liz's street, pretending to search for a house number. She approached the little red car on the driver's side, tapped on the glass, and when Alice rolled down the window, smiled and said, "Excuse me, is your name Alice Morgan? Mine's Amanda Powell." She got no further, because Alice started the motor, swung the wheel and tore off, knocking Amanda over. "Oh dear," Amanda said, "oh dear." She felt her hips and legs, decided she was unhurt, then cautiously got to her feet and walked slowly back to her car.

"It's definitely her," she told Natasha over the phone. "When I introduced myself, she started the motor, drove off, and knocked me flying. But she's definitely Alice Morgan."

"Are you sure you're not hurt, Mandy? And she really knocked you over and didn't come back to see if you were hurt?" Whenever Natasha thought she might have run over a cat or bird she immediately stopped her car and hurried back expecting to see animal entrails plastered on the road. "You're so brave, Mandy," she added.

"Oh, I dunno," Amanda laughed, enjoying the compliment. "Anyway, all's fair in love and war, isn't it? But now we know, don't we? And we can go on from here, can't we?"

"Yes," Natasha echoed, "now we can go on from here."

Chapter 2

Two days passed, then on the evening of the third day as Amanda was having a supper of macaroni and cheese with her children, Annabelle and Christopher, the phone rang. Annabelle answered it, then called: "Mom, it's for you! But it's not HER." (HER was Annabelle's name for Liz, whose imperious assumption that everybody in the world must do as she ordered, irritated Annabelle who preferred everybody in the world to do as *she* ordered.)

Amanda picked up the phone and cooed, "Hello. Amanda Powell speaking."

"This is Alice Morgan."

"Oh, yes? How nice of you to call." She smirked at the children, who held their hands over their mouths to prevent their giggling from being heard.

"I want to know if we can get together."

"I'd be delighted. When would be convenient for you?"

"How about lunch tomorrow?"

"Fine with me. Where shall we meet?"

Alice named a restaurant on Broadway, adding, "It's near my office. Though if you'd prefer somewhere else . . ."

"Oh no, that's perfect. I live in Kitsilano, so it's just up the hill for me."

"One o'clock suit you?"

"Fine, just fine." Amanda sounded like a rhapsodizing pigeon.

"And listen, you won't mention this to Jamie if you see him?"

"I wouldn't dream of it," Amanda simpered.

"Okay, one tomorrow."

"One, tomorrow." Amanda put down the phone and danced around the table, splashing kisses on Annabelle's and Christopher's faces. "Guess who that was?" she asked.

"The lady who knocked you over with her car." Amanda had given her children a dramatic account of her encounter with Alice Morgan in which she narrowly escaped death by rolling over the hood to land on the other side of the car. They had gaped at their mother's torn stockings and the line of bruises that had begun to blossom on her left thigh and thought her truly heroic, as brave as any TV hero. Christopher wanted to know if Amanda was going to arrest Alice Morgan.

"I'll talk to her first. If she doesn't agree to change her ways, I'll turn her in."

Amanda thought her children were the most adorable in the world, though she had to acknowledge that Natasha's daughters and sons were really and truly beautiful — it would be strange if they weren't, with two such beautiful people for parents — and had to admit, too, that her sister Hilda Logan's three children were quite good-looking, though in an anaemic sort of way. Still, there was no denying that Annabelle and Christopher possessed an individual charm all their own, which none of their Powell or McLeod cousins came even close to having. Furthermore, although Annabelle, with her ginger-coloured hair, blue eyes and band of freckles across a turned-up nose, did not resemble Liz in any physical way, nevertheless Amanda foresaw that she was going to turn out to be another Liz. She knew this from the way Annabelle ordered Christopher around; that was exactly how Liz had bullied her and her brothers and sister, first at Rhynewood Manor, their home in England, then at the Big House where they lived after moving to Vancouver. Christopher was a sweet-natured little boy, a male replica, so Amanda thought, of herself — lovable even when naughty. When she looked at her children, especially while they were listening intently, lips parted, to one of her interminable telephone conversations with family members, Amanda thought they looked exactly like the angels she'd seen in Victorian paintings hanging in the homes of her wealthier patients. At these moments, when the children looked so adorable and angelic, she felt such great fear for their safety grip her, body and soul, that she wanted immediately to gather them in her arms and return them to her womb where they would forever be protected from harm.

Now, she scooped out bowls of strawberry ice cream and sliced a banana on top, while Annabelle and Christopher cleared plates from the table, and for a while the only sound that could be heard in the kitchen was that of spoons hitting bowls. After dinner, when the dishes had been stacked in the dishwasher, they sat in the living room and watched the six o'clock news, Amanda in the middle of the couch, the children on either side, leaning against her. Towards the end of the hour when she felt their bodies relax against hers, she turned off the television and announced it was bath time. She loved to see the children in the bath, to watch them emerge, wet and pink-fleshed, and then to stand them on her knees to kiss their bellybuttons while explaining that whenever her grandfather had visited Rhynewood at bath time when she was a little girl, he had done the very same thing with her and her brothers and sisters. Amanda felt this little ritual transformed her from the not-too-bright, average sort of person that everybody in the family said she was into the most fortunate woman in the world.

The next day just past one o'clock, Amanda entered the restaurant, looked around, spotted Alice Morgan's blonde hair, then walked around small, crowded tables to join her. She thought Alice looked decidedly grim. "Is this a vegetarian place?" she asked as she pulled out a chair and sat.

"I don't know," Alice said.

"They usually have small tables and rattan furniture."

"I wouldn't know. I judge restaurants by their food, not by their furniture."

Amanda eyed Alice, wondering why her diffident, reserved brother had become involved with this oversized, less-than-friendly woman, though she had to admit that her golden-blonde hair was a glorious sight and her eyes a truly amazing blue colour that reminded Amanda of cornflowers bordering the northern highway that led to a house trailer in which she had once lived. "Do you work nearby?" she asked.

"Yeah, the accounting firm is a few blocks away."

"I see." While Amanda had an astute financial sense when it came to practical matters such as balancing her monthly budget and buying and selling local properties, accountancy was beyond her. "You type? That sort of thing?" she asked.

"I'm a chartered accountant. I prepare financial statements and conduct audits," Alice snapped.

"A registered nurse doesn't have occasion to deal with accountants," Amanda remarked.

"I'm not aware that nurses did much more than make beds and hand out pills." Fortunately, a waitress appeared at this moment and held out two stained menus. Amanda ignored hers, having decided that any restaurant which offered its customers dirty menus ought to be shut down by city health inspectors. "I'll have a clubhouse sandwich. And a glass of water with ice."

Alice scanned the menu, then ordered the soup of the day and a salad with house dressing. The waitress scribbled something on a pad, grabbed the menus and departed. "I have degrees in commerce and business administration," Alice said. She had already made up her mind that Jamie's sister was a fool, while Amanda, who had not yet formed a definitive opinion of Alice, began to feel uneasy that Jamie had become involved with someone who appeared to lack even the most basic social skills. Amanda moved about in her chair and grimaced, hoping Alice would notice she was suffering from injuries inflicted by Alice and her car.

"How did you and Jamie meet?" she asked.

Alice explained that her firm did what it could to make its art gallery clients' balance sheets look good and, in return, the galleries invited representatives from the firm to openings of artists' works. "It's all a bunch of crap," she summarized.

"I suppose it's something like modern poetry," Amanda said. "Difficult to understand. Have you always lived in Vancouver?"

"I'm from Saskatchewan. East of Regina."

"Oh yes." Amanda's notion of the prairie provinces was sketchy. She thought of these places as desolate, thinly populated areas which people avoided by flying above them at great heights on their way from the security of Vancouver to Toronto or Montreal. "Have you known Jamie long?" she asked.

"Long enough to find out he isn't run of the mill. But I sure didn't realize I was getting mixed up with a poet."

"He's quite well known," Amanda said.

"I don't get what his poems are about, though that doesn't seem to bother Jamie."

"Jamie's very tolerant of other people's limitations," Amanda said.

"He'd have to be, with you for a sister," Alice replied. Amanda now decided Alice was the rudest person she had met in her entire life and regretted not delegating this meeting to Liz, whose experience with political superstars would have enabled her to cut Alice down to size. "Anyway, I contacted you because I don't want you, or Jamie, to think I'm following him around like Mary's little lamb."

"You don't act at all like a lamb," Amanda said. "In fact, you act like the rudest person I've ever met in my life. And I can't imagine why you think you have any right to insult me, since you're the one who suggested we get together. But perhaps politeness isn't essential in your line of work."

"I'm polite when I'm required to be." Alice's face became very red. "That's how I was raised."

"Then I'd say quite a lot was omitted from your education." Amanda got up. "In my profession, politeness to strangers is a requisite." She turned to leave.

"Wait a minute," Alice urged. "We seem to've got off on the wrong foot."

"*I* haven't," Amanda said.

"Please wait." Amanda heard the plea in Alice's voice and turned back. "Look, I don't know how . . . I didn't mean . . . I don't know what to say."

Amanda, realizing she had broken down Alice's barriers, returned to the table and the remnants of the inferior clubhouse sandwich. "You don't know how to tell me that you're in love with Jamie? Is that it?" Her voice was cold and uncompromising.

Alice looked down at the uneaten food on her plate and exhibited symptoms of adolescent embarrassment. "That's about the cut of it," she mumbled. "I didn't know it was going to happen. I didn't know I'd feel like this. Besides, I feel dumb, being older than Jamie and having a face that looks like the side of a barn."

The waitress reappeared and asked if they were finished. "I am," Amanda said. "You can bring me a cup of coffee. And I hope it will taste better than the sandwich."

The waitress was defiant: "Customers like our food and coffee."

"That doesn't speak very highly of your customers," Amanda replied. She occasionally ate out with Liz and appreciatively listened as her sister made derogatory comments about the food and service. She hoped she had done as well today as Liz. She turned back to Alice, who tended to treat waiters respectfully, much as she would acolytes. Alice began to revise her opinion of Amanda. "So what about Jamie? How does he feel?"

The question disturbed Alice and the chair creaked as she moved around on it. "Jamie says," she eventually said, "he can rest with me."

Amanda now switched from sternness to nodding wisely. "Jamie hates admitting anything personal, even with me. So that may be his way of expressing his affection for you."

"You think so? You really think so?" Alice's appeal was so pathetic that Amanda wanted to reach out and pat her hand. "I mean, I've never told Jamie that I . . ." The waitress returned with a mug of coffee and a tiny plastic container of cream which she placed before Amanda, then asked Alice if she was finished. Alice nodded, and they waited until the waitress removed her plates, having been told they weren't interested in dessert. Alice continued: "I mean, I don't find it easy to talk to people."

Amanda nodded. "It's strange how love happens, isn't it?"

Alice suddenly became voluble, describing how she had first met Jamie, followed by the casual encounters that had eventually resulted in Jamie's coming to her apartment, ninety minutes late. "I'd no idea who he was," she said, "or what the hell he did for a living. I thought he must be joking when he told me he taught a college course. Most times, he looked like something the cat dragged in." (Amanda wondered if Alice's frequent use of the word "hell" meant she had been raised in one of those religious sects that consign all but a tiny per cent of the world's population to burn in perpetual fires while those who are saved sit contentedly on clouds which float around in a place called Heaven.) "Then one day Jamie vanishes, and I think he's either buggered off, or dead. Kerist! I went looking for him at his crummy basement suite, I phoned the hospitals and the cops, then he just shows up, acting like nothing'd happened, and doesn't get it when I scream at him."

"Now you know where he goes," Amanda remarked.

"But he still doesn't understand how I feel about him going off without telling me. That's why I call your sister's house. I worry about Jamie, he looks like he's been in the salt mines when he comes back. I know it's dumb, but I worry about him. I want to know he's okay."

Any antipathy Amanda may have felt towards Alice had now vanished to be replaced by unqualified sympathy. "Now listen, Alice —" she began.

"He's told me that he just sits in his old room. But I don't get it. I told him I'd fix up my spare room for him."

Amanda now produced David's theory of why Jamie returned to the Big House. "Jamie's a bit like a salmon that returns to the river where it's been spawned," she said. "Jamie *has* to go back to that room — it's where he was born as a poet."

"I don't get it."

"David — that's our half-brother — says it has to do with Jamie's chemistry. Each time Jamie goes back to the room, he's reborn."

"He looks half-dead to me."

"He doesn't eat much while he's at the Big House. David says he has mystical experiences there. You know, like an Indian yogi."

"And that snobby woman who answers the phone, that's your sister?"

"Yes, that's Liz, our eldest sister. She's a sweet person."

"She doesn't act sweet with me. You'd think me telephoning there was a major crime."

"That's only Liz's manner. You get used to it after a while. You may have seen her picture in the newspaper, she was an MLA for a while."

Like a jigsaw, memories and images came together in Alice's brain. "You mean that woman who caused the big hullabaloo in the legislature and got thrown out?"

Amanda smiled and nodded, pleased that Alice had identified Liz.

"Yes. She accused the Premier of lying and wouldn't apologize."

"You mean she was so green she didn't know *all* politicians are liars?"

"Liz has principles."

"I don't care what she has. Just tell her not to treat me like I'm a piece of shit next time I phone, okay?"

"I have a better plan." Amanda assumed her conspiratorial expression. "Instead of sitting in your car across the street, why not go knock on the door and introduce yourself to her?"

"No, no, I couldn't do that." The volume of Alice's voice changed from a hoarse whisper to a shout, and people across the room turned to look at her. "I don't want Jamie to know!"

"Liz wouldn't tell him."

"No, I won't do it. And I don't want you to say a single word to your sister about me and Jamie, you hear me?" Alice lurched to her feet, knocked the table against Amanda, snatched up her purse, and hurried from the restaurant. Amanda, delighted at the outcome of the meeting, raised a crooked finger to the waitress, asked for the bill, paid it, left a small tip, drove home and immediately telephoned Natasha to give her a detailed account of her meeting with Alice.

Chapter 3

After leaving the Big House, Jamie would sometimes drift along a few blocks to end in Natasha's living room, staring blankly at her and nodding absently when she introduced conversational topics she thought would be of interest to him: book reviews, notices of plays and art exhibits, and other information concerning the arts world. Unlike Amanda, who rambled on about anything that popped into her head, Natasha tried to talk to Jamie about the arts scene, mistakenly thinking that's what he wanted. She and David had received signed copies of Jamie's books upon publication, but Natasha, who believed herself to be a reasonably intelligent person, found the poems incomprehensible, and even David, usually a whiz at deciphering puzzles and crosswords, admitted that Jamie's geometric conglomerations flummoxed him. Their unspoken consensus was that Jamie deliberately went out of his way to be abstruse.

Whenever Jamie showed up, Natasha, knowing he'd only just left Liz's house after a bout of writing, would get the housekeeper to make sandwiches and coffee, then sit and talk at him as he rapidly consumed the food. She would speak first of obligatory matters pertaining to the arts, then move on to the subject closest to her heart: the feeding of the world's hungry children. The difference between Natasha and Amanda's attitudes concerning child poverty was striking, for while it was true that Amanda was a good-natured and emotionally flaccid person, nevertheless any maternal love she experienced was targeted exclusively on Annabelle and Christopher, and she was quite prepared, should the occasion ever arise, to deprive other children of food in order to feed her own. But for Natasha, it was very different: She was unable to look at her own healthy, well-fed sons and daughters without seeing beyond them a vast circle of sad eyes set in the shrunken faces of children dying from starvation, disease and neglect.

"Isn't it just awful, Jamie?" she would say while he hungrily ate another sandwich and gulped down cup after cup of aromatic coffee.

On occasion, Jamie tried to tell Natasha that relief work was pointless because famine was similar to a contagious sore on the human body, which, if cured in one place, would inevitably pop up somewhere else. It shocked Natasha to hear her cousin voice such ugly and unenlightened views, especially while eating, but she never disagreed with Jamie because she was slightly in awe of him, as were all the Powell and McLeod women.

Jamie thought Natasha's attitude toward starving children, especially those who lived in far-away countries, was common enough among shallow-minded, wealthy women, who attempt to soothe their consciences by applying the balm of charity. But Jamie misjudged Natasha, for she was a genuinely compassionate person who experienced acute physical pain whenever she saw images of hollow-eyed, starving children. Her mission to alleviate child poverty began when Jasmine, her firstborn, was nursing at her breast and suddenly she thought: *If my milk dried up, I would have nothing to feed Jasmine.* Thereafter, she was unable to look at her rapidly growing, happily chirping child without simultaneously witnessing the terrifying spectre of a starving child. If Jasmine fretted, Natasha was certain she wasn't getting enough milk, and it mattered not that Natasha's milk supply was so ample she could always expel milk from her breasts, even immediately after nursing. (In spite of Natasha's irrational fear of Jasmine starving, she became pregnant again when Jasmine was six months old. No more than fifteen months separated each of Natasha and David's four children: Jasmine, David and Gloria, who were twins, and Roger. Following Roger's birth, David had advised Natasha to take a rest from child-bearing since their family was now a comfortable size. David was a highly rational man: He saw his children as end products of human biology, whereas Natasha saw them as the product of the passionate love she and David had for each other. (Indeed, Natasha referred to her children as her *passion flowers*.)

Still, while Jamie may not have given Natasha the credit she deserved, he always listened politely to her pleas on behalf of needy children of the world. He knew, of course, that she was the recipient of a large quarterly income that accrued in a trust fund established by her mother, but, interestingly enough, Natasha did not regard herself as a wealthy woman, but rather as an average young mother, deeply in love with her husband, who worried about the well-being of her children as well as about the plight of homeless, hungry children everywhere in the world. She simply couldn't understand how Jamie could be so uncaring about the poverty which rampaged through the world's slums and barrios and gathered up the feverish little bodies with death's scythe. Yet every time Jamie stopped at the house,

Natasha raised the subject, determined to change his mind. Today, Jamie sat and quietly listened once again to Natasha's pleas while consuming sandwiches and coffee. After raising mild doubts concerning the efficacy of her charitable work, he thanked her for the hospitality and departed to careen home on his bicycle, while telling himself he must either get the worn brakes fixed, or purchase a new bike.

That evening, Natasha lay on the couch in her favourite position — head on David's lap, feet on the arm of the couch, slippers dangling from her toes — and complained about Jamie's selfish, uncaring attitudes. (Natasha favoured this position because it enabled her to do so many things: reach up to touch David's face; raise her legs idly to scratch an ankle or foot; invite caresses by taking David's hand and placing it over her breast or thigh; and also it was an ideal vantage point from which to watch David's face and gauge his reaction to things she said.) "Jamie as good as says my relief work is a waste of time and money."

David smiled and stroked Natasha's hair. He had heard all this before and tended to agree with his half-brother, though he would never have said so to Natasha. David was the essence of diplomacy when dealing with his wife; not from self-interest, but because he loved her and never wanted to say anything to upset her. "Jamie questions my motives," Natasha complained. "How dare he!" (She could afford to be indignant with David.) "I don't question the way he writes his poems. You wouldn't like it, would you, if our darling *passion flowers* didn't have enough to eat?"

"Of course, I wouldn't. But you must do as you wish, Tashie. You have every right to spend your money just as you please."

"And something else. Jamie looked absolutely awful. Haggard. He has a girlfriend now. Amanda's had lunch with her."

"I heard about it from Liz."

"From Liz? When did you see Liz?"

"She dropped in at the lab today to say hello. She came out to the university for a seminar on women's rights. So, how's Jamie? His usual talkative self?"

"He said maybe half a dozen words. He makes me nervous, so I just jabber away. Most of the time I've no idea what I'm saying."

"Try silence. That might force him to say more."

"I'd like to have an intelligent conversation with him. But how can I?"

"Jamie's not interested in exchanging ideas. And why should he be, when he's preoccupied with grabbing onto something that's unique?" Natasha was always careful not to raise the issue of whether Jamie's poetry was truly original, because she knew how much David desired to produce original scientific work, but so far hadn't. So she decided to handle David's comment by risking a joke: She invited him to conduct an intimate investigation of her "molecules". David, preoccupied with getting Natasha off the subject of Liz, caressed her face and kissed her, then leaned back and calculatingly examined her. "You know, there may be something in your idea after all."

"Davey! Don't stare at me as if I were some specimen."

"But you are a specimen — a perfect specimen of a beautiful woman, which is why I stare at you. But apart from that, there might be some point to investigating the differences between a beautiful body and an ugly one. If it were possible to determine the cause of your loveliness, it might also be possible to influence fetal development."

"You mean there'd be thousands and thousands of Natashas?"

"No, no. Only that parents would be guaranteed beautiful daughters and sons."

"But parents don't care how their children look."

"Children do."

"Gloria and Jasmine are lovely."

"Of course." David thought he had successfully shifted the conversation from his meeting with Liz, but Natasha suddenly returned to it, wanting to know what else he and Liz had talked about. "Nothing of interest. Liz said some people had asked her if she'd consider running for the Liberals in the next federal election."

"Where would she run?"

"I suppose in this riding. People will remember Stuart." (Natasha's stepfather had been a Liberal Member of Parliament during the Diefenbaker years.)

"So there'd be a family association. I think it's a great idea." Natasha was enthusiastic about any endeavour that would remove David from Liz's orbit of influence. Although she hated to admit it, she knew David's affection for Liz was almost as great as his love for her, the only difference being that she, Natasha, possessed David in a physical and sexual sense, which of course Liz didn't. (At family get-togethers, Natasha invariably engaged in small but overt actions, such as rearranging David's hair or tie, to signal Liz that David belonged to her. Of course, she knew her behaviour was silly, but still she couldn't prevent herself from exhibiting her ownership of David whenever Liz was present.) As a child, Natasha had been in awe of Liz, with three years separating them. But Liz had always been a domineering and impetuous person, while she, Natasha, was quiet and unassuming, much like her mother, and extremely shy, too, and so it had seemed inevitable that Liz would get her way in anything she set her mind to. That was why Natasha had always known that if she wanted David she must deliberately set about capturing him through shrewd planning; and, although she suspected David knew her pursuit of him to Chalk River, after he got his first job there with Atomic Energy of Canada, was part of her long-range strategic plan, still, when she arrived at his room that afternoon he had willingly surrendered himself. She must never forget that. And she knew David still desired her, even though her breasts might not be as firm and high as they once were and her waist was thicker, and only yesterday she had spotted the hint of a varicose vein in her left calf, which had quietly horrified her. Fortunately her face had not changed. Natasha knew this because each morning she carefully examined her face from every conceivable angle in her three-way mirror to see if any wrinkle or sag had appeared during the previous night. When David was away at conferences, she hardly slept, but rolled from side to side, fretting herself into sleeplessness, imagining David making love to some woman attending the conference. When he returned home she tried to hide her feelings, but her jealousy always crept into the questions she asked him. "All very dry and tedious," David usually responded.

"Just a bunch of men nattering on about their pet scientific projects?"

"A few women too, mostly middle-aged."

"But young women were there, too?" Natasha, like an inquisitor of old, pounced on the word "mostly".

"Three or four. They have a tough time competing with the men."

"Oh really? You'd think the men would compete for *them*."

David laughed and kissed her. "If they looked like you, they might. Now, stop it, Tashie." And no matter how many hours David had flown, or time zones he'd crossed, or what time of day it was, by one pretext or another, Natasha would get him into bed and make sure he had not frittered away his virility on another woman: She would strip him and examine every part of his body, while muttering to herself in Punjabi, learned as a child from her mother's Sikh household staff. Then, having assured herself that he hadn't wasted his male essence elsewhere, she would draw him inside to cast out her fear and moan with pleasure when his warm body touched, then pressed down upon hers. Unless David was exceptionally tired, he enjoyed the ritual; after all, knowing Natasha preferred him above all other men was gratifying. Many colleagues' wives were totally indifferent, and thought nothing of getting into bed with other men, and women too.

It was flattering, perhaps dangerously flattering, to have a wife who believed you were the be-all and end-all, and occasionally he experienced profound uneasiness when he speculated what might happen should the pendulum swing the other way and Natasha discover he was not the ideal male after all. Or what if she learned about him and Liz? Suppose she found out that when Liz first heard that he and Natasha were going to marry, she'd said she'd never agree to the marriage and would make trouble unless he agreed to spend a night with her. That he was her half-brother seemed not to worry her; she was convinced her love for him far surpassed anything Natasha felt and believed she had as much right as Natasha to experience the pleasures of sexual love with him. David, who, until that moment, had always thought of Liz as an impetuous comrade, had been forced to contemplate becoming her lover for a single night. Being cool-headed, he worried about the implications of such a coupling, mostly that he might be impotent with her. But events had proved he needn't have had concerns on that score. He had crept along the dark passage between their bedrooms and had found Liz sitting on her bed in a long flannelette night-gown (the Powell girls always wore them), crying. He sat and put his arm around her. "You don't have to do this, Davey," she whispered. "But I must know that nothing will ever change between us." It might be argued that he could have — *should* have — backed out, that Liz had given him the open-ing he needed, that he could have easily just gone back to his room. But he hadn't done that; he had remained to comfort her (so he told himself after-wards), stroking her hair, kissing her cheek, then making love to her, for-ever changing their relationship. Years later, he would try to analyze the steps he had taken to transform himself from brother into lover. But what he could not have known was that Liz would ask him to return, again and again; nor could he have known that their first night together would result in Liz getting pregnant and seriously contemplating having the child be-fore getting an abortion. And so it had come about that David's life had become suspended between Natasha, whom he adored, and Liz, to whom he felt irrevocably bound.

There were times when he felt he was walking along the knife-edge of a precipice and, fearful that a terrible event was imminent, would slip into a black despair as he contemplated his complex relationships with his wife and sister and the comparative futility of his work. He knew some people thought he had married Natasha for her money, and that a few colleagues believed the only reason he held a senior position in the chemistry depart-ment was due to the twenty-million-dollar Frances McLeod Scientific Foundation which Nanda and Stuart McLeod had established following the death of their eight-year-old daughter, Frances, in a canoe accident.

Most of the gossip spread about David was the product of envy; and David himself knew, even as he acknowledged his great good fortune in marrying so beautiful and wealthy a woman as Natasha, that he had married her for no reason other than that he loved her, and still did. And although he realized he might, and probably did, lack the intellect required to produce original scientific work, still he knew he was a competent chemist and much-respected teacher. Indeed, his greatest weakness, he sometimes thought, was not intellectual deficiency, but rather his readiness to acknowledge his limitations, real or imagined. He seemed to lack a strong ego, which might explain why he now found himself strung between two strong-willed, competing women. While outwardly conveying an impression of calm reasonableness, inside he seethed with turmoil and fears. He knew he could never sever his relationship with Liz, fearing it would destroy her emotionally, yet neither could he find the courage within himself to reveal the relationship to Natasha, knowing that the revelation would destroy their life together. He was a trapped man.

Chapter 4

Jamie sat on the edge of Amanda's bed looking at the hump of sheets and blankets under which Amanda pretended to sleep. He knew she was awake, that eventually her head would cautiously emerge, like a tortoise poking from its shell, that she would then warily eye him to assess what sort of mood he was in. Jamie could not recall a time in his life when he hadn't sat on the side of his sister's bed, patiently waiting for the hump that was Amanda to stir and peep out to make sure it was safe to emerge.

Amanda's house was one of those pre-World War One elongated, box-shaped structures built by the hundreds among cedar stumps near the adolescent port of Vancouver. It still had its original steep cedar-shake roof and cedar siding. Inside, the rooms were small, ceilings twelve feet high, walls lath and plaster, coves and corners elaborately moulded, hardwood floors much scuffed, and electrical wiring inadequate to the demands Amanda placed on it. In winter, when Arctic fronts moved from the Yukon to remind Vancouverites they didn't live in southern California after all, the old furnace, made over from a sawdust to an oil-burner, roared continuously, yet failed to heat the bedrooms adequately, or prevent water pipes from freezing.

To live in Amanda's house, David once said, was to experience conditions as they were before the first great war. But Jamie liked the house anyway, and thought it suited his sister, which in fact it did, because the stairs to the second floor were placed immediately inside the front door, thereby enabling Amanda's lovers to bolt up to her bedroom, happily copulate with her for an hour or so, then clatter down and be gone before anyone was the wiser. If a lover wanted to remain longer, Amanda put him to work around the house, thus creating the illusion that she had hired him to redecorate. Jamie was fascinated by the variety of colours on the interior walls and tried to infer from the diverse hues the type of men Amanda welcomed into her bed. He actually had met a few as they galloped down the stairs on their way out: In general, they were young, pleased with themselves, and, misjudging Jamie's reason for being there, seemed not to object to the idea of him occupying premises they had just vacated. Jamie thought Amanda might have gone through thirty lovers in recent years and always intended to ask her if the physical sensations she experienced varied from lover to lover, but before he had worked up a way to frame the question, Amanda had one day mockingly compared men to store cookies, which Jamie understood to mean that, while the packaging might vary, the contents were depressingly alike. She had then smiled at him, patted his hands and said: "But I'm sure *you're* unique as a lover, Jamie." This was before his involvement with Alice, and now he'd come to tell his sister to stop poking her inquisitive nose into his life.

He jabbed the hump of bedclothes and said, "Come out." The hump disintegrated, and Amanda appeared from beneath the blankets. "Why did you do it, Mandy?" he said.

"I wanted to help," she whispered. "That's all."

"It *isn't* all!" he sternly told her. "You just had to find out more about Alice. Isn't that so?"

More of Amanda emerged from the bed covers. "I'm happy you've found someone to love. I'd never do anything to hurt you." Her small plump lips formed a smile of appeasement, which had always worked well with Jamie.

"Alice and I don't want the family involved," he said.

"But you realize, don't you, that Alice's in love with you?" Amanda rubbed her face against his arm. "Does she know how lucky she is?"

"We're both lucky. And I'm not so sure Alice . . ."

"Alice is such a pretty name."

Jamie understood that what he did from now on, how he looked, what he said — in fact, everything about him — would be examined in great detail by his sisters and cousin. (David was the exception, because whatever he knew of his half-brother's private life was passed on by Natasha.) They would probe continually, especially Amanda, until they were satisfied they knew everything about him and Alice, merciless in their invasion of his privacy.

Amanda wriggled beneath the bedclothes so she could get closer to Jamie and achieve the ideal position for exchanging secrets and confidences. Amanda traded in secrets much as people dabble in international money markets: Invest a few secrets of your own and reap profits from hearing those of others. "It makes all the difference when people love each other. Then whatever you do together in bed feels right, doesn't it?" She watched Jamie's profile, looking for a response. "That's how I felt with

Harry before I found out he couldn't give me a baby." She paused, gauging his reaction, and when Jamie remained silent, she rambled on, telling him yet one more time how she had married Bernard Stoltz, mistakenly believing that an obstetrician who personified kindly thoughtfulness with pregnant patients would make a good husband. Then, she had believed that a husband crammed with knowledge of women's reproductive parts would know, more than other men, how to apply loving attention to those parts of his wife's body which ached to be reproductive. What a mistake she'd made! Bernard's warmth and thoughtfulness vanished the moment he left the clinic or delivery room. She painfully discovered that her husband didn't give a damn about women, or their reproductive organs; in fact, the entire process of reproduction appeared to disgust him, and a bewildered Amanda found she was lucky if she could persuade him to make love once a week, and even that ceased after she conceived Annabelle, though somehow she managed to get Christopher out of him three years later. Then Harry Greene had appeared.

He'd travelled to Vancouver from the Northern Interior to attend a lumber-industry convention and was taking an afternoon break, strolling in the area between English Bay and Coal Harbour, when he came upon four-year-old Annabelle, who'd fallen from the end of a playground slide and buried her nose in the gravel. He retrieved her, brushed off her clothes, returned her to Amanda who was sitting with Christopher on a nearby bench, and stayed to chat. He reappeared again, then again, and on that occasion Amanda invited him home for coffee. They never did have the coffee, because once Amanda had put the children down for their nap, Harry took her into his arms, swore he loved her, and ended up in her bed. He stayed in town a week, visiting her each afternoon, then went back north, but returned three weeks later, saying he couldn't live without her. She left a note for Bernard, packed her own and the children's clothes and drove away with him to live in a house-trailer located somewhere between Prince George and Prince Rupert, where she was so bored she wanted to scream (and did scream at the children) except for the nights and early mornings when she and Harry made love. Harry, she always insisted to Jamie, was the best lover a woman could ever hope for.

And everything would probably have worked out, except for one thing: She found she desperately wanted another child; she wanted external proof, as she put it, of her and Harry's passion; she wanted more than the endless stream of secretions that flowed in and out of her. So when she didn't conceive, she drove into Prince George to see a doctor and have tests. Harry also had tests, and the end of their relationship came when the results showed he was infertile due, so the physician informed him, to a bout of gonorrhea he'd picked up, probably from the Vancouver whores he used to visit. The news upset Harry. It was clear he liked children. He played with Annabelle and Christopher and got a big kick out of helping them undress at night when he'd perch Annabelle on one hand and Christopher on the other and prance around the trailer. "They're real cuties," he'd say as he dropped them into Amanda's lap. "Let's have more like them." On learning she and Harry would never have a child, Amanda could hardly bear to let Harry touch her and she believed she had no choice but to leave him; and when she told Jamie about her and Harry making love through the night and early morning of the day she left, Jamie thought it was one of the saddest tales he'd ever heard, made even more poignant by the way Harry behaved: He gave Amanda his car and half his savings. Nowadays, Amanda tried to avoid speaking of Harry Greene because it upset her so much. "He's such a fine man," she would sob, "but I couldn't go on, Jamie, I just couldn't."

Of course, everybody in the Powell-McLeod families knew about "Mandy's escapade" and subsequent divorce from Bernard Stoltz, but only Jamie knew how much Amanda had suffered over Harry, and though he didn't like to admit it, he couldn't avoid thinking that when Amanda spoke of the changes love wrought in a person's life, she knew what she was talking about.

Now Amanda moved closer to Jamie, and he felt her soft breast close to his arm. He had been present at the "birth" of Amanda's breasts when they looked like polyps, and he had been expected to admire them as they had passed through various stages of development. Those were the days when Jamie believed that Amanda was his alter-ego, the days before hair appeared on his chin and pubis and Amanda acquired a rather sickly moral code which caused her to reject a certain proposal he had made, saying, "I'd really like to, Jamie, but we mustn't, because it would be really, really wrong." (Those were Amanda's "really really" days.) The most incredible aspect (to Jamie) of his relationship with his sister was that the things he disliked in other women, he accepted without question in Amanda, and would have been upset had she attempted to change anything about herself. Jamie liked to imagine his sisters and half-brother in settings where their personalities reached fulfillment: Liz he placed in Troy as a character in a Euripidean tragedy, heroically defiant; he positioned David in the Age of Reason, drinking tea with Samuel Johnson or sipping coffee with the French Encyclopedists; stodgy Hilda he put into a George Eliot mid-Victorian setting; and Natasha was metamorphosed into a countess, moving

from salon to salon in Tolstoyan settings. But he had never been able satis-
factorily to objectify Amanda; the closest he'd come so far was to visual-
ize her as an amorous woman in a de Maupassant story, blowsily embracing every man who climbed into her feather bed. Yet even that image was
not truly apt, for while Liz and Hilda always used exclamation marks and
capital letters when referring to Amanda (SCATTERBRAINED, HOPE-
LESS AMANDA!) Jamie knew that in fact Amanda had a shrewd business sense; not only did she own the house she lived in, but also several
other properties along the same street, plus a fourplex where the street
joined the main east-west avenue. She'd told Jamie about her property
acquisitions because, as she put it: "We've always told each other everything, haven't we, Jamie?" So now Amanda wanted to know all about Alice;
and Jamie, who had sworn he'd never keep anything from his sister and
had also reached an unspoken agreement with Alice to keep their relationship a secret, found himself telling Amanda how he and Alice had met and
how their relationship had developed. "You won't tell anybody, will you,
Mandy?" he said.

"Of course not," Amanda fervently promised, even though she knew,
as did Jamie, that everything he told her would be passed on to his sisters
and cousin. "I understand how a couple might feel embarrassed with people
wondering how many times a night they do it, or if the woman really likes
it. *Does* Alice like it, Jamie?"

Jamie nodded. He felt miserable betraying Alice.

"That's good. When I first married Bernard I expected we'd do all
kinds of nice things. But we never did. Women like to stretch love-making
out. I'm sure you do that with Alice, don't you?" He nodded, knowing
Amanda's questions would continue until the last drop of information had
been extracted from him. Fortunately, Annabelle and Christopher arrived
home from school, thereby concluding the inquisition before that point
was reached.

Of his nieces, Jamie especially liked Annabelle. She was incredibly
well organized for a child: She often did the family laundry and prepared
meals for Christopher and herself. She was dictatorial, too, given to issuing streams of contradictory orders to her brother. That he seldom obeyed
them seemed not to matter to either child — it was the giving of the orders
that was important. They knew their mother had lovers, but weren't too
concerned about it. They had once told Jamie, however, about an occasion
when Amanda entered the living room to find one of the men, who should
have been rolling paint on a wall, sitting beside Annabelle with his hand
creeping along her thigh towards her immature crotch. Amanda, so the

children told Jamie, ran to the kitchen, snatched up a breadboard, charged back, brought it down on the man's head, then unceremoniously dragged him from the house and left him on the sidewalk. "We heard his brains crunch, didn't we, Annabelle?" Christopher said. "*I* heard them crunch," said Annabelle. "You didn't, because you were watching TV."

When Jamie later mentioned the matter, Amanda said, "Oh, that guy was an exception. Don't worry, Jamie, I vet the guys thoroughly." (Still, after that incident, Amanda insisted her lovers must leave the house before the children arrived home from school.)

Annabelle and Christopher liked Jamie's company and especially enjoyed walking with him through the University Endowment Lands. Jamie thought perhaps one reason they were keen to accompany him on outings was that they usually stopped at a White Spot for a hamburger followed by banana cream pie. The children weren't exactly mercenary, but saw no reason not to accept any attractive offer Jamie made.

"The kids like you," Amanda always said. "You enjoy them for what they are."

"They're good kids," Jamie always replied.

"You honestly think so? Sometimes I worry about them, not having a father around, especially Chris." After she'd left him, Bernard, knowing Amanda had enough money to live on, not only ignored her, but also behaved as though the two children Amanda had persuaded him to beget in her had never existed.

"We got along without our father," Jamie would point out.

"And why should they need one when they have an uncle like you? I'm sure you're ten times more understanding than any father would be. Will you and Alice have a baby?"

"We haven't thought about it." By now, Jamie's responses to Amanda's questions automatically clicked in. It amazed him.

Amanda rubbed her cheek against his. "Maybe it'll just happen."

When Jamie visited in the late afternoon, Amanda usually asked the children as a great favour if they would make tea. At once, they would run from the room, and within ten minutes Annabelle would return, carrying a tray on which sat a Crown Derby teapot, four cups and saucers, a sugar bowl and cream pitcher. (Jamie remembered the crockery as being part of his mother's favourite tea set, which Amanda somehow had managed to slip away from under Liz's nose.) Behind her would come Christopher, bearing two Crown Derby plates loaded with cream-filled store cookies.

"Oh, how lovely!" Amanda enthused. "A real tea party! Oh, thank you, Chris darling. Just one cookie, please. I mustn't put on more weight.

Thank you, Annabelle darling. What delicious tea, isn't it, Jamie? Annabelle makes the most scrumptious tea. I don't know how she does it." Of course Jamie knew exactly how Annabelle produced the lukewarm, milky fluid, which he found almost undrinkable: She had been instructed by Amanda that as soon as the kettle began to sing she was to turn off the burner, let the kettle sit two minutes, then fill the teapot. "I'd rather drink sewage water than have Annabelle pour boiling water into a teapot," Amanda said. And Jamie was forced to agree with his sister. Even to contemplate that Annabelle might accidentally spill boiling water over herself or Christopher made him shiver. In so many ways, Jamie thought, Amanda was an exemplary mother. Each day she asked the children what they had done at school and whether they'd worked hard and completed their tasks. He was impressed by the fact that as far as he could tell neither child ever lied to their mother, but willingly admitted if they had broken a rule or been naughty. "You know I trust you," Amanda would say to them. "I really and truly do. When you make a promise, I expect you to keep it. You can't go through life breaking promises. You understand?"

Amanda resumed questioning Jamie after the children had gone off to play. "Does Alice know you inherited Grandfather's title?"

"I haven't told her."

"Why ever not? She might enjoy being called Lady Alice."

"We're not married."

"But you will be eventually, especially when she has a baby." Jamie's legs twitched, urging him to get off the bed and scurry away from the house. Amanda tightened her grip on his arm. "It would be wonderful to see *Lord Powell of Hyndhurst* on one of your books. I'd be so thrilled! Not many poets belong to the aristocracy."

"Listen to me, Mandy. I'm a Canadian poet, not some half-wit Englishman writing patriotic couplets to relieve the boredom of being stuck in an outpost of the British Empire. I don't want the title, and I'll never use it. It's an insult." He tried to wrench his arm away from Amanda's plump fists.

"Don't be angry with me, Jamie love. I couldn't bear it." Tears popped from Amanda's eyes and slid over her cheeks. Jamie wondered why he visited Amanda and invited intrusion into his private life. He had known for years how conversations with her invariably progressed: a mixture of insinuations and demands packaged inside repeated protestations of undying affection.

"Cut it out, Mandy," he said.

"I know. And I do try. But it's because of the way I feel about you,

Jamie. Honestly. Don't forget, you know everything about me, all the stupid things I do, my affairs with guys I don't really like because all they
care about is football and hockey. Why can't I find somebody like you,
Jamie? Don't go. If you do, I'll feel I've driven you away forever and the
kids'd never forgive me."

"Stop talking nonsense." Jamie sighed. "You know I'd never walk out
and not come back. Your repentance is a big put-on. But I want you to stop
prying into my personal life. I don't want you arranging lunches with Alice
either, and digging into *her* life. She doesn't know how you operate, Mandy.
But I do. She thinks you're a scatterbrain, like everybody else. But I know
better. You're probably the most shrewd of all of us."

"Oh no, Jamie," Amanda protested. "You and David are the smartest
ones in the family."

"Even if that were true, you have no right to try and wrap me around
your little finger."

"Remember when we were little, Jamie?" Amanda produced a sigh
packed with synthetic memories of a perfect childhood.

"I refuse to discuss anything about our childhood."

Amanda ignored him. "We'd sit on the side of our bed, close together
— just like now — two birds sitting on a telephone wire. Remember how
we'd hold each other? Annabelle and Chris do exactly the same. I must get
up. It must be getting close to dinner time. Stay and eat with us, or is Alice
expecting you? The kids always love it when you eat with us." She slipped
away from him, and was about to leave the bed when feet clattered on the
stairs and Annabelle, followed by Christopher, rushed in.

"Mom!" Annabelle dramatically began, "Chris is looking at that TV
show you told him not to! The one where guys get shot at!"

"Chris!" Amanda remonstrated.

"I didn't know it was *that* show," Christopher protested.

"Yes, you did," Annabelle indignantly said. "I saw you turn it on. You
know what'll happen to you, Chris? You'll become a drug-dealing Killer
Teenager, won't he, Uncle Jamie?"

Jamie temporized. "I'm not so sure about that."

"Christopher must not look at that program again, or I'll have to say
no more TV," Amanda firmly announced. "Now, will you set the table,
please? Jamie's staying for dinner. And don't forget what I've just said,
Chris." The children left the room and Amanda got out of bed, then stood
by it for a moment, absent-mindedly scratching herself while Jamie watched,
recalling the many times in his life Amanda had stood like this telling him
something which she believed was of vast importance for both of them.

The fact that she was thirty-five and he thirty-two made no difference: This was how they had conferred as children and he supposed they would continue to confer in this manner until the day they died. "Every time Liz comes to the house she lectures me on how to raise the kids. It never occurs to her that I may be a better judge of how to raise them than she is. She can be quite impossible. She shows up in the afternoon when I'm sleeping, tells me I'm lazy, and doesn't listen when I tell her I didn't get home until nine that morning. I suppose that's what happens to people who've been in politics. They only pretend to listen. Natasha's told me Liz is thinking of running federally. I wish she would. It's not that I don't think the world of her, I do. She's a marvellous person, but I wish she wouldn't interfere so much." Jamie smiled and refrained from asking Amanda whether this wasn't a case of the pot calling the kettle black.

He got up and went to the bedroom door. "I really can't stay for dinner," he said. "I've got a multitude of things to do."

"The kids'll be disappointed." She crossed to stand close to him and an acrid odour of bodily secretions drifted into his nostrils.

"They'll survive. And remember what I said about probing into my affairs."

Amanda smiled, while raising her hands to her lips in a gesture of prayer. "I promise," she said, "I promise."

Jamie shrugged and left the house. Amanda showered and dressed, then went down to the kitchen where she began preparing dinner, at the same time carrying on a telephone conversation with Natasha in which she gave a detailed account of Jamie's visit, the conclusions she had reached about Jamie and Alice and a suggested course for her and Natasha to follow in the immediate future.

"There," she said to Annabelle, who had listened to the conversation, "now all we have to do is bring Alice into the family." She kissed Annabelle. "Is the table set?"

"Mom," Annabelle said, "you think I'm ugly?"

"Ugly? No. I think you're pretty."

"A girl at school said girls who have freckles are low class."

"That proves she's stupid. How many girls your age can make dinner and do the laundry and vacuuming? Now, go and tell Chris it's dinner time and make sure you turn off the TV."

She watched Annabelle leave the kitchen, then *shooed* air though pursed lips, as she tried not to worry about the disappointments she was sure her plain-faced daughter would experience in the years ahead.

Chapter 5

"You sick or something?" asked Hilda.

Amanda looked at her sister Hilda Logan, standing at the end of her bed, suspiciously eyeing her, much as a visitor stands at the end of a hospital bed eyeing its occupant, trying to decide if the person is truly sick or just malingering. Why was it, Amanda asked herself, that only Jamie seemed capable of grasping the fact that finding her in bed in the afternoon meant she'd been working the previous night? Perhaps their relationship as children had so distorted Hilda's view of her that regardless of anything she did now, Hilda would go on treating her as though she were a lazy and slightly retarded person, even though the rest of the world was prepared to acknowledge that she possessed a modicum of intelligence, for how else could she have got through nursing school and afterwards acquired her degree? And what about the chunk of real estate she owned? Didn't that show she had a few brains? But for Hilda, she remained Scatterbrain Mandy, and apparently nothing could change this.

"I worked last night," she said.

"Oh." Hilda, expensively dressed in a plaid skirt and red jacket, perched gingerly at the edge of the bed, as if Amanda had a horrible, contagious disease. "What's all this talk about Jamie?" she said. "I asked Liz what was going on and she acted as though it was a state secret."

Amanda yawned and sighed. "Liz always acts like that when Jamie's involved."

"She's being ridiculous. So what's Jamie up to?"

"He's not up to anything. He just got involved with a woman."

"Is that all? Then why all the fuss? Isn't it about time Jamie got involved with somebody and stopped acting like a skid-row bum? Anyway, Liz said you've met the woman."

"I had lunch with her."

"So, is she another poet? Somebody in the arts?"

"She's an accountant."

"A what? You're joking."

"That's what she told me. She has degrees in commerce and business administration."

"From where?"

"Somewhere in Saskatchewan. I didn't ask her."

"People say anything. Are they living together? Is that what all the fuss is about?"

"There's no fuss."

"Then why is Liz making such a big to-do over it?"

"Because Alice — that's her name — parks her car across the street from the Big House when Jamie's there working. That's how we found out about her. I went up to the car, introduced myself and was practically killed when she took off." Amanda now gave Hilda an account of her lunch with Alice and ended by saying: "The woman's in love with Jamie, and I'm positive he feels the same way about her. But they don't want us interfering. I guess she just about went crazy the first time Jamie disappeared, because he hadn't bothered to tell her about going to his old room to do his poetry. She thought something had happened to him. I explained David's idea of Jamie being like a salmon returning to the creek where it was born."

"That must have been enlightening." Hilda rearranged herself on the bed and smoothed pleats in her skirt. "Does she know about Jamie's title?"

"I don't think so."

"You didn't tell her?"

"All I did was suggest she introduce herself to Liz. Liz's fine, once you get used to her bossy ways. Alice could sleep at the house, and Jamie wouldn't even know. He only comes out of the room to use the bathroom. But I think she's scared Jamie'll take off if she acts too possessive."

"They're living together?"

"I don't know. At first, she didn't know about his poetry."

"So what's your overall evaluation of her?"

"For heaven's sake, Hiddie, we're not talking about somebody applying for a job. She's a very independent woman — a no-nonsense kind of person."

"Jamie needs somebody like that. Not long ago he showed up at the house and Louise didn't want to let him in he looked so disreputable."

"You must tell Louise that tidiness isn't the most important thing about people."

"If Jamie chooses to look like a bum, then he must expect to be treated like one. *You* may be accustomed to seeing disreputable-looking people in *your* neighbourhood, but that's not the case where I live." Hilda lived at the edge of the exclusive Shaughnessy area and believed it necessary constantly to remind Amanda that the respective location of their dwellings was indicative of their relative value to the Vancouver community. In her view, Amanda always had been, and would continue to be, quite hopeless. She'd had the good fortune to marry a fashionable obstetrician, and what had she done? She'd left him to live with a crude logger. But then, Amanda was one of those irresponsible people whom you see more and more of these days, people incapable of looking after themselves. She invariably left a bad impression on others and failed to grasp opportunities to get ahead in her profession and in society.

Hilda regretted that other members of her family, especially her fabulously wealthy Aunt Nanda, didn't realize how terribly important it was for Hilda's children to meet and mix with all the right people. More than once she had hinted to Nanda that she should offer the use of her home and garden to one of Vancouver's high-toned charitable organizations so that Louise, Jeanette and Max Junior would have an opportunity to meet people from the appropriate class, but Nanda had never responded to the suggestions and remained reclusive, which was a pity, because if Aunt Nanda would only socialize more it would certainly be beneficial for everyone, especially for herself, since making the right social contacts was the foundation for success as a stocks and bonds broker. And Natasha was just as bad. She mixed exclusively with people involved in Save the Children-type organizations. Very nice people of course, but hardly the right sort to be helpful to Louise, Jeanette and Max Junior. Liz could have influenced Nanda to do more, but she had nothing but contempt, so she said, for high society. So while Hilda acknowledged how brilliant Liz was, she couldn't understand how Liz could fail to see how important belonging to the right social group was to the future lives of her nieces and nephew. And why didn't Jamie wake up and realize his title (if only he would use it!) could be of enormous advantage to everybody in the family? When royalty visited Vancouver, he could put on a decent suit, introduce himself and arrange for Louise, Jeanette and Max Junior to be photographed chatting with the Prince or Princess. Jamie was the limit! Really, she seemed to be the only member of the Powell family who knew how to conduct her life properly.

"Did you bring the kids?"

Hilda nodded. "They're downstairs visiting with Annabelle and Christopher. Listen Mandy, you ought to buy some decent clothes for Annabelle. That dress she has on makes her look like a housemaid in a TV series."

"That's the latest in kids' styles. Laura Ashley. She probably put it on to impress you."

"I prefer pleated skirts and blouses for the girls."

"Annabelle and Chris choose what they want to wear. I just pay the bills. It's the easiest way. If they grumble I say, 'Don't blame me. That's what you wanted.' If you'll put on the kettle, Hiddie, I'll make us tea."

"You don't have to," Hilda said.

"You always give me tea when I visit you."

"I'm always up and about."

"I'd be up, too, if you visited me at three in the morning at the house where I'm tending a patient who's dying of cancer."

"Why do you do such awful work, Mandy?"

"It pays well. And I can choose my jobs."

"But you don't *have* to work, do you? I mean, the rent for this place can't be much."

"I own this house." Hilda repressed an impulse to explain that Amanda must not confuse renting with ownership of property. "And I own five other houses in the neighbourhood. And the fourplex on the corner," Amanda added. "Buying houses is simple once you get started. You chop up the houses into suites and rent them. The rent pays the mortgages, and there's enough left over to pay off the principal on one house and cover maintenance costs on the rest."

"I'll make the tea." Hilda left the room thinking that she must speak to Liz about Mandy's inability to distinguish between renting and owning property. It was really quite disturbing. How could a person who lazed in bed in the afternoon own six houses and a fourplex? It was ridiculous, and Liz really must do something about setting Mandy straight.

In the bedroom, Amanda left the bed, stretched, yawned, farted, waggled her buttocks at the doorway through which Hilda had just exited, grimaced, and generally behaved as she had as a child upon receiving a lecture on behaviour from Hilda or Liz. She then scratched her head, slipped on an ancient yellow bathrobe and went to take a shower.

Of all the people who circulated within her small universe, Annabelle most disliked her cousins Louise and Jeanette. She couldn't stand their "superfilicus" (as Annabelle called it) attitude towards her and the way they turned up their noses at her family's possessions. But she valiantly fought back. When Louise talked about the size of their house and the number of bathrooms, Annabelle countered with information that her mother had ten bathrooms, a claim dismissed with jeers by Louise and Jeanette, who looked around the little sitting room and said they supposed her mother had nine other living rooms just as crummy as this one. So when Hilda appeared with the request from Amanda to lay the table,

Annabelle happily escaped, taking Christopher with her: She wasn't going to let her brother be torn apart by her cousins. No sooner had they left the room than Louise told Hilda, accompanied by Jeanette and Max Junior's laughter, about Annabelle's preposterous claim that her mother owned ten bathrooms, to which Hilda replied that Annabelle must be referring to bathrooms in other houses her mother might own. Annabelle, listening outside the doorway, instructed Christopher to lay the table, while wishing she had baked poisoned cookies to serve her aunt and cousins, thus permanently eliminating them from her life. But she had to suffer another hour listening to her cousins' and Aunt Hilda's "superfilicus" talk before they finally left.

As Hilda walked down the front steps she turned to Amanda and said, "Keep me posted about Jamie. Don't forget now." Once the door was closed, Amanda and the children looked at one another, opened their mouths wide and released an explosive, "Phew! Thank goodness that's over!"

Chapter 6

"Is everything going well with you and Jamie?" Amanda asked.

Amanda and Alice were having lunch in a Fourth Avenue restaurant selected by Amanda. It served vegetarian food and was vaguely suggestive of the Middle East. Amanda was spooning a vegetable soup, while Alice coped with pita bread stuffed with a mixture of vegetables. When she chomped on the bread at one end, the vegetables emerged through a crack at the bottom. Since the table was very small, a piece of tomato and some bean sprouts landed in Amanda's soup. "That's an example of fast food in the Middle East," Amanda said.

"Why didn't they keep their damn pita bread there?" Alice replied. "Their food's a mess, like their politics."

"You've been to the Middle East?" Amanda had travelled as far from Vancouver as Prince George and Seattle and her geographic sense was weak.

"Yes. I audited the books of a Lebanese company that wanted to borrow money from a Canadian bank. Their books were a mess too."

"Oh really? Were you able to see much of the country?" Amanda had no idea where Alice could have been. It might have been the moon.

"I had the trots from the minute I landed until the minute I got home."

"Poor you," Amanda sympathized. "There's nothing worse than diarrhea."

"There sure isn't, especially when you have to run down two sets of stairs to get to the toilet."

"How ghastly! I thought all hotels had private bathrooms these days."

"You thought wrong." Alice gave up on the pita bread. "Why did you want to see me?"

"Nothing special. Just to ask how things were going." Actually, Amanda was following up on Liz's suggestion that she telephone Alice and arrange another lunch. After sampling the food, Amanda wished she'd arranged to collect Alice at her office and drive across town to one of the Italian restaurants on Commercial Drive where the food could always be counted on to be good. The places on Fourth Avenue — remnants of the sixties' hippie movement — served lousy food and were too noisy for a quiet exchange of intimate information. Amanda hadn't really wanted to go about things in this way, but Liz had been insistent, arguing they owed it to themselves to find out if the Jamie-Alice relationship showed signs of being permanent. Amanda sighed, wishing Liz had taken on the job herself, then broached the matter that Liz had insisted she raise with Alice. "I suppose you and Jamie are thinking about having a family," she said, then immediately wished she hadn't.

"A what?"

"You know, babies and what-not."

"A what-not?" Alice repeated, her voice shooting up an octave, while her blue eyes opened so wide that for a moment Amanda thought they were going to pop out. "What the hell're you talking about?"

A waiter, who thought Alice might be referring to her lunch, sidled around tables to inquire: "Enjoying your lunch?"

"No, take it away. It's godawful," Alice told him. After momentary indecision, the waiter snatched her plate and moved away. "Has Jamie said anything to you about having a baby?"

"No, no, it's not that." Amanda waved dismissive hands. "I just thought it would be kind of nice if . . ."

"Look, if Jamie wants a kid he can go ahead and have one. I've got no intention of getting mixed up in all that rigmarole." Amanda couldn't believe what she had just heard: Did Alice actually think Jamie could give birth to a baby? For one delirious moment an image of Jamie hopping around like a kangaroo with a baby in its pouch flashed across her mind. (She later told Liz it was very disorienting, to which Liz replied that Amanda always mixed things up and had no business having such a ridiculous thought.) "I'm too old to have babies. Besides, it would interfere with my plans for the future."

"How old are you?"

"Too damn close to forty."

"That's nothing," Amanda burbled. "When I was in maternity I saw lots of forty-year-old women having babies."

"Idiots!" Alice said.

"Beautiful babies, too."

"They're welcome to them, and in the meantime, why don't you stop trying to arrange my life and start fixing up your own?" And with that, Alice got up and left the restaurant.

Amanda paid the bill and went to call on Natasha. She had taken a week off work and her afternoons were now free. "Honestly Tashie," she said, "it was terrible. She just got up and left."

"It must have been awful," Natasha sympathetically agreed. "And you were just asking a question. I mean, you weren't categorically ordering her to get pregnant, were you?"

"That's how Alice takes things, Tashie. She's not a person you can talk to . . . you know, like we talk. She bristles, like a suspicious dog. I wonder what'd happen if she and Liz ever got together."

Natasha laughed. "They might *like* each other. You never can tell about people. Did you mention Jamie's title?"

"I didn't have time. She's the kind of person who's always on the look-out for a fight."

"It's odd that Jamie's got involved with a woman like that. I thought he'd be more attracted to moony-eyed women with hair hanging to their waists. Does Jamie talk to you about personal matters?"

"Hardly ever. I do all the talking. I stick verbal pins into him and try to guess what he's thinking by the way he reacts. Mostly I come pretty close. I should — I've been guessing at his thoughts for years now."

"Isn't it amazing how you can almost feel what a person's thinking when you're close to him? That's how I feel about David."

"You've been lucky, Tashie."

"I know. At times it scares me. I wake up some nights, especially if David's away, in an absolute panic, thinking it can't last, or that I'm not really married or don't have my babies, but simply dreamed the whole thing and will wake up and find I'm still Natasha, lying alone somewhere without anybody who cares for me."

"But why would you ever think such things, Tashie? People who're beautiful never end up alone. Remember what we called you when we were kids? *Gorgeous Tashie.* I used to wish I was as beautiful as you. I was green with envy."

"It's odd what a person thinks of herself, isn't it? Actually, you're pretty, Mandy. Don't you know that? But you don't make the most of your looks. I used to wish I had your nose." They laughed and exchanged confidences about which aspects of each other they would incorporate into themselves were it possible to do such a thing. Amanda loved these intimate sessions with Natasha — the hints, the admissions of deeper emotional compo-nents of her cousin's personality — and was always eager to reveal facets of her own life in the hope she'd learn more about the relationship between Natasha and David, especially what Natasha experienced when she and

David made love. David and Natasha's relationship had always fascinated Amanda because she knew about the strong bond between Liz and David, and she couldn't help but wonder if David ever talked to Natasha about it. As always, Amanda used an indirect approach. "You know, Tashie, I was pretty stupid about sex even after I was married. I didn't understand what love-making was all about until I met Harry. I know Liz and Hiddie think I'm sort of immoral to have affairs, but I don't really make love with those guys. I suppose I'm trying to find someone as nice as Harry. Or a guy like David. When Harry and I had sex I felt I was going to heaven. Do you feel that way with David?"

Natasha blushed and turned her head so that Amanda couldn't see her face. "I suppose I do," she whispered. "When I was pregnant I used to look at myself in the mirror and think my baby had come from God." Amanda had heard before about God's role in Natasha's pregnancies, and she was tempted to demolish Natasha's safe little world by telling her the truth about David and Liz. But caution prevailed, as it always did. As she stood to leave, she said: "I think it's dangerous to love somebody too much, or to feel too strongly about one person. You start thinking that what you feel will never end. You know, like one of those wonderful summers we used to spend at Paradise Island, when the sun never stopped shining and we thought it never would." She squeezed Natasha's arm. "Or like standing in a garden looking at a beautiful flower when all the time there's a nasty grub in the ground destroying the root."

"I have my *passion flowers*!" Natasha proudly cried. "They are proof of what David and I feel for each other."

"Of course they are. But I'm thinking more about what happened to me with Harry. I know what you and David have together is marvellous, just marvellous. That's all the more reason you should protect it, Tashie." She kissed Natasha and departed, satisfied with how the conversation had ended.

Often a comment or gesture has an unintended outcome, and so it was with Amanda's comments on the self-destructive nature of passion, which had so unsettled Natasha that she decided she would become pregnant as quickly as possible. That way she could offer up more proof of the passion she and David felt for each other. As Amanda had advised, she would take action to protect her relationship with David; she would make sure that the passion which burned between them would never flare up into a roaring fire and consume their desire for each other.

Bored with having nothing interesting to occupy her days, Amanda responded to an urgent request from the medical agency that booked her jobs and went back to night-shift work. So, a week later, when Jamie entered her bedroom in the early afternoon, she was half asleep as she felt the bed sag when he adjusted himself on it. She sensed he was terribly angry with her, and felt much like a mouse or small bird might in the presence of a hungry owl. She burrowed further under the covers and waited.

"Why did you say that to Alice, Mandy?" he finally asked.

"I was only trying to help you, Jamie. That's all."

"*Mandy . . .*"

The simple utterance of her name was a more potent chastisement than a stream of reproaches. "Honestly," she whimpered. "Liz said I should ask Alice if —"

"Liz?" Jamie turned and looked down at Amanda whose blue eyes and short, pink-tipped nose were now poking out of the bed covers. Her face resurrected an image for Jamie of a china rabbit he'd once owned and dearly loved and in a rage had hurled against a wall and destroyed. He had tried to piece the fragments together and later, in puberty, ejaculated onto the bits of china, hoping the gooey stuff would enable him finally to reassemble it. Memory of the exhibition of pointless anger which had destroyed his precious rabbit now dissipated the rage that had brought him to Amanda's bedside.

"I love you, Jamie," Amanda whispered. "Annabelle and Chris love you too."

"That's beside the point. Try not to interfere, Mandy. Please." When he reached out to adjust himself on the bed, she grabbed and fervently kissed his hand and began crying.

"I can't help it," she sobbed, "I just can't."

"I know." He leaned on the headboard and looked up at the ceiling to note that enterprising spiders had strung webs across the corner mouldings. He felt Amanda move and her sleep-sour breath drifted across his face. "Alice is upset."

"I didn't mean to upset her. Honestly." As always, Amanda admitted guilt and sniffled apologies; or, Jamie thought, was all the sniffling and sobbing nothing more than practised duplicity, a means to avoid the penalty of his justifiable ire? Of course, none of what Jamie currently felt about Amanda would change their relationship in any way, because she was as much a part of his life as were his personal habits. In fact, he couldn't recall a time when he hadn't identified himself by first identifying Amanda, three years "above him" on the family ladder, and could no more imagine existing without her than he could imagine himself *sans* arms, legs, eyes, cock or brain. "Still love me, Jamie?" she whimpered. He nodded agreement, though in fact he had no clear idea of what "love" was. Many times he had tried to fathom its nature, but had accomplished nothing more than to chase its meaning, like a puppy unsuccessfully trying to bite its own tail. They heard running footsteps on the stairs and hall, and Annabelle and Christopher rushed into the room to stand at the foot of the bed and solemnly stare at Jamie and Amanda.

"There's mud on your running shoe, Uncle Jamie," Annabelle said.

"Which one?" Annabelle reached across the bed and pointed to the toe of one shoe. Jamie moved the offending shoe from the bed.

"So, how was school today?" Amanda asked. "Any problems?" Annabelle raised shoulders, then let loose a melancholy sigh.

"Sometimes I think Mrs. McFadden is totally confused," she said.

"That's normal with people," Jamie remarked.

"*I'm* not confused," Annabelle severely corrected him. "Mrs. McFadden told us to read about Peru in our social studies book. Then today she gave a quiz on Japan, and I didn't get the right answers because I'd read about Peru, and everybody knows Japan's way across the Pacific Ocean and is the last chapter in the book." Jamie watched Annabelle closely, impressed by the degree of moral indignation emanating from her: It seemed sufficient to quell all the wrongdoing and hypocrisy existing in the world.

"You may have misunderstood Mrs. McFadden," Amanda suggested.

Amanda's comment produced a look of judgemental severity on Annabelle's face. "I did not! I always listen careful," she icily said.

"Carefully," Jamie said. "You need an adverb."

"What about the other boys and girls?"

"Oh them! They never read the book anyway, so they answered questions indisgrimly."

"Indiscriminately," Jamie corrected.

"Oh well, it doesn't matter," Amanda said.

"Sometimes I'm more confused than my students," Jamie told Annabelle. "Then they tell *me* what to do. I tend to do things indiscriminately, while they, like you, do things carefully." The children now dumped coats and bags onto the floor and climbed onto the bed. They crossed their legs, put an elbow on one leg, cupped their chins and intently watched Jamie, while he, looking back at them, speculated how they might perceive and judge him. What did Christopher, who seemed hardly aware of what was going on around him, think when he looked at his uncle's face? And what of managerial Annabelle? What did she think? Perhaps they simply accepted him as part of the local scenery. When he looked along the bed at Annabelle, he could see where the flare of her white panties covered her narrow crotch and wondered if she ever thought about the lines and functions of her slender body. Probably not. People did not begin to ask questions about their bodies until those bodies imposed demands on them.

"It's irritable," Annabelle said.

"Irritating," Jamie said. "Mrs. McFadden, your irritating teacher, has made you irritable."

"Darling, it's not important," Amanda said. "Give me a kiss, then go downstairs and make peanut-butter sandwiches for yourself and Chris." Annabelle abandoned her pose to exchange kisses and lie against her mother as she moved a hand over Annabelle's back and gently patted her bottom. Annabelle clutched her mother, then gave a prolonged sigh that rippled through her entire body, releasing its tension. "Okay," Amanda said, "it's over now. Tomorrow things'll start up again, just like new. Now, let me give Chris a hug and kiss." As always, Jamie was impressed by Amanda's nurturing skills. He observed the way she passed her hands over the lines of her son's body and thought that as Amanda caressed him, she not only gathered him into her emotional womb but also removed anything delete- rious that may have touched him during his absence from her care. "Take your things downstairs and hang them up, please," she said as they scrambled off the bed.

"When you caress your kids, psychically, you drain all contaminants and pollutants from their bodies and souls," Jamie told her after the chil- dren had left the room. "Are you aware you practise a form of exorcism?"

Not understanding Jamie's reference, Amanda answered: "Children need to be held and kissed. I'll get up now. Stay and eat with us, Jamie."

"I have a class at seven."

"You'll have time." She pushed the covers away. "I have the most aw- ful job."

"Leave it."

"I can't. They've already gone through three other nurses. The man's mad with pain."

"Wouldn't he be better off in a hospital?"

"That's where he should be, but his sister has enough money for pri- vate nursing and that's what she wants. Did I tell you Hiddie says I must lose weight?"

"You did."

"What cheek! She must weigh thirty pounds more than me." She stood at the foot of the bed. "But people usually don't see themselves. Do you see yourself, Jamie?"

"I try to."

"So do I." She yawned. "But Hiddie only sees other people's limitations. Have you seen Liz recently?"

"No."

"Neither have I." Amanda's misdemeanours had now been forgotten and they were back on their old footing. "I've been meaning to call her, but I'm so exhausted from work the last thing I want is to have someone pointing out my defects. Jamie, would you go down and take the package of hamburger out of the fridge? And ask Annabelle to scrape four carrots."

"I'll do them." He left the bed and walked to the doorway.

"Jamie." He stopped and Amanda went over to put her arms around his neck. "No matter what happens, let's agree we'll never stay angry with each other." Her soft body seemed to melt against his. "Let's always love each other; let's agree that no matter what happens, we'll always go to each other for help. Promise?"

"Okay." He freed himself from her embrace, then left the room.

"There's a cauliflower in the fridge. Cut it in half," she called.

"I'll see to it." He went down the stairs and through the house to the kitchen, where Annabelle and Christopher sat eating peanut-butter sandwiches. Jamie opened the refrigerator, took out the cauliflower and began preparing it, supervised by Annabelle.

<hr />

Jamie arrived ten minutes late for his class and the students, bemused from their task of trying to make sense of John Donne's sonnets and expecting their instructor to clarify them for them, became totally confused when Jamie ignored Donne and instead delivered a lecture on the nature of the psychic womb and its influence on artistic development. When a student asked how that related to Donne's sonnets, Jamie, remembering Amanda's hands passing over the bodies of her children, stared intently at the student and said, "It has everything to do with John Donne's work. In his love poems, Donne sought entry into the universal maternal womb, and in his religious poems access into the spiritual womb of Christ. Read the sonnets again, think about what I've said and we'll talk more about it next class." He escaped, and rode along the traffic-swarming roads to Alice's apartment where, still affected by his concept of a psychic womb, he lay with Alice and made energetic love with her; and as he did so, his semen entered the gateway to her womb and swept around the edge of the rubber barrier she had inserted there to protect herself.

"Did you give Amanda hell?" Alice asked after they had finished.

"Yes," Jamie said. "She means well," he added.

"That's the oldest excuse in the world. It's a bunch of crap! Are you staying the night?" She felt the affirmative movement of his head against her breast and said, "Maybe we should get a larger bed."

"I'll sleep on the couch."

"We can manage here." This particular exchange occurred each time Jamie spent the night with Alice. Alice liked to keep Jamie against her while they slept, though there wasn't ample room for both to sleep comfortably on the narrow single bed. "On Saturday we'll buy ourselves a bigger bed. Right?"

"Right," Jamie sleepily agreed. "Amanda keeps Annabelle and Christopher in her psychic womb," he mumbled. "She exorcises evil from her kids. It's amazing." He twitched into sleep.

"What's so wonderful about that?" Alice didn't want to hear anything good about Amanda. "Don't forget about Saturday. We'll get a king-sized bed. Hey, Jamie! Pay attention to what I'm saying!" She shook him for a minute, then she too fell asleep.

Chapter 7

"Have you met her yet?" Hilda asked Liz.

"No. I'm leaving that to Amanda."

"Isn't it rather odd that Jamie's mixed up with an accountant?"

"He needs a sensible person."

It was a Saturday afternoon and Hilda was quizzing her sister, who always served martinis in the sitting room in honour of her visits; Liz had found that cocktails softened Hilda up and tended to keep discussion of family matters less argumentative. Since Liz believed she alone had the right to criticize family members, she never appreciated Hilda speaking disparagingly of her sisters or brothers, especially of Amanda. Although Liz might agree that Amanda's life was chaotic, whenever Hilda criticized Amanda, Liz rushed to the other end of the spectrum to defend whatever Hilda condemned. None of this appeared inconsistent to the sisters. If Hilda felt free to be critical of Liz's political stands, believing her to be too "left-wing", nonetheless she generally deferred to Liz on matters of family policy and conduct. Hilda's principal family task, as she saw it, was to get Liz out of the Big House, bequeathed her by their mother, and into an apartment. She was even prepared to let Liz come and live with her, provided Liz paid half the expenses. But Liz refused to consider moving, saying she hated apartments and that she and Hilda would inevitably quarrel if they lived together. "We're too set in our ways, Hiddie," she'd say. "The reason we get along is because we don't see much of each other. Besides, where would Jamie go to write poetry?"

"He'd find a place. What does it matter where he works?" Hilda refused to acknowledge any difference between trapping cosmic poetry and writing financial reports. "Does this Alice person still park in the street?" she asked.

"She's not been here since the evening Mandy tried to talk to her and practically got run over."

"Suppose she shows up the next time Jamie comes here? What'll you do?"

"If she telephones, I'll invite her over. Of course, she mightn't call now that she realizes we know who she is."

"Why not ask Jamie to bring her?"

"When Jamie's working, he doesn't want interruptions."

"Do you really believe all that nonsense about his finding poems in the stars?"

"Certainly."

"What does he do when it's cloudy?"

"It doesn't matter," Liz gallantly said. "Knowing the stars are there is what's important to Jamie. Besides, I expect he can see them through the clouds."

Hilda remained sceptical. "What baloney! People at the office think he stole the idea from Star Trek."

"That proves they know nothing of how poetry is created. Another martini?"

"No thanks." Hilda strained as she pushed herself off the couch, fighting weight she had recently gained, and together they walked to Hilda's car. (Hilda drove Max Logan's old Mercedes, which she claimed was comparable to a Rolls-Royce. For Hilda, everything she owned must be of the highest possible quality; she had even convinced herself that her possessions were every bit as good as anything Natasha and David had, and of course Amanda didn't count in family rivalry for possessions, Jamie was a special case, and Liz untouchable.) "One of these days you'll realize you've been foolish hanging on to this place, Liz," Hilda said as she closed the car door. "If Jamie stops coming, I'm sure you'll see the advantages of selling." The sisters exchanged "take cares", Hilda drove away, and Liz went back to the living room, poured what was left in the martini pitcher into her glass, quickly drank it, then walked upstairs to her bedroom, where David sat waiting in their mother's old armchair.

"I'd no idea Hiddie would show up today," she said, and leaned over to kiss his mouth.

"It's the martinis," David said, tasting the cocktail on her lips. "Hiddie's totally mercenary. I really ought to go."

"No, not yet." She leaned over the back of the chair to touch his face. "You look tired. Are you?"

"A bit."

"I can see new lines on your face, Davey." She moved around to kneel and rest her head on his knees. "The way we have to behave is all so stupid, isn't it?" Earlier, David had parked his car on a nearby street, then walked along the lane to enter the house by the back door, and they had just embraced and kissed when Hilda appeared. David, made uneasy by Hilda's hour-long visit, wanted to leave, but he knew a quick departure would upset Liz. They had never meant to have these secret meetings: Liz had sworn she would ask nothing more of him and he had vowed he would never betray his love for Natasha, yet he couldn't prevent himself from returning to the house, and when he appeared, Liz was unable to stop herself from expressing her love for him. Afterwards, they would agree it must never happen again. But it did, and while David understood how desire might build up in Liz, it wasn't the same for him; he desired and loved Natasha, and he wondered if the reason he came back to Liz had more to do with Liz than with himself: He sensed a need flowing from her, like water from an overfull spring, and he felt responsible for stemming its flow before it surged beyond control and became a destructive torrent. People who followed provincial politics in British Columbia knew Elizabeth Powell as a noisy, outspoken termagant, but the woman who lay with David was soft-spoken and filled with a clinging passion. She touched his face again, and he leaned forward to kiss her.

"I promised I'd be home by four."

She stood and began undressing. Her clothes were practical, lacking in decoration — so unlike Natasha, who wore embroidered silk lingerie edged with lace. Once David asked why she wore beautiful garments no one would see, and was surprised when she replied she did it to please him. David thought clothes an insult to both women: Each was beautiful naked. Liz, now almost forty, looked much as she had in her early twenties when, obeying her imperious command, he had first timidly approached, then made love to her. He now slumped with his face against her neck, waiting for his heartbeat to slow.

"If I had a child, would anybody guess it was ours?"

"Do you want one?"

"Just yours."

"I don't know, Liz. I mean, where would it end?" He waited a little, then said, "Are you serious?"

"Only when we're together."

"You mustn't think of it, Liz. Now I must go." He went to the bathroom and carefully washed himself, knowing the slightest hint of another woman's scent would set Natasha on a rampaging hunt for its source. It was easy to misjudge Natasha; she was so quiet, so agreeable, so seemingly passive, but that was the outer shell inside which lived the real, slightly demonic Natasha, who, David knew, had been determined, even as a child, to seize him for herself. Of course he loved Natasha, she was his wife, but the intensity of his feelings for her when contrasted to what he felt for Liz was as a candle compared to a blazing fire. Liz and he were two vines that had grown up to the light by twisting around each other; and while others in the family seemed unaware of Liz's need for him, he had always sensed it, even at an early age. He returned to the bedroom to dress watched by Liz.

"You've decided to run in the next federal election?" he said.

"Some heavies in the Liberal Party approached me."

"In the old riding?"

"It's where I'm best known."

"That would mean running against Gwendolyn."

"It doesn't seem to worry the heavies."

"But it might worry Gwen and Aunt Nanda. Wouldn't it bother you?"

"Not particularly."

"Maybe the New Democratic Party could find you a winnable riding somewhere else." Liz watched David slip on his sports coat. He was always meticulously dressed, even when at home.

"The winnable ridings have already nominated their candidates. And I'd have to rejoin the party. Besides, I couldn't bear to be parachuted into a riding."

"That shouldn't be difficult. I imagine any riding'd welcome a winner like you with open arms."

Liz smiled, and when he leaned over to kiss her, she drew his head onto her breasts. "You have more faith in me than I have in myself, Davey." He kissed her and straightened up. "Anyway, things haven't gone beyond a vague inquiry. Call me during the week."

Liz watched him go, then rolled over and buried her face in a pillow. There were times she could hardly bear being alone, and David's departures after love-making only heightened her sense of aloneness. As a child, she had never questioned her right to command David's allegiance, and it was only after Natasha had appeared as a competitor for his attentions that she had more or less dragged him into her bed, though at the time she wasn't physically attracted to him, but aware only that she must assert her prior right in order to retain her influence over him. (Sexual desire had come afterwards.) Liz still believed she had every right to take what she needed from David, though there were moments she felt slightly contemptuous of him because he so readily complied with her demands; but she realized, too, that it was impossible for her now to form a relationship with anyone else. She had tried; men still approached her, but nothing had worked out. She continued to want only David; only David seemed to satisfy her. Yet there were times when she became quite desperate with the thought of living alone for the rest of her life. Her panic was so great that not even several glasses of sherry followed by sleeping pills at night could prevent the terror from pursuing her in dreams. And of course she could not tell anyone, not even David, about her fears, and to confide in her sisters or in Jamie was impossible, because to reveal weakness would mean forfeiting the power she held over them. She remembered a conversation she'd had the previous year with Nanda:

"Your mother was concerned about you, Liz," Nanda had said. "She'd hoped you'd marry and have children. There must be plenty of men who've been interested in you."

"A few."

"How old are you now? Thirty-seven?"

"Thirty-eight."

"When I was young I dreamed of living alone. That was the ideal way to live, I thought. But then Natasha's father came into my life, and I forgot all that. Now, when I look back, I'm amazed at what I did. I just went off with Cromwell. He saw things in me that weren't there, but it didn't matter very much because I already knew how to respond to men as they wanted. I'd learned that being with your father and grandfather. I suppose it's possible I didn't really love Cromwell, but he took whatever I said seriously, which no one had ever done before. Then when he left me alone at Alderwood when he returned to Spain, I truly understood what being alone meant. He came back once, after France had capitulated. I begged him not to return, but he felt obligated because he'd become part of the Resistance movement. That's when I became pregnant with Natasha. He never knew. Natasha was five when I finally learned what happened to him: He'd died in a Gestapo prison. I thought I'd be alone for the rest of my life. Then Stuart came to Alderwood on his way back to Canada. You know the rest. Now he's gone too, and here I am much as I began. I tell you this, Liz, so you'll understand it's much easier to grow old when you have a companion who'll listen when you speak of things that happened in your childhood, someone who takes what you say seriously. Your mother knew this, which is why she worried about you."

"I'm fine . . . fine." Liz hurried on to prevent Nanda from talking more about how loneliness affects people. "What was my father really like, Nanda? Mother never talked about him."

"He was a very attractive man. David and Jamie look a lot like him, and so do you. But he condemned himself and believed he was a failure. Jamie's everything your father desperately wanted to be. A real poet."

"Not like Grandfather."

"Dad thought ownership of property was the most important thing in life, and he and your father disagreed about that. Dad sold property and managed estates around Hyndhurst and, as you know, he was the agent for Rhynewood before Winnie's mother died and your family moved in . . . though after the war came, Dad got involved in organizing food production. That's what he was knighted for. When the war ended, he joined the United Nations Food and Agricultural Organization, and got a life peerage for his work there. Later the title was changed to a barony, which is why Jamie can call himself Lord Powell of Hyndhurst if he so chooses."

"I think it's unfair David didn't receive the title."

"That's how the system works, Liz. You know that. Your parents formally adopted David after his mother died, but he's still your father's illegitimate son. Winnie even breast-fed him, nursing you and him at the same time. I've never seen two children as inseparable as you and David. But about the title, I think Jamie's right to reject it. Although I'm no politician I think Canada should break away from England. Anyway, this talk isn't getting us any closer to finding somebody for you to spend the rest of your life with."

Liz now remembered Nanda's comments and they made David's earlier departure even harder to bear. It was so true: She and David had been inseparable as children. Yet she had never experienced the impulse to kiss or caress him until Natasha had intruded herself into his life. She had only wanted to be with him, always. She saw him as an extension of herself, a double, with whom she could do anything, to whom she could say anything, except acknowledge their difference in gender. But the news that he and Natasha were to marry had changed everything for her. No longer could she think of David as being an integral part of herself. Suddenly he had become a separate individual and, in her desperation, she believed the only way she could retain her hold over him was by physically fusing their bodies. But it hadn't worked. Now, each time they came together her feeling of separateness intensified and brought with it increasing fear of isolation and loneliness.

Liz showered, dressed, went down to the living room and suddenly found she could not bear to think of spending the next five hours alone in the house. She quickly poured and drank two glasses of sherry, brushed her teeth with mint-flavoured toothpaste, then drove across town to visit Amanda.

Annabelle opened the front door. "Hello, Annabelle," Liz said. "Your mother home?"

"She's still in bed."

"I'll go up." Liz brushed past Annabelle and went upstairs, while Annabelle returned to the living room where she and Christopher were watching television.

"It's HER," she told Christopher, then ordered him to close his eyes as a shoot-out scene flashed onto the screen.

In the bedroom above, Liz seated herself on the bed, politely coughed, then waited. Finally Amanda said, "Is that you, Liz?"

"You're awake?"

"I suppose so."

"I saw David this afternoon and told him about Jamie and Alice. Have you said anything to her yet about Jamie's title?" Amanda yawned and moved below the covers. "I wish you'd come out of those covers so I can see you." The bedclothes heaved and Amanda shot up like a jack-in-a-box. Her hair was a mat of straggling knots and her left breast had slipped from her nightgown.

"You know what I'm going to do one of these days, Liz? Barge into your bedroom at midnight and order you to get up."

"Don't be childish, Mandy," Liz said. She leaned forward and pushed Amanda's breast into the nightgown, went to the dresser and returned with hair pins and a brush. "Why don't you tie up your hair before going to bed?"

"It's not long enough."

Liz began brushing Amanda's hair. "You're letting yourself go, Mandy. You're overweight, your breasts sag."

"I've had two children."

"Don't make excuses. You have to look after yourself."

"I don't have time to exercise."

"Rubbish. You've probably had eight hours' sleep. You should be exercising right now." She brushed Amanda's hair into a pile on her crown, critically eyed it, then swept it back and began pinning it in place. "The children are downstairs looking at television, which isn't good for them."

"It's their Saturday-afternoon treat."

"There are better things for them to do than watching TV."

"You know, Liz, sometimes I think you dislike me."

"Dislike you!" For a moment Liz was disconcerted. "How can you say that?"

"You're always criticizing me."

"Just because I occasionally point out how you mismanage your life doesn't mean I dislike you, Mandy. I'm surprised you could think that, when you must know I've always been very fond of you."

Tears appeared at the edge of Liz's eyelids and, seeing them, Amanda put her arms around her sister. "Sorry," she said, "I know you love me. And I love you too."

"I know you do," Liz said graciously, then sniffed. "Did you shower before going to bed?"

"Too tired. I imagine you're a bit smelly too, when you wake up in the morning."

"There are degrees of odour," Liz said, remembering the odour surrounding her after David left her. "Some are unavoidable, many can be prevented."

"You should smell my patients' beds!"

"I don't want to. Anyway, you should give up night work. You don't really need the money. There, you look quite human now." Liz finished arranging Amanda's hair, and as she stepped back from the bed, Amanda looked up, saw the strain in her sister's face and thought how terrible it was that Liz had let her feelings for David ruin her life. She stifled an urge to ask her if what she experienced with David was worth it all, but because Liz had spoken only once of their relationship, and then only briefly, Amanda realized she couldn't risk a question. She remembered that evening well. She and Liz had been sitting together, recalling childhood memories — some painful, some pleasant — when suddenly Liz began weeping, and while Amanda held and comforted her, Liz blurted out how much she loved David, that she knew their affair ought never to have happened, but fear of loneliness prevented her from ending it. Then just as abruptly as she had begun, she stopped crying, laughed and told Amanda she mustn't believe a word of what she'd just said, it was only memories of her childhood closeness with David that made her talk so foolishly. But Amanda guessed Liz had spoken the truth because she knew what her sister was like: She knew Liz would never surrender any part of the world she had once controlled. Besides, she understood from her own experience that the level of satisfaction a person obtained from a relationship didn't necessarily equate with the degree of one's devotion to it; long ago she had concluded that most relationships functioned in this unequal way. It might be unfortunate, but nonetheless it was true that relationships seemed to involve concession by one person and exploitation by the other, and it might well be that in this instance it was Liz, not David, who was being exploited.

"I'll make tea," Liz said. She went down to the kitchen, which was meticulously neat due to Annabelle's obsessive cleanliness, but was unable to find the kettle. Finally, she went to the living room where Annabelle and Christopher sat looking at cartoons. Hearing Liz come downstairs, Annabelle had switched channels. "Do you know where the kettle is, Annabelle?" she asked.

Annabelle answered with a question: "Is Mom awake?"

"Yes. I'm looking for the kettle to make tea."

"Me and Chris always make Mom's tea, don't we, Chris?" Christopher solemnly nodded agreement.

"Why don't we all make it?" Liz thought the time had come for Annabelle to understand that the weak, cold, milky tea she concocted was undrinkable.

"No! Me and Chris'll make it." Annabelle ran into the tiny dining room, opened a cupboard drawer and retrieved the kettle from beneath a pile of dish towels where she hid it so that no one except herself could make tea for their mother. Annabelle now directed the tea-making operation, and Liz could tell from the expression on her face that Annabelle didn't want any interference, though in the end she did permit her aunt to boil water and pour it into the teapot, while repeatedly telling her that their mother wouldn't like Liz's tea as much as she liked Annabelle's.

"You're probably right," Liz agreed. "I'll carry the teapot." They trooped up the stairs: Annabelle carrying the cup-and-saucer-laden tray, Christopher the plate of cookies, and Liz, the Crown Derby teapot.

Amanda welcomed them with a smile. "Did you give Liz a hand?" she asked.

"She made the tea *her* way, but we know you won't like it as much as ours, will you?" Annabelle said.

Amanda wisely ignored the question, and instead asked Annabelle to get her bathrobe from the closet. "This is quite a party, isn't it? Look at those delicious cookies! Chris, will you kindly bring the chair over for Aunt Liz? Thank you, darling." (Liz had to admit Amanda handled her children well.) They daintily sipped their tea, each acknowledging that it lacked the distinctive flavour of Annabelle's brew; then Liz, after emptying her cup and eating an Oreo, patted Christopher's head, smiled at Annabelle, blew a kiss to Amanda, and departed.

"Come here, I want to tell you something very important." They climbed onto the bed, and Amanda put an arm around each one. "Listen carefully to what I'm going to say. Are you listening?" The children nodded. "If anything should ever happen to me —"

"It won't. Ever," Christopher denied.

"But if it did, I've asked Liz to look after you. I know you get angry at Liz, Annabelle. So do I sometimes, but Liz is a wonderful person. She looked after me and Jamie when we were little, just as you look after Chris. And Liz loves you very much because you're mine. I know she can be quite bossy, but she can't help being like that. It's because she's the eldest in our family."

"Does she know she's supposed to look after us?" Annabelle's lips trembled. The idea that they might lose their mother terrified her.

"Of course. And she's told me she'd love to take care of you."

"I don't know if I could love Aunt Liz," Annabelle said. "Could you, Chris?"

Christopher shrugged his shoulders, and Amanda, satisfied at having planted the seed, hugged them, and they lay on the bed together, dividing up and eating what was left of the cookies.

"Now," Amanda said, "what'll we do this afternoon? How about eating out tonight? Where shall we go?"

"The White Spot!" they cried. "That's where we go with Jamie."

"What a pity he's not here now."

"I'll telephone him," Annabelle said. "Come on, Chris." They ran from the room.

"Careful going down the stairs!" Amanda called, then sighed and lay back on the bed. Dear, dear Liz, she thought, so censorious, yet so dependable and loving; she could always count on Liz. Amanda had no doubt of Liz's strengths, for all her life she had believed Liz possessed qualities of character and intelligence she herself lacked; and now, as she got out of bed, she was struck by the idea that the only reason she, Amanda, could afford to be so disorganized about her own life was that Liz was always so assured and confident about hers. Yet was it not possible that she, Amanda, *deliberately* created confusion in her life so that Liz might then appear to be a tower of strength? After all, when she dealt with her patients she was just as firm and confident as Liz ever was. The problem, thought Amanda, was that in childhood she had taken on a subservient role with Liz and had kept on playing the role, even though she was now able to perceive her sister's limitations and knew in some ways she was the smarter of the two. For Amanda to have such thoughts was tantamount to committing treason and she knew she must never articulate them, because in doing so she would run the risk of destroying the edifice of belief everyone had built about Liz.

Amanda was so shaken by her thoughts that she sat on the bed to regain control of them and reassemble her package of beliefs about Liz's supremacy. How could she have been so foolish to imagine, even for a moment, that her splendid sister, who had supported and guided her throughout her life, was other than she seemed to be? It would be wrong, terribly wrong, for her to betray Liz, even in her thoughts, and she must never again allow herself to think such a thing. She must remember that she had a long, long way to go before she could claim to be as smart and assured as Liz, who was the very best person in the entire world to take care of Annabelle and Christopher should this prove necessary. Of this, she was absolutely certain.

Chapter 8

"Yes, I'd love to. But not that awful place where we had lunch before. You
like Italian food? There's some good restaurants on Commercial Drive.
Oh, okay, if you only have an hour. Don't worry, I'll find it. *Organic* on the
window. I'll be there around one." Amanda put down the phone, whistled
and said "Phew!" She went back to the table where Annabelle and Christopher looked questioningly at her. "That was Jamie's Alice. She's invited
me to lunch."

"I expect she wants to complain about Jamie," Annabelle said. "She
probably thinks he should give her more presents. Girls are like that."

"Flowers and candy," Christopher added. "That's what guys give their
girlfriends on TV."

"We'll see," Amanda said. "We'll see." But on the following day when
she walked into the restaurant and saw the expression on Alice's face, she
almost turned and scurried out — she hated confrontations — but unfortunately Alice had seen her and waved. Alice began talking at once, even
before Amanda pulled her chair up to the table.

"There's no explanation for it. All I know is, it's bloody infuriating.
I've made plans for the next ten years and then this happens. It's a bloody
nuisance."

"What is?" Amanda inquired.

Alice leaned far over the table and hissed snake-like: "I'm in the family way, that's what's the bloody nuisance."

For a moment, in the infinity of moments that skipped past her, Amanda
felt an urge to stand and give an unqualified cheer, but the moment flew
by. Instead of cheering, she let out a dull, "Oh."

"Oh, is it?" Alice ground out. "Is 'oh' all you have to say?"

"I suppose I could say other things. I could say —"

But Alice had no interest in what Amanda might say. "I couldn't believe my ears when the goddamn doc tells me no contraceptive gives a
hundred per cent protection. And he's the same shitty idiot who told me to

use a diaphragm in the first place. Kerist! I could shoot the bastard! I feel so ridiculous." Amanda, anxious to quiet Alice down, asked what she was going to do. "Do!" Alice snapped. "How the hell am I supposed to know what to do? Why do you think I got you here?"

"It's important to watch your diet," Amanda cautiously began.

"Diet!" Alice screeched, which caused other people to look at her. "I don't want to know what to *eat!* I want to be told how to get rid of the damn thing. You're a nurse, aren't you? You should know about such things."

"There isn't much you can do, is there? I mean, you either carry it to term, or you don't."

"That's what I want to know. How to get rid of it."

Amanda looked despondently at Alice. "Well?" Alice categorically demanded. "Well?"

"Does Jamie know?" Amanda asked.

"Why would I tell Jamie? It's none of his business."

Amanda was so numb she could hardly make out the words on the menu which a waitress had handed her. "He might be pleased," she said.

"Listen, just because Jamie tolerates your kids doesn't mean he likes children. In fact, he avoids them."

"Jamie likes children," Amanda obstinately said. "I know he does."

"I suppose you think you know Jamie better than I do?"

"I know him as well as you do," Amanda bravely said. "Don't forget, I grew up with him, and I have a pretty good idea of how he feels about most things."

They glowered at each other for a moment, then Alice said, "I don't want to argue with you over who knows Jamie better."

"You brought it up," Amanda pointed out.

"Don't you get it? I'm in the family way." Among the Powell women, certain words and phrases were too crude ever to utter. "Family way" was one of them. Alice stopped talking when the waitress came for their order. Both chose a green salad with house dressing. The waitress departed and Alice continued. "I'm almost forty, I have a job I like which pays well, and I don't see why I should abandon my career just because a stupid diaphragm doesn't work. What's more, I feel like an absolute fool getting in the family way at my age."

"I don't know what to say."

"Tell me where to get rid of it."

"Ask your doctor."

"Him! He's the fool who told me to use a diaphragm."

"He's obliged to give you information."

"He's an asshole," Alice snarled. Amanda thought Alice seemed more angry with her physician than with being pregnant, and this notion was reinforced when Alice next remarked that jerks like her doctor would never survive in an accounting firm where impeccable accuracy was a requirement.

"I'd hate to be an accountant," murmured Amanda, whose chequebook was a mass of crossed-out figures, smudges, and inaccuracies.

"You need intelligence to be one," Alice announced. Amanda assumed Alice didn't mean to insult her, but simply was a person who seldom thought of the impact of her remarks on others. Liz was like that too, but she attacked other people because she cared for them, while Alice didn't seem to care about anyone, not even Jamie. The waitress brought their salads and two small rolls in a little basket. "You can always tell if a restaurant's good by the amount of bread they give you," Alice said.

"Restaurants never give away anything," Amanda replied. "You pay for everything you get one way or another. I think you should tell Jamie you're pregnant before you decide what to do."

"Tell me what I want to know, not what you think I should do," Alice replied. "Big help you are!" she added.

Amanda said nothing further, and after eating a forkful of salad, got up and left the restaurant without saying anything more. But she did not go home. She drove to Liz's house to share the news.

"That must have stirred Jamie up," Liz said when she heard about Alice's pregnancy.

"She's not telling him. She's going to get an abortion."

"Nonsense," Liz said. "Nonsense" was a word Liz frequently used. "Jamie has a right to know. It's as much his baby as hers."

"Alice doesn't think so. She thought I'd know the name of someone who'd abort it."

"You've not had an abortion, have you?"

"Of course not. But I'm a nurse. And I *do* know where she could go. I told Alice that Jamie'd make a good father."

"I'm not so sure about that. I expect he'd be squeamish about babies. Most men are," said Liz, who knew little about men's reaction to babies. "I'll have to decide what we should do next."

"You won't tell anybody, will you?"

"Certainly not. Now, would you like a drink, or tea?"

"Actually, I'd like a sandwich. I don't know why, but lunching with Alice is very unsatisfactory. I never seem to get enough to eat."

"What else can you expect when you patronize dumps?" They went into the kitchen where they made and ate sandwiches while drinking sparkling cider from bottles.

"Remember how we sat here, eating sandwiches, Liz?" Amanda loved being nostalgic, talking about old times and going through boxes and photograph albums, particularly with Liz who, being a few years older, remembered so much more than she did. She also ventured to ask if Liz had seen David recently.

"He called in the other day," Liz said. The brevity of the reply made Amanda's joints ache with desire to know more about what went on between them when they got together. She could understand why Natasha had fallen for David: Besides being brainy, he was terribly good-looking. But apart from those attributes, and even though he was her half-brother, Amanda had always thought of him as the kind of man who, as she put it to herself, "used" women for what he could get out of them. Their father had been like that. But that's how most men were. Men! The pity was, from time to time women needed them, even Liz. She wished she and Liz could exchange confidences; she wished they could tell each other how they felt during the final moments of making love, when there was no turning back, when every part of you rushed towards that final, cataclysmic second and your body seemed to dissolve into a pool of sweat, smell, and pleasure. Amanda thought it odd that while she had no difficulty looking at a man and imagining him hunched over a woman, she was unable to look at women and imagine them making energetic love as she did with her lovers.

"We don't really know much about each other, even though we're sisters, do we, Liz?" Amanda heard herself say.

"Do we need to? Besides, I'm not sure it's advisable to know too much about another person, even a sister or brother. I value my privacy." And that ended Amanda's tentative effort to pry open the doors and investigate the nature of, and the reasons for, Liz's relationship with David and — even more important to Amanda — to find out what Liz got out of it.

"I have a seminar at four," Liz said, "and I need to look over my notes." Amanda obediently rose and thanked Liz for the sandwiches. She knew when to take a hint. They walked from the house to Amanda's car where Liz, after looking over the car, said, as she always did, that she couldn't understand how Amanda could drive around in a filthy vehicle. As she had on former occasions, Amanda replied that Harry had once told her that a layer of pure dirt on a car was a better preservative than expensive wax, and that the very first thing he did after buying a new car or truck was to drive it over a muddy logging road in order to "shit it up", as he put it. It was a matter of opinion, Liz would then retort, but personally she preferred clean cars, after which Amanda would enter the car, smile at Liz, turn on the motor, rev it up to demonstrate that it was in perfect condition, then drive away.

The sheepdog instinct was a powerful one in Liz, and it never occurred to her that her brothers and sisters might not appreciate being bossed around, any more than it would occur to a border collie that sheep might not want to be herded, driven, and nipped in the legs by sharp teeth. And so Liz went off to the college where she and Jamie taught and, after making a few inquiries, located him in the cafeteria collecting a doughnut and cup of coffee.

"Jamie dear," she began, "so good to see you. How're things going?" She squeezed the arm of the hand that held the paper plate, on which lay a chocolate-covered doughnut. The hand twitched, the plate canted and the doughnut dropped to the floor. Jamie retrieved it and put it on the plate. "Oh, you mustn't eat it now, Jamie! I'll get you another. I want a coffee anyway." She walked back and asked the woman behind the counter to give her a black coffee and a plain doughnut, then went to join Jamie, who was sitting at a table in line with the cafeteria door.

On seeing Liz enter the cafeteria, Jamie's first impulse had been to bolt to the men's room, because he knew from experience that whenever Liz approached him, smiling lovingly and exuding possessiveness, it meant she had some plan in mind for him. As a child, Jamie had believed his eldest sister possessed mysterious sensory devices in her bottom which allowed her to detect his movements, even when she couldn't actually see him; thus, years later, he could still half-believe that a mad dash to the washroom door before his sister spotted him would be quite futile: Liz would simply reach out her arm and nab him before he got there. In his preoccupation with words spiralling around intergalactic space, he had forgotten that Liz was a truly beautiful woman, but was reminded of it now, as male heads turned to watch her walk to the table. He could feel envy radiating from men in the room, including two elderly janitors on their coffee break. As she advanced on him, Jamie wanted to bleat pathetically and tell these men that they should take pity on him, for he was nothing more than a lamb about to be led to its slaughter; his border-collie sister had run him down and deliberately cut him off from the rest of the flock, only to do some terrible thing to him. She was poised to leap upon him, as she had done again and again when he was a child, to pin his shoulders to the ground and demand that he obey her, or *else*. Liz sat at the table, hung her shoulder-bag on the back of the chair, sipped coffee, wrinkled her nose with distaste, and asked once more how he was doing.

"Fine, just fine." Jamie thought he even sounded like a sheep.

"You must remember to look after yourself, dear. You tend to ignore the basic necessities of life."

"No, no," Jamie bleated. "I mean, I don't . . . I mean I do."

"Alice will need lots of support. After all, having your first baby is a —"

"What!" Jamie shrieked. His right arm jerked and the cups of coffee flew off the table.

"We'll move." Liz gathered up her purse and went to another table, Jamie dutifully following. "Didn't you know?" she solicitously asked. "I'm sorry. Truly sorry. I thought you'd be the first to know. But it's wonderful news, isn't it?" (Liz's years in the legislative chamber had made her an expert on tactical assaults.) Jamie looked around the barren, neon-lit room, seeking a hole down which he might scurry and was uncomfortably aware that Liz had placed herself between him and the cafeteria entrance. "Alice must take special care of herself because of her age. I'm sure that she — and you too, Jamie dear — want everything to go well." Liz raised clasped hands. "The baby'll be so fortunate, having you for a father. May I have the honour of being its godmother, Jamie?"

"Yes of course. I'd be delighted," Jamie dutifully mumbled.

"Dearest Jamie." She reached across the table to hold and squeeze his hand. "Dearest Jamie, I love you so much." And that, Jamie thought, was undeniable: Liz *did* love him, as she loved all her brothers and sisters, even totally boring Hilda, although Liz's love for her siblings had never prevented her from mercilessly bullying them (each of his siblings could attest to *that*) any more than it prevented them from becoming enraged when they found themselves trapped once again by the combination of her love and authority over them. Jamie had no doubt his sister would unhesitatingly sacrifice any part of her lovely body, even her life, if by doing so she would sustain a sibling's life. Yet, Liz's sisterly devotion actually terrified Jamie. A sister who loved one's skinny body and inept brain so much that she would die to protect them wasn't necessarily a good thing to have. "You *are* pleased, aren't you, Jamie?" And Jamie, trapped by his habit of obedience to Liz's wishes, sheepishly agreed that he was pleased at the prospect of becoming a father. "I'm so glad," Liz said. "Now, I must run. I'm already ten minutes late." She placed a fond, sisterly kiss on his forehead, then strode to the entrance, watched by the men in the cafeteria, who collectively sighed as she exited, while Jamie, horrified by the message Liz had delivered to him, slowly raised a hand to cover his eyes.

"What the hell have you been up to?" Alice's bellow was so loud Amanda held the receiver away from her ear.

"Me?" she squeaked.

"Yes you, blabbermouth."

"Nothing. I haven't done anything."

"Then how the hell does Jamie know I'm in the family way? And how did that interfering bitch Liz come to know? Eh? Tell me that!"

"I don't know."

"I'll bet! Why'd I think I could trust you?"

"I'm sorry."

"I'll bet you are."

"I haven't seen Jamie for weeks. And I don't know about Liz, maybe she guessed."

"Guessed!" Alice shrieked. "'Oh, guess what, Liz? It's about Alice. I'll give you three guesses. You guessed right! She's pregnant.' Untrustworthy bitch, that's what you are."

"I'm sorry," Amanda said again. "So what're you going to do?"

"Do! What the hell *can* I do after that goddamn sister of yours told Jamie he's going to be a father. So guess what? Jamie expects me to have it." Amanda heard the phone being slammed down, rubbed the ear that had been assailed by Alice's shrieks, then clicked the button until she got a dial tone and called Liz.

"Alice is going to keep the baby," she said.

"What else could she do?"

"She'd planned to have an abortion."

"Nonsense. She has a responsibility to Jamie."

"That's not a very feminist attitude, Liz. I thought you were pro-choice."

"There's more to feminism than having abortions."

"I think a woman has the right to decide." Amanda thought of herself as holding feminist beliefs, though she consistently deferred to men to the point of being rabidly subservient, a trait she'd developed during her years in nursing school when the small amount of self-confidence she'd begun with slowly became eroded by overbearing physicians (all male) who eyed her lecherously while responding with contempt to her timidly expressed professional thoughts on the role of nursing in medical treatment.

"As usual, you're confused, Mandy. Two people are involved in the creation of a child, and those same two people have a duty to feed, clothe and make sure the child is heading toward an assured and safe future." Amanda thought Liz must recently have been reviewing speeches she'd made about child welfare while serving as an MLA.

"Maybe two people do start babies, but it's the mother who carries the baby and does most of the work after it's born. And let tell you something else, Liz, you can ask Annabelle and Christopher in twenty years' time if not having a father around deprived them of one thing."

"Don't be defensive, Mandy. I'm merely pointing out that since two people create a child, it's probably better for the child if they share responsibility for raising it."

"I'll turn Alice over to you. You can deal with her from now on."

"She shouldn't be too difficult to handle. If you'd had more experience handling people, you wouldn't be having any problems with Alice."

After she had hung up, Amanda thought over what Liz had said: Was it true that she hadn't had much experience with people? She wondered what Liz would think of the patients she'd known, say, the one she was caring for now: an elderly priest whose brain was so deranged by disease and pain-quelling drugs that he called his elderly sister, as well as the nun who regularly visited him, "Dulcie", and invited them into bed with him. He called Amanda "Dulcie" too, and invited her to bed, but that didn't upset Amanda since she'd had similar requests from other patients and, oddly enough, the dying priest's request didn't seem to unsettle the nun either; no matter what the priest said or did, she nodded and smiled agreeably. The patient's sister, though, was profoundly shocked and upset, and although Amanda assured her that her brother had no idea of what he was saying, the sister continued to shake her head while saying: "I don't understand. I just don't understand. My brother was such a good man, always so kind to his flock." The sister was drawing on her life savings to pay for private nursing so that her brother could, as she expressed it, "pass over in complete peace". Did Liz have any idea of all that she, Amanda, had witnessed in the course of her nursing career? Did any of her family? She didn't think so. That was the odd thing about her family; everybody presumed themselves wiser and more experienced than herself. For the fact was — and this was something Amanda had slowly come to appreciate — images and perceptions formed in childhood stayed with people and profoundly influenced them throughout their lives. So, regardless of what she said or did now, her family would continue to see and treat her as "Miss

Wet-Pants Scatterbrain", a person incapable of understanding the imperative necessities of birth and death.

A few nights after this conversation with Liz, the priest finally died. That morning Amanda drove home, showered and went to bed. Later that day when the agency telephoned to say another job was waiting for her, Amanda told them she had decided to take a month off, then she contacted Helen Marks, the nurse who babysat the children at night. Helen had worked with Amanda nursing terminally ill patients before her retirement. But retirement bored Helen and she had volunteered her services when Amanda confided her problems finding reliable child care. Amanda ended the conversation by fulsomely telling Helen how much she — and the children too — appreciated her assistance. She then invited Helen to dinner and, after hanging up the phone, made out a grocery list and drove off to the store.

Chapter 9

In the past, human procreation had been an abstract concept for Jamie, something that had little or nothing to do with him, but now it represented a concrete entity residing within Alice's womb. He spent hours contemplating Alice's stomach, as though continued observation would one day be rewarded by the silent opening of a window, thereby revealing the contents of her womb.

"Go look at your own belly!" she would yell at him, but he continued to stare at her, visualizing cells quivering and proliferating in her uterus, forming grotesque patterns, bulging and oozing, quivering and dividing, slipping and slithering, getting ever bigger and more complex. He wished he could crawl inside to watch the process first-hand. Jamie's preoccupation with her insides enraged Alice since getting pregnant was something not supposed to happen to her, therefore when it did there was no need to get "bug-eyed" (Alice's term) and all worked up. Alice also made it clear to Jamie that she blamed Amanda for not helping her get an abortion before he found out about the pregnancy. "Kerist! Why did I think your dumbo sister'd help me out? I should've known she'd blab everything around. And don't just sit there and agree with me! Haven't you got guts enough to defend her? Kerist! You're pathetic!" But mixed with her rage was panic, which appeared, unbidden, to grip her, like the fingers of an unexpected arctic wind. Out of desperation, and because she had no friends, she began telephoning Amanda to discuss the pregnancy, and these conversations helped to calm her. They met once a week for lunch, and Amanda would collect Alice and drive across town to an Italian restaurant. On their second visit there, Amanda told Alice she should stop drinking alcohol.

"What the hell!" Alice snapped. "Don't tell me what I can't drink!"

"If you want to risk a defective baby, then go ahead, drink all you want."

"I suppose you drank nothing but water when you were carrying," Alice sneered. "Carrying" in Amanda's circle was almost as unacceptable as "family way". Alice actually drank little alcohol but had taken to sipping a small amount of rye whisky with meals in order to quell her nausea.

"Milk, I drank milk," Amanda said. "For calcium."

"Jesus!" Alice exclaimed. "Milk! Do I get a reward for this?"

"Yes, a healthy baby." Amanda sounded very professional. "But of course it's your decision . . . your baby."

"You realize this is all Jamie's doing," Alice said.

"Not exactly. All the sperm in the world can't conceive a child unless an ovum is present. You provided that." Alice glared blue-eyed hatred at Amanda, but requested a glass of milk when the waiter took their order. Without being aware of it, Alice had come to rely on Amanda's reassurances that the unpleasant physical sensations she experienced were normal occurrences in any pregnancy; Amanda had explained to Alice that her body was simply making hormonal adjustments to accommodate the fetus.

"Where'd you pick up that medical lingo?"

"Nurses' training and my science degree."

"You actually have a university degree?" Alice continued to view Amanda as a not-too-bright person.

"You can't go very far in nursing these days without a degree. Sometimes I think about going back and getting a master's degree." Amanda was putting on her "Liz act", which was to appear knowledgeable about all things and totally in control of her own and other people's lives.

"Oh yeah," Alice replied. They were eating a spinach salad. Rich in iron, Amanda had told Alice when she had urged her to order it.

"The only way your fetus gets nourishment is through you, Alice, so what you eat is crucial."

"I eat good," Alice obstinately said. "And for God's sake, stop using the word 'fetus'!"

"That's what it is at the moment." Amanda enjoyed putting Alice in her place — rarely was she ever able to do this with anyone. "I know about Jamie's neglect when it comes to proper nutrition, but things have to change now." On and on Amanda would go, telling Alice what foods she must eat and what would happen if she didn't, ending with a vivid description of eclampsia which so frightened Alice that she was unable to finish her piece of Saint Honoré cake and was forced to sit and watch Amanda eat her own piece, then exchange plates and eat what was left of Alice's. Amanda sighed. "Delicious, isn't it? But you must watch your weight. How much do you weigh? You're quite . . ." She paused. ". . . a large woman." (Amanda was discovering that revenge was almost as pleasant as sex.) "Do you weigh yourself every day? Are you visiting your doctor regularly? Which one are you seeing?" Without waiting for a reply, she gave Alice the name of the obstetrician who had delivered Natasha's, Hilda's and her own children.

"I'm doing everything I'm supposed to." The only milk Alice drank was at the weekly lunch with Amanda.

"No fast foods?"

"I hate the stuff," said Alice, who frequently lunched on hamburgers and French fries. Alice resented being catechized and put down. She had no trouble identifying Amanda's tactic for what it was, since her own childhood had been one extended put-down. Yet she seemed to need Amanda's reassurances, so instead of retaliating directly she used Jamie as a whipping horse; and he, aware of what was happening, absorbed the attacks as best he could. At first, the news of Alice's pregnancy had numbed him and, like Alice, he became prone to sudden anxiety attacks, but these finally disappeared one evening when he was visiting Amanda and happened to walk past the bathroom while Annabelle and Christopher were bathing. He went in, lowered the toilet cover, and sat down to watch them. They were engaged in a game called "The Great Battle of Vancouver". (Each child had a navy of plastic boats, toys and animals, and the battle consisted of making waves in an attempt to overturn and sink the opponent's fleet.) Later, as Jamie helped dry the children's warm, water-reddened bodies, he experienced an overwhelming desire to clasp and dry his own child. Would his son or daughter place the same unconditional trust in him as Christopher and Annabelle did? Would his child have a droopy little penis like Christopher? Or a hooked vulval crease like Annabelle? When Amanda came into the bathroom with the children's nightclothes, he helped Christopher put on his pyjama pants, checking he didn't put them on backwards and be unable to find what Christopher called the "pee hole".

"Nice kids, aren't they?" Amanda remarked later, when they were sitting in the living room, drinking the inevitable tea. "You know, I can't remember what I looked like as a child. I don't even recognize myself in the pictures Liz has. What I remember is doing things — mostly with you."

"I remember the scent of you."

"I didn't use scent."

"The smell of your body, I mean. That's how I identified you."

"How awful."

"Somewhere I've read that babies can identify their mothers by scent. I suppose your scent was significant for me because you protected me. Funny, eh?"

"You're different from other men, Jamie. The kids know that . . . that's why they trust you so completely."

"I'm no better than most."

"But you are. The guys who come here are decent enough, but I wouldn't trust them with my kids."

"I'm no different." Jamie was always uneasy when Amanda endowed him with virtues he did not possess. He saw himself as the prey of a host of nefarious impulses. Cowardice alone prevented him from ever acting on them.

"But you are," Amanda insisted. "You've no idea what people hide away." To prove her point, she told him about the dying priest's craving for the woman he called Dulcie.

"We all have 'Dulcies' hidden away somewhere inside ourselves," Jamie said. "Dying liberates our desire and the forbidden can finally be expressed. Listen Mandy, I want to tell you something. I want you to stop using your put-down strategy with Alice. Try not to act so superior. Remember, you were once ignorant yourself about childbirth."

"I'm trying to be helpful," Amanda said, untruthfully.

"Most people are ignorant, don't forget that, except for a tiny area where they've gained a little expertise. I know a little about words, you about health care. Alice knows her field, where we'd both be lost. But she knows nothing about poetry, very little about pregnancy. And why should she? She never intended to become pregnant, or to get mixed up with a poet."

"I think she was damn lucky to meet you."

"The luck was all on my side."

"Jamie, that's not true!"

"I receive more from Alice than she'll ever get from me."

"She loves you."

"I know."

"Do you love her?" The question was coyly put.

"I need her. I suppose I need her for the same reasons I've always needed you. Is your clock right?"

"It may be a few minutes fast, or is it slow? I forget which."

"I must go. My lecture today concerns something my students'll have trouble understanding . . . the nature of artistic vision."

Amanda followed him into the street and watched as he removed the lock from his bike. "Did Annabelle tell you one of your poems is in her school reader?"

"Oh God!" Jamie cried. "Have I come to that?"

"She can't bring herself to ask you what the poem means. She's scared the teacher will find out you're her uncle and ask her to explain it."

"I never know what my poems mean. Tell Annabelle the poem says that everything is illusion."

"Everything is an illusion? Okay, I'll tell her that." Amanda laughed. "Annabelle's such a funny girl. She plans to faint if the teacher says anything about the poem."

"I wish I could do that when people talk to me about my poems, but as a rule I just stand there with an idiotic smile plastered on my face."

Amanda laughed and hugged him. "I don't believe that," she said as Jamie swung a leg over the crossbar. "The kids love seeing you." He gestured goodbye and Amanda gasped as he almost collided with an oncoming car. She watched until he halted at the wide, cross-town avenue, then returned to the house as Jamie furiously pedalled across the street in preparation for climbing the long steep hill that would eventually take him to the college.

As he pedalled, Jamie thought about Amanda's life: nursing dying people, fucking men who were practically strangers, and raising two children. What did Amanda think of when a patient died? Did the sight of death awaken her need to prove to herself she was still alive? People react strangely to death. A few years ago, when he'd seen his mother lying in her coffin, he had found it impossible to believe her life had left. Where had it gone? Into the earth? Up to the heavens? Where could the "life" of "Mother" go? He went through a red light, narrowly escaping being hit by a van. "Get off the street, you goddamn fucking fool!" a man's voice roared after him. Jamie wavered on, barely avoiding parked cars, amicably gesturing to drivers who blared horns at him. He was accustomed to insults and close encounters, too. A few times, on dark nights, during periods of preoccupation, he had run into the back of a parked car, ending straddled across the car trunk, though whenever this happened he worried more about damaging his bike than injuring himself, for on those nights he felt certain nothing harmful could happen to him because his labour of gathering star words from the Milky Way was not yet complete.

A long trailer truck came up behind him, roared by, and for a few seconds he fought the vacuum that threatened to drag him underneath the great wheels. Then the truck passed and he returned to musing about himself. In the past, he had resisted forming relationships with women which had the slightest tinge of permanence; the least suggestion he should shack up made him shy away, then bolt. But the real fear that haunted Jamie was that his poetic vision would desert him; occasionally, when his vision did not return within what he thought was a reasonable time, he panicked and began making plans to escape Vancouver. He imagined himself in places like Patagonia, or the middle of Australia, where street lights were unknown and the night sky blazed with myriads of star clusters. In such a place he would be able to gaze at the sky and see clearly as the words performed their celestial dance before he opened his arms and gathered them in. He longed for ideal creative conditions, while at the same time realized they didn't exist, and that he must make do with whatever stars he could find, however few they were, wherever he was. Of course his moods varied, and sometimes he became so acutely depressed over his personal and artistic limitations that he would spend hours imagining ways he could place himself in situations where death would be inevitable. At such times he was so deficient in energy that his bowels (so it seemed) took hours to move and urine dribbled so slowly from his cock that even frantic rubbing could not invigorate it. Then everything would change and he experienced surges of energy that sent him whistling along streets as expectation (like coitus) accumulated until the moment came when he fled to his room in the Big House, where he sat and waited in frozen ecstasy for the heavens to open and reveal the glory of the words among the stars.

He would have liked to reveal his feelings to someone close to him, preferably a woman, and in fact had come close to expressing his fears to Amanda, but something had always prevented him from opening up. Besides, he recognized that while Amanda would undoubtedly be sympathetic in a tearful sort of way, full appreciation of his dilemma was beyond her. He had once thought Nanda might understand, since he had observed that, like him, she dwelt within a circle of silence, but he had long since concluded that Nanda's stillness functioned as a protective device and bore no resemblance to the stillness which enclosed him as he sat alone, waiting for messages from the stars. He had come to understand that Nanda's stillness had been artificially created, a sheltering cocoon she herself had spun to imprison herself, whereas his was a stillness of spirit which had always been there, all his life, even as a child, surrounding him wherever he went. At one time he thought Liz understood how it was with him and that it might explain why she continued to live in the house in Shaughnessy, but now he was not so sure. Perhaps Liz needed the house for her own reasons; perhaps she needed a place filled with memories to help reconcile herself to the necessities of her life. And Alice, what of her? Could he let loose his terrors on her? Not likely. Adjusted now to her pregnancy, she talked hopefully of their shared future: She would bear their child and they would assemble money for a down-payment on a small house on the east side and move in with their new baby. She laid out plans that made Jamie cringe internally, but he never voiced disagreement with anything she said, only nodded, smiled, watched her dress and undress, observed the internal pressures that were slowly changing her externally, lay with her and gloried in the sexual excitement she aroused in him, not allowing himself to venture beyond Alice's physical being and the heightened sensation both experienced when they came together.

He reached the college, went to the seminar room, eyed the students, and even before removing his windbreaker began speaking of the function of physical sensations as stepping stones to spiritual vision. All mystics, he informed them, utilized excess in order to approach a condition which allowed them to leap from the bodily to the spiritual dimension. When a student asked what sort of excesses he was speaking of, he answered anything would do, provided it heightened physical awareness to the point where consciousness abandoned the body and entered the spirit: Starvation, flagellation, sexual excesses — all had potential. He cited John Donne as an example of a poet who had sought and achieved spiritual vision through sexual excess. "Think about it," he told his students. "Try to imagine how you would go about separating your spirit from your body. You'll probably find it's easier said than done; in fact, some people have concluded — mistakenly, in my view — that the only way to achieve such separation is through self-inflicted death. Think about that, too," he advised his students, then hurriedly left the room before they could begin questioning him.

He slowly pedalled through the web of streets to Alice's apartment block where he chained his bike to a lamp post, identified himself to Alice through the speaker at the outside entrance and rode the elevator to her apartment. Now they sat together eating a late evening meal (Alice had purchased it at a fast-food outlet). She told him how her day had gone, and he supplied an event or observation he thought would amuse her, but he was careful as always not to mention anything of the Powell-McLeod family history: He didn't want Alice to know about his alcoholic father, or how he'd died, or that David was illegitimate; and he certainly didn't want her knowing anything about the ridiculous title he'd inherited. While he supposed it was inevitable that Amanda would reveal tidbits of family history at their weekly lunches, still he hoped he'd made it abundantly clear to his sister that she was to go slow with Alice because it was always difficult to predict how she was going to react.

By now, Amanda and Alice had been meeting for lunch in the same Italian restaurant with such regularity that the waiters knew which table was their favourite. They also knew Amanda enjoyed a glass of white wine with lunch and that Alice drank milk. Amanda, like all expert gossipers, had cultivated Alice to the point where she swallowed information about the Powell-McLeod family as hungrily as she ingested her lunch meal. Alice desperately tried to dig up tales of *her* relatives to balance the conversation, but the sheer weight of information flowing from Amanda silenced her, and the fact that she'd detested her own family and escaped from them at the earliest opportunity didn't help either. In the end, Alice was forced to rely on what she herself had accomplished in her own life, defying Amanda to claim that she, or any other member of the Powell-McLeod family, had achieved as much. It was at this point in the exchange that Amanda decided to drop the information about Jamie's title. "I suppose Jamie's told you he inherited Grandfather's title," Amanda said.

Alice chewed and swallowed a piece of lamb chop, then said, "So what!"

Amanda pretended great surprise. "You mean you don't know about Jamie being Lord Powell of Hyndhurst?"

Alice sliced and chewed more lamb chop before answering. "There's a wimp in our office who says his grandfather was a cousin of the German emperor."

"Our grandfather was a very smart man," Amanda said. "He worked at the United Nations . . . something to do with helping people in Third World countries."

"Big deal!" Alice responded. She then decided to buy time by changing the subject. Later, she would flail Jamie for failing to tell her about the stupid title he had inherited. "These days all I want to do is eat," she said.

"I was the same during my pregnancies," Amanda said, "but do watch your weight." Then she remembered Jamie's admonition not to act superior with Alice, and added, "It's very easy to gain weight when you're pregnant. That happened to me. Anyway, Jamie says he doesn't want the title. This is Canada, he says, and we're not English any more. Stuart, that was Aunt Nanda's husband, he's dead now, helped us immigrate to Canada. But you and Jamie could go back to England if you wanted, though Mother sold our home, Rhynewood Manor, before we came to Canada."

"England's an economic mess. Why would anyone want to go there?" Alice looked at her watch, gestured to the waiter, then ordered a piece of melon. "I don't care much for the English," she said, and Amanda wholeheartedly agreed that the English were an awful people, then passed on to the subject of maternity clothes. She had a few stored away.

"I prefer to buy my own things," Alice said. "Thanks," she said to the waiter, who had placed a piece of melon before her and was waiting for Amanda to order her usual piece of Saint Honoré cake.

"And coffee," Amanda told the waiter, then returned to the topic of maternity clothes. "Natasha had beautiful maternity clothes, but she's quite small. Maybe Hiddie kept hers, she'd be about your size. She's the kind of person who bought new outfits for every pregnancy. Not like me. I always made do with what I had."

"What do their husbands do?" Alice asked.

"David teaches chemistry at UBC, but before that he was with Atomic Energy of Canada. He's very scientifically minded. Hiddie's husband is dead — arteriosclerosis. He was a stockbroker. Hiddie has two girls and a boy." Amanda raised her hand to request the bill. Now, each drove her own car to the restaurant. "I'll see to the bill," she said. "I'm going to have more coffee. Shall we meet here, same time next week? If there's any change, I'll give you a call. I may go back to work. The registry keeps calling." Alice was now on her feet. "You're beginning to show a little."

"You're sure about the bill?"

Amanda smiled. "I've no objection to footing the bill when the company is good," she said. "Listen, Alice, don't blast Jamie for not telling you about his title. He never speaks of it, not even to me."

"Okay." Alice strode through the tables to the entrance and left, while Amanda leaned back and sighed with repletion: The food here was *so* good. When the waiter approached with the coffee pot, she sighed again and ordered another piece of cake. "To go with the coffee," she told him. (The waiter thought Amanda was a love-starved middle-class housewife who substituted food for getting laid, while Amanda thought he was a male chauvinist of Italian ancestry.) She sipped her coffee and was so caught up in planning her next moves with Alice that she didn't notice the waiter when he returned with the cake. She decided that next week she would tell Alice about Aunt Nanda and Natasha and explain how they fitted into the big picture of the Powell-McLeod family. She remained at the table for some time, then paid the bill with her credit card, smiled graciously at the staff and left the restaurant to drive across the city to call on her Aunt Nanda McLeod.

Chapter 10

"Your sister Amanda's not any too bright, is she?" Alice asked Jamie.

"You think not?" Jamie looked across the pillow at Alice's face. He was used to Alice's moods now, and knew something was simmering away inside her. He'd concluded that her habit of hiding what she felt, begun as a child, was so ingrained now that it had become a dominant part of her personality. She was incredibly circumventive; she seldom exposed herself by expressing directly how she felt about anything that affected her personally and generally defended herself from others by responding to them with violently prejudiced or equally coarse opinions. So Jamie understood that Alice's derogatory comment about Amanda's intelligence meant that Amanda had said something (possibly about himself) that had upset Alice. He laid out his usual defence of Amanda. "She hides her intelligence," he said.

Alice glanced at him, then looked away. "She was on to me about some title."

"Oh, that."

"Yes, that!" Alice turned on him. "Why didn't you tell me? And what else is there about yourself you haven't bothered to tell me, eh? You been in the pen? Eh? Maybe you're a homo. You fiddle around with little kids, eh? Goddamn it! Was I supposed to sit there like a dumb-bunny while she smirks away at me and tells me you're some goddamn English lord?"

"It's not important."

"Not important!" Alice yelled. "Can't you get it through your thick head that everything about you is important to me? You've no right to keep things from me."

"You fancy being called Lady Alice?"

"No." Her rebuttal sounded like a prolonged cry of despair. "I just don't want to hear things second-hand." She stopped and looked away so that he couldn't see her face.

Jamie stroked her arm, then put his hand over it to caress her breast and belly. "You'd have to marry me first," he said.

"Did you get anything with the title?" she asked without turning her head.

"There's a house. It's rented out. It was Grandfather's."

"Much rent?"

"I don't know. The guy who bought Grandfather's estate business manages it. The bank receives quarterly cheques."

Alice turned and looked at him. "You mean some bank actually allows you to have an account with it? Those guys must be nuts!"

"The money has to go somewhere," Jamie pointed out.

"Anything else?"

"There was some money from my grandfather." He didn't really want to talk about his inheritance, he wanted to lie with Alice and be silent while passing a hand over her smooth skin.

"How much? And don't tell me you don't know!"

"In Canadian dollars, around four hundred thousand bucks."

"And here I've been classifying you with bums on skid row."

"I once knew the exact amount."

"Don't start telling me what you once knew." Alice sounded dangerous, as though she might assault him physically.

"There was this millionaire I read about who enjoyed living on skid row. He said it relieved him of responsibilities. He felt free."

"Did he now? You have any other little sums of money hidden here and there? In old boots, under your mattress, in jam jars? You have a bank book?"

"Not here."

Alice left the bed and began dressing. "Get up," she ordered.

"Why?"

"We're going to get it."

"Don't get into a tizzy, Alice, I can tell you how much money I've got. Give me a pencil and paper, and if you want, I'll write out a list of assets. Come on. Please."

The "please" did it: Alice unfastened her bra, slipped off her panties, and got back into bed. Jamie put out an arm so she could lie against him. "When our mother died she left the house to Liz, but everything else was divided among my sisters and me, and of course my half-brother, David."

"You mean your sister Liz got the house *plus* a share of the money?"

"Well, she's the eldest, but apart from that I think Mother may have thought being responsible for running the house would keep Liz from having another breakdown."

"Breakdown!" Alice latched onto the word since it suggested a deficiency in Liz. "You mean she went wacky?"

"Heavens no! I mean she was very upset when Muriel died. It was pretty serious."

"Muriel? Who's she?"

"Our nanny and governess when we lived in England. We thought the world of Muriel — especially Liz."

"So why didn't you just tell me that Muriel was some old dame who wiped your backsides, instead of beating around the bush? Now, how much money did you get from your mother? That's the important part of this little chat."

"After the estate taxes and lawyers' fees were paid, we each got just over five hundred thousand dollars."

"Oh lordy!" Alice sighed. "It's not fair. Why do you treat me like this, Jamie? First, you don't bother telling me you're a poet who's well known. Then your sister tells me you've got some stupid title, and *now* I discover you've got money coming out of your ears. Do you think so little of me you can't be bothered to tell me these things? Is that what it is?"

"No." She tried to get away from him, but Jamie held onto her. "I think the world of you, Alice. It's only because I don't think of those things. I've told you everything that's important to me. I didn't ask for that damn title. It got pushed onto me. I want to be known as Jamie Powell, poet. I don't use the money. It just sits in the account. You can have it if you want."

"Exactly how much is there?"

"I suppose around a million."

"Oh Jesus! He supposes he's worth a million give or take a few bucks!" Alice sighed, hesitated, then said, "We could buy a small house."

"I'll speak to Hiddie. She's up on real estate."

"So you don't trust me to buy a house, is that it?"

"Of course not, but Hiddie —"

"Oh, shut up! I don't want to hear any more about your goddamn sisters. I'm sick of them."

"I am too. But still I have to say they mean well." He tweaked her ear. "Know something? If Max Logan — that was Hiddie's husband — was still alive, he'd proposition you."

"Like hell he would."

"Max's favourite saying used to be: 'Them that asks, gets.' "

"He sounds like a real sleaze."

"Actually, he was quite a decent guy. Fond of his kids."

"Did he bugger around with them?"

"One day he solemnly told me he never went after girls under sixteen."

"My uncle used to read the Bible."

"Anyway, do you really want the bother of owning a house? We could move in with Liz. She's often asked me to come and live with her. I think she's lonely."

Alice rolled over onto her back and stared at the ceiling. "I'll have to think about it," she said. "I need to adjust to all this new information." Jamie lay against her, his hand resting on her breasts. She let out great heaving sighs that made her breasts shake and nipples tremble. "I had the wrong view of you, Jamie, I thought you were a struggling artist."

"I get by," Jamie said. "I don't need much."

She turned and her blue eyes were close to his. "You think we should get married? I mean, it seems all wrong. You have this bloody big family, and I've got nobody."

"You have me, you have what's in here." He laid a hand just above the triangle of curly blonde hair. "Isn't that enough?"

"I *don't* have you. I have the tiny little bit of you that your family doesn't want . . . and what's left over from your poetry. So how much of you do I really get?"

"Outside of Mandy, you're the only person I can be at rest with."

"She thinks she owns you."

"No."

"She does. I can tell by the way she talks. Jamie this, Jamie that."

"Mandy likes to have somebody she can boss around. Before I was born she didn't have anyone."

"She tells me I have to improve my diet, and when I tell her I eat good, she corrects my English. She told me I must say 'eat well'. So what's wrong with 'eating good'?"

"Good isn't an adverb. You can eat good food, but you can't eat good."

"Guys in my office say they eat good."

"Then they're eating a virtue, good being the opposite of evil."

"Oh, shut up. You're so bloody smart. So sure of yourself."

"I'm not. Actually, I'm a very insecure person. I'm filled with terrors and uncertainties. Listen, Alice, the next time Mandy delivers her little homily on nutrition tell her you always eat good food, that you say 'eat good' because you discard words you deem unnecessary. That instead of saying 'good food', you say 'eat good' because you consider 'food' a redundant word in that sentence. When I say 'How about it?', do I have to describe in detail what I'm asking? No, because from experience you can make inferences. That's true of most conversations. We simplify."

"Okay, okay. I get the picture."

"That's why people find legalese so insufferable. We're used to living in an abbreviated world where everybody uses acronyms."

"Like what?"

"Like ILY."

"What?"

"Eye ell why. Dee why ell em?"

Alice knew what the letters meant, but was afraid to answer Jamie's question. "Maybe there're some things we shouldn't say," she muttered.

"Maybe." Jamie traced the outer rim of her navel. "Your belly button looks like a volcanic crater."

"Oh, for God's sake! What next!"

"What is next? Well . . . do you want us to get married?"

"I don't know. Kerist! I wish you didn't have a family. We were getting along fine. Now, you push all this new stuff onto me."

"Unfortunately, I can't discard the past. What you see, what you like about me, is a product of the past, just as your past moulded you from a lump of childhood 'unknowingness' into a ferociously independent woman. The past is undeniable and inescapable." He stroked her large thighs and wondered why men generally thought women should be smaller than themselves. Alice matched him in height, weighed more, and was probably physically stronger than he. She could easily pick him up and throw him across the room if she felt like it, but instead she fussed and worried over him and, in their sexual relationship, presented a mixture of passion, delicacy and tenderness.

In the early days of their relationship, Jamie's behaviour had caused Alice to wonder whether she'd got herself involved with a lunatic; but familiarity with Jamie's habits modified those first impressions, and when she was alone in the apartment she would look through his poems, trying to make sense of them, though, to her, they seemed cold and impersonal, not connected with the Jamie she knew. She would stroke the thin volumes, much as she stroked Jamie's body, then carefully replace them in the bookcase where she now displayed them, though they never discussed the contents.

Intellectually, Jamie might be a complicated man, but emotionally was less so (which might explain his enduring attachment to Amanda) and he intensely disliked being involved in any expression of collective emotion. He did not want to share what he felt with anyone. Even more to the point, he had found through experience that what he felt at any particular point in time bore no resemblance to what other people expected him to feel. Above all, he hated speaking about his work, and this as much as anything else was the reason he had never told Alice he was a poet. As to music, he preferred cowboy songs and country music and studiously avoided attending concerts with Liz, who hounded him to accompany her to any event in support of the arts. But he'd found the only sensation a Beethoven or Brahms slow movement aroused in him was an overwhelming need to yawn, and the expressions he observed on people's faces and the conversations he overheard during intermissions, to him, seemed manufactured for the occasion. And he could not bear this: Emotional responses must never be manufactured by people, even though their reactions, as his sometimes were, might be thought weird. Sometimes he'd been overcome with the urge to eat a Mars bar while talking about George Herbert or Henry Vaughan to students, or had experienced an erection when pedalling around the city and seeing the backside of an elderly woman whose skirt had soared as she leaned over to pluck chickweed from a flower border. He viewed these "weird" reactions as the equivalent of a rabbit's ears straightening up when something unexpected appeared in its line of vision.

Before Alice appeared in his life, Jamie's involvement with women had been sporadic and limited to those women who drifted, like broken sea grass, along the edge of the literary ocean. They wanted complexity in a poet, while Jamie, who had more than enough complexity on his hands with star words, wanted simplicity. The women tended to think he was cold and indifferent, while he was of the opinion that they manufactured emotions. The affairs never lasted more than a few weeks, usually terminating with the woman saying, "Well, I tried my best, didn't I?" while Jamie amiably nodded his head in agreement. He wanted to make the best of having sex, while they (so it seemed) preferred to *talk* about having it. Physically, the women ranged from ultra-slender to bucolic plump, but regardless of physical dimensions, all wanted Jamie to join them on verbal explorations through the muddy swamp of emotions. Alice wasn't like that: She compressed her emotions, later venting them in blasts of shrieking rage which had nothing to do with sex. In *that,* she asked for nothing more than to hold Jamie tightly in her warm, soft sheath. She didn't want to talk about her feelings: These were so precious to her that she wanted to hide them, as people do valuable jewels and works of art. Alice and Jamie were alike, in that each was trapped by a fear that made them conceal what they valued most, lest others steal it from them.

"David — how come he's only a half-brother?"

"Our father had an affair with a young woman Grandfather employed. She got pregnant, had David, then died. Mother took him in."

"Honest!"

"Hm-hm."

"So he's illegit?"

"You could call it that."

"That's what most guys'd say. A bastard."

"He and Liz were born just a few months apart. Mother breast-fed him along with Liz."

"Your mother must've been some woman. I couldn't forgive any man who betrayed me."

"David married our cousin, Natasha Powell. Aunt Nanda is my father's sister. She once lived with a man who believed marriage was a union of souls, not an artificial arrangement tying people together. He's Natasha's father."

"Something must have been going on between them besides uniting souls."

"Natasha was a manifestation of their spiritual unity. The guy was part Hindu. Very rich. I learned all this from Mother, who always said I should write a poem about Nanda and Blewthorpe's love affair. That was his name. Cromwell Blewthorpe."

"What a name!"

"He worked with the French resistance during the war. The Gestapo caught him and he died without ever seeing his daughter. He left Nanda everything."

"But isn't her name McLeod?"

"*That's* the real romance. You ready for this?"

"I hate sop."

"So do I. Blewthorpe wanders the world with a bunch of Sikh servants, like an Indian rajah. Then he comes to Hyndhurst, that's where we lived in England, and buys an estate called Alderwood House. When he goes off to fight the Nazis he orders the servants to stay there and guard Nanda with their lives. A few of the servants are still with her, some are a new generation. It's all very symbiotic."

"You're kidding!"

"I'm not. Now, enter Stuart McLeod, son of a Canadian industrialist and federal cabinet minister. He shows up in England to demonstrate Canadian logging efficiency to the English, meets Nanda at Alderwood where he's overseeing the cutting of woodlands on the estate, and falls hard for her. But Nanda tells him she's committed to Blewthorpe, and he sadly departs. The war ends, Nanda waits for Blewthorpe to return, then the war office tells her he's been killed. Stuart returns to England on his way back to Canada after wandering around Europe trying to forget Nanda. So what happens? Nanda explains to Stuart that she must live as a nun for the rest of her life, but Stuart begs her to marry him. She breaks down, he embraces her, they marry, then guess what? Months later my cousin Stuart-Hector is born. He was named 'Hector' after my grandfather. Horrible name, isn't it?" He has two sisters, Gwendolyn and Margaret. Gwennie's a Tory MP. She's desperately anxious for the Tories to form government so she can become a cabinet minister. I see Margaret occasionally. She's an actress and is always at me to write a play for her."

"So what's Stuart McLeod doing now?"

"He died. Car accident. But the family thinks it was a broken heart. Stu and their youngest daughter Frances were on a river when their canoe overturned. Stu got out all right, but Frances drowned. She was only eight or nine. Stu never forgave himself."

"I guess he'd feel real bad."

"He was an expert canoeist. He'd paddled practically every river in Canada, working for the Department of Northern Affairs, surveying resources. He discovered a gold mine in northern Ontario. His family isn't exactly dishonest, but Stu gave information of his find to his father before he reported it to the government. The McLeods are a closely knit family. Stu's father took over Nanda's financial affairs."

"How much money was involved?"

"I don't know. A lot. McLeod invested most of it in Canada Resources Corporation, the family company."

"Did he cheat her?"

"Not at all. The McLeod connection increased her wealth. Nanda settled twenty million on Natasha from Blewthorpe's estate and set up a ten-million endowment fund at UBC in memory of their daughter Frances. All her children have trust money. Poor Stuart, he thought the world of Frances. And here's something else of interest: The McLeods, in a convoluted way, are related to Alexander Mackenzie. Nice people, except sort of conceited. They firmly believe without them Canada wouldn't exist. Of course, they may be right about that."

"What do they think of you?"

"The McLeods seem to have no objection to having a poet in the family. After all, the family's originally from Scotland. Robbie Burns and all that. For all I know, they may even claim descent from one of Burns's bastard offspring. So they tolerate me. Stuart-Hector's a decent enough guy, though he's married to a loud-mouthed bitch, but she did her duty — produced two sons in three years. Amanda tells me that Stuart-Hector has a woman on the side he visits on Sundays after going to church with his wife and boys."

"Your sister pokes her nose everywhere."

"Mandy loves gossip."

"So what about Natasha? Where does she fit into all this?"

"When Natasha was a girl she set her sights on David. He didn't have much chance against her wiles. She's very beautiful and wealthy in her own right. What more could a guy ask for?"

"Are you saying he doesn't love her?"

"No. He loves her. So do I, although we have disagreements about the charities she supports. I tell her they're nothing but tranquillizers that wealthy people like her use to achieve peace of mind. I love Natasha in the same way I love Liz and Mandy. They're interwoven in my past."

"God! What a family!"

"Just average when compared to yours, especially your uncle."

"You know, I ran away from the farm." Alice went on to tell him how one night, not long after she was raped by her uncle, as she slept in the tiny room next to the bedroom occupied by her aunt and uncle, she was awakened by the sound of her aunt crying and pleading, "No. Please no." Afraid her uncle would come into her room and repeat what he had done in the hog pen, she crept from the house and began to walk across the fields in the direction, she thought, of her home town. The fields were large and filled with partially ripe grains which she broke off and chewed to quell her thirst and hunger. At daybreak she saw a road in the distance from which rose clouds of dust whenever a vehicle drove along it. This reassured her, since she had no real idea of the distance separating the farm from her home, only that it took a few hours by car. The sun burned down on her face and arms, and by sunset she was feverish. But she didn't give up. She trampled down a circle of grain and curled up on it. The crushed grain stalks were surprisingly warm, and she slept until a prairie falcon, hunting at dawn, flew down to have a look at her. Its shriek awoke her. The half-ripe grains and stalks had upset her stomach and she experienced ever-weakening diarrhea, so that by the time she reached the main highway she was near collapse. A farmer and his wife driving by saw her in the field, picked her up, drove her to the nearest hospital, then informed the RCMP; but she refused to say anything, and her identity was revealed only when a visitor to the hospital, who'd once seen her at the farm, saw her standing in a corridor. Later, when her parents came to pick her up, they reproached her for her thoughtlessness in running away, but she wouldn't speak or look at them.

Her parents took her home, and during the months from the end of that summer to the beginning of the next, she stole enough money from her parents to buy a pair of tin shears, which, it turned out, she never needed to use because her uncle had been scared off. Then after graduation from high school, she'd packed her belongings into a small case and, without saying goodbye to her parents, boarded a bus to Saskatoon where she found a job in an accountant's office. She was at the bottom of the career ladder but was determined to get ahead, and the president of the small company she worked for encouraged her to take night-school courses in accountancy. When her parents died she received a small inheritance which she invested in the bond market. Combined with the tidy sum her aunt left her — mostly from the sale of the hog farm — she now had the wherewithal to quit her job, move to Regina and enroll at the university there where she graduated with degrees in commerce and business administration, and later earned her chartered accountant's accreditation.

"What an amazing person you are, Alice. So tough and determined to get ahead. Compared to you, I'm a weakling." He moved over her thighs, which she obligingly spread. "So, now that we've heard all about each other's family, shall we get married?"

"I don't know, I don't know." Alice clutched Jamie and pulled him into her. "Promise me something, Jamie. Promise you'll never hate me."

"I will never hate you, Alice. It is just not possible. Please tell me you understand that I could never hate you." Jamie put his nose against hers, they looked intently at each other, and finally Alice whispered, "All right, I understand."

Chapter 11

"It was underhanded of Jamie to get married without telling us," Liz said to Amanda. They were sitting in Liz's living room, Liz in her usual place in a wing chair, Amanda on the couch, flanked by Annabelle and Christopher, who were keen to observe how the news of Jamie's marriage would affect HER, and after that, to go upstairs and spend time in the nursery and bedrooms their mother and aunts and uncles had used as children.

"That was HER bed," Annabelle always said to Christopher whenever they entered Amanda and her sisters' bedroom. "That was Auntie Hiddie's, and that was Mom's."

"Like the three bears," Christopher would reply. He had no trouble imagining his Aunt Liz roaring: "And who's been sleeping in *my* bed?" In his short life Christopher had never once uttered a word to Liz. Once she had asked Amanda if Christopher was retarded. "He never speaks when I'm around," she said. Amanda laughed. "That's because he's in awe of you," she explained; but Liz, who had no idea of the impression she made on other people, especially children, continued to think there might be something wrong with Christopher. She didn't notice that Hilda's daughters didn't speak in her presence either, nor was she aware that Natasha's usually uninhibited children remained clustered around their mother whenever they visited, staring wide-eyed, their pretty little mouths ajar but voiceless. Jamie once remarked to Amanda that such was the power of Liz's physical presence a person felt he had no right to approach her unless armed with a special dispensation. He also noted that Liz, like other people who consider themselves to be superior to others, never questioned her right to censure the behaviour of lesser mortals. Now, she condemned Jamie for marrying a woman she had never met.

"*I* know her," Amanda pointed out.

"Oh, you . . ." Liz said, making it clear that Amanda's familiarity with Alice was of no consequence.

"I think it was the best thing for them to do." Amanda thought Liz was making a big fuss over nothing. "I mean, having an expensive church wedding doesn't guarantee a couple stays together."

"It's what people think that matters," Liz said. She looked at Annabelle and Christopher and asked if they would like to help prepare tea.

"They'd like to explore upstairs," Amanda said. "They like going into our bedroom and imagining us as children."

"Did your mother tell you how she'd wake up at night and sneak into my bed, or Jamie's?" Liz asked.

"Just into Jamie's." Annabelle said. "Mom said you kicked her out."

"Did I really?" Liz's disapproval moved from the children to Amanda.

"Not intentionally," Amanda quickly said. "You'd dream a lot. Once you punched my nose." On hearing that, Annabelle and Christopher looked at each other and giggled behind raised hands.

"You took up too much room," Liz said. "You were quite plump as a child."

"Off you go, children." The children ran out, glad to escape Liz's probing eyes and her criticism of their mother. They raced to the top floor where the beds and dressers provided sufficient stimulation for Annabelle and Christopher to transform themselves into Amanda and Jamie. They opened drawers and usually found some small object (a scarred toy, or perhaps a hankie) to enhance their visit. From there, they went to the adjoining room where Jamie and David had slept, then into the nursery which still held a long table and six straight-backed chairs. Here, Winnie Powell's children had played as children. They visited the bathroom and looked at the old tub in which the Powell children had bathed every night, first the two eldest girls, followed by David, finally by Amanda and Jamie. They looked at the toilet each child had used (Even Aunt Liz had sat on it!) before going to bed, and leaned over the old sink to imagine their uncles brushing their teeth together.

After this, Annabelle and Christopher descended a floor where two large rooms had been rearranged to make five smaller bedrooms to accommodate Winnie's children when, as adolescents, they had asserted their right to privacy. Annabelle and Christopher went into each room, looked at the single bed and named the person who once occupied it. The most exciting part of their explorations on this floor was going into Jamie's old room to look at the little table by the window on which stood an old portable typewriter and a pile of paper. Once Annabelle had touched a key and both had jumped when a letter clacked against the hard rubber platen. Finally, they ventured into the room which had been their grandmother's and where Aunt Liz now slept in the high, mahogany-framed bed. The room intimidated them: It was so redolent with their aunt's presence that they spent most of their time looking over their shoulders, making sure she wasn't there watching them. They peeped into her bathroom to smell soaps and shampoos she used, and Christopher couldn't believe Aunt Liz actually sat on the toilet to do what he did in their toilet at home. They raised the lid of the clothes hamper to glimpse Liz's used lingerie, then dashed out and, as though guilty of some sacrilege, clattered down the broad stairs and into the living room to collapse on the couch beside their mother.

"Well," Amanda asked, "everything still the same?" She put her arms around the children. "They still can't believe you were once a little girl, Liz. They think you came into the world full-grown."

"I certainly *was* a little girl once, and what's more every day I'd have a glass of milk and cookies about this time. So, why don't we go into the kitchen and see if we can't find something interesting?"

For Annabelle and Christopher, this was the best part of their visit because, regardless of her other shortcomings, Aunt Liz always provided something delicious to eat. "So you'll speak to Jamie about introducing us to his new wife?" Liz said as she placed more cream-filled cakes on the children's plates. "Make it clear we don't appreciate being ignored." Unlike their mother, Aunt Liz seemed not to care how many cakes they ate. Indeed, whenever Amanda tried to be firm and protested they'd had enough, Liz would say, "Don't worry, Mandy. These cakes won't hurt them. The bakery uses only pure ingredients," as though this assurance justified allowing the children to stuff themselves with concoctions of sugar, chocolate and whipped cream. At such times Annabelle thought that living with HER mightn't be so terrible after all.

"I'll do what I can, but we'll have to be very careful. We mustn't interfere, Liz. After all, Jamie and Alice are grown people."

"Precisely! You can remind Jamie that we've always gone out of our way to accommodate him."

"But Liz . . ."

"I'm prepared to speak to him if you won't."

"No, don't do that. I'll work on Alice. Okay, kids. Time to go."

The way Liz dismissed her opinions irritated Amanda but she submerged her annoyance by telling herself that Liz always acted in a high-handed manner and that it didn't signify anything. She told herself she would continue to carry on as before, meeting Alice for lunch and suffering her rude behaviour, while trying to influence her and move her in the right direction. As far as she could tell, there wasn't much difference between Liz and Alice: Each had a low opinion of other people and seemed to think that she, Amanda, would put up with anything they said. The irritating part was that Amanda knew Liz would never raise the subject of his marriage with Jamie because at some level Liz realized that her dependence on Jamie was far greater than his on her. Liz couldn't order Jamie around as she did Amanda; the most Liz could do to keep him within her sphere of control was to pay homage to the poet in him and act as priestess in the temple he periodically visited to commune with the stars. And while Amanda didn't object to the drudgery of gathering and distributing family news, still she wished Liz would acknowledge the value of her contribution, and for once stop issuing orders.

When Amanda met Alice for lunch the next week, she did her best to bring Alice around: "You really ought to meet the rest of the family. You can't postpone it forever."

"Give me one good reason." Alice shifted her weight on the chair. Discomfort due to her pregnancy was aggravated by a full bladder. She hated being pregnant, she hated looking down at her ever-expanding stomach, she hated Jamie for having started it, she instantly hated anyone who happened to glance at her, especially men, fearful they would laugh at her. It didn't matter that Jamie told her she looked splendid, for she knew that her bottom was growing proportionately to her protruding stomach, and if she looked like this at five months, what would she look like at nine? "Everybody's looking at me. I can't stand it. God! I feel horrible."

"All pregnant women feel the same," Amanda lied. "We women don't realize when we make love that we're walking into a biological trap. What's more we hate men looking at us and imagining what we did to get pregnant. It's as though they're psychically raping us."

"Speak for yourself," Alice said. "I don't give a shit what men think." That this contradicted what she'd just finished saying seemed not to bother her: Alice was too caught up in immediate reactions and rebuttals to acknowledge earlier remarks. She stirred pasta around the plate before continuing. "I'm scared to meet your family," she finally admitted. "What if Jamie compares me with all his fancy relatives and friends and . . ."

"Look here, Alice." Amanda leaned across the table. "You're married to Jamie now and, like it or not, that means you're Lady Powell. So why worry about Jamie's family? Besides, you've got nothing to be ashamed of."

"I'm not ashamed," Alice quickly denied. "But I'm not used to mixing with people. I don't want your family staring at me and thinking how I got this way." She touched her stomach. "I'm scared they'll turn Jamie against me." Alice couldn't bring herself to look directly at Amanda and reveal her fear of losing the battle for control over Jamie.

"You won't lose him. I've never known Jamie to feel about anybody else the way he feels about you."

"You're not just giving me a line, are you?"

"No. Why would I do that?"

"I wouldn't put it past you." Alice drank some milk, licked drops off her lips, and continued. "I don't know what's going on with him from one day to the next. It scares me. I don't know if I'll be able to bear it next time he leaves."

"Does Jamie know how you feel?" Alice mutely and miserably nodded. "Why not stay with Liz?"

"I want my own place. I don't want to depend on her, or anybody else. And why does he have to go there, anyway? What's so special about Liz's place?" Resentment poured from Alice. "She can't even speak decently to me when I call to talk to Jamie. She treats me like dirt."

"The thing you must understand about Liz is that she acts like that with everybody." Amanda branched into another subject. "How's the house-hunting going?"

"Nowhere. Jamie and I decide to get a house, but *I'm* the one that has to find it."

"Hiddie could help."

"I don't want any help. Get it?"

"I know, I know." Still, Amanda relayed information about a house that was for sale in Point Grey, which Hilda had seen and recommended as perfect for Jamie and Alice. "I drove by it the other day," Amanda added. "It's on a quiet street and could be just what you're looking for."

"How much?"

Amanda ignored the question. "It's a terrific location. Four bedrooms — Jamie could use one as a workroom."

"How much?"

Amanda wished Alice would not interrupt so rudely, and suddenly felt tired of acting as intermediary between the family and Alice who, after all, had made it perfectly clear she didn't want anything to do with the Powell family in spite of the fact that everyone in the family was very nice and totally tolerant of other people's eccentricities. "You know how long it took me to buy my first house, Alice?" Alice glared at her. "Half an hour. I went inside, saw all the defects, told the realtor I'd offer five thousand under the asking price, gave him my phone number and went home. Fifteen minutes later he called to say the house was mine. It's that simple, once you've made up your mind you want to purchase a house. Your trouble is, you haven't really made up your mind to buy."

"That's not true," Alice said. "I just haven't found anything I like." Amanda leaned over her plate to fork strings of pasta into her mouth. "You didn't say how much they're asking for the house."

"There's no point in telling you. The mood you're in, you could go through every single house for sale in Vancouver and turn them all down."

"That's not true." They eyed each other, dislike radiating from them.

"You've made it perfectly clear that you don't like me, and you seem to feel the same way about everyone else in the family, though you don't even know them. Anyway, I'm not going to waste any more time —" Amanda abruptly stopped speaking when she saw tears roll from Alice's eyes and trickle down her cheeks, then said, "I'm sorry. I didn't mean that."

"It doesn't matter," Alice mumbled. "I'm not the best of company these days." That Alice could think she had ever been good company said much about her, Amanda thought. "Jamie's transferred his money into a joint account. But spending so much of it all at once scares me. Jamie says whatever I buy is fine with him, but I can't bring myself to spend such a lot of money. I've always had to be careful."

Amanda slipped into the role of decision-maker. "Have a look at the house. If you like it, then get Jamie to look at it. If he doesn't like it, just go on looking."

"I don't know what to do."

"I do. Leave your car here in the parking lot and we'll go in mine." Amanda gestured at the waiter and asked for the bill.

"No Saint Honoré cake today, madam?" he asked.

Amanda laughed, told him they were late for an appointment, paid the bill, gave him a good tip, wondered what kind of a lover he'd make, waited while Alice visited the ladies' room and decided that regardless of what happened with the house in Point Grey, she would take Alice to meet Nanda.

"Well, what do you think?" she asked as they drove past the For Sale sign and turned into the driveway. "When buying a house, first impressions are important."

"The sign said by appointment only."

"Ignore that. Come on." On leaving the car, Amanda assumed the "superior person" role she'd learned from Liz. She scanned the house and grounds as though she expected them to bow to her. "Rather pleasant," she commented to Alice as she rang the doorbell. A middle-aged man opened the door. "Good afternoon," she greeted him. "My sister-in-law and I were passing by." She gestured towards Alice. "This is Lady Powell. We were on our way to visit my aunt Mrs. Stuart McLeod, when we noticed the For Sale sign and wondered if we could quickly look around. I grew up not far from here. My sister Elizabeth Powell still resides in our home."

"You mean Elizabeth Powell, the former MLA?"

"You know Liz?"

"By sight. Well, my wife's out, but why don't you look around?" He stepped aside, allowing them to enter.

"Charming," Amanda said, "charming." She repeated this word after they inspected each room and even described the rather dingy kitchen and shabby bathrooms as "charming". At the rear of the house a small brick patio and glass conservatory were situated which could be entered through French doors from the living room. "Charming," Amanda once more commented. One side of the garden was fenced with a tall brick wall, the remaining sides with cedar.

The owner pointed to a garage adjacent to the lane. "That's a two-car garage."

"I can see it is," Amanda said. "Well, thank you for showing us around. All very charming."

They walked through the house and out to the car. "They're asking $279,000," Amanda said, "but they'll accept less. Maybe $250,000. They're probably short of money. I'm sure his wife works, that's why she wasn't there."

The prospect of parting with a quarter of a million dollars made Alice cautious. "I'm not sure Jamie'd like it."

"Do *you* like it?"

"I guess."

They halted by the For Sale sign. Amanda took out a pad and pencil. "I'll write down the phone number. You can get more information about the house from the realtor."

Alice licked her lips, then said, "All right."

Amanda wrote down the name of the realty company and the phone number. "It's the sort of house Jamie'd like . . . a smaller edition of our old home."

Amanda drove to West Marine Drive, made a turn and passed through a pair of tall wrought-iron gates, along a curved driveway towards a house that looked to Alice like a royal palace exported from somewhere in Europe and dropped into the middle of a huge expanse of lawn and formal gardens.

"Why're we stopping here?" Alice asked.

"This is Aunt Nanda's house. We can phone the realtor from here. I'll do it for you," she offered as one side of the huge double-front door opened. "Harjinder, this is Lady Alice, Lord Jamie's wife. Alice, this is Harjinder Singh. He takes care of Aunt Nanda's home. His father was Aunt Nanda's butler in England." The bearded man inclined his head and murmured words of welcome while Amanda asked if she could use the phone in his office.

"By all means," he said. "I will inform Mrs. McLeod you are here." He looked at Alice, gestured towards a door, and invited her into the sitting room.

"I'll only be a minute," Amanda said and went across the wide hall to disappear down a passage, leaving Alice to seat herself in a chintz-covered chair beside a window that looked out over a terrace, large garden and magnificent view of the Strait of Georgia. Alice told herself there was no reason to feel panic; she was an independent woman, a certified public accountant with two university degrees and a good job. Why was it then that she felt so self-conscious and wished her skirt wasn't so tight and that she'd worn a coat instead of her windbreaker?

The door opened and a tall, thin woman came in. "You're Alice," she said. "How kind of Mandy to bring you to visit me. I'm Jamie's Aunt Nanda." She offered a hand, and Alice shook it.

"I've not been sure how . . ."

"I know just how you feel. I've always been reluctant to meet new people. Where's Mandy?"

"She's using the telephone. We were in the neighbourhood to look at a house. I had no idea we were coming here."

"I'm so glad you thought of it."

"I feel out of place. I'm not properly dressed."

"What does that matter?" Nanda said. "My home is like any other. When I was a small child I dreamt of living in a little wooden house. It's odd how we dream as children of the ideal way to live, isn't it? I wanted my little house to be in the middle of lovely forest. But things didn't work out like that."

Before Alice had time to concoct a reply, Amanda came in, looking pleased with herself. "There. I've got the ball rolling, Alice. I told the realtor we might be interested in the house if the owners knocked thirty thousand off the price."

Alice was about to tell Amanda she had no business throwing money around that didn't belong to her, when Nanda spoke: "Just like your grandfather, Mandy. Always angling for a bargain."

"There's no fun in buying things unless you bargain." Amanda laughed and joined her aunt on the couch. "You're looking well, Aunt Nanda."

"I consider myself fortunate that I'm so rarely sick."

Alice thought she had never encountered so polite a person as Nanda McLeod. But somehow she must get things straight with Amanda. "You didn't make an offer on that house, did you?"

"Offer? Good heavens, no! I said we might consider it, that's all."

"Because I didn't agree to anything."

"If I'm not mistaken, offers on property are always in writing." Nanda smiled at Alice. "My father was in the real estate business and I picked up bits and pieces of information about the business from him. You know, the way children do."

The door opened and Harjinder Singh entered, followed by two other servants carrying large trays. "You'll take tea, Mandy, Alice?" The trays were set down on a side table, where Harjinder poured tea into three cups, then served them on a smaller tray while another servant quietly moved around offering sugar and milk. Alice, who always drank tea without adding sugar or milk, found herself putting both into her cup, then actually drinking the fluid without a word of protest. She was overcome by confusion, wondering how people could live like this, with servants listening to everything that was said.

"Stuart-Hector spends so much time away, flying to different places," Nanda replied to Amanda's question about her cousins. It was a moment or two before Alice remembered that Jamie had told her about his aunt's children. "Gwen still complains about being in the back row in the House. Of course, Stuart couldn't stand Trudeau, but he always claimed Trudeau was right when he said MPs didn't count for anything except as the backdrop to Cabinet. And Margaret's fine, she's off to Los Angeles, seeing about some film production." The door opened, and Alice turned to watch a woman enter and walk across the room to bend over and kiss Nanda before turning to look at her. "Why Liz, this is a pleasant surprise," Nanda said, as Alice grasped that she'd been set up by Amanda. While one part of her swore revenge, another was gratified the encounter had finally occurred.

"I'm so happy to meet you at last," Liz said. "I still don't understand why all the delay." She held Alice's hand, leaned back and scanned her. "You look splendid, doesn't she, Aunt Nanda? It's wonderful news about the baby. Is Jamie here?"

"Alice and I were house-hunting in Point Grey and decided to call in at Aunt Nanda's on our way back," Amanda explained.

"That's marvellous. Thanks." Liz accepted a cup of tea, and Alice noticed that she waved the tray of sugar and cream away. "A house near here?"

"You know the little street off Bute?"

"Oh yes. I know it. That'll be perfect. Close to me." Liz smiled at Alice, who found that the antipathy she'd directed at the unknown, unseen Liz began to melt away; but before she could think what this might mean, the door opened again and four children ran in, followed by a truly exquisite woman.

"Tashie!" Amanda cried. "What luck! Come and meet Alice." What easy deception, Alice thought, how practised in deceit Amanda was! Was it also true of Jamie?

"Hello, Mother." Natasha herded her children towards their grandmother, then turned to Alice. "It's wonderful to meet you, Alice," she said, holding out a hand. "I'm Natasha."

"Gorgeous Tashie," Amanda whispered to Alice. "Otherwise known as 'The Heartbreaker'. Remember I told you about her?"

Natasha laughed, then said something in Punjabi to the servants who had approached to offer her tea. "Come here, kids," she ordered. "Come and meet your Aunt Alice."

The four beautifully dressed children stood in a row in front of Alice while the eldest solemnly told her they were pleased to meet her.

"These are my *passion flowers,*" Natasha said, pride obvious.

"They're lovely." Like other people before her who have discovered they've been outmanoeuvred by a wilier foe, Alice felt like leaning on somebody's shoulder and openly crying. Liz moved across the room (why did it have to be Liz?) to put an arm around Alice and kiss her, and without warning, Alice leaned on Liz's shoulder and sobbed. For a moment, Amanda cried too, but everybody knew that Mandy cried over every little thing that happened.

"What a pity Davey and Hiddie aren't here. Oh well, it can't be helped," Natasha said. She turned to the servants and spoke to them. At once, the men moved four chairs closer to Alice. The women then surrounded her, happily talking and smiling, and Alice became a prisoner within the wall of their chatter and laughter. Everything Jamie had told her about his family came back to Alice and she wanted to run from the room, because what he had said was absolutely true: Liz was splendidly regal, Natasha lovely and affectionate, Amanda, friendly and helpful, and Nanda kind but distant; and each woman was perfectly prepared to accept her, irrespective of her imperfections and limitations, not because of what she herself was, but simply because Jamie had made her his wife. She understood now why Jamie was uncomfortable with his family, why he ran from them, even why he had formed a relationship with her, and this knowledge filled Alice with terror because she realized that his family, in accepting her, would now attempt to transform her into something resembling themselves, and if that happened, Jamie might reject her. Now, she saw quite clearly that Jamie was attracted by her differences from his family, by her hard-edged personality, her refusal to defer to anyone, or to any system; she saw that Jamie valued her for being herself, and that it didn't matter that she wasn't beautiful, like Natasha and Liz, or rolling in money, like Nanda, because she, Alice, could offer him more than he could ever receive from them. She suspected, as she sat within the circle of their animation and friendliness, that for days afterwards they would appraise her and then would set about, albeit unconsciously, to destroy the uniqueness that was hers. And yet they were all so friendly, so kind; Natasha's children even came over and leaned upon her. The whole family seemed fully prepared to accommodate her; they were so flexible, so ready to enclose her, to abrade away her sharp edges until she finally looked and acted exactly as they did. And they would do all this believing they were helping her and Jamie.

Alice stood and said she was expected at the office where her afternoon work was piling up. Everyone conceded, yes, Alice had to leave, but it was such a pity. Liz offered to drive her to the restaurant parking lot, and as they were escorted to the front door, Harjinder Singh approached to inform Amanda that she was wanted on the phone. "Bet it's the realtor," Amanda said. "Don't leave."

They waited in the hall while Liz described the house in Point Grey to Natasha (how did Liz know so much about it?) and Natasha replied that it would be just marvellous if Jamie and Alice bought it. Amanda reappeared, shaking her head, saying the realtor wasn't interested in pursuing their offer to talk. What everybody took to be Alice's sigh of regret was actually one of relief, for Alice knew she had escaped the first snare, so neatly placed by Amanda, to bring her into the family fold.

Alice squeezed into the bucket seat of Liz's sports car and listened while Liz more or less laid out the pattern for their future relationship, which she might have got away with, except that Alice had already made up her mind that it was not a future she wanted. "We must cooperate," Liz explained, "to make things easy for Jamie." Alice nodded, while thinking Liz had got it all backwards: The time had come for Jamie to begin making things easy for Alice.

"Our father's greatest desire was to be a poet," Liz explained. (The burial service for Alice's parents had been conducted in an Anglican church, and Liz's words 'our father' reminded Alice of it.) "So Jamie's being a poet is especially important for us, don't you agree?" As they drove along the east-west thoroughfare, they could see women, some no more than fifteen or sixteen, slowly parading at intersections, waiting for johns to stop and lower car windows to ask the price of quick relief. "That's an awful sight!" Liz said. "When I was in Victoria, I nagged and nagged at Social Services to do something about prostitution in Vancouver, but the Minister simply passed the buck. It's one big vicious circle: Ministry of Social Services, to police, to city hall, back to the Ministry. Nobody really gives a damn about the women."

"Why should they?" Alice said.

"Don't you think it's awful women sell their bodies?"

"They don't have to," Alice retorted.

"They've been reduced to it," Liz firmly said.

"No. They do it because it's easier to get fifty bucks by taking off their underpants than working for minimum wage."

"You realize a majority of those young women were abused as children and most are on drugs?"

"And you know something else? I was sexually abused when I was a kid. Now I'm a chartered accountant with two degrees. And what's more, I'm also Lady Powell. So what do you make of that? Thanks for the lift." Alice levered herself out of Liz's car. "There's something else, too. I have no intention of sharing Jamie with you, or anybody else. He married me, not you or anybody in your family. So get that straight, okay? Be seeing you." Alice, believing herself the victor in the opening skirmish of what was likely to be a long-term battle, smiled at Liz, slammed the car door, and walked across the parking lot to her car.

Chapter 12

"I suppose we asked for it. I mean, we came on pretty strong. Liz must've been quite upset."

Amanda had just given Natasha a blow-by-blow account of Alice's putdown of Liz, which Natasha secretly enjoyed though she wouldn't have admitted it to Amanda. "I should have warned her," Amanda said. "That's how Alice came on with me. Every time I opened my mouth she'd jump in and attack me. But I doubt if Liz would have taken anything I said about Alice seriously. She never listens."

"But do you suppose it's true? You know, about Alice being abused?"

"Why not? It's common enough."

Natasha shivered. "I'll never understand such things. You read what happens to children in other countries, but you don't expect . . . There's so much vileness in the world, Mandy. It's frightening. How can men think they can do as they please with little girls?"

"Boys too." Amanda had seen many abused children when she'd worked in children's wards; consequently she had little patience with Natasha's tender feelings, which she thought exaggerated to the point of being ridiculous. "When I was in nursing school, somebody — a lawyer, I think — came in and talked to us about family law and children. Of course, I knew absolutely nothing in those days, so maybe that's why I remember what he said about the way some parents view their kids. He compared a man ejecting semen into a woman with a farmer putting seed into the ground, so the woman is regarded as soil by the man and whatever grows in the woman is owned by the man and he has the right to use it as he pleases."

Natasha wrinkled her nose. "Ugh! How revolting!"

"Maybe so. But at rock-bottom lots of men think they own their kids, like farmers own crops."

"Oh, Mandy, how can you talk like that!"

Amanda smiled: She rather enjoyed shocking Natasha. "I didn't say it, the lecturer did."

"It's awful. But what's it got to do with Alice and Jamie?"

"Alice refuses to be owned."

"She's not."

Amanda picked up a Nanaimo bar, popped it in her mouth and a gluttonous smile spread over her face as she chewed it. "I adore Nanaimo bars," she said. "I could gorge myself on them. Alice's attack on Liz was partly my fault. I misjudged her. I thought I'd brought her along to the point where she'd enjoy meeting the rest of us. That's why I took her to Nanda's. It was a mistake. Alice saw it as a trap."

"That's nonsense. All we wanted was to get to know her."

"Remember how we pulled up chairs and sat around her? Remember how we were so charming and accommodating? Well, I've seen enough of Alice to sense what was going on in her head. She's quite sure that we think we own Jamie — especially Liz — and she's determined to get him away from us. That's why she was so nasty with Liz. And Liz didn't know what to say because it was so unexpected. But I know what to expect from Alice now, and most of the time I'm two steps ahead of her."

"Maybe Liz could have been more . . . thoughtful." Natasha thought Liz was an insensitive person, but didn't want to say so to a person who thought the only reason the sun rose each day was to shed light on and glorify Liz.

"It wouldn't have made any difference. I watched Alice's face when you and the kids came in. Jamie's a good-looking guy, but Alice's kid could never look like yours. Never." Natasha smiled and graciously accepted the accolade. "Even *I* feel envious when I see them."

"Oh, you mustn't. Your Annabelle and Christopher are charming."

"Maybe Chris will be handsome, but Annabelle's always going to be a plain Jane. Too bad, because she's a wonderful little person."

Natasha smiled acknowledgement of Amanda's maternal partisanship. "Annabelle's intelligent," she said, while managing to suggest her own children were both beautiful *and* intelligent. Amanda smiled back: Long ago she had decided that while she would always ferociously defend her children she would never imagine they possessed qualities which in fact they lacked. Amanda looked at her watch and said she must leave, the children were due home from school. "You'll go on meeting Alice?" Natasha asked as she rose to escort Amanda from the house.

"Of course. I mustn't let her think she's put anything over on Liz and Hiddie."

"I've never understood people who operate like Alice," Natasha said as she opened the front door and walked out onto the wide gravelled area where Amanda's car was parked.

"You've never had to compete, Tashie, that's why you can't understand. I spent three years in nursing school and three more at university being put down." Amanda opened the car door. "The important thing is to be on guard for it and ready to counterattack."

"Let me know what happens," Natasha said.

Amanda acknowledged the request, put her car into gear, passed Natasha's immaculately polished Jaguar, drove home, and walked into the living room where Annabelle and Christopher were entertaining Jamie.

"I didn't see your bike," she said.

"It's getting a new wheel and brakes."

"A car ran over it," Annabelle explained. "It was Jamie's fault. He doesn't have proper brakes."

"Is that true?" Amanda asked. She sat facing Jamie.

"Sort of," Jamie admitted. "Brakelessness is a way of gauging my relative position in a universe governed by chance."

"You only say that to excuse yourself." Annabelle waved an accusing finger at him. "Even kids know you're supposed to have proper brakes on your bike."

"It's against the law not to," Christopher informed him. "The police will get you."

"It's plain stupid," Amanda said. "Just plain stupid. Are you staying to eat with us, Jamie?"

"No. I must pick up my bike."

"I'll drive you."

"No, no. I'll walk." Jamie stood and limped towards the door. "I need the exercise."

"Wait a minute." Amanda positioned herself between Jamie and the front door. "Has a doctor checked you over?"

"I'm okay, Mandy. I fell off the bike before it went under the car wheel."

"It's a wonder you weren't killed."

"That's what me and Chris told him."

"Christopher and I," Jamie mechanically said.

"Don't make a fuss, Jamie. I'll drive you."

"You're the one making the fuss, Mandy."

"I know more about automobile accidents than you. Which bike shop is it?"

"The one on Tenth."

"We'll put your bike in the car."

"Us too," Annabelle said. Jamie offered no further resistance, and they piled into Amanda's car and went up the hill to Tenth Avenue. "Why don't you get a car, Uncle Jamie?" Annabelle asked.

"Don't like them."

"You'd better get one for when Alice has the baby."

"Alice already has a car. There's the shop." Immediately they entered the store, Annabelle and Christopher went to look at children's bikes. Amanda was adamantly opposed to them having bikes, and so far had managed to resist the pressure they'd put on her.

"Listen, Mandy," Jamie said, "don't let what happened the other day happen again."

"It won't."

"Tell Hiddie to lay off pushing houses at Alice."

"She just passed on information."

"Let Alice find a house herself."

"You don't have to explain anything to me, Jamie. I can see what's going on."

"That's more than I do. I'm here to pick up my bike," Jamie said to a young, grimy-handed man. "New front wheel and brakes."

"Oh, that wreck! Do you actually ride it around Vancouver?"

"I do my best."

The man shook his head partly in disapproval, partly in admiration, and fetched the bike from the repair shop. "Y'know, bikes run better when they're oiled," he said. "You ever thought of getting a multi-geared, ten-speed bike? Easier on the legs," he added.

"I'm a one-gear guy." Jamie squeezed the new brake handles and asked for the bill. While he sorted through the small-denomination bills in his wallet, Annabelle and Christopher took Amanda over to look at children's bikes. "You have any cash on you?" Jamie called. "I need another twenty bucks. I don't have my chequebook."

In the end, Amanda paid the bill with her Visa card, reminding Jamie to reimburse her. The bike-shop mechanic returned Amanda's card while she was still inspecting children's bikes and he began talking about recent innovations in bicycle design. Amanda, who had been loverless for several weeks, willingly listened while imagining his hands (bike grime washed away) touching her sensitive areas. "If . . . and it's only an if . . . I bought bikes for my two kids, would you teach them how to ride safely?"

"Sure would." He grinned. "You bet!"

"We'll be back. Maybe tomorrow afternoon. I've got to take my brother home now."

"That's unnecessary," Jamie protested. "I have a renewed, fully braked bike."

"You also have a badly bruised leg."

"Have it checked over," the man said. "Couple of guys I know got bowled over, thought nothing of it, and ended up spending several weeks in hospital . . . skull fractures. Did you whack your head?"

"I landed on my side."

"Spinal's are as bad. I'd have myself checked out. Hey!" he called as Jamie pushed the bike towards the shop door. "The brakes may need adjusting. Stop by next week. Okay?"

"I'll be in tomorrow," Amanda said. Her smile and tone of voice hinted more could result from the meeting than purchasing children's bikes.

"You bet," the man said. He watched Amanda's broad bottom glide through the opened door, then sighed and returned to mending punctures and dismantling frozen gear systems.

"That guy doesn't know what he's in for," Jamie remarked.

As they stowed Jamie's bike in the luggage end of Amanda's station wagon, Amanda said, "You'll have to tell me how to get to Alice's place." Jamie nodded, aware that when they got to the apartment, Amanda would expect him to invite them in. He knew Alice would hate the intrusion, so before they got there he'd have to think of a way of getting out of it.

"That's it." He pointed to the apartment tower where Alice lived. Amanda smiled and expectantly waited.

"Does she live at the very top?" Annabelle asked.

"Near the top." Somehow he must open the car door and extract himself from this awkward situation. "Some other time . . ." he mumbled.

"Of course," Amanda said.

"It's difficult . . ."

"Don't worry, Jamie, don't worry." Amanda patted his hand. "I know you're in an awkward position. We all know that."

"It's just that Alice has always fended for herself."

"She's amazing," Amanda cooed. "So determined."

"Once we get a house . . ."

"Of course."

(Jamie had never wanted to own a house, had sworn he would never be a slave to property and everything it entailed. His sole concession was the possibility that one day he might buy a piece of bush and build a one-room shack in the middle of it. He'd never held a hammer in his hand in his life, never grown a cabbage or planted a potato, never split wood for a stove, never really prepared his own meals, but that didn't prevent him from believing that a bare-bones existence was the source of high moral conduct, mystical vision and poetic inspiration. He would have liked to share George Herbert's small, cold cottage and partake of bread and water with him, and would've had no objection either to dying, like Herbert did, at thirty-nine, provided the harsh physical regimen had sustained his mystical vision. Instead, he lay each night in Alice's bed, sleeping against her warm cumbrous body, listening to her uneven breathing as she adjusted her position to the burden within her womb; he smelled her sexual odours and the gases she expelled in the night, and when he felt so inclined passed a hand over her shoulders, buttocks, belly and breasts and the hidden lips which so readily parted on his approach; but whenever he did these things he would also feel that doing them was wrong, that he really ought to be lying in a chilled, celibate bed, waiting for the crackling voice of the stars to call him to his poetic labours. He felt this even as he experienced arousal and nuzzled Alice's breasts until she sleepily muttered indistinct words about not venturing too far inside and hurting the baby, then pleasurably sighed once their union was accomplished. It was both wonderful and terrible, because each time it happened, Jamie felt as though the stars were receding and that when he next looked up into the night sky, it would be empty. The contradictions in his life confused him. He wanted to be in Alice's company and felt himself to be at peace with her, yet at the same time he felt that the peace he experienced was a negation of something vitally important to him.)

Jamie became aware that the children, sensing expectancy in their mother, had stopped talking about which bikes they intended to select and were now looking at him. This made him feel as though he was standing on a scaffold with a rope around his neck, waiting for the boards to vanish from beneath his feet, and he felt a momentary hatred of Amanda because he knew her readiness to accommodate his wishes was nothing more than a noose-tightening technique, an illusion of freedom, the giving him of rope to hang himself. The only person he had ever known who was not like this was Alice. She didn't give a damn about the poet in him and hated his brotherly facets. All she wanted was the man in him, the creature that would unfailingly fill the emptiness within her. But Jamie could not eliminate the brother or poet from his life; they were as much a part of his existence as breathing and the pumping of blood through his heart.

"I can't invite you in, Mandy. You have to understand that. You have to realize I'm trying to detach myself from you. I must do this, even if it means not going to Liz's any more."

"You mustn't stop doing that, Jamie. That would be terrible. I won't bother you, Jamie. I promise." As usual, she was close to crying.

"It's not just you, Mandy. It's something in me. Fear that everything will go. Sometimes I wish I hadn't met Alice."

Amanda groped around, found his hand and squeezed it. "Don't feel that way, Jamie. You and Alice think the world of each other. Like what I felt about Harry until everything went wrong. And you mustn't think I object when you say things to me. I don't. I just wish everything was right for you."

"So do me and Chris," came Annabelle's voice from the back seat.

"You hear that, Jamie? Now go on. And make sure you get yourself checked over. Promise?"

Thankful to have escaped and relieved to know the worst was not about to happen (not yet) Jamie pulled his bike from the car and closed the tailgate. He called "See you soon" as Amanda pulled away, watched the car turn at the end of the street, then lifted his bike, entered the apartment block and, carrying the bike, went upstairs. Alice sighed and relaxed when the door buzzer sounded. This was always a bad time of day since she was never certain that Jamie would return.

"What happened?" she said when he limped in.

"I fell off my bike."

"Dope!" Alice said. She wanted to grab him and examine every part of his body just to make sure he wasn't seriously injured.

"I had to get a new front wheel."

"Idiot!" she said when Jamie explained how, unable to stop, he had thrown himself off the bike, which had then rolled on to end up with its front wheel crushed beneath a car.

"I had new brakes put on too."

"That's not the point!" Alice shouted, knowing she yelled to relieve her tension. "You shouldn't be allowed on the streets."

"I don't see how I can be prevented from riding my bike. I'm a tax-paying citizen."

"They ought to make a law . . ." She shunted him into the bedroom, watched him strip and was disappointed when the only evidence of the accident seemed to be a couple of bruises on his stringy legs. Still, she made him get into the shower and ordered him to remain there for ten minutes beneath water as hot as he could stand it while she went back to the kitchen area to assemble dinner. Jamie appeared wearing her pink bathrobe, and they began eating their meal of barbecued turkey thighs she'd purchased from a nearby delicatessen and ready-made salad with dressing from a bottle.

"Tastes good," Jamie said, gnawing bits of meat off a thigh bone.

"I love turkey," Alice said, taking her second piece.

"What do you find so especially endearing about it?" Jamie asked.

"You know what I mean. So don't start lecturing me on the right words to use."

"I'd never do that."

"It's what Amanda does."

"Mandy speaks the language of her childhood and school friends. All my sisters do. They sniff out words and phrases that identify friends and allies. They can't help it. You probably do it too."

"Like hell I do. I don't want to sniff out guys from the same patch as me."

"You could reverse it, and say you sniff them out in order to avoid them."

"Why aren't you running around with old pals?"

"I don't have any." As he spoke, Alice suddenly grimaced and clutched her belly. "What's up?"

"It belted me one."

"Maybe it doesn't like turkey."

"You make the dumbest jokes."

"I know," Jamie agreed. "Once I won a dumb-joke contest."

Alice watched him, then smiled. "I don't know if you're being serious."

"Dumb jokes are serious business. Just think how much money guys are paid to manufacture them for TV." He pointed to the remaining turkey thigh. "Is that yours or mine?"

"You can have it. I've had two pieces." She pressed her belly again. "Oh boy! Talk about whacks."

"It wants the turkey thigh," Jamie said.

"I bought us two each, so it's yours."

Jamie raised the aluminum container and slid the turkey thigh onto her plate. "You need food for one and a half persons," he said. "It's only fair you eat it."

Alice suddenly became very emotional. "When we get our own house with a decent kitchen, we'll have proper meals."

"Of course."

"You want that, don't you?"

"Yes."

"I'll find us a house."

"Of course you will."

"Your sister thinks you need some special talent."

"Mandy only says that to make herself feel important. She has to grab onto little things like that because she's ignored by Liz, Hiddie and David."

"What about you? Weren't you ignored too?"

"In my family, girls were taught to defer to boys."

"No wonder you're so conceited."

"It's one reason."

She chewed at the turkey without speaking. At last she said, "You know, I liked that second house. I would've gone ahead with it if I hadn't found out that Hiddie told Amanda about it."

"Well, if it's not been sold . . ."

"Will you take a look at it?"

"Sure."

"You not saying that to shut me up?"

"No."

"I'll call the realty company tomorrow. We could look at it after work."

"Yes. We'll do that." Jamie got up. "I think I'll lie down." The expression on Alice's face changed to one of fear bordering on panic.

"You okay?" she whispered. "You're not going to faint, or anything like that?"

"Just shaken up." He went into the bedroom and lay down, keeping his eyes closed because when he opened them the ceiling light hazily advanced and receded. "Alice!" His voice was weak and he tried to focus his eyes on the light, but when he did the haze only thickened. "Alice. Alice. I'm . . ." He wanted to call out, but the hazy light turned into a blackness that overtook him.

━━━◆◆◆◆◆◆◆◆◆◆◆◆━━━

"Can you hear me?" a voice asked. "Can you hear me?" Jamie opened his eyes and saw a man's face close to his.

"Yes," Jamie said.

"You're in the emergency ward at Vancouver General Hospital. Can you tell me your name?"

"Benjamin Hector Donald Powell: Lord Powell of Hyndhurst."

The professional curiosity on the face was replaced by amusement. "I see. Is that your real name, or one you use professionally?"

A voice he knew to be Alice's murmured something in the background. "Alice?" Jamie said, and tried to raise himself but slumped back when an intense pain arrowed through his head. He groaned and closed his eyes.

"Your wife's here, Mr. Powell. You can see her in a few minutes. I'm Dr. Gainer and I want you to tell me what you remember about your accident and how you felt before losing consciousness. Can you do that for me?"

"It was my own fault. I was tempting fate."

"A dangerous thing to do," Dr. Gainer said. "Go on."

"I saw the car and fell off my bike."

"I see. Did the car hit you?"

"It went over the front wheel of the bike."

"And what about you?"

"I landed on my side, or maybe it was my back. I don't remember hitting my head."

"Have you experienced any previous loss of consciousness?"

"Not that I know of." The pain in his head was intense; it throbbed and an image of a pulsing jellyfish appeared to hover above the doctor's face. "We're keeping you here overnight, Mr. Powell, so we can run tests and take X-rays. A nurse'll give you something to quiet your headache." The doctor and the jellyfish disappeared to be replaced by Alice, who leaned over to press her cheek against his.

"I'm okay," he said.

"I thought you were dead," she whimpered. Her tears trickled over his face.

"You won't get rid of me so easily as that," Jamie feebly joked.

"Excuse me," a nurse interrupted, and Jamie felt his arm being rubbed, then pricked. "We're going to take X-rays, Mrs. Powell, then he'll go upstairs to neurology. Does Mr. Powell have a family physician?"

"I don't know. He's never sick."

"We'll need information," the bureaucratic voice said.

"Leave her alone," Jamie said. "She's my lady . . ." The cerebral pulsing had ceased and he wanted to make sure the nurse treated Alice with respect, but instead his voice faded and he closed his eyes and slept.

"Come along, Mrs. Powell," the nurse said. "You'll need to fill out some forms at Admissions. We need some particulars about your husband."

⚬⟳⟲⟳⟲⚬

Jamie awakened to find a dark-haired, good-looking woman perched on the bedside, looking down at him. She smiled and said, "Hi. I'm Dr. Barbour, resident neurologist."

"Which TV series did you escape from?" Jamie whispered. His mouth and lips felt as though they had been mummified. "Is there some water?" She poured water into a glass, inserted a bent straw into it and held the glass while he sucked the water. "Thanks," he said. "But I suppose it could work in reverse. Maybe I've slipped into a TV show."

" 'Fraid not. You're in the neurology ward at VGH. How do you feel?"

"I'm not sure. I was told neurologists had pendulous jowls and wore pince-nez."

"Times are a-changing," she replied. "So you're Jamie Powell, the geometric poet. Right?"

"Do you mean am I physically geometric, or do I compose in geometric forms?"

"I guess the latter." She laughed. "Tell me about the accident."

"It's a bore."

"Being bored is part of my job." Once more Jamie explained his reasons for riding around Vancouver on a brakeless bike. "I'm always amazed how supposedly very intelligent people can be so stupid," she commented. "Did you have any loss of consciousness as a child?"

"I don't recall. But if need be, my sisters could give you a detailed account of my childhood."

"That probably won't be necessary. The skull X-rays show nothing abnormal, but we want to run a few more tests just to be on the safe side. Okay?" She turned from the bed, hesitated, then turned back. "We've been asked to put you in a private room. The request came from Canadian Resources Corporation. You work there?"

"Oh Christ! Alice must have called Mandy. Oh lord!"

"The point is, someone will come to get your medical insurance number, that sort of thing."

"Yes, yes, I understand." Jamie suddenly became impatient with the process of treating his physical ailments and all it entailed. He saw himself stuck in a small flower-filled room, locked in with his sisters who would resolutely refuse Alice access to him. "How much longer will I have to stay here?"

"Depends on what the tests show." Jamie knew he was already receiving preferential treatment compared to other patients in the four-bed ward, that the hospital staff had docketed him as someone of consequence; he knew at some point during visiting hours the women in his family would show up, bearing flowers and books and God knows what else; that David would appear too, looking more like the ideal physician than any in the hospital; he knew at some point Alice would plod in, her fetus-filled belly an advance guard, carrying a potted azalea and a Vancouver newspaper. There was a terrible certainty about how each would respond to his incarceration: Amanda tearfully sympathetic; Hilda questioning his diet and exercise regimen; Liz, smilingly unconquerable; Natasha, solicitous; and Nanda, silently supportive. And David? Jamie had never been quite sure what his half-brother thought of him; David moved in mysterious ways (so Jamie couched it to himself), seldom revealing what he thought, never revealing his feelings. He wasn't even sure David liked him. David had always been off somewhere when they were children, preoccupied with matters presumably beyond his younger brother's comprehension; and while it was true that Jamie no longer felt the awe he had experienced as a child for his older sibling and had even gone so far as to say to Amanda that David had totally given up his intellectual life when he married Natasha, nevertheless he often found himself deferring to his brother in much the same way Amanda deferred to Liz. And so when David finally did stroll into the ward, wearing clothes selected in Natasha's presence and approved by her, he would stand beside the bed, head canted and quietly ask Jamie how he felt, chat an obligatory five minutes, then press his hand and depart. Everything would be done quietly and efficiently and would somehow relegate Jamie to the ranks of David's not-overly-bright students. Although Jamie condemned himself for thinking unflattering thoughts about his family, nevertheless he knew his assessment of them was quite accurate. They were so damn predictable, although was it fair to condemn them for that? After all, wasn't he just as predictable? Wasn't it predictable he was going to be utterly bored being confined to this bed? Oh God! Unless he managed to get out he'd be swamped by a wave of solicitations from his family. "Nurse!" he yelled. "Goddamn it! Nurse! I must get out of here."

"It does no good to shout," a doleful voice from one of the beds said. "Press the button. That'll bring 'em."

"Button? Which button?"

"It's hanging at the back of you." Jamie turned his head, saw the word "button", reached up to press and re-press it and immediately heard the sound of people trotting in the passage beyond the door.

"What did I tell you?" the voice said. "Always brings 'em."

Two nurses and the physician hurried into the ward and over to his bed. "Yes? What is it?"

"I've got to leave. Get my clothes," Jamie said. "My clothes, please," he repeated. "I have to get out of here."

"Mr. Powell," the doctor firmly said as Jamie tried to leave the bed. "You can't leave, you're not recovered yet."

"And you don't have clothes to put on," a nurse said.

"No clothes? Of course I have clothes. You think I go around Vancouver naked?"

"You have no clothes here. Your record shows you had on a woman's pink bathrobe when you were brought into emergency."

An image of himself leaving the shower and slipping on Alice's bath-robe floated before him. "Oh Christ, yes of course. Call Alice. Tell her to bring some clothes."

"Why are you so anxious to leave, Mr. Powell?" Dr. Barbour asked. She was once more perched on the bed, the white coat taut around hip and thigh.

"A deluge of sisters will descend on me," he said and even as he spoke he could hear Liz's voice in the hallway: "This must be the room, Mandy." In the gap between the nurses, he saw bunches of flowers enter the room, followed by Liz and Amanda. The nurses separated, the physician aban-doned her perch, and the first Powell wave swept over the recumbent Jamie.

"Darling Jamie," Amanda said, leaning over to kiss him and deposit-ing flowers on his chest as though on a corpse.

"Dearest Jamie," Liz said, and she too leaned over to kiss him and add her quota of flowers.

"We'll leave you," the doctor said.

"Shall I put the flowers in vases?" a nurse asked.

"Please do," Liz said. She turned back and put a hand on Jamie's fore-head as though she doubted whether anyone on the hospital staff was ca-pable of accurately assessing her brother's temperature. "Tell me what hap-pened," she said as the nurse collected the flowers. "You'll probably need three vases," she told the nurse. Then, as the doctor and nurses left the room, Liz and Amanda settled down at the bedside. After a few minutes, Liz left the ward to find out why her brother had not yet been moved into a private room as ordered by Stuart-Hector's secretary at Canadian Re-sources Corporation.

Chapter 13

"It was nothing," Jamie had told his audience of family members. "The accident could have happened to anyone attempting to challenge the universal coordinates which govern life."

Only David had thought Jamie's explanation of the accident nonsensical and became impatient with his wife and sisters when they accepted as reasonable something he considered pure balderdash. Nor was David above thinking that Jamie had conned the family with his fanciful explanation in an attempt to escape their reprobation of his negligent behaviour. After all, much of Jamie's life consisted of conning people into believing he produced work of value. He was fond of his younger brother, but not prepared to adopt the slightly worshipful attitude of the rest of the family. "Come, come, Tashie," he said. "Jamie came close to getting himself killed because he couldn't be bothered to put decent brakes on his bike. Then he spouts absolute nonsense about universal influences and you swallow it. Would you drive around Vancouver without brakes on your car?"

"But don't you think that people can't help but be influenced by happenings in the universe?" Natasha was lying in her favourite position.

"Only to the extent that we're all grubbing around on one tiny speck of matter in an infinity of specks. Or do you think there's a special set of specks for Jamie?"

Natasha reached up to stroke David's face. She knew how David felt about Jamie; sometimes she felt a little bit like that herself, especially when she was with David. Still, most of her opinions about Jamie were formed under the influence of Liz and Amanda, and so she had come to believe, as they did, that there was something extraordinary about Jamie which permitted him to communicate (in a mystical way) with a universal controller. It might be, as David said, nonsense, but still she always felt a little shiver of excitement whenever she thought that the finger of divinity might have touched a member of her family. Further, the idea of a controller of events somewhere "out in the universe" fit in nicely with her belief that "divine fingers" had brought her and David together to generate the passion flowers that had lain dormant within her womb. She remained as romantic today as on the evening when she and David had first revealed their love for each other, then afterwards lay on his single bed and consummated the act which she had dreamt of and longed for all her life. Now, whenever they made love, she relived the sensations she'd experienced the first time David's smooth-skinned body had touched hers. She believed then, and still did, that she and David were, and would always be, "one flesh". And while she suspected there was no scientific or metaphysical basis for her belief that Jamie had a special connection with the universal controller, she secretly hoped it was true.

"The doctors are puzzled," she said. "They can't explain why Jamie became unconscious."

Earlier in the day David had listened to Liz condemn the hospital medical staff, especially the young resident neurologist, for daring to ask if Jamie had had any neurological problems in the past, or the family a history of neurological disorders. "What cheek!" she said. "She practically accused me of concealing information!"

"She was just being thorough," David told her. "After all, we do have a few skeletons in the family closet."

"Those aren't the same thing. And there is nothing wrong with any of our nervous systems!"

"Well . . . physicians look for explanations. And frankly if I were a physician and didn't know Jamie, I might wonder if he was mentally defective, or maybe high on drugs, because both offer reasonable explanations for his careening around Vancouver streets on a bike with defective brakes."

"Jamie explained why he didn't have adequate brakes."

"But it's a nutty reason, Liz. Surely you can see that."

"He's a poet and his mind works differently than other people's."

"I find Jamie's behaviour as incomprehensible as his poetry."

"Lots of modern poetry is like that."

"Maybe." David kissed her, knowing she would continue tirelessly to defend the indefensible.

"Jamie has told me he has to defy the auguries."

"I may be mistaken, but most guys who do that, lose."

"In a way, that's what we do, Davey. Defy the gods."

"Maybe." He kissed her again, caressing her shoulders and breasts. "But we don't live as dangerously as Jamie."

Liz turned onto her side and frantically clutched him. "Is this how we'll go on for the rest of our lives, Davey? Is it? Will you still be sneaking here when we're both seventy? Is that how we'll end up, lying here, help-lessly looking at each other and wishing we'd never started?"

"You began it, Liz."

"You could have said no. Well, couldn't you?"

"I was afraid for you, of what you might do."

"I don't believe that. You wanted to compare me to Tashie."

"I've never done that, Liz."

"Then why do we go on?"

"I suppose because we need each other."

"More than you need Natasha?"

"It's not the same. I don't understand why I feel compelled to do this with you. I do love Tashie, you know that. But it's as though I can't love her unless I also do this with you, as though you have a prior right to me. But I know I shouldn't acknowledge it because it degrades what I feel for Natasha. And God knows what she'd do if she ever found out."

"I think Mandy knows."

"How could she?"

"She guessed. But it's nothing to be concerned about, Davey."

"How did she guess? Did you say something? Did she say she knew?"

"We were just talking . . . I don't know . . . about different things. I don't really remember how it came up."

"Damn it." He left the bed, unable to hide his uneasiness. Liz reached out and tried to detain him.

"It's nothing, Davey. Honestly. Mandy would never say a word to anyone."

"I hope not. I have to go."

"Davey," Liz called as he crossed the bedroom. He stopped to look at her, his face set in condemnation. "You have to understand, sometimes things are difficult . . . being alone."

"I know dozens of men who'd be delighted to marry you, Liz. You're alone because it's what you've chosen. It's not because of what you feel for me. Marriage wouldn't alter that, any more than me being married to Natasha has changed my feelings for you. Listen to me, Liz. Right now I'm so scared I never want to come near you again."

"Davey . . ."

"You've done a lot of irrational things in your life, Liz, but letting Mandy know about us was not just irrational, it was also incredibly stu-pid." David went into the bathroom and she heard water running in the shower. She'd never expected to be the recipient of an outburst of angry condemnation from David, never dreamt he would accuse her of behaving stupidly. But his anger over what she'd blurted out to Mandy was misplaced, because while she believed she had an absolute right as an older sister to criticize Amanda mercilessly, she also knew Amanda would rather die than betray her. David came back and began hurriedly dressing.

"Davey," Liz said, "don't rush off angry with me."

"You don't seem to understand what I could lose," David muttered. "You don't seem to realize the things you say and do seriously affect other people."

"David!" Liz cried. "You don't know what you're saying!" She left the bed and went towards him.

"Don't come near me," he said, hands raised as though to push her away. He slipped on his jacket and almost ran to the bedroom door.

"Davey," Liz begged, following him from the room, through the house to the back door, where she halted in the open doorway.

"Close the door," he ordered. "Don't you realize you're naked?"

"I don't care."

He returned to the doorway and after Liz had moved back, he entered the house, slammed the door and leaned against it. "*You* may not care."

"Davey, you've no reason to worry. Mandy would never say a word to anyone. She wouldn't." She slowly approached him and touched his face.

"It would kill Natasha," he whispered.

"Oh, I don't know." Liz gave an abrupt, pain-filled laugh. "If I know Natasha, it would be the other way around: She'd try to kill me . . . or you." She leaned against him. "Davey, I think I could manage without the sex, but not without seeing you every week. I don't think I could manage that."

David put his arms around Liz and pressed her against him. "I'm sorry for what I said. Let's forgive and forget. Oh God, what a mess." He stroked her head and passed his hand down over her back to her bottom. He remembered her girl's body, how he had enjoyed watching as she dried herself after their evening bath: She was neatly assembled and lithe, but so impetuous in her actions, never thinking of her body per se, only of what she could compel it to do. And she'd changed very little over the years, but he doubted she could now forgo sex because it had become an integral part of their meetings. Of course it was wrong, dangerously wrong, but it was impossible for him to go back and change anything. Besides, while he might worry about Natasha's reaction if she found out, still he wouldn't gainsay that having the love of two beautiful women was a good boost for his ego.

"You won't stay away, will you, Davey?" she asked.

"No, but we'll have to be more careful. It's become too much of a habit."

"But I'm still your sister. So isn't it natural for you to come to see me?"

"I meant talking to Mandy about us."

"It only happened once."

"If it comes up again, tell her the affair ended years ago. Do that. Please! And maybe I shouldn't come as often."

"You decide. I'll dress and walk you to your car."

David waited at the door until Liz returned wearing a tailored green dress with a gold belt — she looked stunning. They walked along the alley to the street where he had parked his car. "I'm definitely going to seek the Liberal nomination," she said. "I can't go on *talking* about political inequality. I have to take action. Besides, I need to get away, I need to —" She stopped, unable to give a reason for leaving, only that she knew she must break free of the claustrophobic atmosphere that surrounded her and her siblings and escape from everything that reminded her of the past.

"If you get the nomination, I'll help you campaign."

"Thank you." She raised a hand of farewell as he drove away, then went back into the house to pour herself a glass of sherry. Her family knew nothing of Liz's drinking. She never drank enough to become obviously drunk, but consumed alcohol constantly through the day, beginning in the late morning with a glass of sherry or port, and she had now reached the stage where she was drinking a bottle a day. She understood very well what was happening, for she remembered how lack of focus, coupled with the absence of a drive to succeed, had turned her father into a morose alcoholic.

The possibility that she too might end this way thoroughly frightened her and largely explained her decision to re-enter politics. Of course there was no guarantee she would succeed in securing the nomination. True, she knew something about women in politics, but her college course was a sketchy, ramshackle affair, consisting largely of biographies of women who had left their mark in provincial and federal politics, coupled with diatribes against the prevailing male clique which, so Liz lectured her students, prevented women from taking their rightful role in the governance of their country. Apart from this, Liz had little to offer, except her notoriety as a provincial MLA. Her grasp of federal issues was skimpy; in contrast, Gwendolyn McLeod held degrees in economics and political science and had two years' experience as a Member of Parliament under her belt. In any case, Liz's earlier political success had had little to do with party policies: They were the outcome of her experience teaching school in Vancouver's east end, the ardour of supporters, and large infusions of cash from members of the McLeod-Powell clan. Actually, Liz was neither intellectually nor emotionally suited to political life: She had little interest in the issues of the day and was incapable of compromise and accommodation. She steadfastly held to her positions, regardless of advice from colleagues or what political winds were blowing. In fact, her entry into politics had been something of an anomaly, since she'd won her seat in a west-end riding never before held by the provincial NDP, a riding party insiders thought was unwinnable: It was a political truism that residents of Vancouver's west end consistently voted for candidates who mirrored their own social and economic interests.

That Liz herself was a member of a relatively small privileged class did not occur to her. At the time of her first campaign she knew little of the world beyond her family and thought everyone more or less lived the way she did. Until going to university, she had spent virtually no time outside the family fold. She had felt close to her mother and sisters and brothers, but had not sought companionship outside the circle of her family and had formed no friendships at school. She attended a private girls' school where the teachers told Winnie Powell that unless her daughter concentrated on her studies she wouldn't have the grade point average necessary for university entrance. "It's such a pity," they said, "because Elizabeth's IQ suggests she could do much better if she applied herself." In fact, although no one in the family except Winnie Powell knew of this, there was a note attached to Liz's school records stating that she had undergone psychological assessment as well as treatment by a psychiatrist when she was in grade five, then again in grade eight, in an effort to uncover the cause of her indifference to her studies and school life in general.

"Darling," Winnie Powell had said to her daughter when she was sixteen, "I'm sure you can do better. You must learn to apply yourself. You're always telling your sisters and brothers they must do *their* best. So it's only right to try harder yourself."

Winnie's cautious warning had the desired effect. Liz raised her grades and went off to the University of British Columbia, although once there she drifted from course to course and showed no interest in campus life. She was unaware of the men, on campus and off, who eyed her with obvious interest. Indeed, she seemed not aware of her own good looks. She wore her thick brown hair short with a fringe resting on her forehead and two curved points touching the outer edge of her high flushed cheekbones and drawing attention to her dark blue eyes. But it was her figure that compelled attention: She was above average in height, blessed with a slender, rounded physique which her carriage accented — shoulders straight, head held high as she confidently (so it seemed) strode forward into a known future. But in fact the reverse was true. She drifted without purpose and more and more she retreated into family life where, due to her mother's failing health, she took on the role of parent to her younger brothers and sisters.

By the time she had left high school Liz had completed her annexation of David. He had become the cup into which she poured the torrent of anguish she'd suffered as a child when her beloved Muriel had died. David absorbed her passionate hatred of their self-destructive father who had stalked Muriel Wickham until she'd finally killed him, and listened quietly as Liz reiterated her lifelong hatred of their grandfather because he'd promised but failed to avert Muriel's execution for their father's murder. As he listened, David developed the idea that, due to these childhood events, Liz had failed to develop emotionally and as a consequence would need his support throughout life. While he had no proof of his theory, barely understanding it himself, nor any explanation for Liz being the only one of the five children (apparently) who had been scarred by the events, nevertheless it shaped forever his relationship with Liz. He encouraged her to become a primary teacher, thinking that teaching small children might be therapeutic and, relying on his advice, she completed the teacher education program at UBC and obtained a position as a grade two teacher in West Vancouver Elementary School. After seven years, she requested and received a transfer to the Vancouver School District and was assigned a grade three classroom in an east-side school. There, for the first time in her life, Liz came face to face with ill-dressed, hungry children who were too tired or too hyperactive to sit still and learn.

Her experience in that classroom changed Liz. Seeing those children turned her into a rampaging crusader against child poverty, eventually leading to her election as an MLA. In her overnight conversion, Liz resembled an archer armed with a single arrow: It was all hit or all miss. She knew nothing about provincial politics and had only the foggiest notions about what political parties stood for which policies. But David was interested in the New Democratic Party and he encouraged Liz to take out a membership. When the 1972 election was called, she volunteered to run for office in her own riding, though her ignorance of provincial politics was so great she didn't know the riding where she lived had never been won by any candidate who espoused left-wing views. When she did learn of this, it didn't faze her in the slightest. She enlisted the support of her family and their friends and, fortified with funds from the McLeod-Powell family, swamped the streets with campaign signs. That she might lose the election never occurred to her, and she astonished party hacks with her assumption that victory would be hers by right, not by effort, or by virtue of sound NDP policies. And she did win, and while she might not have been the youngest MLA ever sent to Victoria, she was certainly the most beautiful and, within a short while, possibly the most notorious.

Once seated as a backbencher, she began her fight to rid the province of its poor children, getting into trouble with the Premier, senior ministers, and practically everyone else in the caucus because she ignored caucus solidarity, had no idea of how to conduct herself in the legislative chamber, and openly attacked the government ministers responsible for education and social services for their failure to live up to their campaign promises. To keep her quiet, she was given a cabinet portfolio which required her to spend time in the Interior and in the North. This didn't work, and Liz was dropped in the next cabinet shuffle. By then she was thoroughly disgusted with the NDP, so she tore up her NDP membership card and crossed the floor to sit as an independent. The media loved that: What Elizabeth Powell actually said might not make too much sense, but she played well in the newspapers and on TV because she was photogenic and provided exciting copy: The old chestnut of "poor little girl becoming a rich woman" was turned upside-down and became "rich woman helps poor little girls and boys." It was a real winner; readers and viewers loved it.

In the 1975 election, the NDP ran a party stalwart in the riding, and Liz ran as an independent. She won a second time with an increased margin, while the NDP was defeated and Social Credit formed the new government. The day she returned to Victoria carrying the same bow and arrow aimed at eradicating child poverty, she was photographed on the steps of the legislature. Inside the chamber, she heckled ministers and insulted the opposition, and more than once was ejected from the chamber for refusing to retract accusations. Then, one day, after accusing the Premier of lying to the people of British Columbia, she was forcibly carried out of the legislative chamber by a sergeant-at-arms, after which she strode purposefully from the building to stand on the front steps and announce she was resigning her seat because she was disgusted with the political process and wanted nothing more to do with it. After this, she retreated into family life. She did not return to her teaching position and lost contact with her supporters, and until approached by the small group of influential Liberals urging her to seek nomination as the federal Liberal candidate in the same riding she'd formerly represented in Victoria, she hadn't given political life any more thought than the minimum required to teach her course at the college.

Up to a point, Liz was aware of her limitations and she realized that if she were to succeed she would need to camouflage her ignorance of federal political affairs with a new issue to which she and her supporters could unreservedly commit themselves. One day while riffling through the back section of a Vancouver newspaper she found it, in a short report of an oil spill in Vancouver harbour. Pollution! A few environmentalists had raised voices warning of the dire effects of air and water pollution, but people didn't seem to care. If the air stank, they said it was the smell of money, and if the rivers filled with industrial waste and sewage, they shrugged and said the ocean was big enough to purify everything drained into it. Pollution! Liz read and reread the short report, took several deep breaths and decided she'd found her issue. She would hammer it as she once pounded the theme of hungry, ill-clad children shivering and waiting at the school entrance before falling asleep in warm classrooms. David could provide the scientific data she'd need to back up her claims. No one could dispute evidence of deadly substances in fish, or of filth gumming nets in the Fraser River, or the blanket of brown haze that hung over the city on hot summer days before slowly drifting into the Fraser Valley and falling as midsummer dew to poison soil and the crops grown in it. How could anyone deny the indisputable? Liz had never been able to understand the capacity of people to close their minds and deny the obvious, especially those things obvious to her. So what if most people didn't seem to care about pollution? She'd soon change their minds. Since Amanda was representative of the average voter, Liz decided to phone her and ask if she was concerned about pollution.

"It's a motherhood issue," Amanda said. "Everyone likes pure water and uncontaminated veggies and fruit. But I don't think it'd win you an election, Liz."

"Why not?"

"Because people don't get really excited about pollution unless it's in their own backyards. And they worry about who'll pay for the clean-up."

"Industry will."

"Industry passes the cost on to consumers. You know that, Liz. And telling people to clean up their act's a waste of time. People know what they *ought* to do, like they know they should stop smoking and boozing, but there's a big gap between people knowing what's right for them to do and actually doing it." Amanda's political acumen surprised Liz. "Anyway, I'll work hard for you, Liz. I'll knock on doors and tell voters what a marvellous person you are."

"I think the issue'll fly. And it'll be even more important in the future. Things aren't going to improve."

"They probably won't," Amanda agreed. "You sound a little off, Liz. Are you okay?"

"I'm quite well." Liz coughed. "A slight sore throat, but that's nothing. Bye, Mandy."

As Amanda hung up, she chewed her upper lip, remembering other occasions Liz had sounded "off" to her and responded to inquiries by saying she had a cold or a touch of laryngitis. But her uncertainty when selecting words and then slurring them forcibly reminded Amanda of drunk people she'd encountered in emergency wards. But that was ridiculous! How could she possibly think of proud, aristocratic Liz as being drunk! She fretted some more, then telephoned Natasha's house and asked to speak to David. "This is probably stupid of me," she began, "but Liz called a little while ago to tell me she's decided to run federally."

"I already know," David said.

"But why I've called . . ." David patiently listened. Every family had a scatterbrain, and Amanda was theirs. ". . . there was something wrong with her voice. She said she had a sore throat, but I could swear she'd . . . well . . . I thought she'd been drinking."

"Liz hardly ever drinks."

"That's what I told myself. But she was slurring words."

"A sore throat would account for that."

"Maybe. But I thought I'd ask if you'd noticed anything. I know you call in to see her."

Aware now that Amanda knew something about his relationship with Liz, David became stiff and defensive. "I don't call in often," he said, "but whenever I do, she always seems fine to me."

"She's going to run on pollution." Amanda had no sooner uttered the words than she realized how silly they sounded. "I mean, that's the issue Liz plans to campaign on."

"It's also what cars, mills, chimneys, and pipes pour into the environment. Sooner or later we'll have to stop poisoning our air and soil."

"Oh, I agree, Davey, I agree. So you think everything's fine with Liz?"

"I've not seen or heard anything to the contrary."

"What did Mandy want?" Natasha asked when David rejoined her.

"Liz had called and got her worried because she was slurring words. Mandy thought she might have been drinking."

"Does Liz drink?"

"An occasional glass of wine or sherry. But drink heavily? No."

"It doesn't fit with her personality." Natasha raised her leg to scratch an ankle. Doing this revealed her elegant legs for David to admire. "Although now that you mention it, once or twice when she's called . . . No, that can't be right . . . I'm only thinking like this because of what Mandy said. I'm quite sure Liz'd never descend to drinking. It's too low class."

"Alcoholism isn't unknown in the middle and upper classes. It's just not as obvious. We're better able to hide our delinquencies."

"But can you see Liz hiding bottles of whisky around the house?"

"No. And I'm sure Mandy is mistaken. If Liz has a sore throat and cold, her sinuses would be blocked. That would account for the slurring."

"Davey darling," Natasha drew up her skirt and critically examined her thighs, "shall we have another baby?" She tilted her head in order to see his face.

"No. We have enough."

"Oh, I don't know. I think of what Mandy said about her love-making with Harry — what was his last name? I suppose it doesn't matter. Remember she told us how she'd reached the point where she couldn't go on?"

"You've reached that point?"

"Oh no. But sometimes I have an urge to have another baby. A very tiny urge. Do you think Liz regrets not having had children?"

"I don't know. I've never spoken to her about it."

"It's odd, isn't it, all the things we never speak of in our family? Mother never speaks of my father, for example. She doesn't even have a picture of him. When I asked her about it once, she said they never took photographs. She's always talked about going to India, but she's never gone. It's funny. She could travel anywhere in the world, yet she hardly leaves the house. We could travel more, too, but we never seem to get any farther than Paradise Island. Remember summers on the island? Remember when we were teenagers and we'd sneak out of the cottage so we could be together? Remember that, darling?"

"Yes."

"And Liz'd be so angry when she found out. She was so possessive about you. Didn't you hate it?"

"I was used to it. It wasn't as bad as it appeared."

"Sometimes I hated her. Did you know that, darling? I'd plan ways to get rid of her. Teenagers are so ferocious, aren't they? Will our children be like that?"

"Probably."

"I hope not. I want them to go on being as lovely and sweet as they are now."

"They'll grow up and we'll age."

"It's awful, simply awful." Natasha reached up to him. "Let's go to bed and make love, Davey. Maybe that's why we never go anywhere . . . because everything we desire is right here."

"Yes," he agreed, "everything we desire is here, everything's inescapably here."

Chapter 14

"Are you back at work?" Amanda asked Jamie.

"More or less." They were sitting in a coffee shop on Denman Street near Alice's apartment. Amanda had called, asking if they could get together because she wanted to discuss something, but Jamie, unsure how Alice would react to Amanda being in the apartment when she was not there, suggested they meet somewhere for coffee. At Alice's insistence, Jamie had given up his suite on Commercial Drive a few weeks earlier.

"You're looking better," Amanda said.

"I'm fine. What would you like?"

"Coffee. Maybe a bran muffin."

Jamie doubled the order and the waitress left. The coffee shop was almost empty, apparently surviving on customer waves at midday and late afternoon when people were hungry, in a hurry and not in the mood to be overly discriminating about what they consumed. "So how's everything with you, Mandy? You wanted to see me about something?"

Amanda sighed, and as her breasts heaved beneath her blouse Jamie thought she'd gained weight since they'd last met. "I'm probably being silly, and I'm sure David thought so when I called him, but anyway you can give me your opinion." She stopped when the waitress came with their order. Amanda sliced the muffin and plastered each part with butter. "I should stay away from butter," she said. "It flows right through my body onto my hips."

"You were telling me about talking to David."

"I had a call from Liz. She's definitely seeking the Liberal nomination, which I already knew, but as I listened to her talking, I had the impression that she'd . . . I can hardly bring myself to say this, Jamie . . . but I had the impression she'd been drinking."

"You mean Liz was drunk!" His voice was squeaky with disbelief.

"Well, I wouldn't go that far, but she was slurring words. And when I asked if anything was wrong, she said she had a sore throat. But I've been fretting about it ever since. She's alone in that house."

"She's at the college too."

"But she goes back to the empty house."

"She chooses to live there." Amanda refrained from pointing out that Liz held onto the house because of him. "What time did she call?"

"In the evening. Half-past eight or nine. Are you eating that muffin?"

"Take half." Amanda sliced Jamie's muffin, took half and began eating it.

"I try to diet, but it never works," she said. "Oh! Remember the guy at the cycle store?"

"Did you get him into bed?"

"He prefers his own gender. But he's very nice. He's taught the kids road-safety rules and he regularly shows up to take them cycling around Jericho Park. I told him you'd ended up in hospital. He asked if you wore a helmet. You don't, do you?"

"No," Jamie said.

"Better get one, Jamie. Bike accidents can cause serious skull damage. I've bought them for the kids. Annabelle's already planning a bike trip around the world."

"Good for her," Jamie commented. "About Liz. Have you spoken to her lately?"

"No. I'm kind of scared to call. Would you telephone?"

"She was fine when she visited me at the hospital."

"I know. I'm probably fussing over nothing."

"We could go over to the house now."

"Well . . ." Amanda glanced at her watch, "when I'm not working, I try to be around when the kids get home from school. I guess there's enough time."

"How are they?"

"Fine. Oh! Apparently somebody in Annabelle's class found out you're her uncle. She told the teacher who then had the class open their readers to your —"

"Don't tell me," Jamie groaned.

"Annabelle was all ready to faint, but they only looked at the page the poem was on. And the teacher said Annabelle must feel proud to have an uncle who was a poet."

"I don't know about that. Well, shall we call on Liz?"

"All right." Jamie paid the bill, while Amanda scrambled in her purse for coins to leave as a tip. They walked to Amanda's car and drove over the

Granville Street bridge to Shaughnessy. "Has Alice located a house yet?" Amanda asked.

"She's sniffing around the first one you and she looked at."

"I *knew* she liked it. Have you seen it?"

"Yes. It's fine. Alice's thought of getting a Vancouver special."

"Oh no! You couldn't bear living in one of those horrible houses, Jamie."

"They're cheap and have lots of room. Liz's house needs painting," he said as they pulled into the driveway.

"I know. I've mentioned it to her." Amanda switched off the motor, got out, went to the door and tried the handle. It turned, the door opened and they walked into the large, square hall.

"I don't remember the house being so dark," Jamie said.

"Mother always kept the hall lights on." They looked in the room where Liz usually sat. "I wonder where she is?" Amanda said.

"The kitchen, the garden? Out?"

"She wouldn't leave the house unlocked. Try the kitchen and garden. I'll see if she's upstairs." Amanda slowly climbed the stairs (How many times had she run up and down these as a girl?) and walked along the passage to Liz's room. The door was partially open and she was about to push it when she heard David's voice.

"Natasha talks about having another child. I'm against it, but she'll probably go ahead. She's gently obstinate."

"That's what I should do." Liz's voice was much lower than David's. It was the soft warm tone of a woman's voice after love-making. Amanda could hear echoes of herself with Harry in it. "I've had to stop short of getting what I really want. I've had to make do, like having you here every other week if I'm lucky."

"Mandy!" Jamie called from the foot of the stairs. "She's not in the kitchen or garden."

Amanda heard Liz's and David's hissing gasps and ran along the passage and down the stairs. "She's not here. Let's go." She urged Jamie towards the front door. "She's not here. Let's go!" They were at the door when Liz called from above.

"Jamie!" They watched Liz come down the stairs. She wore a long red dressing gown and slippers. "I didn't know you were here," she said. "I was resting." Amanda supposed David would exit down the back stairs and through the garden to the lane, which was probably the way he had entered. "Are you all recovered, Jamie? Let's go and sit. Why didn't you let me know you were coming?"

"We can't stay," Amanda said. "We just dropped in to say hello." (She could see the beaded gloss of sexual satisfaction on Liz's face.) "The kids'll be home soon."

"I'll give Jamie a lift home on my way to the college. Okay?" Liz dismissed Amanda with a smile. After sullenly asking Jamie if that was all right with him, Amanda left the house and went home.

"It's so good to see you again, Jamie," Liz said.

"Amanda's told me she's worried about you, Liz."

"Oh, not again! She's always worrying about me, usually about me being alone. She thinks I should imitate her and marry the first man who looks at me. Come on, let's sit. Dear Jamie, I'm so glad you've recovered from your accident. How's Alice?"

"Fine, fine." Jamie realized that Liz had dexterously separated him from Amanda and was gradually leading him to the point where he would automatically bleat responses to questions about his well-being. "It's not as if you're a nobody, Jamie dear," she said. "You're a well-known person and must be careful."

"You mean, it doesn't matter if nobodies are bumped off in accidents?"

"Now, Jamie, you know quite well what I mean." She touched his face.

"Liz —" Jamie began.

But Liz overrode him and began speaking of her plans to gain the Liberal nomination, and after achieving that how she would canvass every voter and talk to them about the need to eliminate pollution from their lives. "Will you help, Jamie?" she asked. "I'm sure having you with me would have a positive influence. You do believe in the need to control pollution, don't you? After all, think of the influence it could have on your son's life. I'm sure Alice will have a boy."

As always, Liz had trapped him by combining beauty, emotional appeal and the remnants of childhood dominance. He knew already, even as he listened to her, that she would win the election. A majority of male voters, after imagining what it would be like to bed with her, would act on their wishful thinking by casting their ballots in her favour, although of course it was always possible for the women's vote to split between those women who saw her as a threat to their security and those who embraced her as a valiant pioneer in the interminable fight for legislative equality. "Don't worry, Liz, you'll win," Jamie said.

Liz grasped his hands. "How wonderful of you to say that, Jamie. You know, I've been having doubts about myself. My self-worth, you know, and whether I'm capable of fighting an election. Having you believe in me makes such a difference. Mandy doesn't think the pollution issue is sufficient. She says people will ask who'll pay for the clean-up, and when I answer 'Those who pollute shall pay,' they'll laugh at me. To be laughed at in politics can be disastrous."

"I don't agree with Mandy. If you stress the need to control levels of industrial emissions, I'm sure people'll listen."

"Yes. We must have stringent controls. But you will help me, won't you, Jamie? I don't have the confidence I had years ago when all I needed to do was stand on a platform and tell people they had a moral duty to prevent children from going hungry. I believed then that everyone would work to change things. I was so naive in those days. Oh, my dearest Jamie, you don't know how much I rely on you and David, and Mandy and Hiddie, too. I know that all of you think I'm a strong person, but sometimes I become so frightened I think I can't go on. I know you think I interfere in your life."

Jamie took and squeezed her hands. "Liz, you don't interfere. What would we do without you?"

"It's wonderful to hear you say that, Jamie." She continued to hold his hands. "I admit I'm a nuisance sometimes. I like people to do things my way, which isn't always appreciated. Years ago, it never occurred to me you'd want to manage your own lives, but I've come to realize we're like the boughs of a tree: If we're to grow properly, we have to separate." Jamie nodded, wondered where Liz had picked up that notion, then condemned himself for doubting her sincerity. The snag was that Liz's belief in her siblings' right to manage their own lives, sincere as it might be, wasn't likely to affect her behaviour: In one breath she would tell them they could go their own way, in the next would order them to follow her directives. "Now, I'll have a quick shower and dress, then I'll take you home. I won't be more than ten minutes."

While waiting, Jamie telephoned Alice in case she was home early and worrying about his absence. "What're you doing there?" she snapped, when he told her he was calling from Liz's. "And next time leave a note so I'll know you haven't buggered off. Or is that too much to ask?" She slammed down the phone, and he knew she was furious because he hadn't asked her to fetch him. Suddenly he became irritated with the women in his life: They professed affection for him, yet expected their needs to take precedence over what he wanted; they claimed to be awestruck by his poetry at the same time they were prepared to stifle him; they refused to acknowledge that if he were to continue to capture the swirling concatenation of galactic words, he must be free to come and go as he pleased; but he must not allow their sinuous arms, their scents, their lips, their breasts, their soft bellies and welcoming cunts to be used as weapons to destroy the only thing of any value in his life. Maybe the women in his life wanted to destroy him because what he saw in the swirling stars threatened their biologic supremacy: Perhaps their urgent cunts — even his sisters' taboo ones — drove them to try to extinguish the fire of his abstract vision. The mysterious swirls of galactic words meant nothing to them — all they cared about was bending him to the will of their bodies. He was opening the front door to leave when Liz came down the stairs.

"Ready?" she called as if she knew he planned to sneak away. She had on a yellow dress and shoes and looked stunning, like a marvellous flower. Surely, he thought, Amanda was mistaken about Liz drinking.

"If you wear that outfit at the nomination meeting, the men there'll fall to their knees and worship you," Jamie said.

"You flatter me." She possessively linked her arm through his as they walked towards her car. "Do you flatter Alice occasionally?"

"Alice equates flattery with being propositioned." He opened the car door for her.

"What a pity."

"Isn't it." He stepped over the car door and settled in the bucket seat. "Maybe you should trade in this car for a family sedan."

"Why ever would I do that?"

"This car is flippant, it suggests a person not to be taken seriously."

Liz started the engine, put the car into gear, but did not press the gas pedal. "I see what you mean," she said, then smiled. "That's why I need you, Jamie. You understand so much."

"Any political organizer could have told you that. You need a car that's commonplace."

"Like Mandy's. I could borrow hers."

"Mandy's is an expensive import, although you wouldn't think so by looking at it. You need a car which symbolizes reliability and conformity."

"Hiddie's old Mercedes Benz?"

"How many people in Vancouver drive around in a Mercedes?"

"I've no idea." She whirled down the drive, crossed the street in the face of oncoming cars, swung the steering wheel, and raced past cars going at the posted speed limit.

"Conscientious representatives of the people drive at or below the speed limit," Jamie remarked.

"Oh, nobody notices," Liz said. "Besides, everyone expects sports cars to zip around."

"Perhaps. But images are also important in elections," Jamie said. "That's why you should own a brown sedan."

"Oh no, not brown! I like my little car, Jamie."

"The nature of public service demands sacrifice." Liz examined his face carefully before deciding he was joking. "So you must ditch all the men in your life."

"I don't have any."

"None!"

"Well, I have you and Davey."

"Okay. You must eat in moderation."

"I do that already."

"And you must forgo alcohol. But you don't drink, do you, Liz?" There was a brief pause before Liz answered: "I have a glass of sherry before dinner."

"Nothing more? No rye, scotch, bourbon or gin? No tequila?"

"No."

"Quite sure?"

They had crossed the Granville Street bridge and Liz moved over into the left-hand lane and turned onto Robson Street. "You have to direct me," she said.

"Go to Denman. So, you have a glass of pre-dinner sherry. Is that right, Liz?"

"What's this about, Jamie? Why are you questioning me?"

"Because Mandy had the impression you'd had too much to drink when you phoned her one evening."

"Mandy! I should have guessed." Liz drew into the curb and stopped. "I'm furious. How dare she involve you!"

"All you need to do is tell me she was mistaken."

She did not look at him, but stared across the street at a shop window. "I may have. I don't remember."

"You mean, you don't remember which evening, or don't remember how much you had to drink?" He waited, then said, "Liz, aren't you going to answer me?"

"I told you. I get panicky sometimes and have a few glasses of sherry." She turned and Jamie saw the shame in her eyes.

"Let's drive on. This is too public." People strolling along the sidewalk were inquisitively eyeing them, and several men looked back at Liz and appreciatively whistled. " 'Where'er you walk'," Jamie sang as Liz moved the car back into the traffic. "Come on, Liz, you better tell me," Jamie said.

"It happens when I'm especially wound-up. I've become more aware of how alone I am. I think of moving."

"You can sell the place. Don't keep it on my account."

"I've thought that now you're married and going to have a family you could take it. Or come and live there with me. If I win the election, I'd be in Ottawa most of the time."

"I don't see you and Alice living in the same house."

"You never know. It might work out."

"When did it start, Liz? Turn right here, it's just down the block. When did you start sipping sherry?"

"Don't put it like that, Jamie."

"You drink a bottle or more a day?"

"No." There was horror in her denial, the horror of what an admission would imply. It reduced her to the level of drunk women she'd seen huddled in doorways in downtown Vancouver. Jamie knew she was lying. "No, nothing like that. Don't be so relentless, Jamie."

"Stop here. It's across the street. Does anybody else besides me and Mandy know?"

"She doesn't know!" Liz cried.

"Oh yes, she does. Don't underestimate Mandy. Anything you haven't told her, she'll either deduce or guess. Why d'you think I'm sitting here? Maybe you could admit things to her you can't to me."

"Sometimes I feel so awful I want to die, Jamie," Liz finally said.

"Don't say that."

"I have dreams about Muriel. She's hanging in her prison cell and I try to cut her down before she dies."

Oh my God, Jamie thought, the defences people build around themselves to keep the world from seeing their anguish! He didn't know what to say, how to deal with his tortured sister. For now, he could do no better than ask how long such dreams had invaded her sleep.

"Years. Ever since Muriel died. I feel guilty because I failed her."

"You weren't in a position to do anything. You were a girl, a child. You should talk to someone about this, Liz, someone better qualified than I am."

"I have."

"A psychiatrist?"

"Yes. It didn't help."

Jamie found and grasped her hand. "Do Davey and Hiddie know about the drinking and the dreams?"

"No. I can't tell anyone." Of course, Jamie thought, it would be easy for Liz to hide her drinking: his own negligence, the fact that she lived alone, that she insisted on a telephone call before anyone visited, that she was impeccable in dress and behaviour whenever she came to visit them. No wonder he hadn't seen the obvious! He felt terrible, as if the props holding up his life had been swept away. How was it possible for the one person in his life he considered a pillar of strength to turn out to be even weaker than himself? "Please don't tell anyone, Jamie."

"Mandy knows."

"But the others. Don't tell them. If I can get away, Jamie, things will work out. I know they will. I'll have something new, I'll forget the past. You won't tell Alice. Promise me."

"All right, but I'm not sure I can avoid it."

"I see." She turned off the motor, but immediately restarted it and fiddled with the hand brake. "It's so humiliating, so humiliating." His help-lessness, his inability to reassure Liz or offer helpful suggestions sickened him. And he was doubly disgusted with himself, because behind every-thing he'd openly expressed to Liz lay anger at her for thrusting her prob-lem at him and intruding even further into his life.

"Talk to Mandy," he said. "I know you see her as a scatterbrain, but actually she's an understanding person, and apart from that, she's had ex-perience with people who . . . have problems."

"I don't have a problem. I just need . . ." she smiled at him, ". . . something new and exciting." The pain she exuded was almost tangible.

"But you won't find . . ." What was he about to say? Trapped by his indecisiveness and his fear, was he going to plead with her not to do any-thing rash? Rash? What did he mean by that?

She patted his arm. "Don't worry about me, Jamie. I can take care of myself." He left the car, then stood beside it, filled with uncertainty. "Say hello to Alice," she said, then whirled off along the street and turned at the intersection. He watched her go, then crossed the street to press the inter-com button and let Alice know he had safely returned.

The following morning, after Alice had left for work, Jamie telephoned Amanda to give her an edited version of his conversation with Liz, which he concluded by saying, "I suggested she talk to you because I'm not much good at reassuring people."

"She'd do better to consult somebody outside the family."

"Maybe. She keeps saying how humiliating it is. She doesn't want people to know."

"That's often the case with people who've got an illness. I've seen it happen over and over again. Men and women who deny they have cancers and believe that strength and determination alone will get rid of their disease. And they're the people who go down faster than the ones who run to the doctor's office every time they have a little ache or pain."

Amanda willingly accepted her new responsibility because she loved Liz — but there was also an element of satisfaction in being called upon to take care of her big sister. She called Liz right away, but got no answer. She's probably at the college, Amanda thought, or meeting with bigwigs in the Liberal Party. No matter, she'd talk to her in the evening when she was generally at home. But when she still hadn't reached her by nine that night, she began to worry. Although she suspected Liz was feeling ashamed that she and Jamie knew about her drinking and for that reason couldn't bring herself to answer the phone, still her experience with drunk people in hospitals led her to think that Liz might have fallen and hit her head. She decided to drive to Liz's and make sure her sister was all right.

But Liz was dead. It appeared that after leaving Jamie she had driven back to the house and consumed a bottle of sherry along with a large quantity of aspirin and sleeping pills. Her body had not surrendered to death without a struggle: The bed was covered with her vomit and her body lay on the floor close to the bedroom door. Amanda blamed herself for not going to the house earlier, even though the autopsy report showed Liz had died the previous night. Her suicide so shocked the rest of the family that they were incapable of communicating coherently when, at the end of the week, they assembled together in the crematory chapel. No one could understand how something so clear to them now hadn't been evident earlier. They could hardly bear to watch the box that held her body disappear through the curtains into the consuming fire; they hated the necessity of receiving the urn that held her ashes; they could barely bring themselves to gather on Nanda's seldom-used thirty-five-metre yacht and cross to Paradise Island to gather on the small headland where Liz had often sat and watch as David and Jamie, sobbing without restraint, scattered her ashes into the anonymous waters below. Afterwards, they walked slowly back to the southward-facing house where Nanda's capable servants provided them with food, which everyone said they couldn't eat, but which all, including Nanda, consumed. Liz's will was then read. The house and its contents went to Jamie and the remaining assets were divided equally among her sisters, brother and half-brother. It was the kind of division of wealth the family expected Liz to make: There was something to comfort and benefit everyone.

Alice had accompanied Jamie to Paradise Island. In fact, Jamie was so distressed over Liz's death that Alice had decided to stay home from work to keep an eye on him, lest he do something desperate. The two-hour trip across the Strait of Georgia made her nauseated, but she resolutely stayed beside Jamie on the deck, although the cold wind made her body shudder and her bladder fill more than once. Her worst moment came when Jamie stood on the cliff edge to throw Liz's ashes into the water. It wasn't much of a cliff, but Alice's fear for Jamie's safety caused her to magnify the size five hundred times and alter its grade from broken slope to sheer precipice. The McLeods were there, headed by Canadian Resources Corporation chairman, Frederick McLeod, nephew of Henry McLeod. Liz's McLeod cousins, Stuart-Hector, Gwendolyn and Margaret were also present, as were Isobel, Stuart-Hector's wife, and their two young sons. Hilda Logan was there too, with her three children, but Amanda came alone because, as she reiterated to everyone, Annabelle and Christopher had been too upset by Liz's death to witness the ash-scattering ceremony. "Liz was their godmother, and they knew she was going to take care of them if anything ever happened to me," Amanda explained to everyone in turn. "Now I'm not sure what to do." Natasha's children were there, and they gathered at Natasha's knees to watch the adults and studiously ignore their cousins. Gwendolyn bombarded Jamie with devastating criticisms of Liberal cabinet members, and Margaret demanded he write a play in which she could star. Fred McLeod attempted to be jovial with Jamie about being a father, but when Alice glared at him, he rapidly scrapped that gambit and went to sit beside Nanda. "Where did Jamie find *that* war horse?" he whispered, to which Nanda smiled, then inquired about his wife's health (she was a hypochondriac). Across the room, Isobel was loudly detailing facts about her sons' activities to Amanda, and Nanda asked herself, as she had many times previously, how Stuart-Hector had come to marry such a thoroughly obnoxious woman who seemed incapable of talking about any subject except herself and her two boys. She never even bothered to mention Stuart-Hector in her monologues.

At some point, Harjinder Singh approached Nanda, bowed and whispered that everything was on board the yacht and they could leave at any time she chose. At once, she stood, which everyone interpreted as a departure signal, and they drifted from the cottage to the yacht, where they clustered in the main lounge because no one wanted to look at the island and remember what they had left behind.

Chapter 15

"Go and look over the house, then decide," Jamie said to Alice.

"What about you? You want to live there?" she countered.

"I've always worked there."

"Does that mean you do, or don't, want to live there?" Alice wasn't sure *she* wanted to live in a house where someone had killed herself.

"I grew up there. I still think of it as my home."

This was a repeat of a discussion Jamie and Alice had been having for days: Should they move into the Big House? Amanda had tearfully told Alice that the soiled bed linen had been taken away, the bedroom carpet cleaned, Liz's clothes removed from the closet and cabinets, and that she had arranged all this on her own since no one in the family had been willing to assist her.

"What did you expect?" Alice said. "Families are always on the lookout for some mick to do their dirty work."

Amanda wanted to protest that *her* family wasn't like that, but the fact was, no one *had* volunteered to accompany her to the house, or help arrange for the cleaning. Of course her sister and brothers were busy people, but this excuse hadn't comforted her much when she had to open the front door and enter the silent house by herself. Afterwards, resentment crept into her thoughts and made its presence known by little, unexpected bursts of anger when she talked to, or about anyone in the family. In the past, Liz had always been the pivot around which Amanda safely orbited, and she had always believed she could afford to be foolish now and then, because the gravitational force exercised by Liz would always pull her back from the edge of self-destruction. She had bequeathed Annabelle and Christopher to Liz on the assumption that she, Amanda, would die first, because from childhood on, for her, Liz had been tinged with immortality. How was it possible then for Liz to have died first? And to die so grossly, so offensively? If Liz must die before her, then surely her death should have been more peaceful! She could hardly bear to recall her sister's dead body sprawled on the carpet and covered with vomit. "I thought I was going to faint," she repeatedly told Natasha. "It was awful, just awful, Tashie. And when I went back to the house to deal with the cleaning company, I felt Liz was walking around the house with me."

"Poor you," Natasha commiserated. She wanted to avoid any discussion of Liz's death. "Has Jamie decided what to do about the house?"

Amanda replied that she hadn't spoken to Jamie recently, then asked about David.

"He looks wretched," Natasha said. "He keeps on saying that he should have known Liz was unhappy. Poor darling."

Privately, Amanda agreed. As the person closest to Liz, David ought to have known more about her situation than apparently he did. She wondered if David's failure to be aware of Liz's drinking problem showed lack of perception on his part, or merely indifference. Indifference to heartache was common enough. But she did not voice her opinion; instead she commiserated: "Poor Davey."

"David's always so sensitive about other people's feelings," Natasha said. "He never stops worrying if he thinks something he's said or done has offended another person. I don't know if he'll ever be able to bring himself to go back to the house."

"That's how I felt at first, but I've been back now a few times. And you know, Tashie, Liz is still there. I talk to her and tell her we still love her and that she mustn't worry about leaving us on our own." Amanda pressed her teeth into her upper lip to prevent herself from crying. Natasha refilled their delicate porcelain teacups.

"If I should die before David, my spirit will stay with him," she said.

"I don't know if such a thing would be possible, Tashie," Amanda said. "Suppose David married again?"

"He wouldn't," Natasha firmly said.

"Would you marry again if you lost him?"

"No. I couldn't. Ugh! Never!" Natasha's shiver conveyed her revulsion of the idea that another man might go where only David was privileged to venture.

"You know, Tashie, it doesn't pay to promise yourself that you won't do something in the future."

"I don't care about that."

"Of course you believe in what you say now. But you can't know how you'll feel five years from now."

"I can," Natasha obstinately repeated.

"I wish I could be that certain about things. I hardly know what I think from one day to the next. One day, I tell myself I'm through with sex, then the next day I spot some guy and think he's exactly the man I'm looking for. And when he turns out to be another jerk, I'm right back where I started."

Natasha blushed. "I've always known David was what I was looking for."

"But doesn't knowing what to expect in bed make it kind of boring after a while?" Amanda couldn't resist that little dig. Natasha was so perfect, so everything Amanda was not: so lovely, so rich. Suppressed anger at Natasha's complacency churned inside her. "Maybe one day when you're out somewhere, you'll see some guy and get a little urge between your legs." Knowing what had gone on between Liz and David made Amanda want to break through Natasha's barrier of self-satisfaction. "If there's one thing I've learned," she said, "it's not to think that what I have, or what I feel, will go on forever."

Natasha cocked her head and looked speculatively at Amanda. "If I didn't know you so well, Mandy, I'd think you were hinting something about me, or about David."

That sobered Amanda and she gaily laughed. She mustn't go too far. "Good heavens no, nothing of the kind. I'm just saying that even when you're content with somebody you can still have spontaneous urges. I'll bet that's true for men too."

"It's not true of me or David," Natasha replied.

"You're so lucky," Amanda simpered. "I envy you." She ate another cookie and changed the subject. "I've been thinking I might leave Vancouver. With Liz gone, there's no real point in me staying here. But then I felt the same way when Mother died. Besides, where would I go? I have no desire to live in the Okanagan or on Vancouver Island. I suppose losing Liz has made me restless. Maybe I should just go back to work. I'm spending too much time going over everything that led to Liz's death."

"You do rather harp on it," Natasha gently said.

"Liz was very important to me."

"That was thoughtless of me, Mandy. I'm sorry. She was important to me too."

"You hated her for getting between you and David. Everybody knows that." The remark came out before Amanda could stop it.

"Shouldn't you say Liz pushed herself between me and Davey? That she did everything she could to keep me away from him? Oh dear, Mandy, we must stop talking like this. It doesn't help."

"I agree. I'd better go before I let fly."

"About what?"

"Nothing. Nothing." Amanda hastily left the comfortable chair by the coffee table. "I'm still angry because nobody offered to help me clean up the house."

"But I thought you hired some cleaning company to do it."

"I did. But I was the one who had to go in and see the mess, and I was the one who found her. Nobody took that into consideration." Amanda began crying, while hurriedly leaving the house, followed by Natasha saying that Amanda ought to have demanded that Hilda assist her.

"It doesn't matter. It's over and done with." Amanda hurried to her car and drove away, leaving behind a disturbed Natasha, who later reported the conversation to David and complained she seemed to have become the focus of Amanda's resentment.

"She accused me of hating Liz. I don't understand it, David. I feel badly that we pushed everything onto Amanda."

"Mandy volunteered. I offered to help."

"That's what I told her." In fact Natasha hadn't, but the failure to assert that her husband had behaved appropriately following Liz's suicide didn't matter now. What mattered was her need to have David reassure her that he had always preferred her to Liz. "Amanda said everybody knew that I hated Liz. That hurt me so much, David, because it isn't true. All I wanted was to spend time with you so that you could see how much I loved you. Amanda can be so vicious. And it happens when I least expect it. I felt she was trying to hurt us."

"She hasn't recovered from Liz's death."

"I understand that. But that doesn't mean she should be allowed to attack me, or you. Have you done anything to offend her?"

"Not that I'm aware of." David stroked Natasha's hair.

"She talks of leaving Vancouver."

David decided he must have a talk with Amanda and tell her to forget the past, even suggest she might benefit by moving to another city or town. He would flatter her, tell her she had the perfect small-town personality, the back-fence-gossip mind-set that would flower perfectly in a smaller community, then make it quite clear she had no right to upset Natasha. He might even hint at unpleasant repercussions if she continued to badger her. Nothing overt, of course, but he must do whatever was required to protect his relationship with Natasha. What he received from his marriage was far too valuable to risk letting it get wrecked, either deliberately or carelessly, by Amanda. But still he had to acknowledge to himself that to enter the room where he and Liz had lain together so frightened him now that he became covered in sweat whenever he contemplated it. Familial obligation had necessitated his offer to help, and he was surprised when Amanda didn't notice his relief after she'd turned down his offer. "There's no point in you getting involved," she told him. "I know you loved Liz as much as I did, Davey, but I feel she'd want me to do things on my own. Maybe it's silly, but that's how I feel." Naturally, he'd agreed. After this discussion, David had telephoned Jamie to suggest that as hereditary head of the Powell family he ought to assist Amanda in getting everything cleaned up.

"Oh sure, we all ought to get down on our hands and knees and scrape up Liz's vomit and shit," Jamie said. "But, being the rotten people we are, we delegate Mandy to hire a clean-up company to do our dirty work."

"I offered to help."

"So did I, so did I. Poor, dear Liz. How she must have suffered, always having to put on a convincing act. It had me fooled." Jamie did not want to talk about Liz's death. He suspected everyone in the family, including himself, was in the process of excusing themselves while blaming others for what had happened, but because he was the last person to have seen Liz, naturally everybody would like to shovel responsibility for her death onto him. A uniformed police officer had already rung Alice's buzzer to ride up the elevator and question him. The officer had been courteous, but clearly determined to get answers that satisfied him.

"You and your sister visited Ms. Powell the afternoon of her death for a particular reason, isn't that correct, Mr. Powell?"

"I've no idea what my sister told you —" Jamie began, only to be interrupted by the officer.

"Ms. Powell drove you from her home to this apartment block on the afternoon of her death?"

"She drove me home on her way to the college."

"You talked during the drive?"

"My sister told me she intended to run in the next federal election."

"That was all you talked about?"

"I offered a few suggestions to help her win the nomination."

"Such as?"

"That she could stop driving around in her sports car and get a family-type car. Little things, like staying within the speed limit — that sort of thing."

"You didn't raise the matter of Ms. Powell's drinking?"

"I did," Jamie reluctantly said.

"How long had you known your sister had a drinking problem?"

"I'd just found out about it from my sister Amanda. I wasn't sure what to do, or say, because of the position Liz held in our family. She was the eldest and handed out advice to the rest of us. We never advised her. The best I could do was suggest she talk to Amanda. I felt terrible, realizing she suffered so much."

"She told you that, Mr. Powell?"

"Specifically, no. The word she used was 'humiliating'."

"You mean that using alcohol was humiliating to her, or admitting she used it was humiliating?"

"Both, I suppose. My sister was a very proud woman. She hated the idea of personal weakness."

"I see. Can you think of any other reason that your sister might have taken her own life? Financial problems? Disappointment in a relationship? That kind of thing?"

"The house was left to my sister by our mother. She owned it. She had a job teaching at the college and also a private income from her share of our mother's estate."

"And her personal relationships?"

How was it possible to tell the officer about the childhood relationships which had moulded, and perhaps constricted, Liz's emotional development? What would the officer make of the information that, as a child, the person Liz most loved had killed their father and was afterwards hanged for murder? How could he possibly understand that she had passionately adored Muriel Wickham, as had all the Powell children, but while the others seemed able to forget their father's murder and Muriel's execution, remembering only Muriel's warm, all-embracing affection, Liz had, through the years, conjured up terrifying images of Muriel being hanged? Could he take in the fact that Liz had misunderstood promises made by their grandfather to save Muriel and had rejected him when he failed to have Muriel's sentence commuted? Could he be convinced of Jamie's personal belief that Liz had been emotionally mutilated by what had happened in her childhood and had surrendered her youth, beauty, intelligence and social position to a single obsession: the death of her beloved nanny? How could he explain all these things to a police officer whose world, so Jamie imagined, was limited to break-ins, assaults, rapes and the occasional murder? And so he had told the officer that as far as he knew his sister's life was free from emotional entanglements. Yet even as he uttered these less than truthful words, he felt he was diminishing his sister's stature, that he'd shoved her off the elevated ledge on which she had sat beside other tragic heroes, which was her rightful place, into the mass of humanity which lived aimlessly, reproduced itself and was quickly forgotten after death. He was disgusted with himself and with his family because he had failed to uphold the dignity and splendour of Liz's life and knew no one else had done better.

"I'm fed up with our family," Jamie told Amanda. "Liz is no sooner dead than we try to forget her."

"I don't," Amanda assured him. "I remember Liz more now than when she was alive. I dream about her. I can hear her telling me to change my life. Are you and Alice moving to the Big House?"

"I don't know." They were sitting on stools in Amanda's kitchen, drinking cocoa and eating cinnamon toast, which Amanda had prepared hoping it would help to cheer Jamie up. He looked and sounded depressed.

"Is Alice still dickering with the realty guy about the other place?"

"No."

"Does she want to live in the Big House?"

"I'm not sure."

"Has she been through it yet?" When Jamie shook his head, Amanda told him: "Take her through it, Jamie. It's lots nicer than anything you could buy. You're lucky to have it."

"We're dismembering Liz. We're taking her apart and getting rid of her. Reducing her to a shadow . . . a memory."

"I'm not. And I don't see how Davey will ever be able to forget Liz after what went on between them."

"Why?" Jamie accepted another piece of hot, cinnamon-laden toast. "What did Davey do?"

"Promise you won't say anything?"

"Of course," he said through a mouthful of toast.

"Liz and Davey . . . you know . . ."

Jamie suspended chewing to first stare unbelievingly at her, then to ask, "Are you saying . . . ?" Amanda nodded. "How do you know?"

"Liz told me. She broke down once and told me she was having an affair with David."

Jamie rubbed his nose, which Amanda knew was a sure sign that he was upset. "Bastard," he eventually said.

"Liz started it, Jamie. Just before he married Natasha."

"Did he have to go along with it?"

"Do any of us have to do what other people demand?"

"Does Tashie know?"

"Heavens no. I thought maybe you'd guessed. When you think about it for a minute, it's pretty obvious. But I suppose everybody thought Liz never married because she'd been traumatized by Muriel's execution."

"She had ghastly nightmares of Muriel being hanged."

"I know. But Liz was in love with Davey. I mean, sexually in love with him. Remember that day we went to the house . . . remember, Jamie? Liz and David were in her room. I heard them talking. If you hadn't called out, she wouldn't have known we were there. Didn't you notice the expression on her face?"

"What about it? She'd been sleeping."

"Do you ever look at Alice's face after you've made love?"

"Are you telling me you can tell when a woman has made love by looking at her face? That's ridiculous, Mandy."

"It isn't. I can look at a woman and know she's pregnant before she knows herself, or at a woman's face and tell if she's had an orgasm in the past couple of hours. That's what I saw in Liz's face. That's why I wanted to get us out of the house."

"Are you telling me David didn't know about Liz's drinking? But he must have. For God's sake, he was fucking her!" Jamie's voice rose. "He'd have smelled the alcohol on her, wouldn't he? Or did he turn his face away, so he wouldn't be reminded he was fucking his sister? The bastard. He made use of Liz, then grabbed Tashie and feathered his nest."

"No, Jamie, no. You've got it wrong. Natasha and Liz fought for David. You never noticed what went on because you were always off in your own little world. But I saw it. They hated each other. They pretended not to, but they did. So don't blame David. They set traps for him and he was bound to step into them."

"Was I so blind I couldn't see what was in front of me?" Jamie moaned and clutched Amanda's shoulders. "Maybe I'm so blind I'll never be able to look up at the sky again and see the words weaving around the stars."

"Don't be silly, Jamie. You have to be patient and wait, like Alice's waiting for her baby to be born."

"It's not the same. I feel something's happened to me. I feel something's left me." He huddled on the stool and actually seemed to shrink. Amanda left her stool and went around the counter to hold him.

"Jamie, darling," she cooed, "Jamie, darling."

"I've thought of leaving Alice," he whispered.

"Does Alice know how you feel?"

"She wouldn't understand." Amanda kissed him and stroked his hair. Throughout their lives she had functioned as the sympathetic ear into which Jamie periodically poured his self-doubts. Privately, she thought his bouts of self-castigation resembled sexual arousal and that the affliction was curable, provided proper therapy was forthcoming. She pressed his head against her breasts and gently massaged his forehead. (Amanda did not expect congratulations, but occasionally she thought it would be nice if the world took time to acknowledge her contribution to the cause of Canadian poetry.) "One of these days I'm going to wake up and find I'm completely empty. That, or discover I'm a mediocre fraud. I mean, ninety per cent of the time I don't have a clue what the stuff I write down means. You know that, Mandy? I haven't a clue. It could be crap. That's what David thinks. I mean, if something isn't set out in an equation, David thinks it doesn't have any meaning. That's how narrow his perspective is. And maybe he's right. Just think, Mandy. Two volumes of crap! I suppose it shows how stupid people in the arts are that they can be so easily taken in by jokers like me who arrange a few symbols on a piece of paper, or throw cans of paint at cardboard and give the end result a high-falutin name like 'Infinity' or 'Universe'. Why did I get into the arts racket anyway? Was it to prove I'm superior to our father? You think that's the reason, Mandy? Liz was always so fucking worshipful of me when I went to the house. I hated the way she kowtowed just because I wrote poetry. It was all wrong."

"She admired you. I admire you too."

"But at least you treat me like a human being. You don't forget that I piss, shit and fart and get constipated when I sit in that bloody room, waiting. You know every detestable thing about me, Mandy. But not Liz. Liz denied that I stank, denied that I sat there and masturbated when I was bored. What a fucking mess we make of our lives, Mandy." Amanda knew that once Jamie became scatological, his bout of self-condemnation was starting to wind down. "I mean, look at us, indulging in self-pity. And David! I hate and envy that bastard at the same time, or maybe envy produces the hatred. But I can hardly bear to think of him fucking our wonderful Liz. Goddamn sonofabitch! I used to look at her body and believe she was untouchable. I behaved as a brother is supposed to behave, even with you, Mandy. Even as a horny adolescent, I never went further than to imagine what my sisters' tits and cunts looked like."

"You saw all that when we were children," Amanda said.

"It's not the same. A child doesn't understand what the body's made for. Mandy, do you think I'm played out? Be honest with me. You've always been honest with me about yourself, haven't you? That's what you've always said."

"It's true."

"So be honest with me, Mandy. Come on, tell me."

Amanda kissed him and laid her face against his. "I don't know if you'll always see words in the stars, Jamie, but I truly believe you'll always be a poet because you seek the truth about things."

He managed to grin. "I can hardly stand myself when I get like this. I feel that everything I am, everything I've ever done, is totally phony. You know, I've never planned out one single thing. I've just waited for things to show up. Look at David: He's planned out his life, he's always had a goal he worked to reach. But not me, I'm a complete phony. I stand in front of my blank-faced students and lecture them on subjects I know little about. Ignorance lecturing ignorance, that's me. Phony! I'm a detestable person." Jamie moved away from her. "Why am I telling you all this asinine stuff? Maybe it's because Alice sees only the best in me and I need somebody who sees the worst. I suppose you're the drain into which I can pour all my moral and spiritual sewage. But you already know that, don't you?" Jamie moved to the other side of the counter to look at Amanda with impersonal curiosity. "What do you do with my sewage, Mandy? How do you process it? Do you get rid of the effluent in bed with the guys you pick up?"

"You know perfectly well I'd never do that, Jamie! Never!" Amanda stared at him, and Jamie was the first to look away. "That may be how you see me. But I've always believed we understood and loved each other. Perhaps I was wrong." It was clear Amanda had been hurt by his remarks.

Jamie suddenly laughed. "Of course we love each other," he said. "You're my sweet, plump-bodied sister whom I leech onto when I'm terrified by what I uncover in myself. I suck reprieves from you, Mandy. In my own way, I'm as much a predator as David. We're both of us pretty sneaky. I present my golden image to Alice and take comfort from you; David fucks Liz and secures his ass with Natasha. You've got to admit it, we Powell men know how to get the best out of life, especially from women."

"I don't know why you condemn yourself so harshly, Jamie. You've never taken anything from me that I haven't wanted to give. And I'm sure David never planned his affair with Liz."

"I know, I know. It's just my juvenile envy. Right?"

"But why should you envy David? After all, he hasn't done any important work yet, and you've had two books published."

"But they're nothing. Not when I set them against what other poets have accomplished." Yet, even as he contemptuously dismissed his poetry, the knowledge that his work could be found within the covers of two slender books on the shelves of bookstores across the country pleased him. He felt confidence rebuilding within himself and began to regret he had so freely dumped his load of emotional offal onto Amanda, who had enough problems of her own. Now he wanted to do something to please her. "Why don't we go over to the Big House and have a look around?"

"I'd like that." She glanced at the wall clock. "Can Annabelle and Christopher come along? They'll be home in a few minutes."

"Why not?"

Amanda smiled. She understood how her brother's mind functioned and recalled his childhood tantrums when he would yell insults at her and pound her with clenched fists, then, after expelling his rage, reinstate himself in her good graces by offering to share his toys. Over the years she'd come to understand that these bouts of self-deprecation were essential for Jamie, a necessary working-out of his complex personality, and that her role, as the less complex, less intelligent sister, was to help him through the bad spots. Apart from that, during the years of early childhood, female subservience to men had been subtly inculcated into her and her sisters; and although Jamie recognized and loathed the deference his sisters accorded him, nonetheless it had become so much a part of their relationships that the sisters, even forceful Liz, were incapable of appreciating how conditioned their own responses were and how inevitable it was they should feel obligated to please him. Amanda could even remember her mother's voice — and her own confusion — when her mother had insisted that she give up a toy to Jamie because he was a boy and one day would be "head of the family". At the time, Amanda had thought the request unfair because she was the elder of the two and also bigger and stronger, but still she had complied, thereby learning her first lesson in female subservience at the same time her brother received his first lesson in male chauvinism. Of course, everyone claimed that gender equality existed in the family, and on the surface this appeared to be true. But relationships in all families operate at deep, subconscious levels, and the Powell family was no exception. Her conditioning to the "rightness" of male dominance explained why Liz maintained the family home to accommodate Jamie, and also why Amanda so readily accepted the role of "scatterbrain sister", to whom Jamie could say anything he felt like because she wouldn't remember or truly understand what he said. And perhaps it also explained why David could so easily take what his half-sister had so passionately offered him.

Although Jamie might understand (to some extent) how gender relationships had affected his family, nonetheless it infuriated him to think a woman of Liz's stature had felt herself to be inferior to him. Yet he also saw how readily he had reinforced her belief of male superiority by playing his "bleating sheep" role and how he supported Amanda in her role of "agreeable big sister" by dumping his verbal excrement onto her. But understanding these things, he thought, had never prevented him from exploiting his favoured position in the family, and probably never would.

As Jamie stood in the kitchen listening to Annabelle and Christopher give accounts of their day at school he concluded that, albeit unknowingly, he and David had used Liz in order to maintain their illusion of male superiority. They were two in a long line of men who unhesitatingly sacrificed women on the altar of male power. So, perhaps, after all, not very much had changed between his own generation and his grandfather's, except that now people had refined their capacity to pretend equality between the sexes existed. No doubt his nieces and nephews would refine this capacity even further. The sorry fact was, he thought, that although he genuinely mourned the passing of his sister, he could not help but be pleased to know that she had stepped forward, as tradition had dictated, and offered herself as yet another sacrifice on the altar of male dominance.

"I hear your class had a look at my poem," he said to Annabelle.

Annabelle, lips parted to expose chewed cookie, nodded and looked embarrassed.

"Everyone was impressed," Amanda said, "weren't they?" Annabelle nodded again. "So you didn't have to faint after all, did you, darling?" Amanda hugged and kissed her daughter.

"Good, good," Jamie laughed, confidence now restored. He ruffled his niece's hair and gave her flushed cheek an avuncular pat. "The last thing I want is to put Annabelle in a position where she has to faint in a last-ditch defence of my work."

All laughed, including Christopher, who had no idea what was going on. Then, after the children had finished their milk and visited the bathroom, they left for the house Liz had given to Jamie.

Chapter 16

"I understand how you feel, Mandy," David said. They were eating lunch at a superior restaurant. "By and large I feel the same, but you mustn't burden Natasha with your personal feelings."

"I'm not sure what you mean by 'burden Natasha'." David spooned up and swallowed some cream of asparagus soup. "I'd like to know more about your involvement with Liz."

David closed his eyes. "I felt as though I was in a nightmare," he said. "I would have stopped it, but Liz insisted we continue."

"Don't blame Liz." Amanda's voice was cold: something rare.

"I blame no one." He opened his eyes and sighed. "Liz was so much a part of me."

"No sexual differences?" Amanda quizzed, letting him know she wasn't going to swallow every explanation he gave.

"That's not the point." He finished the soup. Amanda had hardly touched hers. "I'm talking about the way we thought and looked at things."

"I've always felt close to Jamie," Amanda said, "but I never had sex with him."

David closed his eyes again. "Try to appreciate how imperative Liz was." He wasn't sure Amanda possessed enough intelligence to grasp what he was saying.

"I'm capable of understanding anything you say, provided the words aren't too long. Six syllables are about my limit." David ignored the sarcasm and she continued: "You knew Liz was drinking?"

"No, I did not."

"But how could you be close to her — feel you were part of her — and not know she was drinking?"

"You frequently saw Liz, and were you aware of it?"

"No. But —"

"There! You see? We were in the same boat, Mandy."

"We were not, Davey. You were in Liz's bed, you were kissing her, you were — as you put it — being part of her."

"Don't talk that way, Mandy. Please."

"You expect me to believe you never once smelled alcohol on her breath, or on her body? If you deny it, either you're lying, or something's wrong with your nose." A tray-bearing waitress approached the table to remove David's plate and inquire if Amanda had finished her soup. "Yes," Amanda said and waited until the waitress left after placing dinner plates in front of them containing breaded sole, a small potato, a piece of carrot, and a few zucchini slices. "But I can see how it might happen, Davey." David nodded and sliced the fish. "Though I still don't understand why Liz never told you she was in trouble, or why you didn't surmise it."

"You think I'd deliberately ignore anything Liz told me about herself? And don't drag Natasha into this, or ask how I managed to balance myself between them."

"Look, I'm not trying to dig into your life, but Liz never explained anything to me. She only confirmed what I'd already guessed. I'm not like Jamie who thinks you preyed on Liz."

"You told Jamie!" He became pale and tense. "Who'll you tell next? Can't you keep anything to yourself? Are you out to wreck my life? Is that what you want to do? But if you so much as say one word to Natasha . . . !"

"Don't threaten me, David." Amanda stared back at him until he looked down and moved the food on his plate.

"I'm not threatening you," he muttered. "I'm only asking — okay, begging — you to be reasonable. I mean, Liz is gone. You think I don't miss her? You think I wouldn't give an arm and a leg to have her back? You don't know much about me, Amanda."

"I agree, I don't."

"You think I'm so mercenary that I'd —?"

"No, I don't think that. I know Liz and Tashie trapped you. I can even feel sorry for you, but I also think you should've seen that something was very wrong in Liz's life."

"I did what I could to help her."

"But surely . . ."

"Let me finish, Mandy." Open animosity hung between them before David continued. "In a way, you and the rest of the family are partly responsible for what happened to Liz."

"How dare you say that!"

"In a roundabout way, I should add. Liz knew that you — and everybody else — expected her to be a strong, self-assured person."

"That's because she always insisted she was stronger than us. Right from the time we were kids. Like everybody expects me to be a scatterbrain. It must surprise you, Davey, to find out I've picked up a few things in my thirty-five years. I guessed about you and Liz, but it was easy to keep everything to myself because I wanted to protect Liz. But now she's gone, and resentment builds up in me whenever I'm with Natasha. I feel like lashing out when she goes on about her children and her marvellous relationship with you. She's so complacent about it! That's why I told Jamie — to share the secret with someone I trusted — so I wouldn't unintentionally blurt it out to Natasha. I told him I didn't think you were to blame, how Liz and Natasha fought over you. I told him about Natasha following you to Chalk River and inveigling herself into your bed."

"That's not how it happened," David muttered.

"It's close enough. Anyway, I'm not sure if he believed me. He has a picture of you as the 'big bad wolf' gobbling up his innocent sister and beautiful cousin. But don't worry about me, David. I'd never say anything. The person you should worry about is yourself."

"I'm fine," David assured her. He ate more of the food. "Fine."

"Of course," Amanda politely smiled at David, who smiled back while realizing how badly he'd misjudged his half-sister. Actually, he knew little about her, since all his life, except for Natasha, Liz had been his exclusive companion. His only childhood memory of Amanda was of a plump little girl with wet underpants hanging down her legs who trotted around obediently complying with her eldest sister's commands. Now he wondered if her perpetual smile didn't camouflage a very shrewd mind.

"You're not enjoying your lunch?" he asked.

"I'm not hungry." She ate a small piece of fish, adding, "It's quite good, though." She looked at her watch. "I have to go." (Amanda was in the process of acquiring another rental property.)

She rose and David politely stood. "I'm glad we've had our chat, David."

"It helped." He watched as she walked around the tables, hips swaying, and briefly wondered if what everyone in the family said about her promiscuity were true, then went back to finishing his meal and thinking about her remark that *he* was the one who ought to be worrying. Maybe she had said it for effect, to arouse anxiety in him, to remind him that his future life with Natasha depended upon her willingness to refrain from pricking what she regarded as Natasha's balloon of complacency. No doubt she was envious of Tashie, of her wealth . . . her home . . . her children . . .

even of him. Somehow he must warn Natasha, let her know that Amanda might be looking for an opportunity to make nasty comments about her or, more to the point, about him. But he would have be very, very careful. He ordered more coffee and continued to reflect on his exchange with Amanda. Her perspicacity surprised him, as had her readiness to let him know she was not to be intimidated. Once again he realized how little he knew about his half-sister . . . in fact everything he knew about her had been filtered through Natasha or Liz. According to Natasha, Amanda was financially astute, while Liz despaired over her sister's lifestyle. Of course Liz had always been quick to condemn behaviour in others which she tolerated in herself. But now she was gone and somehow he must accept that he would never again touch her, never again hear her utter his name. Her ashes had vanished into the anonymous waves that heaved against the rocks of Paradise Island, leaving him to protect his marriage as best he could.

He settled the bill and went to his car, intending to return to the university, but for reasons he couldn't explain to himself, drove to the street outside his home where he sat, indecisively nibbling his lips, afraid to enter lest Natasha, in his absence, had learned the truth of his relationship with Liz. He saw with remarkable clarity that his relationship with Liz, which had seemed so unquestionably right and natural when she was alive, had been transformed by death into something perverse and unnatural. He had never doubted his ability to solve problems: The fact he had achieved university tenure at an age when a majority of his colleagues were still struggling up the professorial career ladder was proof of this; furthermore, he'd made a good marriage and had fathered four beautiful children, which served to compound his sense of security and allowed him occasionally to experience contempt for men older than he who were stuck on the ladder of success, or for younger ones who had no foothold on it. He believed, perhaps justifiably, he deserved everything he'd acquired and, on the whole, managed to keep his periodic bouts of self-doubt at bay by reminding himself that he'd always been an indefatigable worker, a person who substituted for intellectual brilliance with dogged application to the task at hand and worried problems like an animal does a bone until the bone finally cracks to reveal the marrow. He told himself that while he truly loved Natasha, still his marriage wasn't only about love; it also involved keeping his wife contented. David did not regard the way he thought of Natasha as calculated. He was completely devoted to her, and more importantly, knew Natasha loved him as passionately as ever. Why then, if he had nothing to fear, was he sitting in his car outside the gateway to his home, uneasily asking himself questions about his life? The contaminating influence in his life was no longer present and he should feel safer than ever before. Contaminating influence! How could he think of Liz as that! He had shared some of the happiest moments of his life with her. They had been inseparable as children and adolescents and had never conceived their paths would ever diverge. He could feel her presence now: sitting beside him in their home, on Paradise Island in the summers, walking, cycling, running. How furiously she had run, not as a trained racer, but like a person who fights a river current that threatens inexorably to sweep her into a chasm where she will perish unless she ferociously struggles onward. He remembered walking to the edge of the cliff with Jamie and how, with head turned and eyes closed — he couldn't bear to look into the urn — he had cast all that remained of the woman who had been the mainspring of his life into the embracing waves.

Images of Liz flowed into his mind: child, adolescent and woman; the child merging into lithe youth, the youth into a stately, apparently self-assured woman. Everything in their lives had been so right, so fitting, so enviable. He realized now that although he'd accepted and enjoyed Natasha's love, his true fidelity had always been to Liz. His affection for Natasha had arisen only after she came to Chalk River and inserted herself into his life. True, he enjoyed being with her, he felt comfortable with her, and there was no doubt she was an immensely desirable woman, eager to receive what he could so easily give. There was no need to think of Liz when he quickened with Natasha and when his hands, lips, and body told him no man had ever caressed so beautiful a woman.

The strange thing was, while he knew that his half-brother's active sex life had coincided with his first publication — a poem in a university magazine — he, David, had remained celibate until Natasha had visited his room in Chalk River. In looking back now, he could see that faithfulness to Liz had governed his behaviour with women, though the odd thing was, he hadn't made physical love to Liz until after he'd become engaged to Natasha. He had never begrudged Jamie the young women who turned up to confirm their image of the poet as a young man — he understood his half-brother was dominated by the fear that one day he might lose his precarious balance and fall off his poetic tightrope, and while he might question whether the end products justified the toil and agony that preceded them and might be genuinely surprised when supposedly knowledgeable people labelled him as one of Canada's most original young poets, yet he didn't envy him, though on occasion he experienced irritation when students asked if Jamie was a relative. When that happened, he felt like throwing the chemistry textbook he'd co-authored at them, demanding to know the difference in effort or result between writing a six hundred-page text and a ten-line geometric poem. Nowadays, he usually denied consanguinity, because now he knew the answer to his own question: The difference was one of kind, not degree — Jamie's spirit soared to the stars while his remained earthbound, tied to the earth's molecules, although Liz had always praised his accomplishments and urged him forward, especially during the stressful years of his doctoral work when he seriously thought he might not make it through his oral examination. Liz had been the spur in his life. Life without Liz! Was it possible that Natasha, knowing how highly Liz valued him, had long ago decided he must be worth possessing, which meant she hadn't fought for him because of his worth as an individual, but only to enjoy a victory over Liz? A laundry van emerged from the driveway, reminding him that each Tuesday afternoon freshly laundered linen, towels and clothes were delivered to the house and a soiled batch collected. Suddenly an image of the laundry room at Rhynewood Manor where servants were permanently occupied washing, drying and ironing the family's laundry appeared before him. There, he remembered, he had experienced a precursor of pubescent change when he'd become fascinated by the rhythmic swing of a maid's breasts as she ironed and folded sheets. Liz must have guessed the reason he was gazing at the maid because she grabbed and pushed him outside the back door into the cold November drizzle as the maid called to her companion: "Did yer see that, Becky? I'll bet that wee cock's gettin' all set ter follow in 'is dad's footsteps." Liz was furious with him for paying attention to someone other than herself and refused to speak to him for the rest of the day. That night he'd gone to her room and told her he'd been fascinated by the way the maid's hot iron had so miraculously smoothed wrinkles in the sheet. Of course she'd known he was lying, but she forgave him, for the alternative — to surrender authority over him — was something she could not bear to do. And had never done. That was why, now, he sat outside his own home, unable to leave the car and enter the house.

He looked at the car clock, started the motor and drove on to the alley at the rear of Liz's house. He parked the car, walked along the alley, entered the house by the rear door, climbed the back stairs to the second floor and went along the passage to the room where his adoptive mother had slept and where he and Liz had made love. He stood by the open door, apprehensive about entering, remembering Liz standing before the mirror, wielding the gold-plated hairbrush that had once belonged to her mother and grandmother as she watched his reflection and gauged his reaction to what she said. He heard noises coming from the bathroom, and trembled, because the only sounds he associated with that room were ones made by Liz. Believing that only Liz could emerge from the bathroom, he let out a cry of terror when a woman appeared in the doorway. The shock was so great he almost fainted, certain the figure was Liz.

"Who're you? What are you doing here? Who told you to come here?" The loud, harsh voice, which he now recognized, jolted David out of the illusion.

"Oh!" David leaned against the wall and tried to laugh, even though he was still shaking. "Of course! It's Alice."

"That's right. Alice Powell. And who're you, mister?"

"Jamie's brother, David. We met on the island. At Liz's funeral."

"I don't remember you."

"We didn't have an opportunity to talk. Excuse me, I have to sit. For a moment I thought . . ." He moved into the room to collapse in a chair. "A shock . . ."

"Jamie and I are moving in."

"Of course, of course."

"That's why I'm looking around."

"Yes. Is Jamie here too?"

"He's at the college."

"I came by to get a book I left here, at least I think I left it here. Anyway, I can't seem to find it. You know how it is when you misplace something and feel unsure where you've left it." The lie he uttered reassured him.

"I usually know where my things are." Alice sat in the chair beside the cabinet his mother had used as a dressing table and Liz as a desk. (Liz's sole concession to make-up had been a light coating of lipstick.) Looking at Alice, David could hardly believe his brother had married so unattractive a woman.

"You're lucky," he said.

"In my line of work, you can't afford to forget where you put things," Alice said. "You need to stay on the ball, otherwise pretty soon you don't have a job any more."

"Oh yes, you're a —"

"Chartered accountant." Alice proudly supplied the information. "What about you? Oh yes, Jamie said you're a pharmacist, something like that."

"Chemist," David corrected. The more he looked at Alice, the more ungainly he found her: She appeared to lack taste, for why else would she wear clothes which emphasized the most unappealing parts of her body?

Apart from the all-too-obvious pregnancy, she wore a red skirt and ill-fitting flowered blouse that clashed with her skin colour. "Do you like the house?" he asked to keep the conversation going.

"Too big. But it's okay."

"If you have more children, you might decide it's too small."

"This is all the family I'm ever having," Alice patted her stomach. "And I wouldn't be having this, except that idiot Amanda couldn't keep her mouth shut when I told her I was in the family way. She blabbed it to Liz, who rushed off and told Jamie what a marvellous father he'd make, which is a lot of bullshit. You have half a dozen kids, don't you?"

"Four," David corrected.

"Kerist! You must be nuts!"

David smiled. At least she was candid. "My wife wanted them," he said.

"Some women are so stupid they think having babies is the only point to their existence."

"Biologically speaking, it is," David commented.

"Oh, come off it," Alice said. "There's more to living than biology."

"No doubt there is," David agreed.

"Tell her there's millions of orphans in the world. She can have one of those."

"I'll mention it to her."

"You do that. Hey, you think me and Jamie should use this room?"

"It's the largest bedroom."

"The idea of sleeping in that bed gives me the creeps."

"I understand how you'd feel. You could replace it."

"I like to make clean sweeps, know what I mean? Amanda said I could borrow her sister's maternity clothes. Hell no, I told her, I don't want cast-offs. I've been buying my own clothes since I left school. No way I'm having guys shove their old stuff onto me. And I'm still not sure about this house. You think we should live here?"

"Jamie works at his poetry here."

"Yeah, I know . . . and I know he's getting pretty strung out because he's not heard the call recently."

"What call?"

"You know." Alice pushed a thumb at the ceiling. "From heaven."

"Oh, I see what you mean."

"So what with me having this," Alice patted her stomach again, "and Jamie being on edge, and us not being sure about living here, we're in a bit of a muddle, know what I mean?"

"Yes, I suppose I do."

"What d'you think of the Lord Powell crap?"

"I tend to agree with Jamie. But on the other hand, if you'd like to —"

"Me? You think guys'd take me seriously if I told 'em I was Lady Alice Powell?"

"They'd have to, surely." David thought there was something comical, yet rather touching about Alice asking whether he thought she was a suitable person to bear a title. He was beginning to understand why Jamie was attracted to her. Maybe she was physically ungainly and deficient in the social graces, but her lack of guile made it easy to forget these defects and see only her thick blonde hair, bright-blue eyes and fine clear skin.

"I'll bet you can't believe Jamie got mixed up with someone like me. No class, eh?"

"The only person I judge is myself," David said.

"Who d'you think you're fooling? You've been sitting there giving me the once-over, asking yourself how Jamie could be such a fool as to get mixed up with a hag like me."

"I never presume things about other people." He stood. "I have to be getting home. Meeting you here was a bit of a shock," he said, "but I'm glad we've had a chance to talk."

Alice followed him along the passage. "For a minute, I thought you were a burglar." David wondered if she was following to make sure he actually left the house. Then she asked if he had a key.

"Why, yes. To the front and back doors," he said and became offended when she asked for them. He silently turned over the two keys while saying, "Each of us has a set. After all, this was our home."

"Maybe it once was," Alice replied. "Now, it's Jamie's and mine."

"Of course," David said after a pause. He continued to look appraisingly at her for a moment, then opened the back door and stepped out. He stood on the brick path and listened as the door was closed and locked. The finality of the bolt entering the lock made him feel as though part of his life had suddenly been sliced away. He walked to the alley gate, looked back at the house, then opened the gate, quickly walked along the alley to his car, and drove away.

That evening, after considerable thought, he told Natasha of his encounter with Alice, putting their meeting in as favourable a light as possible, explaining at some length how he'd finally decided to call at the house to make sure nothing had been disturbed. Natasha agreed it was a good idea: "There must be valuable things in the house."

"I almost keeled over when Alice walked out of the bathroom," David said. "Quite a shock."

Natasha agreed. "Mandy says she can be obnoxious."

"Everything was okay once we'd sorted out who we were. She was quite pleasant. She and Jamie will probably move in. She's worried about Jamie. He's uptight about not seeing more galactic words."

"Oh, they're bound to reappear soon." Whenever Jamie's demonic drive to wrench words from the stars came to Natasha's attention, she attempted to make the process seem as normal as possible, rather like observing a lunar eclipse or a shooting star.

"She asked for my keys to the house."

"Did you hand them over?"

"I had no choice. She pointedly informed me the house now belonged to her and Jamie."

"Honestly! Did she say that?"

"When I explained we had keys because it was our family home, she said it was hers and Jamie's now. Which it is." He tailed off and shrugged. "It's not worth fussing over. Listen Tashie, I had a call from someone at UCLA this morning. A fellow by the name of Schwartz — he worked with a Nobel prize winner years ago — was supposed to present a paper at a conference in Mexico City next month, but it seems he's had a stroke, quite serious I gather. Anyway, I've been asked to replace him. My first reaction was that they ought to get someone from Schwartz's department, especially since the paper discusses chemically induced atmospheric changes, but I gather from what the guy said that everyone in the department is off doing other things, and since I'd published a couple of papers on the subject, would I oblige? So I agreed to fill in. I think I can cobble something together. It's quite an important conference. The point is, will you come with me?"

"You want me to?"

"Yes." He wanted her near him to ensure she would never be infected by Amanda's malicious insinuations. He felt the only way to keep their relationship intact was for them to go off alone and relive the days they'd spent in Chalk River when they'd been isolated from the family, aware only of the rapture they experienced when they came together.

"Then I'll come. We'll stay in Coyoacán. The air's not so polluted there. How long is the conference?"

"Three days."

"We could use the Can-Ray jet. The children love it. Maybe we could go on to Acapulco."

"I thought, just the two of us."

"You don't want to take the children?"

"We could escape from them for a few days. Go back to the way we were in the past."

His remark astonished Natasha. She sat up and put her face close to his. "But, darling Davey, why would we want to escape? We still have everything we had in the past. Well, don't we? I haven't changed. I'm the same as I was. And so are you. So our past is here with us. Isn't it?"

"I'd like us to be alone somewhere where no one could interfere with us."

"Oh, Davey, my darling," Natasha reached up to pull his lips down to hers, "no one's going to interfere with us." But as she moved to press her lips against his, she realized he was not looking at her, but at someone or something beyond her. She felt as if an icy barrier had been inserted between them, drew back and turned to see what he was staring at. "What is it? What are you looking at?"

"Nothing," David muttered.

"But what was that strange look on your face?"

"It's just that I'm uncertain about what I should do."

"Uncertain! Uncertain about what?"

"I mean . . . I'm afraid of what could happen."

"Afraid!" Natasha retreated to the end of the couch. "Afraid of what?"

"Since Liz died."

"Liz!"

"That's why I thought that if you and I went away . . ."

The thought that Liz, even though she was dead, could still affect her life changed Natasha's fear into rage. "I don't want to hear what you thought!" she stormed. "I won't be dragged off to Mexico so that you can talk about your wonderful Liz. All my life I've had to put up with you — and everybody else — telling me how lucky we were to have Liz. Well, I won't have you pushing her into my life any more." She hunched against the arm of the couch, staring at him, hands and lips trembling, regretting having exposed her resentment and wishing she could retract what she had just said. She waited for David to speak, desperate to hear him tell her he loved her, but when he did nothing except continue to stare fixedly at her, she jumped up and ran from the room. David groaned, then pressed both hands over his eyes as people do when they strive to prevent themselves from seeing their world about to disintegrate.

Chapter 17

"You're not looking well, dear. Is something wrong?" Nanda looked across the low table at Natasha. "Is it to do with the children?" She glanced at the two servants positioned by a larger table laden with tea things, who in turn glanced at each other, then quietly left the room. "You look worried. That's not like you."

Natasha looked through the window at the cloud-laden sky, down at the cups on the table, then finally turned and looked at her mother. "I don't know how to put it," she said. "I'm probably imagining things." She stopped, and Nanda patiently waited. She knew that Natasha, unlike her half-sisters Gwendolyn and Margaret, was slow to express her feelings, though as a child she'd been quite different. Natasha hesitated for a moment, then spoke: "I expect I'm fussing over nothing, I'm sure I must be. Davey was talking the other evening about going to a conference in Mexico City and whether I should accompany him. I thought we'd take the children, then go on to Acapulco for a few days. It would be a break for all of us. But then, when I looked at David's face and into his eyes . . ." She halted, breathed deeply and continued: "I don't know what it was, Mother, not exactly, but when I looked into his eyes, I wasn't seeing the David I'd always known. I felt I was looking through his eyes at another person, at somebody hiding inside him."

"David has nothing to hide from you, dear."

"I know, it's silly to feel like this. I do trust David, I know he loves me, but something came between us as we were talking. It terrified me."

"Perhaps he was thinking about a scientific problem." Nanda's notions of how the scientific world operated were practically medieval: Years ago she and her brother had read Marlowe's *Faustus* together and she still conceived of scientists as alchemists eager to trade immortality for temporal profit, pleasure and fame. "Perhaps you're being a little too possessive, dear."

"Possessive!" Natasha was genuinely astonished. "How is it being too possessive to suggest our family spend a few days in Acapulco?"

"But David may have been thinking it would be more enjoyable for the two of you to get away on your own."

"Are you suggesting I'm pushing what I want onto David?"

"No, no. You're always most considerate with him."

"It was something to do with Liz." The words and the name burst from Natasha. "He said he's been afraid since she died."

"Did you ask why?"

"How could I?"

Nanda waited before cautiously saying, "Well, years ago David and Liz were very close."

"No closer than David and I are!" Natasha quickly and fiercely asserted.

"I'm talking about childhood." Natasha stared at her mother. Anger and resentment momentarily made her beautiful face ugly. She didn't want to acknowledge that Liz had once been the dominant force in David's life; she wanted to forget that her own persistence was what finally had forced David to notice her and become susceptible to being moved from Liz's sphere of influence into her own. The turning point in Natasha and David's relationship (Natasha thought of it as "the great divide") had begun late one sunny morning when Natasha, then a student at UBC, had walked past the clock-tower near the library on her way to a class and heard a familiar voice: "The world's come to a pretty pass when a cousin skips past me without stopping to say 'how do'." David was sitting on a low wall near the library entrance.

"I didn't see you." Natasha was embarrassed. "I'm sorry."

"No excuses," David said. "I suppose you expected me to be struck dumb by your beauty. Was that the idea?"

"No, no. Honestly, I didn't see you."

"You were preoccupied, I suppose, thinking about the guy you're on your way to meet. Right?" She blushed, because there *was* a man in a course she took who'd expressed a desire for "a deeper relationship", which Natasha interpreted to mean "having sex", and she wasn't interested in that.

"I'm not meeting anybody," she said. "I was just thinking about getting something to eat."

"Oh, I see. You actually suffer pangs of hunger? So my next question is, do you also suffer pangs of love?"

"Davey!" Although he was a graduate student and she merely meandering towards a lowly Bachelor of Arts degree, she wasn't sure his academic superiority privileged him to patronize her.

"Well, since I'm hungry too . . ." He got off the wall. "Let's eat together. You have classes this afternoon?"

"No," she said, happily forgoing her seminar on sixteenth-century Florentine art.

They had driven in Natasha's car to a Greek restaurant. "Marvellous food," David explained in his graduate-school voice, tolerant of her inexperience with Greek food. "I often eat here with friends." Natasha pretended to enjoy the retsina which David said he and Liz (that hateful Liz again!) drank when they came here. But she was certain something special had passed between them that afternoon, even though he treated her as a younger sister (which she hated) telling family jokes, bestowing casual pats on her hand and dabbing quick kisses on her cheek when they parted. Oh, how she'd treasured those kisses! At the end of other meetings, often at the same Greek restaurant, she always managed to turn her head so that David's lips landed squarely on hers. She'd despaired when David finally got his doctorate and moved East. Desperate, she cooked up reasons to complete her degree at the University of Ottawa, and a few days after arriving there she drove to Chalk River where a surprised but delighted David yelled: "Tashie!" before he hugged and kissed her. After that everything went as she had hoped and planned: In his room, in his narrow bed, they were finally united. Although she never spoke of this to anyone, not even David, she believed that a mystical being was responsible for bringing them together and not even death could separate them now, for their spirits had been joined and they would walk side by side forever and forever. The overwhelming passion she felt for David had continued undiminished during the years of their marriage and enabled her to believe, even after the shock of what she had seen a few days earlier in David's eyes, that they were still bonded together in a mystical union that could never be severed. As she sat now, drinking tea, she found herself getting impatient with her mother, who apparently could do no better than issue vague generalities about the nature of relationships; obviously, her mother didn't understand that she had a special relationship with David.

"You know, dear, it's impossible to anticipate how you'll feel when you lose someone who's been close to you. There's a huge gap in your life. I expect that's what's happened to David, and I'm sure you'd feel exactly the same way if someone you loved died." Natasha panicked, not because of the spectre of her own death, but because she found it impossible to conceive of losing David, or to imagine that one of her passion flowers might one day die. Oh God, she silently prayed, as images of death flickered through her mind, do not let death come to my loved ones. During her moment of terror, she was quite prepared to pay homage, even to sacrifice herself, to any god that offered life everlasting to David and her children. Perhaps that was why she'd been so frightened the other night when she'd looked into David's eyes: She'd seen death hiding there, and had been so appalled by the sight that she'd had to run from the room to escape it, though afterwards she told herself she'd overreacted. After all, it was perfectly natural for David to feel upset about Liz's suicide. She shouldn't have brooded over the incident, she should have talked to him about it as she'd always done in the past when some little thing came between them. Yet she hadn't said anything to him, and her increasing uneasiness about the incident had driven her to confide in her mother, who in effect was now telling her she had turned a molehill into a mountain. "You worry over nothing," Nanda now said.

"I felt as if I'd lost David."

"You read too much into it, Tashie. I think you —"

"What? What?" Natasha, eager to be enlightened, leaned towards Nanda.

"Perhaps you could tell David you'll go to Mexico City with him. Without the children."

"But it won't be the same now. I can't rid myself of that feeling I got when I looked into his eyes."

Sure now that Natasha was experiencing fear that David no longer loved her, Nanda patted her daughter's hands. "You're being plain silly, Tashie. Just plain silly." Nanda had often used these words in the past when dealing with the irrational behaviour of her children and usually it had worked.

"Maybe I am." Realizing she would get nothing more from her mother, she said, "I must go."

"Don't forget what I said," Nanda called as Natasha left the room.

"I won't," Natasha called back. "I won't."

That evening she returned to her favourite position on the couch beside David, fully intending to follow her mother's advice, but she found she could neither speak of the conference, nor express willingness to go with him. A knot of anxiety tightened inside her as she looked up at his face in the hope he would raise the subject and ask her again to accompany him.

A few evenings later, he did raise the topic. "I won't be going to Mexico after all. UCLA called to say one of their faculty had volunteered to read Schwartz's paper."

Natasha's relief expressed itself in excessive annoyance with the Los Angeles people. "But how could they do that, after you'd gone to all the trouble of preparing something? It's despicable."

"I gather they looked at Schwartz's material and decided they could put something decent together, which is all I intended doing anyway," David said.

"It's still despicable. Didn't they even thank you?"

"Of course. As a matter of fact the guy was apologetic, saying if he'd only looked at Schwartz's notes in the first place, he'd have seen they were usable. Anyway, UCLA'll be holding a conference on atmospheric pollution next year and he asked if I'd present a key paper. A consolation prize I guess."

Natasha was so relieved she sat up and hugged him. "It'll be the best paper at the conference," she said. Where David was concerned, Natasha was intensely partisan.

"I can hope so," David said.

"Darling, you mustn't undervalue yourself." She kissed him, then returned to her usual position, took his hand and placed it over her breasts. "We could still go away for a few days, just the two of us," she said.

"Of course," David agreed. Natasha pressed her hands on his and felt her oppressive anxiety slowly dissolve. She wanted to sob with relief and make love with him right there on the couch, or on the floor, she didn't care, didn't care either if anyone saw them, all she wanted was to affirm that their bond of love was still intact. And perhaps she and David would have made love, except that Maria, the children's nanny, after first tapping on the door, entered the room to inform them that Roger, their youngest son, had a slight temperature, an announcement that sent Natasha hurrying to the room where four matching beds held her passion flowers. She kissed and caressed the little boy who complained of stomach pains, then held, kissed and caressed the others who, resenting the attention given their young brother, suddenly discovered they too had stomach pains. "I think they could all do with some analgesic, don't you, Maria?"

Maria, who had been raised in a barrio near Manila where death was expected to reap an annual crop of children, smiled and agreed. She invariably agreed with Natasha because, before coming to Canada, she had been warned that rich North American women were impulsive and irrational and the best way to stay on good terms with them was to agree with everything they said. She had also been told that rich North American men would expect her to have sex with them, although so far that hadn't happened; in fact, she sometimes wondered if Mr. Powell was even aware of her existence. When Natasha learned that Maria sent half her wages to her family, she impulsively doubled Maria's salary and with her assistance contacted the local priest and donated funds to the church to build a medical clinic for women and children of the barrio. Natasha could hardly bear to listen when Maria talked of the hopeless position of women in the Philippines, who bore child after child, many fated for death before they were a year old, and she assured Maria that the new clinic would help change that by teaching women about family planning. Maria's response to Natasha's reassurance was much negative head-shaking and muttered words about the influence of priests and the Catholic church.

Sometimes Natasha spoke to David about the clinic ("my clinic", she called it) and was disheartened by his response: Change could not come about in countries like the Philippines, as long as celibate priests ruled the roost; until priests married and suffered the agony of watching the birth and death of their own children and saw their own wives prematurely age from endless child-bearing, conditions would never change. And behind David's comments, although Natasha did not know this, lay his belief that disease and high child mortality operated as population controls and that to assuage those afflictions would result in far greater maladies: overpopulation, destruction of forests, and soil depletion, followed by famine and proliferation of further diseases. Privately, David thought the only certain way to control population growth in the Third World was through wholesale sterilization, because, even in countries like China where rigorous attempts had been made to limit reproduction, the population had doubled since the end of the Second World War. In fact, population, like the national debt, had a nasty habit of doubling, even quadrupling, once a critical point was reached. Well-meaning people never seemed to grasp that while conscience-driven charity might appease their personal guilt, ultimately it compounded the problems of those they intended to help. Naturally, David kept his opinions to himself and merely nodded and "*tch-tched*" whenever Natasha spoke about her charitable activities.

Natasha took the bottle of pink liquid from Maria and smiled with adoration as each pair of lips opened to receive the raspberry-flavoured medicine. Then she returned the bottle to Maria and, as each child lay down, she leaned over to place a kiss on its forehead. Natasha and her children formed a mutual adoration society: The children thought they had the loveliest mother in the world, who provided everything they wanted, while Natasha believed no mother had ever had been so blessed with four such perfect children.

"Everything okay with Roger?" David was in bed, reading. During the early days of their marriage, Natasha had found David's habit of getting into bed to read disconcerting; she thought people went to bed to make love, or to sleep. David's logical reasons defeated her: What, he had asked, was the difference between sitting in a chair to read and lying in bed to read, or, come to that, reclining in a tub of hot water to read? It was a matter of personal inclination, and Natasha, whose only inclination at the time was to get into bed for the purpose of making love, had been forced to agree that reading in bed made good sense. Ten years of marriage had not altered David's reading habits or lessened Natasha's desire to lie in bed for the sole purpose of making love. During the short grey days of winter, when rain fell with a persistence that reduced sky, land, mind and body to a sodden uniformity, David would remain in bed for hours on weekend mornings, which meant Natasha also stayed in bed, which in turn meant the children invaded the bedroom to crawl over their parents and weren't made to dress until lunchtime. The memories of these mornings were among Natasha's happiest, for nothing in the world felt quite as pleasurable — except of course making love with David — as having her children snuggle under the covers and lie against her.

David never quibbled over Natasha's romantic notions of how their children had been conceived, or her obsessive devotion to them. How could he, when the children were the result of her equally obsessive devotion to him? In the past, he had been successful in maintaining a balance between his involvement with Liz and his marriage to Natasha, though he'd always known that he hung suspended between them on an emotional high-wire. But everything had gone surprisingly smoothly, and he had believed he could continue for the rest of his life to tread the thin line that separated the two women who, in every conceivable meaning of the word, controlled his life. He had never fooled himself about any of this: He knew the house in which he lived was owned by Natasha and that even if his salary were added to the interest he earned from his share of his adoptive mother's estate, his total income would still be minuscule compared to Natasha's. An act of will enabled him to isolate himself from the knowledge that their home and large garden, their two cars, the children's nanny, the couple who prepared their meals and cleaned the house, and other luxuries were all paid for with money from Nanda's trust. His only financial responsibility was for their monthly household expenses. Since Natasha had no real idea how a majority of people lived, she could believe that she and David lived a simple, even frugal life, and in a way she was right since neither was inclined to extravagance. They seldom went out or entertained, and the only time they were away from home was the summer months, which they spent on Paradise Island.

David liked but did not love his children. He was sexually satisfied by Natasha and, until Liz's death, believed he had loved her. Now, he realized he had never loved Natasha, *could* never love her, because his love for Liz took precedence. And more: The shock of her death had forced him to the realization of just how deeply he'd cared, how compulsively he had loved her, how dependent he was upon her presence in his life, for since she'd gone he'd felt an inner emptiness, the only explanation for which was that Liz had taken half his being with her down into the waves. All that remained now of their love was fear, a fear so terrible it could drive him to crouch in a corner and refuse to leave a room, lest he be attacked. But by what, or by whom would he be attacked? He lay in bed, listening to Natasha happily telling him how the three older children had suddenly developed tummy aches which could be soothed only by a spoonful of harmless analgesic plus her hugs and kisses. As she talked, she removed her clothes and dropped them here and there on the floor. "Have you ever noticed how pretty the children's lips are? Such sweet little lips! I adore kissing them. Davey, can you imagine ever spanking their little bottoms? Even when they're naughty, it's only baby naughtiness." Naked, Natasha sat on the bed, nightgown in hand. "Shall I put this on?" she asked, raising the gown. This was her way of asking David if he wanted to make love, as her earlier striptease had been performed so that he might see her at angles designed to lever his attention from the book.

There had always been the same combination of innocence and cunning in the way Natasha courted David; for he had never courted her, nor for that matter Liz. He had sought neither, but rather had responded to them on a physical level, the only difference being the bonding of childhood he'd experienced with Liz. Rarely, very rarely, he felt contempt that they would give so much of themselves and be satisfied with so little from him. But perhaps that was the way love worked: It was the great deceiver, compelling people to give, yet be satisfied with receiving little in return. He thought perhaps there was small difference between Natasha crying out as she moved to sexual fulfillment (as she was now) and a religious pilgrim ecstatically sobbing while kneeling before a shrine: In each instance, the person surrendered autonomy. Ah, that was it! That explained why he was now experiencing fear, why he felt as if he were being cut off from something immeasurably important to him. At some point early in his life — he couldn't be sure when, since he'd been unaware of it happening — he had surrendered his soul to Liz, and the terrible truth of this was that Liz hadn't commanded him to lie with her out of her love. No, she had not loved him; she had wanted only to reinforce control over him. He felt hatred for her as he now churned upon Natasha and pressed his lips against her open mouth and felt the hot, muted scream release her from sexual strife. All of us, he thought, every one of us without exception, at some point in our lives, surrenders personal autonomy to someone else, or to an idea or goal, because to do this thing was part of the human condition, an inescapable necessity of life, like eating and sleeping, pissing and shitting, and yes, like fucking (he was doing *that* now), and like dying, which was probably the greatest necessity of all. And, for David, that was the rub, the horror of existence, for while he attempted to experience forgetfulness as he crouched over Natasha, he could never forget, even during moments of exquisite pleasure, that the act he performed was nothing less than a prelude to his own death. He had experienced these moments of pleasure with Liz, too, and already she was in the grave. No, he was with Liz now . . . that first night . . . quickening . . . stark need overcoming the taboo . . . overwhelming his natural reticence . . . the curve of her breasts under the nightgown. No. He was with Natasha, waiting, calculating the time it would take for her crescendo of moans to rise until a brief scream and prolonged shudder told him she'd been freed from desire's prison. How strange to have your flesh inside a woman . . . so strange . . . the distance was so short, yet you felt you were travelling so far . . . so far . . . as though you were scaling an incredibly smooth rock face . . . scrambling . . . scrambling . . . until finally you reached up . . . your hand . . . your arm . . . you were over the top . . . lying face down on the warm curve of . . .

"It's always the same," Natasha whispered. "Always. Isn't that how you feel, Davey?" Caught up in memories of Liz, he nodded assent, then pressed his lips against her crushed breasts. "What would we do without each other?" she asked. "I couldn't bear it." When he did not respond she clung to him and reiterated: "I just couldn't bear it."

Chapter 18

"I'd like to have another baby," Natasha said to Amanda.

"Does Davey know?"

"I'd never do anything without telling David."

"Absolutely nothing?" Amanda teased. "Maybe he's already guessed, because you're *trying* harder?"

"Oh no, it's not like that." Natasha blushed and laughed. She regretted expressing her desire for another child. She should have known Amanda would reduce her maternal impulse into nothing more than having sex. "You know what I mean, nothing important." She changed the subject. "Have you seen Alice or Jamie lately?"

"No. Have you?"

Natasha shook her head. "I suppose they've settled in by now. David ran into Alice at the house. She asked him for his set of keys. He said she was quite obnoxious."

"That's her style. She's defensively rude. Before you can retreat and take cover, she goes bang, bang, bang; but it doesn't really mean anything."

"I've never been able to understand that sort of behaviour."

"You've never been forced to swallow insults, Tashie, or have people put you down."

"I've had *you* make digs at me," Natasha said.

Amanda laughed in reply, and after a momentary pause Natasha joined in. "I'm sort of an archaeologist, Tashie. I disturb the surface of things to find out what's going on underneath."

"Why bother with me? We grew up together, so you know all about me."

Amanda cupped her chin and cheek in her right hand. "It's a funny thing, but you can live with people for ages and still not know what they're thinking, or what's going on inside them."

"You should have been a psychologist, Mandy."

"I'm not interested in curing people's neuroses. What I want to know is what's bubbling under their skins. You listen to me talking, and I do the same with you, but we may be thinking something completely different from what we're saying. I thought I knew most of what went on inside Liz, but in fact I knew next to nothing. Liz died without dropping her mask. We grew up together, Tashie, so we *suppose* we know all about each other. But we don't. We wear masks. And I know from experience the only time most people drop them is when they're dying. I've seen it happen."

Natasha's uneasiness was evident in the way she moved on the chair and rearranged cutlery on the table. Finally she said, "We can't give all of ourselves to others. It's too dangerous. It would be like belonging to one of those ghastly cults where people confess sins and afterwards get trapped by what they've said."

"Those people don't stand up and confess anything that matters to them. Men don't say: 'Lord, forgive me, for I beat my wife,' or women: 'Lord God, help me stop hating my child.' People don't reveal important things about themselves. Do you tell me what's important to you?"

"There's no reason I should. Well, is there?"

Amanda shrugged and smiled. "I agree, there's no obvious reason."

Natasha licked her lips and the muscles in her throat moved. "Why do you go on at me, Mandy? It's as though you're suggesting there's something I ought to know about myself, or about somebody else, that I don't."

"That's just me being gossipy. I like to plant seeds here and there in order to get my crop of gossip sprouting. Then I select the strongest shoots and feed them. But since Liz has gone and Jamie's so involved with Alice, I've got no one to gossip with except you."

"There's Hiddie," Natasha suggested.

"She's hopeless. All she thinks about is keeping up with the Joneses." Amanda refilled the kettle and put it on the stove. "I'll make another pot of tea."

"Remember how Max used to dress up Jeanette and Louise and parade them in front of his awful friends? Hiddie must have hated that."

"Max treated his girls like princesses. He couldn't bear to think that one day they'd stop being his little sweethearts, wearing knee-high white stockings and shiny Mary Janes; he hated to think of them changing into women, because then his predatory pals'd swarm after them. There's lots of guys like Max. They don't want to give up adoring their little girls and having the exclusive privilege of seeing them naked. I feel a little like that about Annabelle, but for a different reason. I'd like to stop Annabelle growing older because I don't want her to go through the torment of adolescence. She'll never be pretty. Not like your girls. She could end up letting some jerk fuck her because she thinks it's the only way she can get a man. I should know. That's the way I was at sixteen. Were you like that, Tashie?"

"Me? I wouldn't have dreamt of letting any man touch me."

"But you never had to make yourself think you were in love with some pimply-faced goofball. You always knew you would get David in the end. Did you have lovers before you married him?"

"Oh no," Natasha whispered. "I never met anyone I liked well enough."

"Sex is easy once you get started. You must know that by now. Just take off your panties and somebody gets a five-minute high, though you might not be the one who gets it because you're either too scared or too anxious." Amanda gave a barking laugh of self-derision. She dropped two tea bags into the Crown Derby teapot and filled it with boiling water. "That says a lot about me as a teenager. It's incredible what you'll do when you think you're in love." She stirred the tea. "You must know that, Tashie."

"Why are you talking like this about yourself, Mandy?" Natasha said.

"Probably because Liz is gone." She dropped more fig bars onto the plate. "I'm disoriented." She examined the interior of the milk jug to gauge how much was left. "It's an odd feeling, because when I lived with Harry I didn't see Liz for months and months. But I knew she was there, that I could always pick up the phone and have a gossip with her."

"I ought to go."

"Not yet. I need to talk to you about something that's bothering me." Amanda looked into the teapot, then poured tea into their cups. "Liz's gone . . . permanently gone."

"Does that have anything to do with me?"

"In a way. It has to do with —" She glanced at Natasha's face, saw fear and dismay, and paused for a moment. "It's nothing to worry about, Tashie. It's about Annabelle and Chris. I'd arranged with Liz that if anything happened to me, she'd take them. Of course, I don't expect anything to happen, but you can't arrange things once you're gone, can you? Anyway, I'd explained things to Annabelle and Christopher. They weren't too upset . . . you know how kids are. Jamie and I were the same. We thought Mom would never die. And I certainly didn't expect Liz to go. So . . . I want to ask you if you'd be their guardian . . . you know, if anything happened to me."

"David and I would be happy to look after Annabelle and Christopher." She sounded relieved. "You mean David too, don't you?"

"Yes, of course," Amanda said. "Didn't I include David? Sorry. I meant you and David. Thanks, Tashie. I've been worried. I'll have my will changed, now you've agreed."

Natasha ate half a cookie, drank some tea, glanced at Amanda from beneath lowered eyelashes, then said, "David feels the same as you . . . I mean, about Liz suddenly going."

"He said something to you?" Amanda was apprehensive.

"Only that he felt afraid."

"Afraid? I see. Well, who isn't afraid? Once in a while I get so scared I practically pee my panties, though I know there's really nothing to get so frightened about. Did you tell David that?"

"I'm not sure what I said. Afterwards, I thought maybe he was afraid we might stop loving each other, that our love had burned out. Remember how you once said people who feel passion for each other can get burned out?"

"Did I actually say that? Well, I guess it's true enough." Amanda stuffed a cookie into her mouth and slowly devoured it.

"Didn't you mean it?"

"Of course I meant it." She drank some tea. "Are you really going to have another baby?"

"I'd like to."

"I thought David was against it."

"I think I can persuade him."

Looking at Natasha over her raised cup, Amanda thought her cousin as naive today as she'd been as a girl, while Natasha, looking at Amanda, wondered what lay behind her casual chatter. One part of Natasha wanted to jump up and run, lest Amanda say something terrible that would destroy her life, while another part kept her at the table longing for Amanda's reassurance that everything was going to work out. She still didn't understand why she had begun to experience moments of panic, only that it had started the evening David had asked her to accompany him to Mexico. She believed there was no objective reason to feel as she did: her relationship with David was the same as always, and so was her daily routine. Each day after David went off to the university, she filled the hours between his departure and return, driving the three older children to their respective private schools, answering mail (usually requests for money from charities), shopping, and visiting her mother. She hadn't realized she had no close friends until the fear had begun to eat away her sense of security. She'd discovered there was no one with whom she could talk, not even her mother. David, who had always been the pivot on which her days contentedly turned, had become (though this was hard to acknowledge) the source of her fears. True, she had returned to reclining on the couch in the evenings in her favourite position, but an uneasiness lay behind everything she said; she felt there was another person inside her head who was watching David's face as he responded to her, and she even experienced (and this was terrible for Natasha) a slight detachment when they made love. She told herself it was silly to worry; after all, she still had David and her four passion flowers, which made her the most fortunate woman in the world. But the little nagging fear remained, and because her mother had provided nothing to comfort her, she was sitting, now, at Amanda's kitchen table, fiddling with the silverware while trying to overcome her own natural reticence and the mistrust she'd always had of Amanda as a person, so it seemed to her, who had an unhealthy desire to pry into the intimate lives of family members.

"Is something wrong, Tashie? What is it?" Amanda's voice was soft and invited confidences. She patiently waited while Natasha sipped cold tea before replying.

"I think . . . David . . . I think maybe . . . he no longer loves me." The words came out in a gush of despair.

"How can you say such a thing? David adores you."

"I looked at his face, into his eyes, and saw his wish that *I* was dead instead of Liz. I could see it in his eyes. It was there, Mandy. I saw it."

"Tashie . . ." Amanda reached across the table to hold Natasha's hand and prevent her from touching the spoons. "How could you possibly see that? Aren't you imagining it? Well, aren't you?"

"I'm not. He said he'd become afraid, and I knew he was thinking about Liz . . . thinking he couldn't go on loving me because he misses Liz so much." It was finally out: The fear had found words to express itself.

"Natasha!" The unexpected sternness in Amanda's voice quieted Natasha, as the voice of authority stills the irrational sobbing of a child. "Are you listening, Tashie? Because what I'm going to say is important." Nursing had taught Amanda much about human fear. In her time, she had leaned over and clasped the hands of many frightened, dying patients, as she now leaned over the table and compelled Natasha to look into her eyes. "Look at me, Tashie." Natasha responded with a whimpered "yes".

"David was very close to Liz and probably feels he should have known she was in crisis. He feels *guilty*. I know, because I feel that way too. You have to understand years ago, when they were kids, Liz and David thought of themselves as being one person. Jamie and I were the same. You feel protected, as if you have two faces, one to defend yourself at the front, the other on guard for your backside. I'll bet your twins are the same way."

"They *are* close," Natasha whispered.

"There! You see?" Amanda triumphantly said. "I'm not saying they'll feel the same when they're adults, but — and this is extremely important to bear in mind — if one of them accidentally died, the other would feel he or she was responsible for what happened." Amanda hoped she sounded convincing.

"Davey and Liz weren't twins."

"It doesn't matter. What counts is how they felt about each other in their formative years. Look, Tashie, until you came along and appropriated David, he and Liz spent all their time together. People used to say they acted like a couple who're engaged."

"That's not fair, Amanda. You make me sound like a thief. I didn't steal David from Liz. He loved me and wanted to marry me. He said he'd always loved me."

"Of course he loved you, of course he wanted to marry you. He still loves you and sees himself as the luckiest guy on earth. But that doesn't prevent him from feeling guilty about Liz, because now that she's gone, he can't help remembering everything that went on between them when they were growing up."

"What? What went on between them? What are you saying?"

"Tashie! Stop imagining things!"

"Then tell me what he and Liz did when they sneaked off together."

"I do believe you're still envious of Liz." Amanda leaned back and critically eyed Natasha. "You don't want Liz ever to have been part of David's life. That's your problem, Natasha."

"I'm not envious!"

"You are, and what's more, you can't admit you deliberately followed David when he moved to Ontario."

"I didn't! I went to Ottawa to take courses at the university there. I didn't even know Chalk River was anywhere near Ottawa."

"Tashie! That's not true. Everybody, including Liz, knew you'd gone after him, so what's so wrong with admitting it? You were in love with David, so why *not* go after him?" Amanda raised questioning eyebrows. "Well?"

"You all thought I had no right to take David away from Liz."

"That's absolute nonsense, Tashie. First off, it wasn't our place to tell you and David what to do. We thought David was lucky to get you. For heaven's sake, Tashie! You're not only gorgeous, you're rich!"

"Davey's never cared about me having money." Natasha always denied that her wealth could possibly have influenced David. Their marriage was the outcome of impassioned love.

"That's right. He wouldn't care if you gave away every cent, say, to me." Natasha managed a smile. "Tashie, listen to me: Make the most of what you have. Get David into bed and exhaust him with so much love he won't be able to think of another woman." Amanda's laughter became raucous and lewd. "Make him work, Tashie. Don't let him think you're there for his convenience. Tell him the city's filled with hungry guys — I should know, I cash in on their hunger. For God's sake, Tashie, stop looking shocked. I know you wouldn't dream of doing what I do. I know you and David have a wonderful relationship, but all I'm saying is the quickest way to wreck what you have is to be suspicious and let your suspicions take over until finally . . ." Amanda raised suggestive hands.

"I don't want to play the role of dissatisfied wife, Mandy. I'm afraid I'll lose David."

"Listen Natasha: Don't forget I have a stake in what happens to you and David. We're family. I admit sometimes I have twinges of envy because you have so much of everything, but, believe me, I'd feel terrible if anything went wrong in your life. And there's something else too. I've seen some pretty awful things happen to couples who doubted each other." Tears flowed down Amanda's cheeks. "You don't know one-half of what goes on in relationships. You and David are two of the luckiest people in the world. So hang on to what you have."

Natasha, who always cried from joy, now gave a preparatory sniff before tears of relief drifted from her eyes. Amanda went around the table; Natasha stood, they held each other and released more tears. Amanda loved every moment of it, but Natasha was embarrassed by her show of emotion, though she was able to say: "I'm glad I spoke to you, Amanda, I was making myself sick with worry."

"I could see you were," Amanda sobbed. "We must always be open with each other, tell each other what's bothering us, no matter what it is."

"Yes, we'll do that. And I should apologise, Mandy, because I've always thought I couldn't talk to you, that you were . . . you know . . . a bit of a scatterbrain."

"It's partly true, I guess. And I do love to gossip, though you'd be surprised how well I can keep secrets, so you needn't worry I'll repeat anything you tell me."

"I've always concentrated everything on David and the children. I don't have any friends."

"Well, you have me."

Amanda used a tea towel to wipe her eyes, while Natasha took a dainty handkerchief from a bead-embroidered straw bag, purchased at a store that sold articles made by South American women. Natasha did her bit to help these oppressed women by purchasing serapes, wall hangings, scarves, sandals, handbags, and little carvings, which she then donated to charity-organization sales, or used as gifts. Now she offered Amanda a Peruvian serape. "It doesn't suit me but it'll look marvellous on you."

"You mean, it'll hide how plump I've got?" Amanda knew the serape was being offered as payment for services received. During her years of private nursing she'd learned that wealthy people were incapable of seeing anything, including basic kindness, except as a service that required payment. Sure, Natasha had come seeking help and was grateful for the assistance she had provided, but now that their tears were dried, they could revert to their habitual roles: Natasha, friendly but reserved; Amanda, eager to help, yet envious of her cousin. To demonstrate her appreciation further, Natasha next said she had some clothes that might be suitable for Annabelle.

"The trouble is," Amanda said, "Annabelle has very definite ideas about what she wears."

"I'm sure Annabelle would like these." And so Amanda wouldn't think she was trying to get rid of old clothes, Natasha added, "Some of the skirts and sweaters haven't ever been worn."

"Annabelle's so funny about her clothes. But why don't we come over Saturday? She can try them on."

"Of course. We'll have a tea party for the children. By the way, how do Annabelle and Christopher get on with Hiddie's kids?"

"Not well. Annabelle thinks the girls are silly."

"I'm relieved to hear that — Jasmine and Gloria can't stand them."

"I suppose we should feel sorry for them, and for Hiddie too. She put up with a lot from Max, knowing that when he came home at night he'd just left another woman's bed and she had to be satisfied with the leftovers. At least you don't have that problem. I'll walk you to your car." They left the house and strolled along the street, chatting about the minutiae of their lives. "So, you aren't sure about the baby?" Amanda asked.

"I probably won't. David isn't —"

"For heaven's sake, Tashie, if you want another baby, then go ahead and have one. David's not the one who has to carry it for nine months, then labour for hours and hours to bring it into the world."

"I know, I know. But I tell myself the reason I have the impulse is because I felt useful when I was carrying and nursing the children. Now I feel so useless."

Amanda stopped and laid a hand on Natasha's arm. "Look, Tashie . . . you employ a nursemaid, two housemaids, a cook, a gardener-handyman."

She counted them off on her fingers. "You're an economic benefit to the community. Have you ever thought of that?" They stopped by Natasha's car. "Compare yourself to me. I create nothing. I only bank rental cheques." They laughed.

"You say that to make me feel better. Anyway, thanks for everything." Natasha dabbed a kiss on Amanda's cheek, got into her car, waved, smiled and drove away, while Amanda went back into her home to hunt through papers on which were scribbled seemingly endless phone numbers. She couldn't find what she wanted and, after much frowning and lip-chewing, picked up the phone and dialled a number. "This is Amanda Powell speaking," she said, her voice thick with politeness. "Is Hilda Logan still in her office?" She waited a moment, then said, "Listen Hiddie, I'm sorry to drag you away from your stocks and bonds, but I thought you might have David's office number. I've mislaid mine. Oh, to ask him about a chemical listed in some cookies I bought. Don't bother, I can call him at home. How're you, Hiddie? And the kids? Oh, sure, they're fine. Annabelle's planning to cycle around the world. Oh, little things like crossing oceans don't worry her. It's the big things, like making sure the bathroom's clean. Sure, we'll get together soon. Okay. Bye." Each time the sisters spoke to each other the conversation terminated with Hilda saying they must get together, and Amanda agreeing they must. Usually it got no further than talk because Amanda, knowing Annabelle's dislike of her cousins, never pursued the matter, and Hilda, so it seemed, forgot the suggestion the moment she put down the phone, presumably because Amanda was of no use to her in bettering the social status of her children.

Amanda returned to the kitchen table, dug a writing pad and pen out of the drawer, and began writing: *Dear Davey, I've had no luck reaching you at the university, and I don't want to call the house, which explains why I'm writing this note.* Having set that much down, Amanda leaned back and scratched her head with the pen. Composing sentences was a laborious task, yet the curious thing was, once she knew what she wanted to say, she wrote easily, as an extension of her spoken words. (Amanda had never understood the reason for the high marks she used to receive on her university term papers because she experienced agony writing them and had a low opinion of the final results.) *Tashie was here today and I could see she was upset about something. Of course, being Tashie, she had trouble letting go. But it finally came out. She's afraid you've come to hate her, Davey. She's afraid what you really and truly wish is that she was dead, instead of Liz. So please, if you value what you have with Tashie, smile at her more, look and act as if you love her, which I know, really, you do.*

Love, Amanda. She put the note into an envelope, sealed and wrote David's name on it. She looked at the clock and decided there wasn't enough time to drive to the university and back before the children came home from school, so she slipped the note in the drawer with the writing materials, told herself she must deliver it the following day, then forgot it. She made more tea and, while waiting for Annabelle and Christopher, reflected on her conversation with Natasha: Fear opened people up. It had been like a knife going into an oyster shell to crack open and expose the usually ultra-reserved Natasha, but she'd done it and been rewarded with a peek into her private life. She'd seen Natasha's resentment hidden beneath the smooth facade; she'd seen her suspicion that maybe there'd been more to Liz and David's relationship than simple childhood affection. Oh yes, she could see that Natasha's suspicions were very real and she could predict that Natasha would use every trick in the book to ensure David never strayed from her bed. She'd start to impose demands on him, and if he fell short of what she wanted, she'd find a way to punish him: She'd let him know he was living in *her* house and that everything in it belonged to her, and she'd do these things because she wouldn't be able to resist retaliating. Amanda told herself she mustn't be too hard on Natasha: Natasha sincerely loved David and was truly frightened that he wished her dead instead of Liz. Of course, Liz had had absolutely no right to step between David and Tashie — it was cruel of her to have done that; and as for David, how could a person feel much sympathy for a man who married a woman passionately in love with him and then carried on for years and years with his half-sister? It was despicable. It really was. Poor Tashie. Amanda wished there was a way she could warn her. But there wasn't, and she mustn't be tempted to reveal anything about Liz and David. She heard the front door rattle, then the hollow sound of shoes racing along the long, narrow hardwood hall.

"Mom!" Annabelle shrieked as she tore into the kitchen. "Mom, Susan Jones said Uncle Jamie's poem stinks!"

"I wouldn't take any notice of that," Amanda said.

"That's just her opinion," Christopher offered. He'd picked up that rejoinder at school and used it to rebut Annabelle's remarks addressed to him, which naturally infuriated Annabelle because she believed that she alone was endowed with a papal right to deliver dogma.

"Of course it's her opinion," she cried. "She wouldn't say it if it wasn't! You can be so stupid, Chris!"

"Don't get worked up, honey," Amanda said. "Does Susan have an uncle who has a poem in your reader?"

"She doesn't have anything. She's just a crummy, stupid brat, and I hate her!"

"That's no answer, darling. But if she says anything again, just tell her that lots of clever people like Jamie's poetry and think it's good enough to include in your reader."

"They're not cleverer than Uncle Jamie," Christopher said.

"I don't suppose they are. Anyway, it's not worth getting into a stew over. Now, come here and give me a kiss." As always, Amanda kissed each of her children and passed a hand over them from head to bottom, making sure nothing adverse had happened to their bodies (and souls) during the day. She poured glasses of milk and gave each child two cookies, then sat at the table, watching as they ate their snack and drank their milk.

Annabelle would soon be ten, Christopher seven. It was hard to believe they had been in her life that long. As she sat and listened to Annabelle's piping voice and Christopher's solemn, considered responses, she could not imagine life without them. They were talking about their birthdays and, after much discussion, decided to celebrate jointly. Annabelle counted the days between her birthday and Christopher's, divided the number by two, checked the wall calender and came up with the date of November 19.

"Who're we going to invite, Annabelle?" asked Christopher.

"Not Susan Jones. Not Jeanette and Louise."

"We have to invite Mom," offered Christopher. "She gives us presents."

"If you'd just have waited two seconds, Chris, I was going to say we would invite Mom. You're so impetual! You never let me say anything!"

"'Impetuous' is what you mean, Annabelle," Amanda said, thinking the word ironic, coming from someone who never gave her brother much of a chance to *be* impetuous. Amanda loved to watch her children, and now she leaned on the table, chin on hand, observing the expressions flickering over their faces as they chattered away. She thought of her children as being intelligent, far more intelligent than she'd been at their ages, but of course she had to keep in mind that she had been none too bright as a child, everyone said that, and she still wasn't very smart. Her one regret was Annabelle's deficiency in looks. It was a pity, because Annabelle was such a sprightly little soul. "Is it tomorrow you bike with Don?" she asked. She thought there was something touching about the way the man from the bike shop continued to cycle with the children.

"Sunday. But only if Chris learns to changè gears proper."

"Properly."

"That's what I said. We're going up the long hill and around UBC."

"There's lots of cars there." Images of the children being struck by cars appeared in Amanda's mind.

"It'll be in the morning when there's hardly any traffic. But . . ." Annabelle released a great sigh, ". . . I could be an old lady by the time Chris learns to change gears."

"You could walk your bikes up the hill," Amanda suggested.

"Mom! No one pushes bikes up hills!"

"We did."

"That was in the olden days. Now, you don't. You have to change gears, and Chris always gets it wrong. I don't know why, it's so-o-o simple."

"You know, Annabelle, when I was taking my nurse's training, people would get impatient with me because I didn't do things the way they wanted. And you know what happened? I got worse, instead of better. Do you know the moral of that little story, Chris?" It was safe to ask Christopher this question, because he'd heard before of the miseries she'd suffered trying to do things in the approved way.

"Guys won't learn if you put them down too much!"

"Did you hear that, Annabelle?"

"That's what *I* was going to say," Annabelle indignantly replied. "And I would have, except Chris got there first. Really Chris, you're getting to be positively improbable!"

Feeling thoroughly amused and delighted with her children, Amanda went around the table to hug and kiss them again. "How lucky I am, having two of the sweetest *and* smartest children in the whole wide world!"

"Well, there's a few things I don't know yet," Annabelle admitted. "But I know more than most guys in my class. And lots more than Chris!" She paused, then said: "Don't I, Chris? And what's more, I'll always know more than you because I'm three years older."

"I wouldn't count on that if I were you, Annabelle. When I was a girl I was absolutely sure I'd never be as smart as my sisters and brothers, but now I think maybe I'm as smart as any of them." She laughed and threw up her hands. "Perhaps even smarter! So what do you think of that?"

Chapter 19

"You're looking glum, Jamie," Amanda said. "What's up?"

He had appeared at the house as Amanda was on the verge of going to bed. She'd gone to answer the doorbell, looked through the security eye and seen him on the doorstep. When she opened the door, he shuffled in, looking even more disreputable than usual. They went into the kitchen where Amanda heated milk and made mugs of cocoa. "So, what's up?" she asked for the third time.

"Nothing," Jamie eventually said.

"Have you and Alice settled in?" Jamie nodded his head and noisily slurped cocoa. "It's good that you didn't have to buy furniture or anything." He nodded again, and Amanda, with an unusual show of impatience, said, "Jamie! I wish you'd say something, not just sit there like a dumb-bunny. Am I supposed to guess what's happened?"

"Nothing's happened."

"Well then, why're you —" Amanda gestured, and knocked her mug off the table. "Damn it!" she said, looking down at the bits of crockery and spilled cocoa. "Why does everything in our family have to end in such a mess!" She angrily gathered up the pieces of mug and wiped up the fluid with paper towels. "That was Annabelle's Easter mug when she was five."

"I'll get her another," Jamie muttered. He wasn't familiar with an angry, irritated Amanda.

"You don't have to get anything for Annabelle, or for me. You have to bring some sanity into your own life!"

"I'll go." Jamie left the table only to be caught by Amanda at the kitchen door.

"Don't mind me, I'm out of sorts. Come back." She kissed his forehead. "You look so miserable." Jamie allowed Amanda to lead him back to the table, and once he was seated, she stood beside him, stroking his hair and face. "Is it because Liz isn't there?"

"I don't know."

"Do you miss her?" He nodded. "Me too. That's why I'm down in the dumps. At least, I think it's that. Does Alice know you're here?"

"I dunno."

"Maybe you should call. I mean, she gets upset if she doesn't know where you are. I'll do it."

Jamie suddenly smashed his hand on the table and shouted, "She doesn't get it! She doesn't understand I want to be left alone!" He slurped more cocoa. "Liz understood. You know what I think? I think Alice is driving everything away. I'm finished! I'm finished!" His voice rose to an hysterical pitch. "Finished!" He sagged over the table. "I might as well go somewhere and cut my throat."

Amanda had dealt with patients who cried out for death to release them from unending pain, but she'd never expected to hear her own brother despairingly say he too wanted to end his life. She felt waves of terror engulf her; she was not made to be the rock to which other family members clung during times of crisis. That had been Liz's role; just knowing Liz was there, standing solidly in the midst of the raging stream of life, had allowed Amanda, and probably Jamie too, to skitter around, knowing they were attached to her by a lifeline that would haul them to safety if ever they got into serious trouble. Now with Liz gone, Amanda had enough trouble keeping herself and the kids afloat in the life-torrent, never mind having to worry over Jamie. Of course she loved him and enjoyed her role as ever-accommodating sister, but she had no intention of sacrificing herself to him, as Liz had: She had to think of her own and her children's futures. Besides, she was becoming a little impatient with Jamie; he apparently didn't care a fig whether Alice suffered and worried over him, provided *he* got what he wanted. She'd always been prepared to admire and support her poet-brother, but things had changed now and, while she might not particularly like Alice, nevertheless he had married her and now she was carrying his child. It wouldn't be right to silently stand by while Jamie sacrificed Alice on the altar of his galactic star-word gods. "I think you're making too much of this, Jamie," she began. "Just because your words don't show up when you want them to doesn't mean that —"

"What d'you mean, don't show up?"

"When you go to your old room."

"You think I whistle and they appear like pet dogs?"

"I'm not sure. I don't know what they do," Amanda cautiously said, aware she'd stumbled into dangerous territory.

"You're not sure, because you know nothing about it! Everything's fine as long as I listen to you gab about afternoon fucks with guys you've picked up from God knows where. But when I have a problem, you don't want to hear about it."

"That's not true, Jamie! I care very much about your problems! But I don't pretend to know anything about poetry, or how it comes to you. So I don't see why you attack me when all I do —" Amanda was so upset she couldn't continue. She went back to her chair and sat with her head turned so Jamie couldn't see her face.

"I'm sorry." Amanda heard the apology, but did not move. "Mandy . . ." She knew he was standing beside her. "I've messed things up, Mandy. I don't want us to be a mess too. We go back too far, we go back to me crawling into your bed at night after I'd had a bad dream."

"We were happy then. Don't you think we were, Jamie?" She did not look at him.

"As happy as most kids can be. Are Annabelle and Chris happy?"

"I think so. Most of the time. They don't have to face the problems we had. Losing our father, moving from England, and now having Liz go."

"We had one set of problems, they'll have others to deal with. Problems are relative to what you know and where you are at any given time."

"Oh, Jamie, I do miss Liz. I miss knowing she's there, sort of like a parent. It's true, I hardly ever followed her advice. But knowing I could get it was so important. Do you ever feel like that, not sure about things?"

"I'm not sure of anything these days. I used to think the greatest awakening in my life took place on the day you pulled down my pants, played with my penis until it stood up, then told me if I ever tried to put it inside you it would fall off and you would die, all this because we were brother and sister."

"Surely I never said anything like that!"

"You did. We go back to you graphically demonstrating gender differences. You theatrically imposed ethical strictures on me, then played the role of temptress to test my moral stamina and aptitude."

"Oh, Jamie!" Amanda laughed. "The things you say!"

"So what happens? I discover that the moral precepts I've acted on all my life've been reduced to a shambles by the people closest to me. I've also — belatedly — come to appreciate that, compared to hypocritical Liz, you are a highly moral individual."

Amanda went around the table to embrace him. "Jamie . . . don't be too hard on Liz. She suffered . . . really suffered."

"I never saw evidence of it."

"She hid it from you. Liz knew you thought of her as being strong and capable."

"I outgrew that view of her, years ago."

"No, Jamie, you didn't . . . any more than you've outgrown what you feel for me." Amanda rubbed her cheek against his. "Well, aren't I right?"

"Perhaps."

Amanda sighed and stepped back. "I'm going to telephone Alice. You don't want her to chew her nails to the quick, do you?"

"She doesn't chew her nails."

Amanda shook her head like a reproving teacher. "But she does! She's hardly got any nails left. If you go off the deep end now, she'll have to start on her fingers!"

"Why should I take responsibility for what Alice does?"

"Jamie! You married her, you pushed your penis into her and started the baby she's carrying! What do you think you are, a cuckoo bird?"

"It's the female that lays eggs in other birds' nests."

"I don't care which bird does which. You know quite well what I mean. Shall I make more cocoa?" Amanda carried the telephone over and placed it before him. He managed a painful, slightly servile grin before dialling the appropriate number.

"I'm at Mandy's," he said. ". . . Just to say hello. I'll be home soon. Yes. I know." He replaced the phone. "Satisfied?"

"Are you sure you called her? I couldn't hear her voice." He held out the phone, inviting her to use it. "No, but I know how sly you are, Jamie. You've always been able to fool me."

"Unintentionally." He watched Amanda going about the business of making more cocoa and decided that the expression of amiable expectancy usually present on her still-pretty face had been replaced with one of anxiety — or was it misery he saw there? "You don't look particularly happy, Mandy," he said.

"I told you, I miss Liz. And I worry about Natasha. She was here the other day saying she thought David hated her."

"Maybe she's suddenly realized David married her for what she *has*, not for what she is."

"No. I can't accept that."

"Please yourself."

Amanda mixed hot milk into the cocoa powder. Her hand trembled as she tilted the saucepan. "Anyway, how could you know? You hardly ever see Natasha and David."

"Two points, Mandy: Tashie would have married Davey even if he was a liar, cheat and God knows what else. She *wanted* him and nothing else mattered. And while it's true I don't see much of Davey — in point of fact I never did see much of him — still, I've seen enough to know he's a cool customer, always on the lookout for a way to get ahead. He's an operator, an opportunist, like our father and grandfather — and if you want to know what *they* were like, ask Aunt Nanda. Did Mother ever talk to you about Father?"

"Only that he was handsome and wanted to write poetry."

"He was a drunkard! And he tried to rape Muriel!"

"Don't, Jamie," Amanda said. "Anyway, I don't go along with what you say about David. I know he genuinely feels terrible about Liz, and worries about Natasha."

"I'll bet he worries!"

"Don't dare say anything to Natasha, Jamie. I wouldn't have told you, if I'd thought you were going to turn on David."

"I'm putting things in their proper perspective, Mandy. That's all. Tashie has this big illusion about herself and the world. She actually believes if she gives away twenty thousand bucks a year — or fifty, or a hundred thousand — that would solve the world's problems *and* her own."

"She doesn't believe anything like that, Jamie. It upsets her knowing so many children die of starvation and disease. It's because she's a mother and worries about her own children. I'm the same. I'm always worrying about Annabelle and Christopher." She pointed a finger at him. "And you'll be the same too, when the baby comes. You may think you'll go on being the same old Jamie, but once that baby enters your life, once you know it can get ill, or get a high temperature and maybe die, you'll change. And you won't feel the same way about the starving kids you see on TV either. Because you'll understand that there's really no difference between your kid and those. That's what upsets Tashie so much. I'm sorry for her because she can't enjoy what she has. All she really cares about is her relationship with David. Maybe he's a conniving S.O.B., I don't know. I just know until now she was happy in the relationship."

"Phew! What a speech!" Jamie offered a pacifying smile. "I'd no idea you felt so strongly about our cousin." He sipped cocoa and cautiously watched her. Amanda had surprised him by knowing how to get at him, how to slip beneath the persona he exhibited to the world and squeeze the inner, real Jamie.

"I've spoken to Davey about Liz's death. He feels as though half his life had been cut away. I believe him, Jamie."

"For God's sake, Mandy. If I'd been coming here and fucking you whenever I felt like a change from my wife, I'd feel put out too, if you went and kicked the bucket on me."

"Did you ever want to do it with me, Jamie?"

"Sure, when I was eleven."

"Then don't damn Davey."

"Now wait a minute, Mandy. I may have had a passing urge to get inside your underpants when you were lusciously pubertal and practised your seduction techniques on me —"

"I didn't have techniques."

"They came naturally, so you weren't aware of them. Let me finish. Even though I was pretty asinine in those days, I'd been around enough to know where to put a stiff cock, and I knew, too, how soft your breasts were because you'd made me touch them so I could say nice things about them. Remember how you used to ask me to smell the latest scent you'd poured over yourself? I could've advanced on you then, and probably you wouldn't have said no. But it never happened, Mandy. It never happened because I understood you were my sister. That's the difference between me and David. And you understood that I'm your brother, and no matter what we may or may not have felt about each other, there was always a line between us."

"I used to wish we weren't brother and sister. I still do, because apart from Harry you're the only person I like to be with. You're the only one who knows what I'm really like inside, though we seem mismatched, don't we? I'll never understand your poetry."

"Neither will I."

Amanda laughed. "How can you write something and not know what it means?"

"I'm like most people, I function mechanically. There's not much difference between people and insects, or fish. If we even remotely guessed what was actually going on in our lives, if we grasped the implications of our actions and the consequences, do you think we'd behave as we do? Of course we wouldn't. Do you think Liz and Davey realized what could happen to them? No. What Liz wanted was six inches of David inside her cunt. That's all she cared about."

"Jamie, please don't."

"And Davey was only too happy to provide it. When Liz let you know what was going on, why didn't you tell her she was heading for disaster? Why, Mandy, why?"

"I suppose because I knew she wouldn't listen." The phone rang, Amanda answered it, then passed it over to Jamie and heard him say, "Yes . . . yes . . . I'm just about to leave . . . yes . . . fifteen minutes." She took the phone from him and returned it to its place on the wall.

"You'd better go," she said. She followed him through the house to the front door, where she held and kissed him. "I love you, Jamie," she said. She followed him to the sidewalk and waited while he undid the lock on his bicycle. "The words'll come back. I know they will."

Jamie lifted his bike onto the road and straddled it. "I wish I had your optimism. Look, Mandy…in the past I've asked you to stay away from Alice, but she's not having an easy time. Maybe you'd visit her."

"I promise." He waved, then rode off. She watched him pass through patches of street lighting, then returned to the kitchen, tidied up, and went to bed to lie awake, going over the conversation with Jamie and, while reflecting on it, to be amazed that Jamie should think so highly of her. Years ago, when she'd compared herself to other members of her family, she'd found herself profoundly deficient in the attributes possessed by her brothers and sisters and cousin. David was intellectually remote; Jamie, poetically remote; Liz, morally and, later, politically remote; Hilda, business-acumen remote; Natasha, ah Natasha, remote by reason of beauty and wealth. How could she possibly match them? *Those* members of the Powell family used their minds, while she wasn't even sure she had one; she appeared to do whatever thinking she did with her genitals, not her brains, and learning in a Fine Arts course that Renoir ascribed his paintings to his genitalia offered little consolation because she knew her genitals were totally disinterested in art of any kind; all they did was produce a monthly supply of sticky blood — they still did, of course — and stimulated vague internal urges and aches whenever she saw pictures of nursing mothers. And it was true, she *had* practised little tricks and come-ons with Jamie. Why not? He was a convenient male, and she knew she could tease him and still be safe; she could instruct him to place his fingers on the white skin of her dish-shaped breasts, practice rolling her hips against him, invade his room in her nightgown and, while sitting on his bed, draw his attention to the clump of hair sprouting at the vee between her upper thighs; she could even lie beside him to practise resting her head upon his shoulder in the position she planned to assume when she met and married the man of her dreams. She could even, oh, so casually, while speaking of matters far removed from fleshly desires, move a hand over the bed covers to find out whether her strategic moves had affected Jamie's anatomy. After all, there was no point in perfecting techniques if they had no effect, always taking into account that Jamie was three years her junior as well as her brother.

It seemed strange now to have Jamie admit to temptation and to imagine how she might have responded had he granted his hands freedom. Probably with shock, because a huge gulf separated her little tricks from the act which supposedly followed. He must have understood the reasons for her behaviour, and maybe, unconsciously, she knew them too. That was why Jamie was so special for her, why she regretted she would never be able to find anyone else in the world like him. Jamie was a unique person, like Liz. David, Hiddie and Tashie might be above average, but they lacked the qualities that set Jamie and Liz apart from the common run. It was easy to pinpoint Jamie's uniqueness: He was a rare bird because he saw something in the stars no one had ever seen before, but Liz's distinctiveness wasn't so easy to establish; after all, there was no shortage of people who protest social injustices. These people persistently popped up, like aggravating nettles in severely regimented gardens that defy surface elimination because their roots probe deep into the soil. So what was so special about Liz? Perhaps it was simply the way she carried herself: the air she had, suggestive of immortality, as though she were a true descendant of the Athenian gods, a person whose thoughts and actions were beyond the ken of average people like herself. It made no difference that Liz often irritated her and ignored what she said, because no matter how she behaved no one ever tired of looking at her beautiful face and body. There was something exciting about the way she would walk into a room and stand there, as if in command of sufficient forces to decimate anyone who dared disagree with her. Amanda remembered how as a plump adolescent she used to sit on Liz's bed and watch as she dried her hair after showering. She felt no envy that the line from Liz's shoulders to her hips and thighs possessed sculptural grandeur, while her own waistline hardly existed, or that Liz's skin was marvellously smooth and cream-coloured while hers was pinkish and blotchy. Her principal feeling about Liz had been one of awe, and she'd found it hard to accept that her body and Liz's had been conceived in the same womb and that the functioning of their bodies was the same. Yet Liz must have felt with David the equivalent of what she felt with Harry; and when she entered Liz's bedroom that terrible night and found her lying on the floor covered in her own vomit and excreta, she'd learned, truly learned, there was no difference between her body and Liz's. She remembered kneeling beside her sister to touch her cold body, then in a frenzy washing it and slipping a nightgown onto it before calling the police who, after the officers saw what she'd done, warned her she could be charged. But she'd simply ignored their threats. All she cared about was restoring a modicum of dignity to her beloved sister, making sure she was treated with the respect she deserved. Amanda ended her reflection by crying a little, then rolled onto her left side, touched the empty half of her double bed, regretting a man was not there to hold her, sighed, and slept.

❧

"Why did you have to go to Amanda's? How long were you there? Don't you care about me being stuck in this mausoleum all by myself? Now I wish we'd stayed in the apartment."

"We'll move back," Jamie said.

"We can't. Somebody's rented it."

"We'll find another place."

"I don't want another place," Alice stormed. "I just want to know why you bugger off and spend hours with your sister."

"But I hadn't seen Amanda in weeks." They were lying on the new bed in the newly carpeted, refurbished room where Jamie's mother and elder sister had once slept. He thought the maple-veneer furniture Alice bought had transformed the comfortable lived-in room into one which best fitted a second-class hotel. The old bed, the soft boudoir chairs, the dressing table and the high chest of drawers were now stacked in Liz's childhood bedroom, and occasionally he slipped into the room to sit in one of the chairs, not because he wanted to think about Liz, but because sitting there allowed him to think that not too much in his life had changed after all, that the great universal wheel which in the past had governed the seasons of his life would continue to spin as it always had; sitting in the chair, above all, enabled him to believe his poetic vision had not failed and soon he would be seated again in his old room, looking up at the sky, watching word patterns writhe among the stars.

Contemplating that there might be no more in his future than what floated in Alice's belly was almost more than he could bear: His impulse was to run before the creature inside Alice squirmed out and damned him to a lifetime of servitude. His fears puzzled him, because he had always enjoyed children: They were amusing and viewed the world with unjaded eyes. He could even enjoy the terrible artificiality of Hilda's daughters, which they'd acquired under their father's tutelage. Actually, he found Jeanette and Louise slightly humorous, for they assumed their role of sophisticates was beyond reproach: skirts impeccably arranged, heads attentively cocked while others chatted, smiles of rigid appreciation on their pouting lips — poses that would guarantee, they thought, successful entry into the adult world. Periodically, when visiting Natasha, he'd accompany her to the nursery and was always impressed by the liveliness of her children. But his favourite was Annabelle. She embodied everything he enjoyed in a child: acute perception, naivety and puritanical morality. He did not agree with Amanda that her plainness was a misfortune, but then he valued intelligence above looks for, as he pointed out to Amanda, intelligence was the only quality that remained relatively unchanged throughout a life span, the rest being transitory. But she'd not been impressed by what he'd said, arguing that while brains might get men what they wanted, beauty had always been, and would continue to be, the single most important asset a woman could possess if she wanted to stroll along the great avenues of a successful life. This was self-evident, she told Jamie, surprised that so knowledgeable a person could be blinded to the importance of looks to a woman.

"I don't feel right in this house," Alice said. "Half the time when I enter a room I expect to find somebody there."

"You're used to living in a place without memories," Jamie said. He put a hand on her stomach. "This will create layers of memories." He moved his hand over her groin onto her thighs.

"You don't blame me for not having sex?"

"No."

"I want to. But I'm scared something bad might happen inside."

"Don't worry."

"Maybe the reason you're always out late is because you're off with some woman."

"I'm not doing anything like that."

"Then what are you doing?"

"I cycle around . . . waiting."

"You were at your sister's, that's not cycling."

"I happened to pass Mandy's street."

"But why d'you have to cycle around at night? You might get hurt. Why?"

"I've told you. I'm waiting."

"But what about me? What about this?" She grabbed his hand and placed it on her belly. "You don't understand what it's like being a woman."

"I plead total ignorance."

"Don't be a smart ass. You don't know what women go through, having guys look at them. You don't know how men talk."

"You could visit Mandy."

"Why can't she come here? Eh? I'll tell you why. Your family thinks I'm a nobody." Alice's suspicions of Jamie's family were aggravated by increasing physical discomfort. Her back and legs ached, she was constipated and felt comfortable only when stretched out in bed. She didn't believe Jamie when he explained why he cycled around streets at night. She felt alone and deserted and was sure he went off to have sex with another woman, and her suspicions were compounded by her resentment of his family who, she now felt, were going out of their way to ignore her, apparently forgetting her own rejection of them. When Jamie suggested she invite the family to visit, she snapped at him, saying she wasn't up to entertaining "dozens of people" and summarily rejecting his suggestion of hiring a caterer. All this added to Jamie's depression, the core of which was his fear that perhaps he was finished as a poetical gatherer of star-generated words. He was convinced that he and Alice had betrayed themselves and their relationship by trying to normalize it. By marrying and moving into the family house they had ruined what they valued most about their relationship: secrecy and isolation.

"If you want, we can get a townhouse. Or we could sell this place and go away."

"How can I go anywhere? Look at me. I feel like a fat sow. My uncle raised pigs . . . the sows always had saggy bellies, waiting around to have piglets. Waiting, waiting, waiting: That's all I'm good for now. I can't enjoy anything. Nothing. I hate it." She began to cry noisily, while Jamie stroked her face and tried to assure her that things would be fine once the baby was born. "They won't!" she shrieked. "They won't be fine ever! Never! Don't tell me things'll be the same when I know they won't. God, why did I ever get involved with you? I got along fine by myself. Well, didn't I? I had a decent job."

"You still have a decent job," Jamie pointed out.

"I'm not talking about that. I'm talking about . . . What's the point of saying anything to you? You —" She abruptly halted and substituted glares for words.

"You mean your overall lifestyle?" Jamie asked.

"Don't talk down to me, mister, as if —" Glares were now replaced by more sobs. "You don't care about me, that's the trouble."

"Do you care for me?"

"Why the hell d'you think I'm here in this goddamn bed, eh? Why d'you think I'm putting up with this?" She slapped her belly and Jamie winced. "God! You're *so* dumb!"

"So why do you suppose I'm lying on this bed with you?"

"How the hell am I supposed to know how you feel?"

"By now, you should." Alice's response to this was to grab and to drag him onto her so that his body curved over hers. "Oh, Jamie, tell me it'll be okay, tell me nothing'll go wrong. I get so scared. I'm afraid it won't come out and they'll have to cut me open. I'm afraid it'll be dead."

"I can feel it moving right now. Feel it."

"I know. It kicks all the time. But maybe there'll be something wrong with it, maybe it'll have two heads, like a piglet my uncle showed me once."

"The doctor says everything's fine."

"Those guys make mistakes all the time. I'm not brave, Jamie, I'm a real coward." Alice went on to explain how necessity had compelled her always to wear a brave face, then recounted her agonies in the presence of men who joked about her figure and stood near her to tell obscene stories about women with oversized boobs and hairy cunts. "You don't know what I went through, Jamie. I wanted to cut my breasts off. Once I actually got out a knife and touched them."

"Don't," Jamie whispered. "Please don't." They made love as best they could, and afterwards smiled at each other like a pair of shamefaced, sweaty adolescents who had somehow managed to satisfy their rampant desire without taking the ultimate step. Perhaps it was her sobbing, combined with the gentle orgasmic trembling, that finally eased Alice's tension and allowed her to sit on the toilet and have a bowel movement. Afterwards, Jamie stood in the shower and soaped her.

"I feel better," she said. "I can't stand it when my innards get out of whack."

Later that same night, Jamie was awakened by a torrential rushing noise that surrounded, then overwhelmed him, like a great trans-Pacific wave breaking and pinning him down. For a while he lay perfectly still, listening to Alice's uneven breathing and to a distant pulsing that beat out the words "Come, come." Finally, he slowly and with extreme caution slid from the bed and padded along the hall to his old room where he crept to the window to peer out at the clear night sky. His fingers trembled as he inserted paper in Liz's old portable typewriter before he sat down to wait for the moment when the heaven-conceived words would tire of their dancing and consent to drop from the skies into his waiting hands.

When Alice awakened in the morning, thinking Jamie was already up and making breakfast, she went down to the kitchen, then through the first floor rooms before returning to the bedroom, where she saw Jamie's clothes piled on a chair. She realized then where he might be and going along the hall peeped into the room to see him sitting at his table, naked and absolutely still. She stood in the doorway, indecision showing in the way she chewed her lip and flexed her fingers. After a few minutes she went downstairs and telephoned Amanda to leave a message on the answering machine: "Lord Powell is working and must not be disturbed under any circumstance." Then she went into the kitchen, made herself breakfast and sat at the kitchen table to drink her morning coffee (She had chosen to ignore Amanda's advice and drank several cups a day). She felt terribly alone and a little afraid in the soundless house. She decided she would go to the office even though it was Saturday, but she found she was too upset to go through the motions of dressing, organizing the contents of her briefcase, and starting the car. An hour passed before she once again crept up the stairs and along the passage to peek into the room where Jamie sat, still naked, still motionless. Unable to bear the terrible uneasiness that possessed her as she looked at him, she went downstairs and dialled Amanda's number again. This time Amanda answered with a cheerful "Hello, Amanda Powell speaking." Alice told her she couldn't stand the silence of the house a minute longer and begged her to come over and talk to her. "Oh, you poor dear," Amanda chirped. "Don't worry. I have one errand to run, but after that I'll be right over."

Hearing Amanda's sympathetic voice and knowing she was prepared to rush over relieved Alice's anxiety for the moment. She showered, dressed, tidied the bedroom and returned to the kitchen where she sat and waited for Amanda's arrival.

Chapter 20

"I don't know what really happened," Amanda explained to Alice. It was evening, and they were in the sitting room with the curtains drawn and the lights on. "I was just a little girl . . . Mother was in Canada visiting Aunt Nanda. David and Liz were with her. Of course, Hiddie, Jamie and I cried when they left and complained to Muriel — our nursemaid — it wasn't fair that Liz and Davey got to go on a holiday and we didn't. But we quickly got over our disappointment. Muriel took us on outings and once on a picnic. I can remember going to a beach with her and our father. He drove us in Grandmother's old Daimler. It was a huge car, you could practically walk into it. We went across some fields and down a little valley to the beach. We had a lovely day. Then everything changed. Policemen came to the house . . . Muriel was taken away . . . Mother came back and Muriel was found guilty of killing Father. It's such a sad story." Amanda sniffed and hunted through her handbag.

"There's Kleenex in the bathroom," Alice offered.

"Muriel died in prison." Amanda wiped her eyes with a wad of crushed tissues she dug out of her handbag. "It was so sad. Jamie and I didn't understand what was going on. All we knew was that Muriel had left us. Mother cried a lot."

"But she was only your nursemaid."

"I know, but Muriel was a wonderful person. She'd been with us since Liz was born. Mother thought the world of her. She looked on Muriel as a younger sister."

"So what did this Muriel do? Make a play for your dad?"

"Oh no, nothing like that. Muriel was very proper. Muriel would never do anything like that."

"She must've done something!"

"Muriel would never do anything like that!" Amanda made it clear that the subject of the Powell children's nanny was sacrosanct.

"I thought I had the worst family in the world, but yours sounds just as bad," Alice said.

"I wouldn't say 'bad'," Amanda said, "more like 'unfortunate'. I should check on Annabelle and Christopher." After spending the day with Alice, Amanda had driven home to bring Annabelle and Christopher back to the Big House. They were now sleeping in her old room, after being lectured by Amanda on keeping quiet because Jamie was working.

"Your kids are kind of cute," Alice said.

"Aren't they?" Amanda left her chair. "Sometimes I wish Annabelle was prettier."

"Forget that," Alice said. "She'll get by. Take me. I was the ugliest girl in Saskatchewan and look where I am now . . . sitting in a comfortable chair in a nice house with a gut full of baby. I've even got a title I can pull out if some smart ass tries to put one over on me. Let me tell you something, Mandy . . ." This was the first time Alice had used her diminutive. "Good looks don't count for that much. What counts most is determination."

"That's not how girls think."

"Don't I know it! The silly little idiots swallow near everything a guy tells them, and where do they end up? In strip joints, or on the streets. So if Annabelle ever complains about not being pretty, take her around and show her the streetwalkers, show her the strip joints, then ask her if that's where she wants to end up, or worse, in a dumpster with her throat cut. For crissake! Get on the ball, Mandy, tell her that one day she'll meet a guy who'll be sharp enough to see there's a real cutie behind the plain face. Tell her what she's got inside her bra and panties is as good as what any film star's got in hers."

"I doubt whether there'd be much point to that." Amanda sighed copiously. "When I was fifteen I thought my chances of getting a man were zero."

"Mine were below zero. But look, Jamie's told me you've had more than your share."

Amanda produced a smile which she hoped embodied modesty and experience. "A few," she admitted.

"So, was one any different than another?"

"Well . . . Harry was different. But the others. I guess it's like trying out different brands of vanilla ice cream."

"Or beer."

"Or breakfast cereal."

"Or store cookies."

Amanda giggled and Alice grinned. "You know, I've always hoped I'd come across a man like Jamie," Amanda said.

"You don't mean you wanted to . . . ?"

"Of course not. Nothing like that. It's just that Jamie understands so much, at least about me. But then we grew up together. You never had a brother or sister?"

"Having me finished off my parents."

Amanda smiled politely in reply, left the room and climbed the stairs to the room where as a teenager she'd looked in the mirror each day, convinced no man would ever want to marry her because she wasn't slender and good-looking. (In those far-off days Amanda hadn't yet grasped that a man and woman could copulate without being married.) Annabelle and Christopher were lying tightly against each other, and as she leaned over to kiss them (How could she *not* kiss them?) Annabelle opened her eyes. "Mom, do I look like you when you were a kid?" she asked. The question surprised Amanda and she wondered momentarily if it were possible that Alice's and her comments had been telepathically communicated to Annabelle. But then she reminded herself how often children ask difficult questions when least expected, and so she whispered, "You're much, much nicer," a reply that seemed to satisfy Annabelle.

"Has Uncle Jamie finished his poems?"

"Not yet."

"Me and Chris sneaked a look at him."

"You shouldn't have." Amanda laid a reproving finger on Annabelle's cheek.

"He didn't see us. Does he always write his poems without clothes on?"

"I don't know, dear. I've never seen him writing poems."

Annabelle digested this, then said, "I don't like Alice much."

"You'll get used to her. Go to sleep."

"I have to pee."

Amanda escorted Annabelle along the hall to the bathroom adjacent to Jamie's room, waited while Annabelle used the toilet, then whispered, "Don't flush it. It makes too much noise." She ushered Annabelle back to the room and bed.

"You think Uncle Jamie's cold, Mom?"

"No."

"Everything okay?" Alice asked as Amanda came into the sitting room.

"They're fine. Annabelle had to pee. I told her to use your bathroom, though it won't matter if Jamie finishes working."

"Does he usually take this long?"

"I've never been here when he goes after the star words. Liz took care of everything."

"It's kind of nutty, isn't it?"

"Maybe it's not much different from the way other poets write."

"I wouldn't know. He's the only poet I've ever had dealings with, and I sure won't get mixed up with another."

"You and Jamie get along well, do you?"

"Pretty good."

"You could almost say you and Jamie were fated to meet."

"Fate! What a bunch of crap!" While Alice might ferociously deny the possibility that invisible forces determined the course of a person's life, in fact, deep down, she wasn't so sure.

"I suppose I meant coincidence. Like me meeting Harry."

"You mean chance."

"I suppose I do." Amanda did not care enough about fate, destiny, or chance to argue the point with Alice.

"Then for crissake say what you mean, instead of slinging bullshit." By this time, Amanda's social smile had frozen into a rigid grimace and once again she decided Alice was the most unpleasant, objectionable woman she'd ever met, worse even than certain nursing supervisors she'd known. Then Alice surprised her by apologizing: "Sorry, Mandy. Once I start shooting my mouth off, I can't stop. You've been real decent coming over. I'm not good company at the best of times, and since I got in the family way I can hardly bear myself. I'm so damned uncomfortable."

Amanda decided the moment had arrived to begin teaching Alice a few rules of social intercourse. "You shouldn't jump on people, Alice," she began.

At once Alice became defensive. "It's the only way I know how to behave. Anyway, I was just setting you straight. That never hurts anything. Well, does it?"

"No. But you're like people in those strange religious sects, Alice. You're so certain you're right and everybody else's wrong."

"I've got a right to my opinion."

"Of course I was taught to respect other people's opinions, even if I disagreed."

"Real liberal type, eh? The only opinions I ever had were ones knocked into me. That's the difference between us, Mandy. You got taught . . . I got facts rammed into me. The rest I discovered for myself."

"But we're in the same boat, Alice, trying to survive."

"Is this a lesson in how to act like Lady Alice, or what?"

"No. But I could help you not offend people so much. That's only if you want me to help." They looked at each other, one pair of blue eyes studying another pair.

"Y'know, Mandy, some ways we're alike. The difference is, you've learned how to be sneaky and I haven't."

"No. The difference is I like people, and you don't, especially men."

"You're right there. I detest them."

"Even Jamie?"

"I don't think of Jamie as a man, exactly. I think of him as being . . . well, what he is. All's I know, he's different from the rest of the assholes I've met in my life. And believe me, I've met some dillies."

"I heard something," Amanda said. "Listen." She ran into the hall and Alice lumbered after her. "The toilet," she whispered.

"Does that mean he's finished?" Alice whispered.

"Perhaps."

"Go and find out." Amanda nodded, slowly ascended the stairs and crept along the hall to peer into Jamie's room. The chair was empty, and she hurried into Liz's bedroom. That was empty too. She scooted along the hall to the back stairs and listened there. Then, as she ran back along the hall towards the main stairs, she heard a floor board in her old room creak and entered the room to find Jamie, looking down at Annabelle and Christopher.

"Jamie!" she urgently whispered. "Jamie!" He turned, saw her and joined her in the hall.

"What are the kids doing here?"

"Sh, sh," Amanda hissed. "I came to keep Alice company." He looked haggard, and Amanda was forcibly reminded of people she'd seen as a student nurse in hospital emergency wards: filthy, usually skinny, often dying human remnants discarded by a society that could no longer squeeze any profit from their labour. That had been Amanda's first encounter with human misery, and though their physical condition repelled her, her soft, sentimental nature responded to the agony of loneliness she saw in their eyes and she wanted to reach out and console them by pressing them against her breasts. Of course *that* wasn't permitted, although, in a roundabout way, her early experiences in emergency wards had set her on the path that ultimately led her to caring for the terminally ill. There was nothing macabre about her desire; she simply wanted to help people over the greatest hump in their lives: the necessity of death.

"Where's Alice?"

"Downstairs." Amanda noticed that Jamie's ribs bounced against his skin with each heart beat and that his male organ was rigid. She thought his erection must relate in some way to the agonizing process of netting star words, and its presence didn't especially bother her because from childhood she'd followed Jamie's physical development until he'd vanished into the steamy jungle of adolescence. But she did not want her children to wander out into the hall and be confronted by such a provocative sight. "Put something on, Jamie," she said. "You're shivering."

He looked down, became embarrassed, and turned away. "Yes, yes. Sorry. I didn't notice. Didn't know you were here."

"Shall I make you something to eat?"

"Yes." He moved away.

"You've finished working?" Amanda followed him along the hall to the bedroom.

"I'm through."

"You'll come down to the kitchen?"

"I couldn't believe my eyes when I saw the kids in your bed. I thought I'd been transported back in time, or I'd somehow got to your house. What's the time?"

"About midnight."

"How's Alice?"

"Fine."

"There's a lot Alice doesn't understand. And listen, Mandy, she's not as tough as she sounds."

"She's like most people, Jamie, she's built a shell around herself."

"Like clams and oysters, aren't we? Hard outside, defenceless inside."

"Put something on. You'll catch cold."

"Poor Liz . . . once her shell was pried open . . ." He started to enter the bedroom, then stopped. "We're lost in eternity. You know that, Mandy? We're drifting . . . it's almost unbearable." He went into the room and Amanda hurried down to let Alice know Jamie was hungry.

"Scrambled eggs, he likes those," Alice said. "He'll always eat scrambled eggs, toast and tea."

"Sometimes Jamie and I used to sneak down in the middle of the night and make sandwiches. All of us kids would, and practically empty the fridge. Mother would come into the kitchen and say, 'What in the world are you doing down here? Don't you realize it's the middle of the night?'" Amanda poured six beaten eggs into a frying pan. "And we always said, 'We thought it was the middle of the day, Mom.' Isn't that right, Jamie?" she called as Jamie, now showered and dressed, came into the kitchen.

"Remember what Mom said when she found us eating sandwiches in the middle of the night? She didn't really mind, did she? You know, I've come to realize how tolerant Mom was of all the silly things we did." Amanda put four pieces of bread into the toaster. "When you're a kid you take things for granted."

Jamie was sitting at one end of the long kitchen table, with Alice cater corner to him. "All I ever took for granted," Alice said, "was that parents ignored their kids and uncles fucked their nieces."

"So much depends on experience," Amanda said as she spooned eggs onto a plate, rapidly buttered the toast, placed the pieces around the eggs and delivered the plate to Jamie.

"You bet it does!" Alice took a piece of toast from the plate. "Which means you can't generalize."

"Let's not belabour the point," Jamie said. "Let's agree there's variation among the scum who're annealed to the planet." He forked eggs into his mouth.

"Jeez! All I do is point out there's differences in experience, and he reduces me to scum."

"It's metaphoric," Jamie said.

"That's even worse."

"I'm going to bed," Amanda said. "I'll take the kids home in the morning. 'Night."

"Thanks for the help," Alice called as Amanda went towards the back stairs and when Amanda turned to wave acknowledgement, she saw Alice reach out and take Jamie's hand.

Amanda slept in Hiddie's old bed and in the morning awoke to find Annabelle and Christopher curled beside her. The watch she'd worn throughout her years of nursing informed her the time was eight. When she told the children they'd be going home for breakfast, they objected: They wanted to eat with Jamie. In the end, they waited until Alice and Jamie appeared and as soon as they did Christopher said he and Annabelle had seen him naked.

"Weren't you cold?" Annabelle asked.

"I had on my deep-freeze suit," Jamie replied. "No shivering or shaking in that. It's an excellent way to beat the cold." Everyone was at the kitchen table, eating cereal, toast and jam.

"You didn't have any suit on," Annabelle said. "Me and Chris —"

"Chris and I."

"That's what I said. Me and Chris saw you, and you didn't have nothing on."

"Deep-freeze suits are transparent."

Annabelle appealed to her mother, but before Amanda could answer, Alice said, "He's bullshitting you." Annabelle looked first at Alice, then at Jamie, and the expression on her small, freckled face was one of disapproval. The word Alice had used only compounded the seriousness of Jamie's offence, and Annabelle let them know that not even a star-trapping poet was permitted to sit naked at his desk. What if Susan Jones found out?

"I get stars on my school work," Christopher proudly announced.

"I'm sure your stars are much superior to anything I ever get," Jamie replied.

"I get A's," Annabelle told them. "Don't I, Mom? Stars are for little kids."

"It's as important to get a star at six as it is to get an A at nine, or a Ph.D. at twenty- or thirty-nine," said Jamie. "It's a progression of events taking place in time, and without one event occurring the others can't happen. Which means they're all equally important. But one thing you have to remember is that no matter what you look at — at me, your Mom, Alice, Christopher, or up at the stars, you're always looking back in time. There's no place in our universe where you can look forward in time."

"For Christ's sake, don't confuse the poor kid. She doesn't know what you're talking about," Alice said. "Nor do I."

"Yes, I do," Annabelle asserted. "He means me and Chris'll get older, but I'll always know more'n Chris because I'll always be older and smarter than him."

"You can *imagine* a future," Amanda suggested.

"You can imagine anything, but no matter what you conceive of as your future, it'll get lost in the eternity of time because you've projected it into time past."

"Me and Chris are going to ride our bikes around the world. Then we'll cycle from the north pole to the south pole, won't we, Chris?" Christopher happily nodded his assent.

"We have to go," Amanda said. "Come on, kids."

They collected their belongings and, escorted by Jamie, walked to Amanda's car. "Did you catch any words?" Christopher asked Jamie.

"A few," Jamie said.

"What do they look like?" Annabelle said.

"A mess."

"Come on, kids, get in."

Amanda got into the car and started it. "Alice looks well," she said.

"Is that a professional assessment?" Jamie closed the car door and Amanda lowered the window.

"Just one woman looking at another and hazarding a guess."

"Thanks for your help, Mandy. See you, kids." He raised a hand, the children called goodbye, Amanda drove off and Jamie went back to the kitchen to stand by the table. "I hope things didn't go too badly," he said.

"So-so," Alice told him.

"I have a few things to tidy up."

"Sure. Go ahead." She looked and sounded indifferent. Jamie went to the kitchen entrance, then returned to the table.

"I thought you knew what would happen," he said.

"I do, I do. But I'm wondering what it'll be like when we have a baby around here, screaming its head off."

"We'll manage."

"I sure hope so." She got up and began gathering plates up. Nothing more was said, and after a brief pause Jamie left the room.

───※─────

Early in the afternoon Jamie went cycling and, after wandering around Stanley Park, went to Nanda's where he hunched in a chair across from her, moodily staring at the carpet. For a while, little was said. Tea was brought in and served, Jamie drank some, then put down the cup and appeared to forget about it. At last Nanda spoke: "So, you and Alice are settled in?"

"Yes."

"Is she comfortable there?"

"Oh, I guess. It's easy for me, I'm returning to what I've known for most of my life. But it's not so easy for her."

"My Lord?" Nanda's servants always used Jamie's title when addressing him. Now, a servant held a teapot over his cup.

"No more."

"That will be all, thank you." Nanda was meticulously polite to servants, although Jamie often wondered whether her unfailing courtesy was a product of indifference, not consideration; somewhere he had read that hangmen and torturers prided themselves on being punctilious. "How much longer before the baby's due?" she asked after the servants had left the room.

"A couple of months."

"Alice still works?"

"Yes. She can't stand having nothing to do."

"That's understandable."

"We'll need help when the baby comes. Do you think your people might know of someone . . . maybe someone to help with the baby and another for cooking and cleaning?"

"I'll inquire. Have you seen Hilda recently?"

"No. We have nothing to talk about except the weather."

"She was here last Sunday. Her usual monthly visit. I gather she's thinking of getting married."

"Well, let's hope the guy isn't another Max Logan."

"I agree, that marriage was unfortunate. But Hilda was in love with Max Logan. She's a lot like your mother, Jamie. Whenever Hilda visits, I have the eerie feeling that it's Winnie who's in the room with me. The likeness is amazing. Hiddie *had* to marry Max Logan, just as Winnie had to marry your father. That's how love operates, especially for women. I'm sure Winnie and Hilda knew the kind of man they were marrying. Winnie forgave your father again and again, and I expect Hilda did the same with Max. Forgiveness is something women excel at. It's either that, or transforming their love into hate. Winnie wanted to hate your father, but she could never manage to do it. She always loved him."

"Was my father so bad?"

"No. He was a disappointed man . . . he condemned himself because he came to believe his youthful desire to become a poet was nothing more than a pretentious charade. He wrote a good deal of poetry as a young man — he had special notebooks and he talked and read poetry all the time — I should know, I was on the receiving end. But in his early twenties he realized he was only repeating what he'd read and that his work wasn't original. He hated the idea of being second-rate. You're what your father dreamed of becoming, Jamie. A real, published poet."

"He didn't miss much," Jamie savagely replied.

"You say that because you've been successful. But your father lost self-respect, he began to drink, then went after Muriel — and other women too, I'm sure. He came to see me one afternoon and tried to explain how he felt. He said he had to get away or he'd fall apart. But I told him he was behaving despicably and sneered at him."

"I can't believe you'd do that, Nanda."

"But I did. I *wanted* to express contempt for him; it satisfied something in me, because up to that point he'd been so dominant in my life. It amazes me to think of it now, but I was raised to think of my brother as the more important child in our family. He was everything. I was nothing."

"So Father went down and you ended on top?"

"You could say that."

"Am I like my father?"

"No."

"You say Father wanted to escape his failures. So what's the difference between that and me wanting to escape my family because I feel they're suffocating what's inside me?"

"Jamie . . ."

"And now I'm stuck in *another* family." He jumped from the chair, and Nanda hastily stood to follow him.

"No one is forcing you to do anything, Jamie."

"No one forced Father to stay with Mother. He could have run."

"He had no money. It was all Winnie's." They arrived at the door to the room and stopped. "He came to me for help. I could have given him money. I had plenty. Instead, I treated him with contempt."

"He probably deserved it."

"Don't judge him harshly, Jamie." Nanda placed her hand over his to prevent him from opening the door.

"Why not? If we make fools of ourselves, we deserve what we get."

"Your father was desperate that day he came to Alderwood."

"How do you know I'm not desperate? How do you know I don't want to get on my bike and pedal off into nowhere? I sat in my room staring at the words . . . but they wouldn't come down. You hear me? They wouldn't come down! I'm through. Finished."

"Come and sit."

"Don't manufacture sympathy, Nanda."

"I don't intend to sympathize. I reserve my sympathy for those truly in need."

"You mean, I don't qualify as one of the starving millions you dole out charity to?"

"Jamie! I can't allow you to speak like that."

"You don't lose anything being altruistic . . . not one goddamn thing!"

Nanda could feel anger radiating from him, but she was unsure if it was directed at her, or at himself. "I'm sorry if I've said anything to offend you." She stepped away from the door.

"You haven't offended me, Aunt."

Nanda could always gauge where she stood with Jamie by the terms he used to address her. "Aunt" was the word he used when they were furthest apart. Still, she wasn't going to confront him: That was something she would never do. She had always deferred to her father and brother, except for that single occasion she'd turned her brother away, and now she must defer to Jamie because he was head of the Powell family. "For a minute I thought I had."

Jamie opened the door and went into the hall where a servant waited at the main entrance. Nanda followed him from the house onto the wide steps where his bike was propped against a pillar. "You remember William Blake's poem about pity and mercy?"

"I'm terribly ignorant about English literature. Is Blake the man who wrote 'Tiger, tiger'?"

" '. . . burning bright . . .' "

"Your father used to chant it. So, what did William Blake have to say about poor people?"

"He believed the upper class created poverty so that they could feel morally superior when they bestowed charity on the poor. 'Pity would be no more if we did not make somebody poor; and mercy no more could be, if all were as happy as we.' I realize you're not like that, Nanda, but others are. And another thing, have you ever thought where the billions flowing into the charitable organizations you support go? How much of it ends up with people who need it?"

"I often ask myself that question."

Jamie swung his leg over the bicycle seat. "Perhaps I'm mistaken, but I think charity morally degrades the giver and the receiver."

"You have a right to your opinion," Nanda coldly replied, "but I've never felt that helping suffering people degraded *me*."

"No doubt." Jamie decided to be polite.

"And I should point out that charity is part of our Christian heritage."

"Does that necessarily make it good? We have an unlimited ability to deceive ourselves, Aunt."

"I can't accept that, Jamie." Nanda was upset. "Are you accusing me of exploiting misery in order to satisfy something in myself?"

"I'm saying people are often most self-serving when they're being charitable." He smiled. "You could be one of the few exceptions to the rule. Take care, Nanda," he said as he pushed himself off and rode away.

"Come again, soon . . . and bring Alice with you," Nanda called after him. He acknowledged the invitation with the wave of a hand. She watched until he rounded the curve in the drive, thinking what a pity that such an intelligent man had so little sympathy for those less privileged than himself; while he, passing through the wrought-iron gate, thought it a pity that a woman as perceptive as Nanda failed to see that the ultimate purpose of charity, regardless of the presumed goodwill of those who give, was to maintain the status quo and make sure that beggars will never be choosers, and men and women, and children too, everywhere in the world will continue to flow unimpeded into factories, into brothels, and onto country roads and city streets ready to be exploited by those who hold and wield economic and political power.

He rode along the darkening streets, scurrying from street light to street light, sometimes racing across an intersection as the yellow light turned red. Inchoate thoughts dominated his mind: A single word would erupt to spark off streams of incomplete memories and fragmented ideas: . . . Natasha as a child competing with Liz for David's favours . . . oh, splendid imperious Liz! . . . As a boy he'd spent so much time, so it seemed now, trying to grab her attention, hoping she would bestow her favours on him, however briefly . . . but Liz was always preoccupied with David, whom he feared, especially when he silently stood and watched him and Amanda, appraising them . . . the day Amanda imposed her "Thou shalt not" upon him and demonstrated the tabooed act: how, where and why, then afterwards engaging him in tests to find out if he'd learned the lesson . . . and at Rhynewood, Muriel whom he'd loved . . . who'd always known there was more to him than his family realized . . . as a child, awakening in the dark, terrified, being lifted from his bed by Muriel, lying against her flannelette nightgown, listening to her heart beat while she told him he mustn't be afraid . . . Oh, the bewilderment of childhood! . . . the terrifying uncertainty that enters a child's life when a person upon whom he depends disappears from his life . . . he hadn't understood why Muriel had suddenly vanished, or why he and his sisters were removed from their known world: the house, gardens, fields and woodlands of Rhynewood, to settle in an unknown, alien city . . . then finally the day came when he considered himself mature enough (was he twelve? thirteen?) to know the truth and he'd demanded an explanation from Mother . . . Liz refused ever to speak of Muriel; Hiddie merely shrugged when he brought her name up; David advised, "Forget it, Jamie. It's just one more episode in your life"; and Amanda either cried or skidded around the question like a runner trying to avoid tumbling into an open cesspit . . . his nervousness in confronting his mother . . . his brutal adolescent arrogance . . . she'd broken down and incoherently told him the story . . . disgusted with what he'd heard . . . loathing for his father and pity for Muriel who'd allowed his father to seduce her: "taken Muriel behind some bushes" was what Mother said . . . then months later, while Mother was on holiday in Canada with Liz and Davey, Muriel had gone to his parents' bedroom . . . stabbed his father for reasons which were — so Mother said —"too complicated" for him to understand . . . maybe they were . . . It wasn't until his own personal

conflict — his unending battle between body and soul, for as early as sixteen he'd become obsessed by his unresolved poetic aspirations and frustrated sexual drives — had erupted that he was able, finally, to get a fix on
the relationship between Muriel and his parents: He saw Muriel as an es-
sentially innocent young woman utterly devoted to his mother; his father
as a morally weak, sensual man who callously manipulated Muriel's emotions and sexual desires to the point where she believed she must kill him
in order to protect the children under her care and eliminate from Mother's
life an evil which couldn't be extirpated by means other than death, or by
any person other than herself . . . *Muriel'd sacrificed her life* . . . because
she'd loved Mother and loved Liz, Davey, Hiddie, Amanda and himself as
she would her own children . . . Dear God! . . . Why had Muriel believed
her sacrifice a necessity when not one of them justified it? . . . . He shouted
at the empty street: Why? Why? Why?, then suddenly burst into laughter,
mocking himself for imagining there could possibly be an answer to his
question. He turned into a silent tree-lined street, pedalled along, then entered the driveway of his home, parked and locked his bike against a convenient wall and walked through the house to the kitchen where Alice sat,
waiting for him.

Chapter 21

"The girls and Max Junior have known Conrad for years," Hilda said. "He's very fond of the children, but naturally they'll keep the Logan name. It's well known in B.C."

"Hm-hm," Amanda agreed, thinking the Logan name was just notorious among a limited circle of women.

"Aunt Nanda's hosting the reception."

"That's helpful."

"Conrad's family'll be there. And all the McLeods are coming. We're inviting a few company people, too."

"You mean, you've actually invited the nobodies!" Amanda's sarcasm went unnoticed. Hilda was quite immune to little digs. To get through her tough outer skin you needed to insult her openly.

"And Conrad insists that since we're starting a new life together, we must have new things in our home."

"Of course," Amanda agreed. "You will need new silver, new china, new crystal, new everything." Amanda had gleaned the reason for Hilda's visit.

"I'd prefer stainless steel, but Conrad was brought up with monogrammed sterling silver. It would be useful to have both."

"I'm sure," Amanda said. An image of Hilda's putative husband chewing silver forks and knives flitted through her mind. She remembered having met Conrad Knight. He was a crony of Max Logan. She had wondered if Conrad would get around to propositioning her as Max once had and she recalled now how Max had told her that the best thing that could happen to any young woman was to be sexually indoctrinated by an older, experienced man — as Max put it, "by a guy who knows which ropes to pull".

"Will Louise and Jeanette be bridesmaids?"

"No. I'll ask Natasha to be my matron of honour. I would have preferred Liz, naturally."

"Naturally," Amanda agreed. "But why Natasha? Wouldn't Aunt Nanda be more appropriate? Natasha might think you were slighting her mother."

"I'll think about it. I suppose I could always ask you." Hilda didn't notice the anger that flushed Amanda's cheeks, but then she'd never taken into consideration anything her younger sister might have felt. Usually Amanda tolerated Hilda's offhand treatment of her, but this afternoon she experienced active dislike of her sister. Hiddie presented such a contrast to Liz who, even when she was bullying you, showed affection and spontaneous generosity which varied from hugs and kisses to gifts of perfume, an elegant blouse or silk scarf she'd seen in the window of an exclusive boutique. Being with Hiddie served to magnify Liz's generosity and the degree to which she'd given of herself to the family — to David, she gave herself; to Jamie, her support and time; to Hilda, money following Max's death before help from Nanda was forthcoming; and for herself, always affection and unending advice. Dearest Liz, how she missed her, especially now, as she contrasted Liz's thoughtfulness to Hiddie's total preoccupation with herself and her own affairs. Now that Liz was gone Amanda tended to remember the best of her, infusing her memories with more import than they warranted and going so far as to speculate that Liz might have sacrificed herself to David because she thought that if she didn't give herself to him, his marriage couldn't be sustained. She remembered Jamie once saying that Liz had the makings of a heroine in a Greek tragedy, except for her conscious realization that her fate was cosmically ordained. It was a pity, she thought, that Liz had not achieved quite that degree of grandeur, for really and truly she deserved it.

"You seem preoccupied, Mandy," Hilda said. "What are you thinking about?"

"About Liz. Remembering how generous she was."

"Was she? I never noticed."

"She helped you," Amanda angrily said.

"Oh that."

"Yes. That."

"What in the world's the matter with you, Mandy? I've come to give you good news, and all you do is snap at me. Where are the children?"

"They're cycling."

"You allow them to go out alone?"

"They're with a young man from the shop where I got their bicycles."

"You surprise me, Mandy. I'd never allow Max Junior and the girls to go off with a stranger."

"He's not a stranger."

"Well, whoever he is, I'd certainly check him out."

"I have."

"Well, make sure he's not a pederast. There's a lot around."

"I'm quite sure he's not."

"Hm!"

Hilda's expression of doubt escalated Amanda's irritation to an explosive level. "For God's sake, Hiddie! You were married to a guy who dressed up his daughters and exhibited them to his dirty-minded pals! You've got no right to tell me I'm not looking after my kids!"

"Max did no such thing!" Hilda refuted.

"Oh no? Well, let me tell you the day Max propositioned me he told me twelve-year-olds were fair game."

"That's ridiculous! Max was a kind-hearted man who loved women and couldn't help himself from issuing invitations for sex. It meant nothing."

"Except you only had sex with him every three months or so. Right?"

Hilda actually smiled. "Quiz, quiz, quiz. You know what your problem is, Mandy? You've never gotten over how you wormed your way into a marriage with a man who didn't want you . . . and now you pry into other women's lives, hoping to discover they've been as miserable as you have. Well, let me tell you something." A heavy blush settled on Hilda's face and neck. "I had a good relationship with Max. Which is as far as I'm prepared to go with you, because my private life is none of your business."

Hilda grabbed her handbag and made for the front door, trailed by Amanda who couldn't resist one final dig. "Nevertheless I'm supposed to provide you with an expensive wedding present? Right?"

Hilda turned on her. "I don't care what you do," she snapped. "I don't know what's the matter with you today, but don't bother to attend the reception if you can't be more pleasant."

Amanda watched her leave, then telephoned Natasha. "I've just had a set-to with Hiddie," she said. She was in the middle of the narration when footsteps clattered along the hall and Annabelle rushed in, followed by Christopher and Donald Gowan, the young man from the bike shop. "I have to go, Tashie, the kids've just got back from cycling."

"He did it, Mom!" Annabelle shrieked, "He did it! Chris rode to the top of the hill!" The children's oversized helmets lent piquancy to their small faces; Amanda thought they looked like storybook elves peeping from beneath toadstools.

"That's wonderful, Chris."

"We stopped and changed gears at the bottom of the hill," Don explained. "I dunno why we didn't think of it before. Chris suggested it."

"*Me* and Chris did," Annabelle corrected. "Don rode behind and gave Chris a push up the really steep part. But that's all right, isn't it, Don? That's not cheating, is it?"

"Sure is all right!" Don agreed. Amanda had had several conversations with Don and knew he was a third-year biology student at the university, worked part-time in the bike shop, and had been terrified when he first discovered his sexual orientation. He was the only male of three children and knew he'd never be able to meet his parents' expectation that he marry and have a family. This had come out when Amanda had tried to seduce him.

"So, Chris finally did it, eh? I knew he would. I knew he'd master that hill. Want to stay for a sandwich, Don?"

As always, the young man demurred at first, then after being coaxed by Annabelle and Christopher, sat down to eat with them. Annabelle did most of the talking while Christopher, like a true champion, modestly acknowledged the accolades.

"We rode past the gate to Aunt Nanda's house," Annabelle said. "Don didn't believe it was our great-aunt's house."

"The next time you cycle that way, call in. She'd be pleased to see the children."

"I'll tell her I can ride up hills," Christopher said.

"We went past the university," Annabelle announced.

"We saw Uncle David," Christopher told her. "We waved at him, but he didn't see us."

As Amanda heard David's name she remembered the note she'd written, which still lay in the drawer. "David's in the chemistry department. David Powell, you may know him."

"I took a course from him. Tall, good-looking guy."

"Do you know our Uncle Jamie?" Christopher asked Don.

"No."

"My brother," Amanda explained. "He's a poet, he teaches at Langara."

"I don't know many people," Don told them. "I'm an average sort of guy, trying to get my degree and not sure I'll make it."

"You'll make it," Amanda assured him. "If I can get a degree, anybody can." She smiled at him and wondered if she should make another attempt to get him into bed. It was such a pity that she went against his grain, so to speak, but perhaps he'd had one or two unsatisfactory sexual experiences with women and had reached the wrong conclusion. It was easy to do that;

she, for example, while married to Bernard had concluded she was sexually frigid, which was as far from the truth as the distance separating the north and south poles.

When Don got up to leave, Amanda accompanied him to the door where she laid a detaining hand on his arm and said they must get together soon for a long chat. "There's so much I want to know about you. I'm incredibly curious about everyone I meet. I like to find out everything about them, absolutely everything."

"There's not much to tell about me," he replied.

"Oh, you'd be surprised." She squeezed his hand, waved goodbye and returned to the kitchen. "Listen kids, I've got to run a short errand. I'll take you to the library on my way." She took out the note she had written to David. "Aunt Hilda's getting married. That means we'll have to shop for a wedding present, so while you're at the library try to think up ideas for a present. You could write out a list. And Chris, you'd better take off your helmet."

"Okay," he said reluctantly.

When they reached the library she reminded them to go straight to the children's section, then blew them a kiss. "We'll go to Oakridge Mall when I get back and see what's there. And we'll eat at the White Spot. See you soon." While driving to the university, she reviewed techniques she might deploy to get Don into bed with her: She might ask how he could be so sure of his sexual preference. As a future scientist, he must know that extensive data must be assembled, collated and interpreted before any definitive conclusion can ever be reached. It followed that her bed would be an ideal location in which to undertake an investigation. Who could say what might happen once he was there? Why, it might prove to be a wonderful experience! Of course she need not focus wholly on Don Gowan: She had hospital connections, and if they didn't produce a willing intern or resident, she could always drift into a bar or club. But for the moment she'd concentrate on Don. What a nuisance sex was. When it first appeared in your life, you hardly knew what was happening: You experienced vague yearnings that made you sigh and act moody and sentimental. Later, you longed for someone to fill the great emptiness you felt inside your body, and while you didn't know what or whom you wanted, still you spent years searching for it, hoping the unknown would suddenly materialize to give you everything your woman's heart and body desired. Then suddenly one day you became aware of small lines on your face and an occasional gray strand in your hair, which you immediately excised as a surgeon does a cancer. After that, you examined your body daily in the bathroom mirror and while you were saddened to see your breasts lose their youthful firmness, you were pleased to see that your body hadn't noticeably aged. The real problem was, most men regarded women over thirty as so much dead mutton. She'd once nursed an eighty-five-year-old retired professor of anthropology who'd told her that her sexual drive had remained as active in her seventies as it had been in youth, but while society found it acceptable for men in their sixties and seventies to boast of continued potency, it forced women to feel ashamed of theirs. It was all due to the ancient association between female sexuality and child-bearing, she'd explained, which meant post-menopausal women inevitably lost rights to sexuality, for if they continued sexual activity, they would deprive younger women of male seed which was required for maintenance of the species. At the time, Amanda'd only half-believed the dying woman's words, but her own grey hairs and facial wrinkles had finally forced realization of her own aging and explained in part why it was increasingly difficult for her to tend terminally ill patients and why she took longer and longer breaks between jobs. But she missed the social contact, especially meeting her patients' sons and grandsons who, with surprising frequency, ended up in her bed. She regarded these sexual exchanges as perquisites of her demanding, stressful job.

As she drove along, she told herself it was unreasonable for a person to expect to get everything in life she wanted; indeed, she was among the most fortunate of people, for she had a secure income, good health, and two children who loved her in spite of her limitations. Yet memories of her months with Harry Greene told her something was missing from her life and the absence of this essential ingredient probably explained why she'd carped at Hiddie: She was envious Hiddie was getting married and would have a man in her bed every night. Yet she had no right to be jealous. After all, Hiddie hadn't had an easy time of it, trying to maintain her social position while raising three children and holding down a demanding job. She ought to be ashamed, she told herself, acting so spitefully, and because she knew she'd never be able to bring herself to apologize for what she'd said, she decided to make up for it by presenting Hiddie with an extra-special wedding gift. She glanced at the envelope resting on the passenger seat beside her, and it suddenly became clear to her that she had no right to interfere in David's life. She drew into the curb, opened the note and read the few lines she had written. What had she imagined the message would accomplish? Did she intend to intensify David's guilt? Was she hoping Natasha would find out about Liz and that a catastrophic explosion would then take place in her supposedly idyllic life? Was it possible that she was not only envious of Natasha, but also of Liz, because the passion required to break down social and moral taboos and drive her into her half-brother's arms was more powerful than anything she herself had experienced? Was Liz's passion so great that she had no choice but to surrender to it, or else perish? It must have been something like that — some awful, terrifying necessity, like total surrender to a drug — a requirement that overwhelmed normal, everyday needs — for surely David wouldn't have risked destruction of his marriage merely to satisfy amatory inquisitiveness, nor Liz, her independence, just to extend the proprietary rights of childhood into adulthood. And what about herself? Had the feelings of love, resentment and envy she'd had as a child remained unchanged? the awe of Liz? caution with David? resentment with Hilda? love for Jamie? You could flatter yourself that you'd discarded childhood emotions, but the fact was, most people carried them forward into adulthood. How could any individual ever discard those things which formed the very person they'd become? She could see Liz now, rushing around the gardens at Rhynewood, organizing their games as she wanted them to be played, David supporting her, Hilda resentfully complying with orders, herself eagerly obeying to curry favour, and Jamie, not really caring how they were played, or who directed them. But what about Natasha? Oh yes, she was there too, hovering on the sidelines, quietly watching, waiting for a chance to sneak in and capture David. And she'd nearly succeeded, too, when she became pregnant the first time she and David had sexual intercourse, thereby forcing Aunt Nanda and her mother, who may have thought first cousins oughtn't to marry, to consent to the marriage. For that matter, everyone in the family had reached differing decisions about what was necessary in their lives, so why should she worry about what happened to them? Why should she care? They had cut the cloth of life in the pattern they believed best suited them and she was under no obligation to point out their mistakes. She'd accepted responsibility for her own mistakes — her bad marriage, leaving Harry — but she wasn't obliged to take responsibility for correcting errors made by anybody else. She lifted the envelope, shredded it and the note, opened the window, and as she turned the car around, let the scraps of paper float from her hand and disappear into the wind.

"Okay, where's that list of ideas?" she laughed as she walked into the children's section. "Let's get going, kids. We've got important things to do. We must put aside all unnecessary matters and concentrate our energies on the necessities of life. Come on, come on, let's go."

Chapter 22

"What should we do, Jamie?" Amanda whispered. "Natasha won't see me."

"What did she say when she phoned?"

"Something about David not coming home. She was crying and I had trouble hearing the words. Then she hung up, so I thought I'd better go over and see what was wrong. But when I got there, the maid told me Natasha wouldn't see me. What's happening, Jamie? What's going on?"

They were standing in Amanda's living room, their postures more suggestive of a pair of foes engaged in armistice negotiations than a brother and sister discussing a family matter.

"You should have telephoned David, not me."

"I tried to! I called his office and left a message there. I got somebody to go to the lab, but he wasn't there either. I'm sorry if I interrupted something important, but there was nobody else."

Jamie moved as if he intended to leave, then turned, and there was cold fury in his voice when he harshly said: "Hasn't it occurred to you that it was your damn tittle-tattle that sparked this off?"

"My . . . ?"

"Has it never occurred to you people want to be left alone? Well, has it?"

For a few seconds, it seemed as if Amanda would react as usual and begin crying. Instead, her face lost its normal blush, then reddened intensely as anger flowed through her body. "That is not true, Jamie — and you know it!"

"It's not? Well, let me remind you of something. I explicitly asked you to stay away from Alice. And what did you do? You deliberately concocted a scheme to contact her."

"Alice telephoned *me*, she asked me to meet her."

"Only after you'd scared her, behaving like a cop, asking why she was sitting in a parked car in the street."

"How can you say that, Jamie? How can you?"

"Because somebody has to say it! Then, when she got pregnant and came for advice, what did you do? You got together with Liz and put pressure on her to have the baby, though you knew she'd come to you about getting an abortion."

"I can't believe you're saying these horrible things! I can't believe it! I told Alice she could get an abortion if that's what she wanted. I told her to ask her doctor."

"Oh sure, you did that. And you also set Liz after me, and when I told her what Liz had said, she assumed I wanted her to have the child."

Amanda collapsed into a chair, held her hands over her face, then as rapidly removed them to say: "None of it is true, Jamie. You want someone to blame because things aren't going well for you."

"So what did you do next? Just think for a minute what you did. What you did next was tell me about David and Liz. But telling me wasn't good enough, you had to tell David that you'd told me."

"I confided in you because I couldn't keep it inside any longer."

"Oh sure, you had to let me know that you knew all the intimate secrets of Liz's life. But even *that* wasn't good enough for you! You had to put the screws on David too. Apparently it never entered your head David might tell Liz we knew."

"That's not right, Jamie. I didn't say anything about Liz and David until *after* Liz had gone. I'd known about it for years, but Liz knew I'd never tell anyone. She never discussed it with me."

"Why the hell would she talk to you, or ask your opinion, when she knew damn well the damage you could do with your unending tittle-tattle?"

"Are you suggesting I'm responsible for Liz's death? Is that what you're saying, Jamie?" Amanda left the chair to stand close to him, looking directly into his eyes. "If it is, you can leave right now, because I never want to see or speak to you again." Brother and sister stared at each other, silently battling, erasing memories and pleasures they'd experienced together over all the years of their lives. Finally Jamie looked away.

"Sorry, Mandy," he mumbled. "Sorry. As usual, I'm trying to dump my pent-up mind-sewage on you. Forgive and forget, eh?"

Amanda backed away from him before answering. "I'll forgive, but I don't know about forget. I've always thought you were the one person I could trust." She sat on the couch, turning her face away.

"Your trust was probably misplaced anyway," Jamie said.

"I guess it was." She felt the cushions move as he joined her on the couch. "Remember how we used to sit side by side when we were kids? Remember how we told secrets?" She felt him move until his hip touched hers. He reached out to clasp her hand. She tried to pull away, but when he refused to release her hand she acquiesced and let it lie in his. "I'm so utterly wretched, Mandy." She glanced at him and momentarily smiled before looking away again. "But I'm not so far gone I'm unaware of what I say, so if I've hurt you, I've done it consciously. I suppose I wanted to share my frustration and fear. Mandy, you're the only person I'll ever be able to talk to. I can't tell Alice what I'm feeling because she has enough fears of her own to cope with. Besides, she wouldn't understand, even though she wants to. It's terribly important to Alice that she be the person who sympathizes with me — not someone in the family. And I don't blame her for not understanding my situation. Thousands of things are beyond my understanding."

"Me too."

"But you've never pretended to understand things, that's the difference. I think maybe I have. Listen Mandy, it looks like I may have to quit writing. I've managed to turn out two volumes. Maybe that's enough. I'd probably be repeating myself anyway, and who wants that? There must be a limit to what star words can do for any poet. I think maybe I've reached my limit. I've laid out my few itty-bitty ideas — they're all I'm ever likely to have. I'd have to switch forms and pretend I've created something new, something never before seen. Other poets — artists too, especially painters — do it all the time. I'd be forced to write a half-baked novel or, God help me, short stories, and I might even get decent reviews because reviewers would know I might be asked to review stuff they churn out. But they'd let me know they were waiting for the cool, cool waters of another volume of geometric poems. I can see it all so clearly, Mandy. And I won't do it. I won't. I won't debase myself. I won't let anybody crucify me!"

Amanda reassuringly squeezed his hand. There was really nothing else she could do. From the time Jamie had first begun to talk, she had been his confidante, his source of solace. (As a plump adolescent, she'd wondered if everything Jamie had confided in her had been transformed into body fat.) "Jamie, you've already accomplished more than most people do in a lifetime. You don't have to explain or justify anything."

Without realizing it, they had moved on the couch so that their bodies were now touching. Amanda slipped her hand from his and put her arm around him, and they sat in close, companionable, restorative silence. Finally Jamie said, "Maybe I'll call in at Natasha's on my way home."

Amanda put her head on his shoulder. "I didn't mean what I said about never speaking to you again."

Jamie slipped his arm around her shoulders and hugged her. "I'd better go." Amanda smudged one of her tear-dampened kisses on his cheek, then accompanied him to the door and asked where his bike was. "I'm using Alice's car. In case I have to tear home."

"I'd forgotten you could drive."

"I possess the same driving gene as every other North American, and have a licence to prove it."

"Phone me if you find out anything?" He got into the car. "Jamie, you think I should try to get in touch with David?"

"How can you, if you don't know where he is?" He started the motor, waved, then drove off. Amanda shivered, as if to throw off her uneasiness, went back into the house where she once again dialled David's university number, replaced the phone when there was no answer, then set about making herself a pot of tea and some toast. The meeting with Jamie had been stressful, even frightening, especially when he'd accused her of being responsible for Liz's death. Amanda knew she would never forget that terrible moment when it had seemed as though a relationship she thought indestructible was being torn asunder. How could Jamie accuse her of driving Liz to her death? Or even *think* such a thing! It was scary. Sure, she realized that things Jamie said were because of his own pain and stress, but nevertheless it revealed a facet of her brother she hadn't known before. The more she thought about the episode, the further away she got from her initial shock, the more upset she became. That he worried about Alice and was frustrated by his inability to capture more galactic words was understandable, but he had gone too far: He'd twisted things in order to make it seem that she, Amanda, was responsible for things that had happened in the past and what might happen in the future. Of course, people habitually rearranged their histories — she did it herself — but it had never occurred to her that Jamie would imagine that her gossip was the immediate cause of Liz's death and exonerate David of all responsibility. After all, David was the one who, in the role of epicure, savoured majestic Liz, then moved on to enjoy exotic Natasha, sampling each woman much like a wine-taster assesses the colour of wine, smells it, then sips and rolls it around in his mouth before spitting it out and passing judgement. Yet that wasn't entirely fair to David: She knew he was racked by love for both women. Still, she had warned him, hadn't she, that day they'd had lunch, when he'd tried to intimidate her? Oh yes, she'd looked David straight in the eye and stood up for herself. Maybe she'd kowtowed to her brothers and sisters in the past, maybe she'd deferred to David and allowed Jamie to judge her by revealing her innermost thoughts. For all she knew, Jamie was criticizing her right now, or perhaps he and Natasha were laughing about her, because beneath her cousin's reticence and politeness she'd always thought Natasha felt contempt for because she was neither beautiful nor wealthy.

She experienced a surge of anger as she remembered her lifelong appeasement of her siblings. She was the family clown, the scatterbrain, the little girl who had moved from messing her underpants in childhood to messing up her life as an adult. And she could see how willingly she'd undertaken the role assigned her. Of necessity, a family selected one of its members as clown so that they'd always have someone to deride and laugh at in order to retain or restore confidence in themselves. But that was over! From this minute forward to the end of her life she would be as harsh and critical of her family as they'd been of her. No one, not even Jamie, had sympathized with her during her awful years with Bernard; not one person had expressed sympathy during the months of torment following her agonizing separation from Harry. Whatever happened to her was regarded as yet another example of her silly blundering through life. Once, Liz openly doubted if she had what it took to be a competent nurse, which was terribly hurtful and unfair because her professional training far exceeded Liz's. Remembering how in the past she'd submissively bowed her head and accepted her siblings' judgement filled her with fury. How could she have been so stupid, so willing to be laughed at, so willing to be their lickspittle? Well, no more! From now on, she'd live her own life; there'd be no more prolonged telephone chats and afternoon visits to gossip about family matters. She was a changed woman. She went into the hall and examined herself in the mirror to see if her commitment to change had altered her appearance, but there was nothing different to see, except perhaps a slight compression of her lips, which she thought made her look more unattractive than ever. She was so preoccupied with examining her face for evidence of her new resolve that she didn't immediately hear the doorbell, though it was situated on the wall behind her. "Damn!" she muttered and went to open the door. Standing outside, his back to her, was David.

"David! What're you doing here?" she asked. This was a first. David had never condescended (as Amanda thought of it) to visit her before.

"May I come in?" He looked exhausted.

"I didn't expect to see you here. Sure, come in."

"I suddenly thought of you." David stepped past her and went into the living room. "You're the only person left I can talk to."

"I'll take your raincoat." He removed the coat and handed it to Amanda who walked back into the hall to hang it on the coat rack while he continued talking.

"I could always talk to Liz. All my life I've talked to Liz about my problems, about things that bothered me . . . whether I'd be able to complete my doctoral work . . . whether I had what it takes to make a go of it in chemistry. But that was before the other happened . . . before I went to Chalk River, before Natasha appeared . . . if I'd known about Liz then . . ."

"I'll make coffee," Amanda said. "We can sit in the kitchen." He obediently followed her to stand by the kitchen table. "Do sit," Amanda said, and at once he pulled out a chair and sat down.

"The physical part didn't change our relationship much. It wasn't that important, only an extension of our close relationship as children — a confirmation of what'd always existed between us. I'm not denying that the physical existed, don't misunderstand me: It was crucial in the sense that it removed barriers that may have developed between us, but it wasn't a sexual relationship, not like what exists between me and Natasha. Of course I love Natasha, but if I'd known about my feelings for Liz before I agreed to marry Natasha . . ."

"Natasha'll appreciate that," Amanda murmured.

David continued as though she hadn't spoken. "Liz allowed me to express my fears, to acknowledge my limitations, something I could never do with Natasha. Never. I could tell Liz what I'd discovered about myself — that I was deficient in originality. She understood and didn't blame me. But I couldn't tell Natasha; I couldn't reveal any weakness to her. And Liz revealed her weaknesses to me. You — and everybody else — saw her as a strong, authoritative person, but she wasn't really like that. She was very vulnerable; that's why she couldn't let me go. After Muriel was gone, I was the only one who understood just how fragile Liz really was. She talked about getting back into politics, but I don't think she could've made it. She knew it, and so did I; but I never imagined knowing that would drive her to . . . I have to talk to someone about this."

"You have to explain things to Natasha."

"I can't. I'm afraid of what might happen. I've not been able to go home."

"So that's why Natasha was practically hysterical. I called Jamie and he's gone to see her."

"You had no right to do that."

"For a change, why not think about what *you* had no right to do? Why not stop whining about how much you miss Liz? Haven't you got the guts to tell your wife that all the while she was bragging about her perfect marriage you were sneaking off and fucking your sister?"

"I'll go." David brushed past her, and she could feel his body shaking as he went by.

Amanda followed him into the hall. "Let me tell you something, David. If you don't tell Natasha, I will, because I'm sick and tired of having her compare her wonderful life to my miserable existence." David had halted in the doorway and turned to watch her. "So you choose."

"You're really a vicious person, aren't you?" he said. "I thought maybe, for once, you could rise above the level of petty gossip." He left without his raincoat. Amanda watched him drive away, closed and locked the front door, then took the raincoat (it was new and expensive) and stuffed it into the garbage. She did not want to be reminded of the unpleasant scene with David each time she walked along the hall. (That she could have hung the coat in a closet did not occur to her.) Afterwards, she hunted through the kitchen cupboards until she located a bottle of rye, which she kept to loosen up timid lovers. Amanda had seen what damage alcohol can do to men and women and seldom drank, a highball or two at family celebrations. She poured the whisky and as she raised the glass, her hand trembled so that some of the contents spilled. A line of sweat appeared on her forehead, and for a moment she thought she was about to faint. Then the spasm passed, and she was able to lift and drink from the glass. You pay a price for trying to be confident and brave, she told herself, especially when you've been in a subservient position all your life. A little practice would be needed before she would be able to appear as strong and assertive as Liz. Because David was wrong about Liz, quite wrong. Liz had been strong, much stronger than David, but he judged her by the standards he used to assess himself. Maybe Liz seemed vulnerable because she opened her thighs to him — for a woman, the ultimate surrender. But, like Jamie, David was in the process of recasting his own history, and would, no doubt, hold Liz responsible from now on for whatever went wrong in his life. People always blamed those who've been closest to them for their own failures. Oh yes, she'd seen lots of people passing the buck. Maybe Liz had killed herself because she had nowhere to pass the buck and was unable to bear looking into her future, or if she tried to see ahead, all she could imagine was her descent into a private hell.

Amanda drained the glass, while reminding herself that Liz, being alone so much, had undoubtedly sat like this at a table with a bottle and glass, although she, unlike Liz, was not alone: She had Annabelle and Christopher. She continued to sit for a moment, then stood and put the bottle into a cupboard and washed out the glass.

Jamie stood by a window in Natasha's living room, looking out on the rain-slick patio, waiting to learn if Natasha would see him. The maid, looking apprehensive, had shown him into the room after he'd said: "Tell Mrs. Powell it's important for me to speak with her. I am her brother, Lord Benjamin Powell." The maid was used to admitting Jamie to the house, but she'd never before heard him talk like this. After a few minutes, a brief, nervous cough let him know Natasha had entered the room.

"Amanda telephoned me at the college," he said.

"I wish she hadn't."

"Well, she did. So, why did you call her?"

"Nothing, it's nothing."

"For God's sake, Tashie. I'm dragged out in the middle of class and informed there's an emergency. I rush to Amanda's where she tells me you've phoned, that you're hysterical, and will I try to find out what's going on. So she's either suffering from an overdose of imagination, or you're pretending nothing's wrong. Which of the two is it? Better tell me, because I don't have any time to waste."

"I didn't ask you to come here." Natasha's voice was tight with reserve.

"That's enough for me." Jamie made for the door without looking at her.

As he turned the door handle Natasha whispered, "David didn't come home last night." He turned, leaned against the door and watched Natasha's facade crumble. "He didn't call. I don't know where he is. I don't know what's wrong." She ran to the couch, flopped onto it and hid her face in the pillows. Jamie recrossed the room to sit and listen to Natasha say she didn't know what was wrong, or what she'd done to upset David.

"You haven't done anything," Jamie said.

"I must have." She turned her head to look at him and he saw she'd been transformed from a poised woman into a wailing, confused child. "I must have." She sniffed and wiped her face on a cushion. "You needn't stay. I can manage."

"No doubt you can." He paused then said, "Has David spoken to you?"

"What? Spoken to me about what?" She began sobbing again and hid her face in the cushion.

"Have you talked to your mother?"

"I don't want Mother to know about this. It would upset her."

"Being upset once in a while doesn't hurt anyone."

"She mustn't know. She doesn't like David."

"How do you know that?"

"The way she talks about him, and how she behaves with him. You don't know Mother like I do."

"Probably not. Until a few minutes ago I thought I knew you."

"David won't talk to me any more. He hates me." She sprawled on the couch as though abandoning all reason and rectitude.

"Has he said he hates you?"

"He doesn't have to say it, I know it."

"Have you asked him why he's upset?"

"Of course I have. But he's been so distant . . . I feel he's moving away from me."

Jamie looked at Natasha's slouched body, past the cushions that covered her head, over the arm of the couch, at the door which was now opening to admit David. Jamie stood, crossed to the door, nodded as he passed David, and then left the house.

"I can't bear it, I can't bear it," Natasha sobbed. When there was no response she looked around, saw the empty chair, sat up, and saw David. Colour drained from her face and she began whimpering, "Where have you been, where have you been?"

"I have to tell you something," David said. He did not move from his position by the closed door.

"I've been so frightened. Where were you?"

"You have to know something . . . something about me and Liz." Natasha stopped whimpering and leaned forward, hands on her knees, tense and watchful. "From the time you and I got married, Liz and I —" He got no further.

Natasha launched herself at him, shrieking, "I'll kill her! I'll kill you!" David didn't try to defend himself, other than to close his eyes as her fingernails ripped at his face while she shouted, "I'll kill her! I'll kill you!" As he sank to his knees Natasha ran to a table, snatched up a vase of flowers, then raced back to hurl it at his bowed head. He slumped forward onto his hands and knees, while she, after looking around, rushed across the room and dragged a heavy wrought-iron standard lamp to where he crouched. "I'll kill her! I'll kill you!" she screamed again as she smashed the lamp down on him. The shade split, the large bulb shattered and glass shards struck his neck and hair. Natasha raised what was left of the lamp to vent her rage once more, but her body suddenly froze, then convulsed, and she looked around the room as though just awakened from sleep. "David!" she cried, then dropped the lamp, slumped to her knees and reached out to touch him with a trembling hand. "David, David," she whispered. She touched his head, then withdrew her hand and stared at the blood on it. Slowly, very slowly, she rolled him over and gasped when she saw his face transformed into a bloody mask. "Oh, David, oh, David." She began to cry and bit her clenched fist to stifle her sobs. Convinced she'd killed him, she kept repeating his name: "David, David." It was true: People did kill what they loved most, she'd just proved that, because she'd loved David more than anyone, more than her mother, more than her passion flowers. She had killed him because he'd allowed Liz to steal something which was exclusively hers. Yet hadn't she always known Liz was capable of grabbing what she wanted? Hadn't Liz always believed she "owned" everyone in the family and could do as she pleased with them, especially David? Her hand brushed David's chest and she could feel his heart steadily beating: He was alive! She reared up as rage flooded through her, arousing the impulse to attack again. Yes, David deserved to be hurt, he deserved even to die because he had betrayed her, because he'd forgotten she was the one essential person in his life.

David licked his lips and began speaking. "I want to explain."

"I don't want explanations!" she screamed. "I wish I'd killed her! And you too!"

"Go ahead."

"What do you mean, go ahead?"

"Kill me. If that's what you want."

"I trusted you! I never withheld anything from you!" She wanted to inflict pain on him, she desired to humiliate and torture him to the point where he would beg for mercy; yet she wanted, too, to wash the blood from his face and apply a magical balm that would heal him immediately. She wanted him to beg for forgiveness, she wanted him to tell her he'd been coerced by Liz, or blackmailed . . . She closed her mind to the thought that he'd compared her to Liz, that he'd given and received more with Liz than with her. No, she would not think of that, she could not bear to think of that. She had surrendered herself to him, every inch of her body, every part of her inner self while he was carrying on with his sister. She hated him! She loathed him! "I'll never trust you again. Everything was lies. Lies! Lies!"

"I never lied to you."

"What was it then?"

"Tashie . . ."

"Don't use that name!"

"Natasha . . ." He tried to sit up and winced when he put pressure on his right arm. "There's something wrong with my shoulder," he said.

Natasha wanted to say she didn't care if every bone in his body was broken, but years of loving him defeated her. She wanted to tell him he must leave her home, but instead she assisted him to rise and helped him to a chair.

"I think it's broken," he said, after he had touched his shoulder. "I didn't realize I was so fragile."

"I'll call Dr. Gerard." She went to the door, then stopped. "I wanted to kill you," she said. "I can't believe I really wanted to kill you."

A weak, tentative smile formed among the mess of blood on David's face. "You came close to succeeding," he said.

"I can't believe it, I can't believe it." Natasha opened the door, closed it again and looked at him. "It's the end. You know that, don't you? It's the end." She looked at him steadily. "And I loved you so much." She opened the door and went to telephone the doctor.

Chapter 23

"Why assume *I* know where he is, Aunt Nanda?" Amanda asked.

"You usually know everything about the family."

"Because I pry into everybody else's life, is that what you mean?"

"Don't get upset, Mandy." Nanda smiled at her niece.

"I have every right to be upset. Jamie implied I caused Liz to kill herself, now you get me here and suggest I'm bound to know where David's gone. Well, I don't. (This wasn't true — she did know.) What's more, I don't *want* to know anything more about David and Natasha, or about anyone else in the family. All I've ever done is show interest and to care about everyone, then when something goes wrong, I'm scapegoated and accused of being the family gossip. But I never said a word about Liz and David's affair until after Liz died. And the only reason I told Jamie was because I felt so much pain." Amanda pressed both hands into her breasts. "I kept quiet when Natasha said she was worried about David. And then David, who's always treated me as though I'm mentally defective, actually threatened me if I didn't keep quiet about their affair. I don't want to see any of them again, ever. I thought Jamie . . ." Amanda began to cry. "All my life I've been close to Jamie, told him everything about myself, trusted him completely; but now he's twisted things and says I'm responsible for Liz's death. Liz didn't mind me knowing about the affair; she knew I'd never breathe a word about it to anyone. And I never did until she died and I felt such pain."

Nanda leaned forward and poured more sherry into the small glasses. "I'm sure you're the soul of discretion, Amanda," she said. "The reason I asked you about David is because he might have got in touch with you to find out how Natasha and the children are doing."

"I'm the last person he'd call." Amanda sipped the sherry and held up the glass. "This is what Liz drank. Poor Liz . . . I looked up to her. I thought there was nobody like her in the world." She emptied the glass. "She'd always lecture me when she found me in bed in the afternoon. Of course,

I'd worked the previous night, but that didn't matter to her. According to her, nobody should be in bed at four in the afternoon, for whatever reason. But the next time she came to see me, she'd bring a little gift to make up for having criticized me. I understood her."

"Of course, of course." Nanda now regretted thinking Amanda might be able to provide information about David's whereabouts. It was clear she was filled with resentment towards Natasha and David and believed they'd treated her badly. While she didn't doubt that Amanda's tongue was too loose, she didn't think for a moment that responsibility for the rupture between Natasha and David could be attributed to anything Amanda had said or done. Amanda's childish habit of chattering endlessly to appease and amuse her cousin and brothers and sisters had simply been continued as she grew older, but it wasn't something that would affect people's behaviour — Amanda couldn't be held responsible for that. At family gatherings, Nanda had more than once seen Jamie walk away from her when she was in the midst of a sentence; maybe she thought the world of Jamie, but if a person's general behaviour is any indication of feeling, it was clear to her Jamie had no real affection for Amanda, but used her as a convenient receptacle into which he could dump his problems. Still, Nanda's prime concern was for Natasha, who was seriously depressed since her fight with David and his subsequent disappearance; in fact Nanda was so worried she'd suggested Natasha contact the police, or put the matter into the hands of a private investigator. Natasha would have nothing to do with either suggestion. She'd stared at her mother, compressed her lips to prevent herself from crying and silently moved her head from side to side indicating *no*.

"I wonder if I might ask a favour, Amanda?"

"I suppose," Amanda replied, knowing what was coming.

"Would you visit Natasha? I understand how you feel about Jamie unfairly blaming you for something that was outside your control. But I'm sure Natasha doesn't feel that way, and she desperately needs to talk to somebody. I'm worried about her, Amanda, very worried."

"If she won't talk to you, why would she open up with me?" Amanda said.

"Natasha knows I've reached a time of life when I have little sympathy for the stupidities of my children, which isn't to say I didn't do equally stupid things in my own youth. But it's a matter of age: Once you've passed a certain age, you have little patience for entanglements people get themselves into, and I'm afraid my impatience shows through when I speak to her. I really feel like saying, 'For goodness' sake, girl, pull yourself together,' which is the worst thing to say to someone going through a bad time. She needs someone like you, Amanda."

"I'll do what I can, but she may refuse to see me."

"Persist! I know what Tashie's like, and I know being persistent works with her. When she was a child she'd get into terrible stews over little things, shake her head and refuse to speak to me, but in the end she always came around. The difference is, I had more patience in those days. I understand your reluctance, Amanda, but I'd truly appreciate your help."

Since the women now knew Nanda had got what she wanted from Amanda, both stood and Nanda escorted her niece to the door. "I'll call you," Amanda said.

"Of course." Nanda dabbed a quick kiss on Amanda's cheek. "Next time you visit bring the children."

"They ride their bikes past here sometimes."

"Really? Well, tell them to stop for a visit."

"I'll do that." Amanda walked from the house, then looked back and asked, "Did Hiddie thank you for organizing the wedding reception?"

"Of course. Why do you ask?"

"I just wondered. Sometimes we take things like that for granted."

"Both Hiddie and —? What's his name?"

"Conrad."

"Oh yes, Conrad. Not a name I like. Both thanked me."

"Good."

Once away from Nanda's influence, Amanda's willingness to visit Natasha and offer help faded rapidly. Resentment at the way her aunt had manipulated her surged through her. One result of the painful process of rethinking her relationship with her family was that Amanda was now thinking she would completely break contact with everyone. She'd done much crying in her bedroom at nights and at the kitchen table during the days, turning over and over in her mind how difficult it would be to move away. Perhaps she could go to Kelowna, or another town in the Interior, maybe even start a new life in Alberta; maybe there was another Harry out there somewhere, anxiously waiting for an Amanda to appear in his life. Surely there must be hundreds and hundreds of Harrys in the world just as there were hundreds and hundreds of Amandas, eager to meet, embrace and live happily ever after.

A lingering sense of family loyalty (she *had* given a promise) caused her to drive to Natasha's and ask the maid to speak with her.

"What do you want?" Natasha said as she entered the room. "If you've come to gloat, you can leave."

"I haven't come to do anything of the kind," Amanda said. "And let me tell you something, Natasha, I've put up with more than enough insults from this family, and I don't want any more from you." She moved towards the door, fairly certain how Natasha would react.

"Don't . . ."

The word was sufficient to get Amanda back to the chair. "You're in a bad way, Tashie," she said. "You look awful." It was enough to crack the dam. Natasha's lips parted, and she began sobbing.

"I want to die, Mandy!" she wailed. "It makes me sick to think of it. With his sister!"

"You wouldn't mind if the affair had been with some woman at the university, or a student?"

"Of course I would mind. But Liz!"

"Oh, stop it!" Amanda ordered. "Either be unhappy, or get mad, but don't do both. If you're unhappy, you'll take David back . . . if you're truly angry, you won't want to see him again, ever. So which is it?"

"You are so hard," Natasha whispered. "You don't understand." Amanda found she enjoyed being classified as tough-minded and unsentimental.

"Bullshit. I know just how you feel, Tashie. Personally, I think you're well rid of him."

"Don't say that! You know nothing about David!"

"I suppose you know everything about him? You know so bloody much you didn't have an inkling he was fucking Liz? Well, I knew. I guessed that Liz had somebody. One Christmas when we were all at Liz's I saw her standing beside David and I could sense something going on between them."

"Didn't it sicken you?" Natasha had stopped sobbing.

"I thought it was stupid, but I could also see how such a thing could happen. There was no way Liz was going to let you march off with the man she'd staked out as her property. But I doubt if she ever thought of having sex with him until you let everybody know *you* had."

"I didn't!"

"Of course Liz started the affair. I'm sure of that. David would never have had the guts. Maybe he thought Liz'd be satisfied with a few fucks on the sly, I don't know. Men are so stupid. But once Liz'd got him into her bed he was hers for good. You got the leftovers, Tashie."

"Stop it! Stop it!" Natasha screamed. "I wish I'd killed him. I wish Liz weren't dead so I could kill her too."

"Well, she *is* dead, and David's left. So why not smarten up and forget it?"

"I can't. I wish I knew where he's staying."

"Well, don't expect me to tell you. How am I to know?" (In fact, David had telephoned Amanda and supplied her with a number to call in case he was needed at home, a number which Amanda had traced to a woman who taught at the university.)

"Why be so unpleasant, Mandy? There's no reason for it."

"I have to admit I'm not sorry you've been knocked off your pedestal. It makes us equal. One of the odd things about our family is that no one ever wants to know anything about me. We talk about you and David, about Jamie and his wonderful poetry, and about Hiddie and her misfortunes with Max. And we used to talk about Liz and her experiences as an MLA. We even talked about your mother and hint how lucky she's been to have snared two such terribly wealthy men. And — if Liz wasn't around — we'd talk about Mother and the awful life she had with our father. We talked about Muriel too, and what must have gone on between her and Father before she killed him, and shivered when we imagined what she must have felt when she was taken out of her cell to be hanged. We talked about our grandparents, especially Grandfather Powell, and how he got to be Lord Powell of Hyndhurst. And if David wasn't around, we'd talk about his mother, and we always said she must have been very beautiful because David was so handsome. And remember how we talked about your father, who fascinated us because he was part Indian and fabulously rich? And how your mother ran off with him? We thought it was so romantic! But there had always been one person who was never spoken of in our family because that person was totally uninteresting. Guess who that person was, Tashie? Me, Miss Scatterbrain. None of you ever gave a damn about me. I just was there. I was somebody who was supposed to listen while Jamie whined, Liz lectured, Hiddie censured, David ignored, Nanda tolerated, and you arrogantly allowed me to be admitted into your presence. But now, Tashie, you're down where I am. Now we're equal. If you want to kill David, then go right ahead and do it, but don't expect me to find him for you. If I were you, I'd go to the nearest beauty salon and get a facial and my hair done, then I'd drift into a hotel bar to pick up some guy to fuck the rage out of my system. I'll tell you what: You fix yourself up and we'll go out on the town and find a guy for you. It shouldn't be difficult."

"I'd never do such a thing."

"You prefer to imagine torturing David? Well, too bad. You'll just have to sit here getting skinnier and skinnier as your skin gets muddier and muddier and the bags under your eyes grow larger and larger." Amanda smiled. "Tell me something, Tashie. Is David the only guy you've ever fucked?"

"I don't see why I should tell you. And don't use that awful word."

"Let me tell you something, Tashie: A woman falls in love and so she thinks the guy she loves has got to be extra special. But he's not. He's just your average slob, only she doesn't know that because he's all she's ever known. If you want to find out what men are like, stroll downtown some night and ask a prostitute; they've got lots of experience. Honestly, Tashie, you don't need to put yourself through all this. Nobody gets awards for self-inflicted misery."

"I didn't start it," Natasha fiercely said.

"I agree, you didn't, but you keep rubbing your sore. Anyway, I've blown my top and feel better for it. We understand now where we stand with each other."

"You enjoy dragging me down, don't you?"

"I just want you to know I'm not simple-minded."

"I never thought you were."

"I've learned a lot from my dying patients. You know, the class system stops operating when it comes to getting sick and dying. I remember nursing a woman dying of cancer and the walls of her bedroom were covered with pictures of herself as a young woman. She was beautiful, lovelier even than you, Tashie. There were paintings of her too, naked, and when I sponged her body, or did anything that involved exposing it, she shut her eyes because she couldn't bear to see it. She told me she wished she'd killed herself while she was still young and beautiful."

"What's that got to do with me?"

"I guess nothing. Did I tell you I'm thinking of moving? Maybe to Kelowna. Harry and I stayed there one night. Perhaps people in Kelowna'll think I'm smart. It's odd, but I've always wanted to be near my family, physically near Jamie and Liz, you and David, even Hiddie. But now I want to get as far away as possible. Odd, how we change, isn't it? A month ago, you were a complacent matron; now, you're just one more miserable woman. The world's full of them. Liz wasn't like that: She never revealed how she felt, not even to David."

"Where would you go?"

"I told you, Kelowna."

"I mean, if we went out together."

"Oh that. I dunno, one of the hotel bars, I suppose."

"What would we do?"

"Do? You don't have to do anything, Tashie. You just make yourself available."

"It's vile to think of doing something like that."

"People do it all the —"

"I don't want to hear what people do." Like a child, Natasha covered her ears.

Amanda glanced at her wristwatch. "The kids'll wonder where I am," she said as she got up. Natasha followed her to the main door.

"We'll remain friends?" she pleaded as she opened the door.

"Of course." Amanda smiled as she departed, pleased with the way she had conducted herself, satisfied that for once she had bettered Natasha. She did not go directly home, but drove along Sixteenth Avenue down the hill to an area that had been marshland when Vancouver was first settled. There she stopped to look at a small insignificant house. What a come-down for David, after living for years in Natasha's splendid home! She was tempted to go to the door and when David opened it to tell him she had just left the company of his wife who was filling in the long evening hours by sitting in hotel bars and picking up men. David deserved to be knocked down a peg or two because he'd been too cocksure; he thought he had the right to judge others by standards he set. People like David — and Natasha too — who behaved arrogantly needed to be given their quotient of hu-miliation: They needed to know what it feels like to be insulted — as she had been insulted during her years in nursing school; not that her treat-ment was the exception — oh no, most of the other seventeen- and eigh-teen-year-old girls — for that's all they were, just girls — had sobbed themselves to sleep after being verbally torn apart by their instructors. It had taken two years of nurses' training to feel sufficiently trustworthy even to empty bedpans, and it was not until near the end of the course that she regained the confidence she'd started out with and could calmly ap-proach patients to take their temperature or pulse rate. In every part of her mind and body, she, Amanda, knew what it was to experience humiliation, which was why she could feel such satisfaction at the spectacle of a teary-eyed, humiliated Natasha. She told herself that no one, no matter how pow-erful a person might be, ought to be allowed to escape experiencing those horrifying moments when you are reduced to absolute servility, because unless individuals experience humiliation they can't feel compassion for people less fortunate than themselves. Yes, it was terribly important for every human being to be humbled once in while — one might even go so far as to say that to experience humiliation was a necessity of life. Amanda smiled, looked at herself in the rear-view mirror, decided to leave well enough alone, pursed her lips and awarded herself a kiss, put the car into gear and drove home.

Although Amanda could return home with a feeling of satisfaction, Natasha continued to fret over the conversation and to amplify Amanda's derisive comments, which resulted in an even more intense retrospective loathing of Liz and increase of fury directed at David. But beyond this, she felt contempt for herself and for the way, so she now thought, she'd played into David's hands, disregarding the fact that she'd been the one who'd always taken the initiative with David, the one who'd pursued him across the country, the one who'd seduced him, the one who'd made sure their relationship ended in marriage. Now, in order to transform him from the perfect lover and spouse into a trickster and liar it would be necessary for Natasha to transform herself too, from seducer into "innocent young woman corrupted by powerful male". She magnified Amanda's words, turning them into harsh mockeries, then trembling and covered in sweat, she'd recall the therapy Amanda advocated and writhe in disgust when she imagined herself doing that. She'd always seen her body as belonging exclusively to David and it was unimaginable that another man — a stranger — might put his hands on it. How would she ever be able to bring herself to undress in front of a man she would never see again? Her hatred of David increased proportionally to the intensity of the images of herself with another man, since she held David responsible for whatever she imagined. In her entire life, Natasha had never been inside a hotel bar. In fact, she'd never stayed in a hotel. As a child, whenever she travelled, she'd moved from airplane or car to a house, then from house to house owned by the McLeods, or one of their relatives, or by an executive of Can-Ray Corporation. Consequently, the more she fretted, the more fixed in her mind was an unrealistic image of a hotel bar filled with lewd men, watching and waiting for women to appear. She dreamt she walked into a long, dimly lit room where white-jacketed men rapidly poured liquids from bottles into glasses while heads turned and eyes appraised her as she seated herself at a table. She felt the presence of someone at the table and knew it was David, but he seemed not to know her, for he began talking to Liz, who'd appeared from nowhere, and Natasha knew, without actually seeing it, that they were naked and making love on the floor in front of everyone. Her own shrieks of hatred became blended with Liz's cries of ecstasy: "Look at them!" "Look at us!" "Kill them!" "Kill us!" and at that point she awakened.

One afternoon, using the need to shop for the children as an excuse, she drove into The Bay parkade. She purchased socks and underwear the children did not need, left the store and walked the few blocks to the Hotel Vancouver where she dawdled for fifteen minutes in the shops in the lobby, purchased a bottle of perfume, then drifted around the immense foyer until she found the cocktail lounge. She entered it and was surprised to find it bore no resemblance to the bar she'd conjured up in her feverish dreams. It was quiet, and the bar itself unobtrusive. Hardly anyone was there. She seated herself at a small table in a commodious, cushioned chair. Two men sat at a table not far from hers, preoccupied with scribbling on papers which covered the table and taking an occasional sip of coffee. When a waiter appeared to ask what she would like, she ordered a sherry. "Sweet or dry?" he asked. She hesitated, then said, "Sweet. No, I mean dry." On the far side of the lounge a young man and woman sat close together and Natasha decided they were a honeymoon couple.

"Thank you," she said when the waiter returned and placed a small glass of amber-coloured liquid on her table.

"No problem." He remained, prepared to carry on a casual conversation. "Been shopping, eh?"

"Oh . . . a few things."

"You're a guest?"

"Guest?"

"Staying here in the hotel?"

"No. I live in Vancouver."

An elderly man and woman entered the lounge and settled at a table. The waiter left to serve them. "We stayed at the hotel on our honeymoon," the man told the waiter. "So my wife and I thought we'd come back for our fiftieth wedding anniversary."

"Things have changed since then," his wife said.

"Congratulations," the waiter said. "And in all those fifty years you never had a single fight?"

"Not true," the man said. "She did the fighting and I did the worrying because a few years later we were flat broke. You're too young to remember the Depression. Anyway, can you dig us up a small bottle of champagne?"

"You bet we can." He went to the bar where a prolonged discussion took place with the bartender. The bartender then spoke into a house phone, and after a few minutes another waiter appeared bearing a tray holding two chilled champagne glasses and a bucket of ice in which stood a bottle of champagne. Almost immediately a young woman, wearing a green apron, entered carrying a vase holding two magnificent roses. The vase was placed on the table, the champagne opened and poured, after which the three hotel staff stepped back and gently clapped their hands as the man and woman toasted each other.

"That was a nice gesture," Natasha said when the waiter returned to stand by her table, as if that was his post.

"People who've survived fifty years of hearing each other repeat what they've been saying since day one deserve to be congratulated," he said.

Now reminded of the brevity of her marriage to David and the evil associated with it, Natasha decided to leave. She opened her handbag, then remembered she had no cash. Cash was something she seldom handled; she paid for everything by cheque because her accountant had counselled against credit cards. The same accountant also had advised her to use her full surname, Natasha McLeod-Powell, when she signed her cheques. "I know this sounds ridiculous," she explained to the waiter, "but I don't have any money with me, or any credit cards. Will you take a cheque?"

"Sorry." His attitude changed from impersonal friendliness to one of open speculation, as though he were thinking: *Not another one of those! Funny, she doesn't act like one.*

For Natasha, it was a moment bordering on panic. She looked at her watch, only to discover it was long past bank-closing time and she had no idea how to work a bank machine. Glimpsing the diamond wristwatch (Nanda's gift to Natasha on her twenty-first birthday) caused the waiter to change his mind about his customer: Even a high-class prostitute wouldn't wear a wristwatch studded with diamonds while cruising for customers.

"Tell you what," he offered, "make out a cheque to me and I'll pay for the sherry."

"You will? That's very kind of you."

"No sweat," he said.

"I've no idea how much it is," she said.

"Five bucks'll do." He watched while she made out a cheque for twenty dollars. "Nicholas Parsons," he said when she asked what name to put as payee. "But call me Nick."

"Thank you so much," Natasha said as she handed him the cheque.

Nick Parsons looked at the cheque while saying, "I hope you'll come back." He repeated her name. "Powell? I've heard that name somewhere."

Natasha now became nervous lest his query reveal her social status and that information about her presence in the hotel might be conveyed to her mother. "It's a common enough name," she said.

"A woman . . . ? Sure, I remember now. Liz Powell. She was in politics. Any relation?"

"No, no." Natasha gathered up her shopping bags and prepared to escape. Why had she come into this place to expose herself?

"Natasha McLeod-Powell," he repeated, looking at her signature on the cheque. "Oh! You're Mrs. McLeod's daughter. Is that right?" Natasha nodded. "Wow! I'll have this cheque framed. Mrs. McLeod is a real big contributor to the arts. Half the theatres in town survive on her donations." Natasha had to laugh: The idea of someone framing her cheque seemed preposterous. "Wow! McLeod!" He moved to one side and proffered a hand to assist her to rise from the deep, heavily-cushioned seat. "Would you mind if I ask you a question? I just can't resist. What does it feel like to be rich?"

"I don't really know." The question disturbed Natasha. "I suppose I feel the same as other people."

"You think rich people have the same worries as ordinary folks?"

"I don't know. I suppose so."

"Don't mind me, Mrs. Powell. But I'm a real curious guy. When I'm not being a waiter, I work in the theatre; that is, when I can get a part. There's not much work around now."

"Acting must be very interesting." Natasha, shopping bags in hand, made for the entrance, escorted by Nick Parsons.

"Yes, it can be. I hope you'll come again," he said.

"I'll see. I'm not sure what I'll be doing in the next little while," Natasha replied and practically ran from the hotel and along the streets, anxious to regain the security of her car.

Chapter 24

She couldn't tell anybody about her overwhelming desire to return to the hotel lounge — she hardly dared admit it to herself. She told herself over and over that she was the mother of four children and had no business being interested in any man except her husband, even though he'd been unfaithful. Further, she must never allow herself to be placed in a position which conceivably could result in unsavoury publicity. Her mother had explained time and time again that society columnists were always eager to print information about the McLeod family. Now, Natasha trembled as she envisaged her mother reading: "Rumour has it that Natasha Powell, wealthy daughter of the immeasurably wealthy Nanda McLeod, visits a certain hotel lounge for reasons other than an afternoon aperitif. We wonder why?" She groaned with anxiety: She had been taught to avoid publicity and must never under any circumstance allow her name to appear in a newspaper. But Nick Parsons wouldn't be bothered by publicity, would he? The reverse — he'd like it. An actor who worked as a waiter for a living would be keen to bring his name to people's attention, at least so Natasha imagined. She fussed unendingly and every day scanned the social columns before passing on to the international scene to find out where new famine cysts had erupted on the global body, which meant more children dying of starvation, which meant greater contributions to charitable organizations she supported whose employees rushed around the world like so many Saint Georges to fight dragons of hunger. After days of indecision she went to the bank and withdrew money from her account. She told herself she mustn't go anywhere without plenty of cash.

"Professor Powell was in yesterday," the teller said. "It's good to see him recovered from his skiing accident. There're so many nowadays. It's almost as dangerous as driving a car, isn't it? Nobody's safe anywhere, are they?"

Natasha agreed it was so and quickly left. She drove to the Vancouver Hotel car park where, no matter how full, entry was assured anyone driving a Jaguar, then walked through the hotel to the lounge. He was not there. A middle-aged waiter came to serve her and she ordered a dry sherry, paid for it, then got up and left. After her departure the waiter asked the bartender: "You seen that woman before, Tom? The one that ordered the sherry and hardly touched it?"

"No. Why?"

"I've seen her somewhere." It was true: The waiter *had* seen Natasha. He was one of a team of waiters hired by the catering company which Nanda had employed to serve food and drinks at Hilda's wedding reception. He'd actually held a tray from which Natasha had lifted a glass of champagne to toast the smiling bridal couple. (Hilda and Conrad Knight were back in Vancouver after spending a two-week honeymoon in a Puerto Vallarta condominium owned by the Can-Ray Corporation: Hilda, enclosed in a new, glossy shell of physical satisfaction, and Conrad possessing a newly acquired machismo which he displayed by continually tapping Hilda's rump, much like a rider flicks his crop over the haunches of his mount. There were no flies on Conrad: He was determined to let the Powells and McLeods know he was master in Hilda's house and bed.)

"It's irritating," the waiter told the bartender. "I like to remember where I've seen people. You'd be surprised how they react when you address them by name. It'll double or triple your tip. That's one thing I've learned in this business: Guys pay good money to be recognized. But she didn't leave nothing, just ordered the sherry, then took off."

"Probably in a hurry for an appointment." The bartender was bored with dissertations on how to get larger tips out of customers. He'd heard it all before and, besides, wasn't convinced the way you treated customers affected the size of the tip you got. Some guys were generous, others skinflints.

"No. I think she was looking for somebody. Wait a bit. I know where I seen her! At a fancy wedding reception."

"So what!"

"So what, he says! So what! Listen Mac, you should of seen this place on West Marine. What the hell's the name of the old dame who owns it? Jeez! The dough some of those guys have! Y'know what champagne they was serving? Bollinger! That's class for you. Anyway, if that sherry dame comes in here again I'll tell her I've seen her before. Yes sir."

Natasha did come back to the lounge, but on this occasion the waiter on duty was Nick Parsons. He saw her enter to sit at a table close to the entrance and immediately went to greet her. Her nervousness was apparent. "A glass of sherry, Mrs. Powell?" he asked.

"No. I came to ask you a question: If someone from a newspaper asked you, you wouldn't say I'd been here, would you?"

"Certainly not! My second name is Discretion." No reporter from any Vancouver newspaper had ever come into the lounge and asked him about anyone. So why would she ask such a question?

"Thank you." She lifted her handbag as though to leave.

"Look, I'll be through work in fifteen minutes. Maybe we could have a coffee?"

He watched indecision ripple across her face and manifest itself in the way she raised and lowered the bag. "I suppose we could."

"Would you rather wait in the lobby?"

"Yes, I'll do that." He watched her go, then went to the bar.

"Tom, would you do me a favour?"

"Okay, okay. But you'll owe me one."

"I told her fifteen minutes. That means forty-five minutes before old Jack shows up."

"I'll manage. But don't forget you owe me one!"

"I won't."

Natasha sat in the hotel foyer, opposite the reception desk, watching people pass, all seemingly absorbed in their own thoughts. This was an alien world to Natasha, who rarely entered hotels and had never approached a reception counter to make an inquiry. She was not an unintelligent woman, merely limited in experience. Almost everything had come to her through intermediaries and, except for bearing children, she'd never had to face the day-to-day anxieties experienced by most people: She didn't know what it was to worry about finding or losing a job, or having enough money for rent, or sufficient food and clothes for her children. True, she'd acquainted herself with problems of famine-stricken children around the world, but her knowledge was far from being firsthand. All her life she had been protected by thick layers of fiscal insulation and, while vaguely aware that a world existed beyond the walls surrounding her, she knew little about it. Gossiping with Amanda had functioned as a pipeline and allowed her to believe — except for the money — that she lived like other young mothers.

"Hope I haven't kept you waiting too long." The navy blue blazer and raincoat made Nick Parsons look more like a hotel guest than employee, but an actor, Natasha thought, would be bound to know how to dress appropriately for any occasion.

Natasha stood. "I don't know where we might go. I seldom come downtown," she explained.

"I have an idea. Do you have your car?" She nodded. "Then why don't we go back to my place and I'll make us some coffee?"

"I'm not sure . . ."

He reached out and pressed her hand. "Don't worry," he said. "I just love your name. Natasha . . . It suits you. Did your mother read *War and Peace* when she was pregnant with you?" They went through the hotel to the car park and Natasha's car. He did not comment on the car, but told her he got around Vancouver by bus.

"My cousin rides a bicycle."

"Sensible, but risky — especially downtown."

"You'll have to direct me." She followed his directions, hardly aware of what she was doing, or where they were heading.

They turned off an alley and entered a carport. "I have a basement suite," he said.

"I've no idea where we are," she admitted.

"We're on the hill that looks north over the city. We drove south on Quebec, then west on Thirteenth. If you lived in one of the suites above . . ." he unlocked the basement door, ". . . you'd be able to see the roof of the Vancouver Hotel and downtown Vancouver." The rooms were small, the ceiling low, everything immaculately clean and tidy. "I can't stand living in a messy place," he said. "That's the reason I live on my own, though it's more expensive. You rent a place with somebody else and pretty soon dishes accumulate in the sink, floors aren't swept, beds not made. The list's endless. It's less stressful to live alone. Let me take your coat. Ah . . . here's my cat." They were standing in the tiny kitchen when a tabby cat came in, stretching and yawning. He scooped up the cat and introduced it. "Diefenbaker, meet Natasha."

"What an odd name for a cat."

"He's an odd cat. Give me your coat." She followed him into a small sitting room where he put the cat onto a rocking chair and laid her coat over the back of it. "Shall I make us coffee? Or do you want to just sit and talk?"

"Perhaps we could do both. Though I can't stay long."

"In that case, we'll forgo coffee and conversation and do this." He put his arms around her and kissed her. "I mean, this is the real reason why we're here, isn't it?"

The bedroom was even smaller than the sitting room, with a tiny, curtained window. "I don't think I ought to do this," Natasha protested as he undressed her.

"That's what you may *think,* but the fact you're here means it's right." The bed was narrow and the sheet cold to her back. "You're beautiful," he said. "It's the first thing I noticed about you, before I fell in love with you. Do you like me?"

"Yes." She whispered the word. Surely being there meant she liked him.

"A lot?"

She did not reply, simply waited, eyes closed. Maybe Amanda was right in saying men's sexual actions were the same: Any man might do what Nick Parsons was doing right now and whatever *she* felt would be a product of her own desire, not his. She'd always known she was beautiful, but still it was wonderful to hear Nick Parsons tell her so. Had he really fallen in love with her? David seldom spoke of love, but it hadn't mattered because she'd always known that he loved her. Or had he? She felt a stab of pain as she questioned David's love for her while exquisite pleasure surged through her loins each time Nick Parsons entered, withdrew and pushed further inward with each stroke. When she was a child, she and Stuart McLeod had often walked through the garden to stand on the shallow dyke at the edge of their property and watch the tide creeping over the serrated mud-flats through the marsh grasses before it rippled hesitantly at the dyke's foundation, testing the slope, receding, rising, again and again, until the moment of fullness came, as it did now, in herself, rising and receding. "My husband had an affair with his half-sister," she said. "For years and years it went on, and I didn't know."

His face was pressed against her breasts. "The world's filled with people who love other people they're not supposed to."

"How do you know what goes on in the world?"

"I keep my eyes open."

It was unbelievable! How had she ended in this hard, narrow bed in a tiny, low-ceilinged room, talking to a man she hardly knew as he lay between her thighs and moved his lips over her breasts? Ought she to have known this would happen? Ought she to have known her pleasure would be greater with Nick Parsons than it had been with David for a long time? She could hardly remember what their first days together had been like, when physical ecstasy had intoxicated her and all she'd wanted was to embrace David. "We mustn't do this again," she said.

"What's to stop us?"

"I have children."

"I have Diefenbaker." She wanted to explain that there was a vast difference between them . . . that quite apart from the fact she had children, her position in the communal fabric made a relationship impossible. She could now see and smell everything that was wrong with the suite: stains on the walls and ceiling, mustiness in the air and the odour of cat urine. "Besides, I like you. I enjoy fucking you."

"It's impossible." The word "fucking" upset her. She'd heard the word only once in her life when Amanda had used it. That was bad enough, but now the word sounded even coarser and turned their physical ecstasy into something crude and mechanical.

"I have to go," she repeated. "Please . . . I have to."

"I want to keep you."

"I have four small children. I must go."

"Of course." He moved away, stood and looked down at her.

She left the bed and was surprised she didn't feel embarrassed standing naked in his presence. "May I use your bathroom?"

"Sure thing." He walked in front of her through the kitchen to open a narrow door; following him, she noticed a birthmark on his left buttock. "Take your time," he said and stood aside to allow her to pass by him.

"Thank you," she said and closed the door. It was the size of an aircraft toilet, the shower, toilet and washbasin all jammed together. She soaped and wiped herself with toilet paper, glanced at her face in the little medicine-cabinet mirror, opened the door, returned to the bedroom, and was shocked to see Nick going through the contents of her handbag.

"I'm looking for your phone number," he hurriedly explained. "You're not listed in the phone book."

"Why would you want it?" She began dressing.

"To keep in touch. That is, unless you're going to contact me." He picked up and passed her brassiere to her.

"I'd prefer it that way." It was strange that in his presence she could make habitual, intimate gestures while dressing, such as leaning over to ensure her bra was snug around her breasts and wriggling her hips as she drew up her pantyhose. He even reached out to support her as she inserted each foot, and by his action insinuated an intimate relationship.

"Lovely dress," he said as he handed it to her. "Expensive?"

"Not really."

"Life must be so simple for people like you," he said.

"No simpler than any other life."

"No money worries. No job worries. You ever had a job?"

She slipped on her low-heeled shoes. "No." As he gave her the handbag, she remembered she'd left it in the sitting room with her coat, which meant he'd deliberately gone to get it. "Quebec will take me to Forty-first Avenue?" she asked as she put on her coat.

"It will." He followed her to the door. "Natasha, I must see you again."

"I'm not sure."

"I know what you're thinking about me," he said.

"I'll see."

"Promise?"

"Yes, I promise." It was not until she turned into the driveway of her home that she remembered she hadn't given him her phone number, nor asked for his. Later, after she had taken a shower, while looking into her purse she found that, except for a five-dollar bill, the money withdrawn from the bank was gone. This was a shock, because to that point she'd believed what he'd said. In itself the money didn't matter, but what the theft said about him and how he felt about her was upsetting. To remember how readily she'd responded to him caused her shame.

"Diefenbaker and I miss you," he said when he telephoned.

"You took money from my purse," Natasha sobbed. "How could you do that?" When he'd gone through her purse, he must have found the little book where she kept the family's unlisted numbers, including the number of her private line.

There was a pause before he replied. "Habits formed in childhood stay with us as adults."

"I'd have given money to you if —"

"If I'd asked? But I'd never ask. I want to see you again. I want to make love with you again." She put down the phone, and when he telephoned the next day she begged him to leave her alone.

"I can't," he said. "I love you. Maybe I stole money from you, but that doesn't mean I can't love you. I do. You are so beautiful, Natasha. I must see you again."

That same day Natasha went to see Amanda.

"You're looking much better," Amanda told her.

"Mandy, I want to ask you something." Amanda's lips parted as she listened avidly to Natasha's incoherent account of her meeting with Nick Parsons. "He phones every day. What should I do?"

"You think he's fallen for you? Maybe it's a trick to get his claws into you?"

"I don't think it's that." Natasha slowly shook her head. "That's the awful part. I think he's in love with me."

"What about you?"

"I like him." To like Nick was a necessity, for if she didn't acknowledge she liked him, then she'd be forced to admit that sordid desire alone had driven her into his bed. Even now, Natasha couldn't bring herself to tell Amanda how she'd felt when she lay with him in the darkened room.

But Amanda put the question: "How was it, Tashie? That's the important thing. If a guy gave me what I wanted, I'd see him again."

"Even if he stole money from you?"

"Well, maybe not, but a good time in bed is worth a lot, isn't it?" Natasha blushed. "Was he as good as David?"

Natasha's face flushed a deep red. "The same as when David and I were first together."

"Like when Harry and I first did it! Heavenly, isn't it? If he was that special, I'd see him again, but I'd leave my money and jewels at home."

"Would you really?"

"I sure would. That heavenly feeling is rare. Is it ever! And I should know. Two-minute fucks in back seats of cars and once-a-week frigid fucks with Bernard were all I knew before I met Harry. That's how long I had to wait. I'd risk it, Tashie."

"I'm not as brave as you, Mandy. Suppose David comes back? What if he answered the phone when Nick called?"

"Tell him since you've forgiven him his affair with Liz, he can forget an itsy-bitsy liaison with a waiter."

"I couldn't do that. I don't want David to know."

"You want to play the role of ever-forgiving wife, eh? Well, it's up to you."

"It's not that. It's just that Nick wouldn't fit in, that's what I mean." Natasha wrenched the admission from herself. Amanda looked as though she might sarcastically reply, but ended by shrugging. "And I'm not being snobbish, Mandy," Natasha assured her.

"Have I said you were? Why don't I look him over?"

"Well . . . I'm not sure if . . ."

"Why not? Besides, don't you want someone to tell this guy to stop phoning you? Well, don't you?"

"I suppose so. Yes, I do." What a relief! Amanda would handle everything and her problem would go away. "If he agrees to stop phoning, would you give him this?" She dug into her handbag and produced an envelope, while Amanda told herself Natasha had come prepared.

Amanda held the envelope to the light. "Is this money, Tashie? That's stupid, really stupid. The guy'll think he's got you in his back pocket."

"I want him to have it."

"I'll talk to him and decide. If he strikes me as a real sleaze, I won't give the money to him, okay?"

The following afternoon, Amanda, wearing what she called her "lounge-lizard" outfit, wandered into the Vancouver Hotel lounge, sat and looked around, trying to convey the impression she spent hours every day sitting in similar settings.

"Can I bring you something?" She recognized him immediately from Natasha's description and had to admit he was good-looking, with a smile designed to engage the attention of women, combining friendliness and flattery, attributes that women find difficult to resist.

"I'll have a dry martini," Amanda said.

"Dry it shall be," he said. She observed him as he went to the bar and decided he was physically well set up, slightly above average, but nothing special.

He returned, placed the glass before her, then stepped back and waited while she sampled the drink. "It'll do," she said. "Is your name Nick Parsons?"

"It is." The smile disappeared.

"You've been telephoning my sister-in-law, Natasha Powell."

"I've called her a few times."

"Even though she told you not to? I'm here to have a talk with you." She looked at her watch. "Natasha's told me you finish work about this time. Is that right?"

"Yes."

"Good. I'll finish my drink and wait for you in the lobby."

She watched him serving other customers and talking to an older man who had arrived to take over his station. She placed a ten-dollar bill on the table, then walked through to the lobby and waited.

"I don't see there's much to talk about," he began as he approached her. "This is something between Natasha and me."

"It *was* between Natasha and you."

"I happen to have fallen for her. I love her," he said.

"That may or may not be true, but the fact remains you stole money from her. How does that fit in with loving her?"

"I don't want to talk here."

"It's as good a place as any." She took the envelope from her pocket. "I don't know how much money's in here, or why Natasha's prepared to give it to you, but one thing I know for sure is that if you don't stop telephoning her, I'll make it my business to inform the police of the theft."

He looked around the lobby to make sure no one could overhear them talking. "The police won't do anything unless she lays a charge."

"You'd be surprised what police will do when a complaint is made on behalf of someone in the McLeod family. Nothing public, of course."

"I love her."

"Natasha's married and has children."

"Her husband's cheated on her. She told me."

"I happen to know she still loves her husband."

"I fell for her the minute I saw her."

"Take this — and leave her alone." For a moment, Amanda thought he was going to break down and cry, but he snatched the envelope from her hand and quickly walked through the lobby and out into the street, followed by Amanda who watched him run across Georgia Street and leap onto a bus as the doors were closing. She went along the street to where her car was illegally parked, tore a violation ticket in half, stuck the pieces beneath the windshield wiper of a nearby car, then circled through streets to Burrard Street Bridge and drove over False Creek to Kitsilano and home. It was sort of sad, she thought, that Nick Parsons was deficient in the attributes required by those who moved in the McLeod circuit. The McLeods either ignored the Nick Parsons of this world or walked all over them. She could even feel sorry for him, though probably he was nothing more than a sexual sleaze who traded physical assets for whatever he could get. Still, it was possible he'd actually fallen for Natasha, and there was no doubt he'd opened *her* eyes — Natasha now knew she was capable of enjoying sexual pleasure with someone besides David. And that must have come as a real shock because she'd always claimed she and David were perfectly matched in every way, though you might think David had disproved that assertion by his long-standing affair with Liz who, Amanda must assume, gave more to David than the facile emotion Natasha provided.

Amanda rummaged around in the baggage of her thoughts and, more by intuition than by logical processes, decided that Natasha and David's marriage was finished. Years ago, Natasha had snatched David from Liz, then triumphantly flaunted the apparently acquiescent David and the four children begotten in the marriage in Liz's face, which meant that now Liz was dead, having David around to prove she'd captured the prize was no longer a necessity. It felt strange to realize that a marriage which she, Amanda, had once believed would go on forever, had turned out to be nothing more than a contest between two strong-willed women — a battle which, in a curious way, both had lost. Though that's what happened, she mused, when you became obsessed with possessing a person without whom you felt you couldn't continue to live. It was scary to think that maybe the compulsion to have David was what had really killed Liz; it was awful to think that the sister she'd loved and admired so much had been imprisoned by the need to possess her half-brother and that the only way she could escape had been to kill herself. Amanda remembered how she'd always regretted she wasn't like Liz, that she'd had none of Liz's beauty or courage or intelligence. Instead, she'd floundered and muddled along, going from hope to hope, from one man to another, trying this, then that, always hoping somehow she would develop into someone like Liz. Now, she saw that Liz was like a person chained to a rock in the face of a rising tide, while she, Amanda, ever hopeful, had survived, and would continue to survive, by discarding anything and anyone that did not match her expectations. All of which was quite, quite incredible. She sighed, drew into the curb, parked and locked the car, then slowly walked along the street to her house.

Chapter 25

Natasha wasn't sure how much longer she could go on. She was doing something she'd never believed possible: pretending to love David. She'd told herself she shouldn't deny him sexual pleasure, that she truly wanted to be reconciled, that he would soon forget Liz's death and they'd rediscover the wave of mutual passion that had carried them along so successfully in the past. She believed she was prepared to forget and wanted to demonstrate her forgiveness, but her body refused to cooperate. She had no idea what David felt now when they made love and she wondered if he suspected that her passion was manufactured. Although they'd spoken of the need for reconciliation, she'd told him that things between them could never be the same again, so perhaps he attributed her subdued response to that, though *his* love-making (could she call it that?) remained fervent. The difference was in her, she knew that, and she couldn't account for it, because she truly wanted to re-experience the abandonment of self that had always occurred when they came together, but instead she became acutely aware of her body and of the mechanics of the sexual act. The sweat that had once lubricated her breasts and belly and allowed her to writhe snake-like beneath David was now obnoxious to her, and she wanted to leap from the bed and run to the shower to wash it away. She told herself eventually things would sort themselves out and she would experience once again the delirium of desire that would make her tremble with feverish weakness as she waited for David to approach her. She thought of consulting a psychiatrist, but she was too proud to reveal herself to anybody, especially someone who might judge her as deficient. She had gone to Amanda, intending to be open with her, but she had been unable to get beyond the simple acknowledgement that she and David had a long way to go before they would attain the degree of intimacy and trust they'd formerly had.

"Though perhaps I should say, *I* have a long way to go," she added the afternoon she'd visited Amanda. "Because David seems —" There she stopped, unable to speak further about David, and while they continued their conversation for another hour, nothing helpful emerged. Amanda had thought it was unreasonable of Natasha to expect to receive advice without revealing more of her problem and finally concluded that Natasha's "perfect marriage" was in fact over, but of course she didn't say so to Natasha, who kept repeating the only thing she and David needed was to make a few minor adjustments to their marriage, which might have been all very well, Amanda thought, if the two of them were starting out from something tenuous and working towards a stronger, more harmonious relationship, but Natasha had commenced her relationship with David by plunging into a sea of passion to float on endless waves of delirious sexual and emotional intimacy. How could adjustments be made to something supposedly so perfect? Surely the nature of perfection meant you could neither add to nor subtract anything from it. Perfection was complete in itself, and when you tried to modify or alter it in any way, it ceased to exist. Maybe that's what had happened to Natasha. She'd trapped herself in the idea of perfection and had lost everything, because the airy, insulating balloon of joint rapture which she'd persistently conjured up had simply vanished following the revelation of David's liaison with Liz.

During the Christmas holiday, Stuart-Hector telephoned Natasha from Florida and after delivering the usual festive greetings, went on to pontificate that experience had taught him it made no sense to demolish a house because the roof leaked: You simply fixed the leak and went on living in the house. His unsought advice grated. Of course, he meant well, but you knew he was the sort of man who always stresses the importance of family values, even when they might not apply to him. (Stuart-Hector was now separated from Isobel and happily cohabiting with his former secretary.) Still, Natasha patiently listened because she knew Stuart-Hector held her in high regard and had always admired what he referred to as her "integrated" marriage, meaning that, unlike his own, Natasha's marriage perfectly integrated all the positive aspects of a marital relationship. Yet his remarks were no comfort to Natasha because they didn't address the revulsion she now felt whenever David touched her, although he'd patiently explained to her how he felt trapped between his love for her and prior allegiance to Liz. In fact, he'd made every effort to explain what had happened between him and Liz, and while she could understand how a close childhood relationship could profoundly affect people when they became adults, her appreciation of his dilemma did not result in any alteration of how she felt deep within. "I'm grateful for your understanding, Tashie," he'd say. "There were times when it came close to being unbearable." And no doubt it was her profound sense of betrayal coupled with her inability to express her new feelings that prevented Natasha from opening the inner doors of passion to welcome David into her arms again. All she could do was to hope that the passage of time would dim her memory of Nick Parsons and that before long her desire for David would return to bless their marriage.

She didn't immediately spot him because he was leaning against a lamp standard which, combined with the poor January afternoon light, had the effect of blending any person standing there into the background of walls and trees. When recognition came, something crumbled in her, and she swung the car into a driveway, backed out and, defying oncoming traffic, crossed into the other lane.

She drew up, opened the passenger door and, after some hesitation, Nick got in beside her. Natasha, who was on her way to her weekly appointment with her hairdresser, drove haphazardly. "What are you doing here? You were supposed to go away. I gave you money to go away. Why did you come back?"

"I did go away." He was shivering and she turned up the heat to high. "To Edmonton. There's a theatre there."

"Why didn't you stay? Why come back?"

"I couldn't help it, Natasha. I had to see you. Don't tell me it's crazy, I already know that. But I had to." Natasha halted at a red light, then reached out and touched his face. He kissed her hand while repeatedly saying, "I love you, I love you. God, how I love you." Cars behind blared horns and she pulled her hand from his to drive on. "Are you back in your basement suite?" she asked.

"I'm staying in a motel on Kingsway."

"What about Diefenbaker?"

"Guys I know took him. Diefenbaker doesn't care where he is as long as somebody feeds him."

"Direct me. I don't know my way around that part of town."

They drove in silence along the broad Kingsway and left it to pull up beside a small motel cabin. "It's cheap. Winter rates," he said. "After a while you get used to the funny smell." There was a double bed, a small chest of drawers, a partitioned shower and toilet, and an old gas range underneath a wall cupboard.

"How can you stand it?" Natasha said.

"I can stand anything provided you're with me." He held and kissed her, and his breath was slightly foul as though decay had entered his body.

"I mustn't," Natasha whispered as he opened her raincoat to push impatient hands beneath her blouse and skirt. "Don't . . . don't." Afterwards, at her request, he left the bed to supplement the thin sheet and blanket with her lined coat. "You're so thin," she said, watching him. "You've lost weight."

"Pining for you." He adjusted the coat, then got back into the bed to burrow beneath the covers and mouth her breasts, before moving down to her belly and from there to do something David had never done even when their passion was fresh and brightest.

"What do you feel for me?" he asked afterwards. "You've never said you loved me. You just want me to fuck you, is that it?"

"I love my husband," she said. But did she?

"You *imagine* you love him. In fact, you love me." He began kissing her and the scent of her secretions was on his lips. "Say it, Natasha, say it," he urged.

"I must love you," she whispered.

"Say 'I love you, Nick.' "

"I love you, Nick. But *why* do I love you?"

"You mean, why does a woman who drives a Jaguar and lives in a mansion fall in love with a bum like me?"

"You're not a bum."

"I am. A thief, too. Remember I stole money from you? You paid me five thousand bucks to bugger off. Remember? But in spite of all that you love me. Say it again, Natasha. Say: 'I love you, Nicholas.' "

"I love you, Nicholas."

"I love you so much that if we can't be together I don't want to go on living. Say that, Natasha, say that."

"I won't. I can't."

"But you *are* going to say it, Natasha, my beautiful, my love." He vanished beneath the covers, and she began to pant in anticipation as his lips slowly moved from her breasts to the place she thought of as her hidden grotto where a man, after payment of an appropriate tribute to the gods of love, was granted the privilege of knowing ecstasy. But something had gone terribly wrong: The special bond she'd once believed was exclusive to her and David was now reduced to a mere physical reaction that at once fascinated and repelled her. She recalled things Amanda had said about men, how they assumed whatever they offered women in bed was what they desired. Nick reappeared: "You *will* say it, Natasha. I know you will, because you want me to take you up the mountain of ecstasy 'til you reach the top and can throw yourself off . . . to fall, endlessly fall. So say it, Natasha."

"I love you so much that if I can't be with you, I don't want to go on living."

"There. It's easy to say, isn't it?" He disappeared beneath the covers again and she felt his lips brush her nipples, then hover at the entry to her secret grotto. He reappeared, like a swimmer surfacing. "I mean every word, Natasha. Do you?"

"Yes. Don't stop." Before Nick, she'd thought it unbecoming for a woman verbally to impose sexual demands; rather a woman must let a man become aware of the existence of her needs by insinuating herself into his awareness.

"Maybe you think you can say anything you please to me. That it doesn't matter what you say, because you can always shrug me off. Is that all I am, Natasha? A guy available to lick your cunt?"

"No!" she cried. "Don't speak like that. You know I think the world of you." The coarse, brutal words appalled her. "You know I'd do anything for you." There: She'd made the admission. Now she screamed as his lips touched her, even while wondering if David had reserved such intimate caresses for Liz. She felt enormous hatred for both of them.

He emerged and acrid sexual odours swirled around her. "Ugh! We stink — physically and morally."

"Are you trying to humiliate me? Trying to make me feel ashamed?"

"No." He lay upon her, his face against hers. "I'm trying to tell you that we live in a schizoid world where everything and everybody stinks. But I never cared about any of that until I fell for you. I never understood before that there could be an absolute need in my life. I thought life amounted to eating, drinking, pissing and shitting and being laid occasionally. I thought I could survive, that I could get by. Hell, I'd been doing that since leaving school. After all, what was I? A two-bit guy who thought he had the makings of an actor. It's a big laugh to think you'd even bother with a guy like me. There're dozens around just like me. You want me to line a few up for you? Why did you have to walk into my life? I was surviving quite nicely with Diefenbaker and my illusions. Now, I haven't the courage to go on without you. I don't want to go on living and have to know that each night you'll go to bed and shimmy up your nightgown for some other guy to fuck you. What's he like, Natasha? I can't bear to think of him lying between your thighs. Natasha. I can't stand it."

"We'll work something out."

"I've trying to tell you, we can't. I'm not going to be stuck in some dump like this and hang around waiting for you to call once a week for a lick and a fuck."

"Don't talk like that. It's hateful."

"It's the truth, Natasha."

"No. If you really think I'm like that, why did you come back?"

"Have you listened to me? I've told you what happened. I've told you what we have to do and you agreed. Remember? You said —"

"I know what I said. But you made me say it. I can't leave my children. Let me go." She panicked and struggled to escape from him, while he pressed down on her. "No! No! I won't listen to you. Let me go." He suddenly stopped trying to restrain her and lay face down on the bed. She scrambled away, snatched at her clothes, quickly put them on, made for the door, then stopped to look back at him.

"Nick?" she said. When he didn't reply, she returned to touch his head. "Isn't it enough that we can meet? You needn't worry, I'll help you."

He raised his head and hatred could be seen in his narrowed eyes and throat-tightened voice. "Just go," he said, "just go." She hesitated, then returned to lie on the bed beside him and cry silently. After a while he lifted his hand to touch her face and wipe away the tears. "It doesn't matter," he said. "Don't cry any more. It's not worth it. *I'm* not worth it."

"Promise you won't do anything. I'll come tomorrow. I'll bring you . . . I'll arrange things."

"I don't want money." He turned to look at her, and there was so much pain in his eyes she wanted to hold and comfort him. He managed to smile. "I used to think I was a pretty cynical guy who more or less knew everything. Now I realize I know bugger-all. I'm sick with love, Natasha . . . sick with it. And I can tell by looking at you that you haven't caught my disease. You don't like me to say so, Natasha, but what you want —"

"Don't say it!" Natasha cried out. "Don't use those horrible words! I know what I feel. Why do you think I'm crying? Why do you think I'm lying here with you? You think I'm the kind who goes around picking up men? You think I want this to happen? I'm terrified." Then, like a child who's been suddenly frightened, she felt the need to empty her bladder. "Can I use your bathroom?" she said.

"If you're going to piss, I want to watch."

"Oh no. Please."

"Oh yes. Please. Can you shit too? I'd like to smell it. I'm sick with love, so sick I want to know each detail of your life. Let me watch you."

In the end, his desire and her full bladder allowed her to pull down her underclothes and squat on the rickety wooden seat while he stood in the doorway watching. When she was finished, he ripped off several pieces of toilet paper and wiped her. "Oh, Natasha, Natasha," he moaned. "Where would you ever find devotion like this?"

"I'll be back tomorrow. I promise." He pulled up her clothes, then pressed his lips against her forehead. "You have enough money?" she asked. "Enough." She hunted through her purse and found several bills. "Tomorrow," she promised as she pushed the money into his clenched hand. "Tomorrow," he echoed.

She put on her coat and went to the door. "You promise?" she said, not knowing what she was asking of him. She could hardly bear to look at him sitting on the bed: naked, skinny, nondescript. Why did she experience a desire to stay with him and offer comfort?

"Just leave, Natasha. You'll feel better once you're in your car driving away. Take my word for it. Never hang around a dump like this. You came here to get something. You got it. Now get out. Go on!" he suddenly shouted. "Get out!" She left, quickly drove away, turned up the heater and after driving a few minutes decided she'd just undergone a degrading experience, which she mustn't allow to happen ever again. At home, she showered, threw the clothes she'd worn into the garbage, put on fresh ones, then went to visit with the children, who were having their evening meal. She kissed and hugged each child, then sat to watch them, feeling horrified as she recalled that Nick's lips had driven her to such heights of torturous passion that she'd actually agreed to abandon her exquisite passion flowers. How could she imagine a life deprived of their beautiful faces, dark eyes, and pretty lips which she loved to watch as they opened to reveal their innocent activities and little quarrels, the mountains of their molehill world? She wanted to clasp them to her body and remember how she'd carried them in her womb and had experienced pain as they left that maternal haven to slip out into the fearsome world. How could she ever have allowed gross physical desire to threaten the futures of the most beautiful creatures in her life? After they'd eaten she watched them bathe, dried their silky-skinned, supple bodies, then placed her hands around their faces and looked into their eyes, as though hoping to discern there the pattern of their futures, because soon — all too soon — they would commence the alterations which would take them away from her. What would they think if they knew that their adored mother had been sprawled out on a damp sheet in a cold ugly room, sweating and moaning while the tongue of a penniless waiter touched the most secret parts of her body?

Shame invaded her and she felt she had no right to touch her children: She had befouled herself and was carrying the stench of her vile promiscuity. Until this moment she hadn't truly understood that trust in its mother is the greatest necessity of a child's life, the anchor that holds it in place on the placid surface of childhood and prevents it from being carried off into a realm where trust and love do not exist. She told herself what had occurred that afternoon would never happen again; she would beat back her errant desires until they became subservient to her will. The sweet aroma of her children's warm bodies reminded her of her own and Nick's sexual odours. No, she would never go near him again, never again would she succumb to those unseemly indignities. To remember he'd been present while she emptied her bladder humiliated her. She felt she must be blushing and she hid her face in the children's nightclothes so that Maria could not see the evidence of her moral turpitude, which surely must be imprinted on her brow for all to see. Years ago, women caught in adultery were branded on the forehead, and hadn't she read somewhere that in backward Islamic countries adulterous men and women were publicly executed? Oh God, what had she done? She clutched the children as though she would use them to defend herself. She felt her heart pounding and realized her panic was being communicated to them. "It's nothing, nothing," she whispered. "Mommy just gets upset when she imagines how bad she'd feel if anything ever happened to any of you. That's all." She managed to laugh. "See? It's all gone. All better. Now, I have to go and see if Daddy's home." She kissed them and went downstairs to the living room where David sat, turning the pages of a *National Geographic* magazine. He did not look at her and she was afraid of what might happen if she began talking. And so they sat there: David, carefully turning pages, Natasha watching him. After a while, she said, "Shall we have dinner? It's ready." At once, he set the magazine aside, stood and waited for her to precede him across the hall into the dining room where they sat at the oval table, picking at their food, awaiting (like condemned prisoners) the moment when the facade of their marriage would split itself open to reveal it had wasted away to nothing.

"What shall we do?" Natasha whispered. "What shall we do?"

David raised his head to stare at her. His lips parted as though he wanted to speak, but no sound issued forth. His throat convulsed and he got up and left the room. Natasha continued to sit at the table until the maid came in to clear the dishes, then she arose and went into the living room where she lay face-down on a couch, her face hidden in the cushions.

Chapter 26

"You mustn't blame Natasha too much for what's happened," Amanda said. Amanda, Jamie and Hilda were sitting at Amanda's kitchen table, drinking their habitual tea and eating lemon tarts from the supermarket, while discussing the apparent collapse of Natasha and David's marriage and attempting to concoct a plan to bring them together again. But, as is often the case in such circumstances, they found it easier to diagnose the problem than to solve it. "Finding out about Liz was a terrible shock to her."

"Maybe David behaved like a fool," Hilda said, "but he's not the first man to cheat on his wife and won't be the last. Women have to expect that."

"But men don't usually cheat with their half-sisters!" Jamie said.

"What's the difference?" Hilda said. "It's still another woman. Let me tell you, the first time I found out about Max I felt as if my whole life was falling apart. But I forced myself to focus on Max's better side — fortunately there were good points." Amanda and Jamie nodded. "Natasha's always taken things to extremes. Like thinking her kids are perfect . . . and how she refers to them. Her *passion flowers!* It's ridiculous! And embarrassing! As good as telling us what she and David did in bed."

"Maybe that's how she felt," Jamie tentatively said.

"David would never have married Natasha if she hadn't got pregnant."

"What was so wrong about Tashie going to bed with David and getting pregnant?"

"If she'd complained to Aunt Nanda, there'd have been hell to pay if David hadn't agreed to marry her. And I'll bet he knew it."

Amanda picked up and nibbled at a lemon tart like a rabbit going around a lettuce leaf. "Natasha got pregnant because she was in love. It happens all the time. Anyway, the person truly responsible for the mess is gone now," she said. "Liz couldn't let David go. It's as simple as that."

"There's nothing simple about it," Jamie commented.

"I meant, Tashie's being in love with David and going to bed with him was simple and normal, but the way Liz behaved wasn't. Yet you two want to blame Natasha for the bust-up of the marriage."

"I don't want to do anything of the kind," Hilda said. "I'm just saying that the quickest way to break up a marriage is to expect perfection in it. That's all. I recognize Conrad's limitations. I know he's not particularly bright and has his fair share of male conceit, but apart from that he's quite acceptable." Amanda and Jamie nodded, recalling Conrad's possessive slaps on Hilda's capacious rear-end.

"You mean he gives a good account of himself in bed?" Amanda quizzed.

"I said, he's acceptable — which covers a variety of things. Marriage doesn't consist entirely of sex, Amanda."

"There's not much to a marriage without it," Amanda dryly remarked.

"Is this some damn marriage counsellor's conference, or what?" Jamie asked. "I'm not enthusiastic about getting involved in other people's mess-ups. I have enough of my own."

"But Jamie!" Amanda reproachfully said. "You promised you'd talk to David."

"I'm still prepared to do it, but I'm not going to gossip about his marriage. I don't give a damn how many times a week they have sex, or why David got into bed with Liz. Who knows and who cares, except you, Mandy? I can see you're itching to ask Hiddie how often she and Conrad go at it, but I refuse to sit here and listen to your tittle-tattle. I've already said I'd try to knock some sense into David's head, and you two'll try the same with Natasha. Agreed?" Amanda and Hilda, silenced by Jamie's outburst, nodded. "Good. Then that's settled." He got up. "I'll telephone you after I've seen Davey. And you can call me, but that's it. No more discussions about who did what and who's responsible for the mess."

"He's edgy these days," Hilda said after Jamie left the house.

"Alice isn't the easiest person to live with and Paul cries a lot at night."

"All babies yell at night. Maxie slept all day and was wide awake all night. But I took it in stride."

"I'm sure you did."

"And Max always did his fair share when the children were small, not like some men who think changing diapers is beneath them. He liked children."

"Especially girls."

"That comment was uncalled for, Mandy. Fortunately, by now I'm enured to your snide remarks and can ignore them. But let me tell you, Max was as devoted to his children as they were to him, and he never said or did anything out of place with Louise and Jeanette. Never. What's more he taught them how to behave in public, which is more than your or Natasha's children know."

"Max said twelve-year-old girls were 'fair game', and he told me he'd proved the point with a friend's daughter."

"I know all about Max's stories. And that's the point: They were only stories. His ambition was to be thought of as a modern-day Don Juan. Poor Max. He scared away more women than he ever seduced." Hilda got up and walked along the hall to the front door, Amanda following. "You see Natasha first, then call me, so I'll have information before I go and see her. We have to coordinate things, Mandy, so don't handle this in your usual scatterbrained fashion. Remember, one of the great necessities in life is accurate, detailed communication. Right?" The delivery of that verbal blast carried Hilda out the front entrance, leaving Amanda fuming, telling herself once more that she was finished with her family. Now that Hilda was safely remarried it appeared that she felt free to whitewash memories of her dead husband, transforming Max Logan from a skirt-groper and ogler of little girls' underpantries into an ideal family man. Amanda might have been amused by Hilda's attempts to sanitize his reputation, but she'd always been certain that a hidden agenda lay behind Max's fondness for dollying up his daughters in fancy clothes, and while she didn't want to blacken his reputation, still she knew how sneaky and circumventive men could be when they wanted to manoeuvre themselves into situations that offered opportunities to exploit and gratify their secret urges. Amanda had often observed the closed-up, withdrawn expressions on Louise and Jeanette's faces, which reinforced her suspicions that more had gone on between Max Logan and his daughters than having lunches in elegant restaurants. Of course, she couldn't be absolutely certain, but when she looked at her own children's faces and saw expressions there that revealed their reactions to what was happening around them, it was easy to conclude that *her* children were surrounded by an essential innocence which Louise and Jeanette seemed to have lost years ago.

Of course everyone knew where Natasha had gone after leaving David, although why she'd elected to live with Nick Parsons in an East Vancouver basement suite when she could have rented an elegant apartment overlooking English Bay was something Amanda had difficulty comprehending. Jamie claimed it was the product of a masochistic streak in Natasha, who sought physical, social and sexual degradation in order to appease her guilt about possessing wealth in a world otherwise dominated by poverty, disease and unrelieved misery; Hilda maintained Natasha did it for the same reasons people join religious cults and kneel before repulsive, heavily bearded gurus who are interested only in getting their hands on their disciples' money, although as far as Hilda knew, Natasha's capital was safely locked away in a trust, thank goodness; and although Amanda nodded as Jamie and Hilda offered explanations for Natasha's behaviour, her own opinion was that Natasha was simply in love with Nick Parsons and as indifferent to her surroundings as she, Amanda, had been when she fled with Harry Greene to northern B.C. It was really quite obvious, and although she'd agreed to function as the family's first ambassador, she felt sure Natasha wasn't about to change her mind, at least not yet.

<hr />

"But Tashie," Amanda said, falling back to her second line of attack, "the children miss you. I've told them you're on holiday. But . . ." Amanda trailed off, implying that pretence with Natasha's children couldn't be prolonged indefinitely. They were sitting in Nick Parson's basement suite, which Natasha had regained by paying the tenant to move out.

"If David doesn't want them, they can come here."

"They couldn't possibly come here, Tashie."

"Lots of children live in places worse than this."

"Maybe, but that's how those children've always lived. Listen, I understand why you have to be with Nick Parsons, I felt the same about Harry."

"This isn't the same."

"We always think what we personally feel is different to what others feel, Tashie, but really there's no difference. When Harry kissed me, I'd feel as if the world was melting away. I wouldn't have cared if somebody had walked into the trailer at that moment and shot me."

"There's more than that between Nick and me."

Amanda shrugged. "I can tell you what's going to happen if you stay."

"I won't hear it." Like a child, Natasha clamped hands over her ears. "Go away, Mandy."

"Is this where you came the first time, Tashie?"

"That's got nothing to do with what I feel for Nick. Or what he feels for me."

"And just what *does* he feel for you?"

"I don't see why I have to explain anything to you, or anybody else."

"Maybe you're doing this to pay David back, to make him suffer."

"I'm not. I've stopped loving him, that's all."

Amanda got up and stood by the small table, looking at the stained wall and low ceiling. A large cat padded in to stretch, yawn, then spring onto and settle on Natasha's lap.

"This is Diefenbaker." Natasha rubbed the cat's ears. It obligingly purred.

"I was watching Jasmine yesterday." Natasha stopped stroking the cat. "And she suspects something. I'm sure she does. The other children ask if I've spoken to you on the phone, if you're having a nice holiday and so on, but Jasmine's stopped asking about you because she knows I'm lying. She's losing her innocence, Tashie." Amanda opened her purse, to search for her car key. "It's a shame, she's such a lovely girl." She walked towards the basement door.

"Nick said he couldn't go on living if I . . ." Nastasha's voice trembled.

"The guy's playing another trick on you, Tashie. You paid him to go away. So what did he do? He came back to say he couldn't live without you. And you fell for it. The next time he says that, offer him a knife, then walk out."

"He means it. You don't know Nick."

"I've met dozens like him. Cheap bums. Wise up, Tashie. You're being taken for a ride. How much money have you given him?"

"None."

"You're lying. I'll bet you've given him thousands. So why not come to your senses and realize it's not just your own life you're ruining, it's your kids' lives too?" It was amazing, thought Amanda, that she, the family profligate, should be talking like a bluenose to the one person in the family whom everyone had always viewed as the personification of marital fidelity.

"I suppose you think you're a perfect example of how to be a good wife and mother?"

"I don't claim to be anything, but I've never let a five-minute fuck interfere with my kids' lives."

"Go away!" Natasha suddenly shrieked. "Get away from me! Leave me alone! Who gave you the right to interfere in my life?" Amanda's answer was to shrug and walk out, behaviour that was far more humiliating to Natasha than any bitter verbal condemnation Amanda could have delivered. The shrug communicated Amanda's indifference; it conveyed that she didn't care what happened to Natasha, and that frightened Natasha because all her life she'd been surrounded by people whose principal occupation was making sure nothing untoward happened to her. The ill-lit, dreary room in which she sat suddenly became a prison into which she had been thrown, like waste into a pit. She shivered and clutched the cat, which yowled and scratched her hands before she allowed it to spring from her lap and rush away to hide beneath the bed where she and Nick slept and made love. Love! Was what she felt for Nick, love? Or was it nothing more than a recurring need to scale the highest peaks of sensual pleasure, to experience, as Amanda had described it, the melting away of the body into an indescribable throbbing bliss? Was it nothing more than lust? And was she — a woman in her thirties and mother of four children — merely experiencing what any adolescent girl felt during her first love affair when she lay on the back seat of a second-hand car, successively surrendering lips, breasts and loins to the urgent lips, hands and loins of a sweating, clumsy youth? There had to be more to what she and Nick felt for each other: A man does not tell a woman he can't live without her; a woman does not surrender a fine home and adoring family unless . . . She heard footsteps, the door opened, Nick entered and turned on the weak overhead light.

"What's up with you?" he said as he crossed to the table.

"Amanda was here."

"Did you tell her to get the hell out?"

"She lost patience with me and left. Where have you been?"

"Visiting at the lounge where we met. I thought I might get my old job back."

"Why? You don't need to work."

"It's what I ought to be doing. I envied those guys." He moved to the back of her chair, and after pressing her shoulders, moved his hands down onto her breasts.

"I have to go back home," Natasha said.

"No. I won't let you."

"I have to. The children . . ."

"She tried to scare you, eh? Kiddies wailing for their mommy and all that crap?"

"I know it's not important to you. But I swore I'd never allow what I felt for you to come first, before my children."

"And so now that you've had — what is it? nine . . . ten days of undiluted fucking — you can —"

"Please, Nick."

"For God's sake, you don't care what I do with your body, providing I don't talk about it." He squeezed her breasts. "You know what I'd really like to do? I'd like to get my teeth into your cunt and rip it out, I'd like to rip your throat out and watch you die. Once you were dead, I'd slit my own throat, because I'd know then that no other guy could ever kiss your tits and feel your cunt." He pulled her up off the chair and began kissing her face and throat. "Know what I did this afternoon?" He laughed. "I went to the bar on the off-chance a guy I knew'd be working the floor." He laughed again. "An old woman was sitting there, so I went up to her and said, 'Aren't you Mrs. — I've forgotten what name I used — Brigadier-General So-and-so's wife?' All so obvious. 'No, no,' she wasn't, she said. I chatted her up, I told her she must allow me to buy her a drink." His laughter became uncontrollable, like a rasping cough. "I went to her room. Oh sure, she knew I'd pitched her, but she wanted what I had to offer. She wanted me between her thighs. Will you be like that when you're old, Natasha? Will you have fat thighs and a wrinkled ass? I gave her a good run for her money too. Old women never stop wanting it, you know that, Natasha? They can't get enough of it. Is that how you'll be, Natasha, eh? Letting a guy like me screw you for a hundred bucks?" He manoeuvred her into the dark bedroom and pushed her onto the bed. "Saggy tits, fat belly. Is that what'll become of my sweet little Natasha?" He lay across her, and she could smell the alcohol on his breath and clothes. "I lifted a couple of hundred from her wallet." His body shook with racking laughter. "But she won't tell, because if she did, she'd have to explain what I was doing in her room. God, Natasha, I loathe myself. I want to die. Let's get it over with. Look at me. A paid fucker of old women. Look at you. You don't care about anything except having me fuck you. We're not fit to live, Natasha. You know that. You can no more go back to your kids than I can go to Hollywood and become a film star. We're a cosmic joke. You've bought me, haven't you? You'll work me over, then throw me out, won't you? When I can't give you what you want any more? That's true, isn't it? Admit it! Admit it!" He clutched her shoulders and violently shook her, while she mutely stared at him. "You want to know why I went with that old woman, Natasha? Eh, do you? Do you?"

"I don't care."

"You don't? I did it to prove you didn't own me. Oh Christ, oh Christ." He began to sob. "It's lies. I'm a liar, Natasha. When I open my mouth I spew lies, like a kid vomiting."

"You don't lie when you say you love me, do you?"

"Maybe I do, maybe I thought I could leech thousands of bucks out of you . . . enough to carry me for a few years. Oh God, oh God, I can't go on like this, Natasha. There really was an old woman sitting in the bar, probably somebody's grandmother, maybe in town to consult a specialist, maybe she has a heart disease or cancer. Why do I look at people and degrade them in my imagination? Why can't we make love and then die? I tell myself there's nothing wrong with us loving each other. I tell myself you're like other women: You want to feel a man burrowing in you, you want to feel his head moving between your thighs. That's all natural in women, isn't it? Then something goes wrong, Natasha. I can't think. I start asking myself if I really love you. I walked along Granville Street and had a look at the women and girls, the way their asses moved, like yours when you walk. There's no difference. Some were beautiful, some plain, some ugly; but they all have what you have, Natasha. And the guys I saw, they're like me. It's crazy. Any one of them could be on top of you, like I am, and if you closed your eyes, would you know the difference? We're crazy, Tashie, crazy. That's why we have to make an end to it before we wake up. I've thought about it. I know how to manage it."

"No," Natasha moaned. "No, I can't."

"But Natasha —" He stopped sobbing and was now reasoning with her as parents do with irrational children. "You must see that if what we think is so unique and special is the same thing that millions and millions of people do every day, that's *sold* by teenage kids who bargain with old guys who drive around in cars, then there has to be something crazy about us." He paused. "Well, isn't that right?"

"They don't love."

"Love!" he jeered. "Love! You call what we do, love?"

"You could have left me alone. You chose to come back and stand on the road where you knew I'd see you. If you think I'm no better than the women you see in the street, then leave me alone. Go on, get away." She pushed at and struck him as she tried to free herself, then both collapsed and lay still as the telephone, which rang so seldom they tended to forget it, rang.

"Probably for you," he whispered.

"No. It has to be for you."

"It's not listed in my name."

"Answer it, Nick." He went into the little kitchen and she heard him pick up the receiver and say hello.

"Nothing," he called. Natasha quickly left the bed and went to stand by him in the kitchen. "Probably someone misdialling. Is there anything to eat?" He opened and looked into the refrigerator. "You're not the best provider in the world, are you, Natasha?" The phone began ringing again. He picked up the receiver, listened, then replaced it. "It's malfunctioning. Phones do that."

Natasha leaned over to peer at the cradle that held the phone. "There isn't a number on it," she said.

"It's probably an old phone somebody hooked up."

"Isn't that illegal?"

"Guys have to get by somehow."

"Unplug it," Natasha said.

"Why? It can't bite us."

"Unplug it!" She suddenly grabbed the phone, jerked it and the cord flew out from behind the refrigerator. They stared at the two exposed wires.

"Somebody made a bad job of connecting it."

"Throw it away!"

"Why? I'll move the fridge and connect it again."

"No! They'll get the number, they'll fix it so they can hear us talking!"

He laughed. "You read too many spy stories." He picked up the phone and pointed it at her. "Your mother's spies're taking pictures of you. Snap, snap, snap. Tashie with her pants down, having it from the rear. Tashie on the kitchen table, legs open. Hey guys, take a look at that gash." He moved the phone as though shooting a movie and Natasha responded by snatching up the cradle, smashing it into the receiver and hitting his eye. He cried out, dropped the phone and leaned over the table, hands over his eye.

"Oh, Jesus!" he groaned. "You smashed my eye. Jesus! Can't you take a joke?"

"If you ever speak of me like that again, I'll . . ." She left the kitchen and went into the bedroom where she began collecting the articles of clothing she had brought with her. He followed her into the room.

"What are you doing?" he asked.

"A man who loves a woman doesn't talk to her like that," she said.

"Men and women say anything. They enjoy hurting each other. A lot of women get a kick out of filthy talk."

"Not when they love each other. They respect each other's feelings."

"Natasha . . ." He managed to get his arms around her. "Remember, I'm a no-good bum and petty thief. I always talk that way about women. Those are words I learned as a kid." He caressed her. "If you go, I'm finished. You're the only woman who's given every part of herself to me. I know your family think I'm sucking money out of you, but I wouldn't care if you turned in every cent of it and we had to live on the streets. Maybe I'm not much good, Natasha, but while I have you I can convince myself I'm capable of becoming something halfways decent. Don't go, Natasha, don't go. Don't leave me, Natasha. Natasha!" His voice rose to a wailing shriek as she pushed him away and walked towards the door. He rushed to the kitchen and returned carrying a paring knife. "You're making me do this, Natasha." He brought the knife to his throat, while Natasha stood by the half-opened door, white and shaking. "Watch . . . watch. You're doing this to me, Natasha. Remember that." Natasha gasped as blood dribbled down his throat, then cried out "No! No!" and rushed over to wrench the knife away from his throat. The cut in his skin was small: no larger than a gash accidentally made while shaving, but to Natasha it appeared immense and the blood flowing from it like a torrent.

She took the knife from him, forced him to sit at the table, while, fingers violently trembling, she applied Bandaids to the wound. They did not speak, and when she had stopped shaking she made a pot of tea, which they half-heartedly drank. Natasha could not look at him, because in the brief moment she'd rushed over to drag his hand away from his throat, her passion for Nick Parsons had vanished to be replaced with disgust at herself and something akin to loathing for him. She remembered the sexual things she had done with him, and to recall her behaviour filled her with acute embarrassment. How could she have done these things? How could she have exposed herself so completely? Amanda had been the one who had assessed Nick accurately, and she, Natasha, had been too weak to call his bluff; but his judgement of her had been as accurate as Amanda's of him. From the first moment he'd seen her, he'd guessed she was looking for something she wasn't getting from her husband, which he was prepared to provide, for a price. He'd trapped her by pretending love. How could she have been so foolish as to believe that? Probably his going to Edmonton was a lie. Oh, what a fool she'd been, what a fool!

"Everything you've told me is lies," she said. "So don't bother to make up any more stories."

"Maybe one or two things," he admitted.

"Such as going to Edmonton."

"That was true — I have family there."

"What? Who?"

"Well . . . actually a woman . . . and a little girl."

"You're contemptible! And so am I for believing you loved me."

"It's true — I am utterly contemptible, except for one thing. I love you, Natasha."

"I don't believe you."

"I hardly believe it myself, but it's true."

"Are you saying you have a wife? Oh, why do I ask? What do I care?" Her hands twisted the fabric on her purse, snapping it.

"There's no reason you should care. Anyway, I'm not married to her.

Janice calls herself my wife because of the child. Most of the money I got from you's gone to her."

Natasha stood. "What a fool I've been. Don't you realize how ashamed I feel?"

"People do far worse things than you did, Natasha." She went to the door and put her hand on the door knob. "Okay, so I'm condemned, but why not let me have my say? Okay?" She waited by the door, her back to him. "You pushed yourself into my life; I didn't ask you to come into the lounge, or return to it. I didn't force you to come here. So just remember that when you put on your self-righteous act and blame me for everything. Sure I took your money. Why not? You're wallowing in it like a hog in a mudhole. You got what you wanted — a guy who'd give you all the sex you'd dreamt of, or read about in cheap novels. You got all that, lady — and at a cut-rate price! So now you want to bugger off back to your kids and husband. Okay, that's fine; it's what I expected at the beginning. But something unexpected happened, Natasha. I fell in love with you."

"You aren't."

"You think I'm playing games? No sir. Maybe just now I was playing, when I nicked myself. Hell, I want to keep you here with me." He smiled and gestured. "Y'know, when I went to Edmonton with the five grand you gave me, I really thought I could make it with Janice. Get a bar job. I mean, she's got a good set of boobs, nice ass. What the hell, all the equipment's there, just waiting for some guy to have fun with. And she likes having me fuck her. So why didn't I stay? Because of you, Natasha. And you know something else? Until you came along, I never waited around for any woman. Never! If she didn't show on time I was gone. And something else . . . you drove by half a dozen times in that street and didn't see me. That made me feel lousy. Of course, it wasn't your fault. You thought — or did you ever bother to think about me? — that I was down in Hollywood becoming a film star." The cat had returned to settle in Nick's lap, and he automatically stroked its head. "Cupboard love," he said, when it began to purr. "Okay, I've had my say, you can go now. Why don't you go? Go on, leave. Open the fucking door and go. Or d'you want me to fuck your ass first?"

He moved as if to stand, and Natasha fled to her car, started it and raced away. She looked into the rear-view mirror as she turned onto Quebec Street and thought she saw him standing in the lane holding Diefenbaker, but decided she was mistaken, that he didn't care enough to make a final gesture. She began to cry, and tears were still flowing when she rang the bell at Nanda's house. She hadn't seen her mother for several weeks and imagined the meeting would be difficult and that Nanda would censure her. Instead, her mother smiled and said nothing more than, "Hello dear, how're you keeping?"

Natasha collapsed beside the couch to hide her face in Nanda's lap and sob. She rocked, as people do when afflicted by severe pain. "Oh, Mother!" she repeatedly cried. "Oh, Mother, I didn't understand." Finally she got onto the couch to lie with her face pressed against the blouse that covered Nanda's shrunken breasts.

"These things happen," Nanda said after Natasha eventually quieted down. "And when you least expect them. Your life seems to be going along just fine, when suddenly, for no apparent reason, everything collapses and you can't understand it because you think you've been doing your best."

Nothing further was said. Of course Natasha might have said she wanted more than soothing platitudes from her mother, and Nanda might have pointed out to her daughter the dangers of sexual entanglements, but nothing of this was uttered by either because Natasha was unable to feel anything but shame for her behaviour during the past two weeks and Nanda's concern went no further than pacifying her eldest child to ensure she returned to her children. David was not mentioned, although Nanda assumed a reconciliation would eventually take place. On balance, she thought David's follies equalled those committed by Natasha, and it followed therefore that one set of offences cancelled out the other. There was a good chance, she thought, that harmony would be restored to the marriage of David and Natasha Powell and that it would continue into the future as if nothing had ever occurred to disturb it.

Chapter 27

"Has Jamie met with David yet?" Amanda sat in an armchair opposite Alice, who was perched in a cushioned rocking chair nursing her son Paul, one vast china-white breast majestically exposed. Amanda remembered her mother having purchased the rocker, then afterwards deciding it didn't blend with the living room decor and retiring it to the basement from which it had been rescued by Jamie after Alice had told him that a nurse in the maternity ward had informed her a nursing mother required only four things: a good rocking chair, an ample supply of milk, three dozen cloth diapers and a towel-lined apple box in which to put the baby when it was not nursing. Of the four, Alice had three: the rocker, an abundance of breast milk and dozens of diapers; but instead of an apple box, Alice and Jamie's baby reclined in a beribboned bassinet, a gift from Nanda.

Whenever Amanda entered the nursery to be confronted with Alice's breasts and nipples from which thin white fluid copiously oozed and spurted, she invariably reflected on how gingerly she had once broached the subject of breast-feeding with Alice, because for some reason she'd assumed Alice would find nursing her child repugnant. But Alice had surprised her by saying, "You think I'd go to all the trouble of manufacturing the stuff, then waste it? Like hell I will. I'll put it where it's supposed to go — into the kid."

Shortly after Paul's birth, the running of Liz's house (Amanda still thought of the house as belonging to Liz) had been taken over by a Sikh family recommended by Harjinder Singh. Gurdev, the head of the family, spent most of his time in the front hall, the mother did the cooking, two daughters functioned as house and nursery maids, and a son worked in the garden when he wasn't attending classes at Simon Fraser University where he was studying for a degree in economics. Amanda assumed Gurdev was a relative of Harjinder Singh and was always ready to chat with him, but Gurdev never uttered a word in her presence (he communicated by bowing, pointing, or opening and closing doors) and the young women more or less ignored her. She had never even seen the mother.

When Amanda asked Alice about the family she shrugged and said, "Don't ask me. Ask Jamie or your Aunt Nanda. They dug them up from somewhere. They were here when I came home from the hospital. I think they're from Fiji." Alice revealed a racist streak in her dealings with the family: She couldn't get their names straight and addressed them with the words "Hey, you!", which embarrassed Amanda, who had overheard enough adult conversations as a child to know that one should always be polite with one's servants in order to offset the possibility that some day in the future, when the masses revolted, they would attempt to kill you if you were male or rape you and steal your jewellery if you were female. Also, Amanda was impressed by the changes in the house since the family had moved in: They demonstrated the kind of unseen efficiency noted in superior hotels, for although Amanda never observed them engaged in household tasks, nevertheless floors and furniture were polished, carpets vacuumed, and silver and brass ornaments buffed to a sparkle. Indeed, the light reflected by the polished surfaces had the effect of making the house brighter and more attractive than it had been in years. Outside, the son, whose good looks made Amanda's mouth water, pruned shrubs and trees, edged errant borders, swept the drive, and generally tidied everything up until the house and its grounds re-emerged as the imposing structure it had been in the days when Amanda and Jamie lived there as children.

One afternoon, Amanda had tried to start up a conversation with one of the young women by inquiring whether she and her sister had found the Vancouver climate much different from that of Fiji. She didn't get far with her opening gambit.

"We came from London," the woman replied in her impeccable English. "I and my sister and brother were born in England."

"Oh . . . I thought you were from Fiji."

"Really?"

"I don't know where I got that idea." Amanda gave one of her light social laughs.

"We came to Vancouver in order to oblige my uncle, Harjinder Singh." The woman was scrupulously polite, but beneath her response Amanda could detect a layer of contempt, which made her uneasy and caused her later to try to soften Alice's attitude towards the family. She got nowhere.

"London, Fiji . . . who cares? If they don't like the way I treat them, they don't have to stay."

"I get the impression they're under some sort of obligation to Harjinder Singh."

"So what! They're being paid, aren't they?" Alice had little time for people who claimed there were finer places in the world than Canada. She might have passionately hated her family and one hundred percent of Canadian men (except for Jamie) but that didn't prevent her from being chauvinistic about her homeland.

Although Amanda found fault with Alice's relationship with her servants, she had no criticism of Alice as a mother. In fact, Amanda was of the opinion that Alice had done remarkably well when actually called upon to produce the infant: She'd gritted her teeth and evicted the seven-pound six-ounce child from its lodging place in just under three hours. "To hell with lying around moaning and groaning," Alice had informed Amanda, who came to the hospital a few hours after Paul's birth. "I had nine months of misery, and that's enough for me. So, what d'you think? Does he look like Jamie?"

Naturally Amanda agreed that Paul bore a striking resemblance to Jamie. Alice re-asked this question every time Amanda paid one of her frequent visits to offer advice on the nurturing of infants, most of which Alice ignored, and should Amanda persist and emphasize, for instance, the need for cleanliness, Alice would dredge up some memory of childhood hours spent on her aunt's and uncle's farm and silence Amanda (temporarily) by asking whether she'd ever watched sows feeding a dozen piglets. "Well, I have," announced Alice when Amanda shook her head no, "and I'm telling you, as long as those piglets were fed on schedule they were as happy as clams in sand." What was Amanda to do with a person who apparently couldn't distinguish among a suckling pig, a clam and the son of a poet and peer of the realm? However, Alice's comments did not deter Amanda in the slightest from offering advice over the phone and during visits; after all, she had her reputation as health expert to maintain and so she made sure that snippets of information about immunizations and other public health services were slipped into conversations with Alice, and while Alice might rudely reject the information offered, Amanda noticed she often followed her advice. On occasion, she discussed deadly childhood diseases, to which topics Alice violently reacted, accusing Amanda of deliberately trying to frighten her. "I dunno why you tell me about those awful things," she said, "Paul's as healthy as a weed."

"Of course he is," Amanda soothed. "He's a lovely baby, and you're doing marvellously well as a mother, Alice. But you have to be aware of what could happen, that's all."

Today, as she followed Alice downstairs to the living room, Amanda asked again, "Did Jamie talk to David? Did he tell you what David said?"

"I got the impression David said bugger-all," Alice said, "but sometimes it's hard to figure out what Jamie's talking about. Hell, the only time

I'm certain what he's driving at is when he crawls across the bed and gets on top of me."

Amanda, feeling obligated to defend her brother, countered, "I usually understand what Jamie says."

"Bully for you," Alice said. "Bring us some tea," she ordered Gurdev, who was standing in his usual position in the hall. He hurried to open the living room door for them, then closed it after they entered the room. "I dunno why Jamie got those people, but I wish they'd pack up and go back to wherever they came from. That guy just stands around in the hall all day and doesn't do a goddamn thing."

"Listen Alice, I don't think you should speak so . . . well . . . so rudely about the servants."

"I'll speak as I please in my own house. If they don't like it, they can bugger off."

"That's not what I meant," Amanda protested.

"I don't care what you meant."

The door was now opened by Gurdev, and a daughter pushed in a tea trolley (something else Jamie had found in the basement). "Mother never liked that tea wagon," Amanda said.

"Well, I do. Shoo! Go away!" She waved the servants out of the room, poured tea and invited Amanda to help herself to the sliced cake. "I can't bear to have people standing around watching me eat."

"You'll get used to it."

"I won't. You really think Paul's doing okay?" Alice revealed her anxieties at odd moments. "You really think he's growing? I mean, I don't notice much difference in him."

"Paul's doing very well."

"But what about his brain? I mean, you're always being told that women my age have a greater chance of having a retard. Could you tell that by looking at him?"

"Paul's a normal baby, Alice."

"I guess." Alice chewed her lip. "You're sure? I mean, you're not just saying that to shut me up?"

"If there were anything wrong, your physicians would tell you."

"I don't trust those guys." Alice was referring to her obstetrician and pediatrician (both female). She continued to nibble at her lip. "I don't want anything to go wrong."

"It won't. I'm sure of that."

"God knows what Jamie'd do if Paulie turned out to be a retard." Amanda cringed at hearing Alice say the word "retard" again; once was bad enough.

"Jamie'd do what most fathers do, Alice. He'd continue to love Paul. Listen, you're sure Jamie didn't say anything specific about his meeting with David?"

"Next to nothing. Hey, you think I was wrong not to have Paul circumcised?"

"I've heard the procedure's going out of fashion."

"It's a Jew thing."

"I believe it's done for hygienic reasons, to prevent disease."

"So what's hygienic about chopping a little piece of skin off a kid's dong? Why not cut off his nose to prevent colds, or his ears to prevent earache? Eh?"

Amanda sighed. She had come to the house this morning, knowing that Jamie had seen David the previous evening and was hopeful her brother would be home and tell her what David had said. "So Jamie didn't get anywhere with David?"

"If he did, he didn't tell me."

"Oh dear," Amanda said.

"Why bother now? Everybody knows what David was doing with his sister."

"Half-sister."

"Does it matter which half was fucking which half? So why didn't you tell him — or her — to quit?"

"I suppose I should have."

"You were under Liz's thumb, right? You were too scared to say anything. You don't have much in the way of guts, do you?"

"I'm a real coward," Amanda agreed. "But I did speak to David. I told him it could lead to disaster, which was better than doing nothing. Anyway, what else could I do?"

"Know something? You Powell guys set yourself up as being superior to other people, but underneath it all you're a bunch of creeps — you probably even think your shit doesn't stink." Amanda defended herself by telling Alice that any sense of superiority that she, Amanda, may have started out with had been pounded out of her during nurses' training. But Alice wasn't interested in Amanda's experiences. "You treated me like dirt when we first met," she reminded Amanda.

"You mean, like you treat your servants?"

"Oh, them!" Alice's face reddened. "For Christ's sake, do I have to go around apologizing for everything I say and do? You think I don't see the way those two bitches take a dig at me every time they open their mouths? And you too! Going on about my kid getting sick from this or that disease. I didn't ask them to come into my house, and I don't invite you over either.

As far as I'm concerned the whole lot of you can get the hell out, and stay out!"

Amanda and Alice gazed into each other's eyes, blue into blue, neither, it seemed, willing to back down. They were still staring at each other, like two snarling dogs, nose to nose, unwilling to back off, when the door opened and Jamie entered the room.

Amanda turned to look at Jamie, then got up. "I'll be going," she said, moving to the door.

Aware he had walked into the midst of an argument, Jamie held out a detaining arm. "Just a minute, Mandy. What's up with you two?"

"Alice seems to think I've been too critical of her."

"Critical!" Alice flared. "I've had it up to my eyeballs with people standing around and sneering at me. Nobody around here likes what I say or do. I'm fed up. Fed up, you hear me? Fed up!"

"Is that true, Mandy? Do you criticize Alice?" Jamie's voice was dangerously quiet.

"No. I do my best to help her." Amanda began to cry.

"Those damn servants you brought in, they're always looking at me as if I should be ashamed of myself. They treat me like I'm some act in a circus sideshow." At this point, Alice broke down and began sobbing too. "I'm trying to do what's best for the kid," she wailed. "But the way everybody acts when I'm nursing him, you'd think I was feeding him poison."

"Are you saying the servants insult you?"

"I don't know what I'm saying. I wish I'd never had a baby. I wish I'd never met you and got mixed up with you and your goddamn family! Leave me alone! Don't touch me!" she shrieked when Jamie reached out to touch her hair. Amanda walked back from the door to kneel beside Alice and take her hand.

"Alice," she said. "I think you're a marvellous mother. I think it was wonderful the way you gave birth to Paul and decided to feed him yourself."

"I don't believe you," Alice wailed. "I don't believe anything people in your family say. You're a bunch of manipulating bastards. I've known what you thought of me from the first time we met. All you ever wanted was to keep Jamie from me. You think I'm so stupid I don't even know how to feed my own kid. You think I'm a big-assed, big-titted dumbbell."

"Alice, I don't think anything of the kind. I may have once thought you and Jamie were not suited —" But Amanda was not permitted to tell Alice that she had long ago revised her opinion of Alice as a suitable mate for her brother, because Jamie approached her, leaned over and put his face close to hers.

"Get out!" he hissed. "Leave us alone. Get out, and don't ever come back!"

Amanda went, although when she thought of the incident later she was never quite sure how she'd actually persuaded her legs to guide her feet across the room, into the hall and out of the house to her car. Oh, she'd carried herself upright enough and didn't glance at Gurdev who trotted over to open one side of the big oak door to allow her to exit: Under no circumstance would she ever allow anyone, especially a servant, to see how much she had been hurt by another person's vindictive words. Jamie's savage words "Get out" were branded on her memory and, in Amanda's mind, were as final as Liz's still, naked body sprawled on the bedroom carpet because they signified the death of her relationship with Jamie. Of course, in the past, there'd been times when Jamie had raged at her, accusing her of being everything from a fool to a shameless whore, but he had never ordered her out of his life. "Listen to me, Jamie," she whispered as she drove along the streets, "you've got it all wrong. I've never tried to come between you and Alice. I've only tried to help. Jamie, you've got it all wrong, I don't begrudge you Alice. I'm happy you've found Alice. Jamie, please, don't push me away." From street to street, Amanda drove, talking as though Jamie sat beside her in the car.

On reaching home, she parked the car and, shoulders hunched, walked the few paces to her house. When the phone rang as she closed the door, her heart thumped and she ran to the kitchen, hoping the caller was Jamie. But it was Helen Marks, anxious to chat about inconsequential things before inviting Amanda to have lunch with her at a newly opened restaurant on Commercial Drive. "I've heard the food's divine," she said. Amanda couldn't bring herself to say no, and because she knew Helen was lonely and worried about her health, she decided to mention her second thoughts about moving: "I'm thinking of returning to work," she told Helen and immediately detected an increase of liveliness in Helen's voice as she inquired about Annabelle and Christopher. "They're the same. They often ask about you." It was sad, truly sad, Amanda thought, how Helen's spirits leaped when Amanda told that little white lie: "Oh, do they? Do they? They're such wonderful children. Annabelle's so bright and Chris so lovable . . . the kind of little boy every woman wishes she had for a son." Helen's comment went a long way to ease the pain in Amanda's heart. "I'll tell the kids you called, Helen. And I'll see you tomorrow at one."

She sat at the kitchen table and pondered why her resolution to leave Vancouver had suddenly slackened, especially after Jamie had implied he never wanted to see her again. She'd observed Jamie's attempt over the years to escape from the family, and in a hazy sort of way she understood why he believed it was necessary to separate himself from his brother and sisters. And she understood, too, why he had rejected their grandfather's title and insisted on being known as a "Canadian" poet: He wanted to cut the umbilical cord that bound him to an English heritage. Yet their mother had never been able to acclimatize herself to Canada. She preferred a society where social position was determined by class, not money; and while it was true she had chosen to leave England of her own free will, her exile from her homeland had not diminished her "Englishness", but rather served to emphasize it. Her mother had not escaped the past by fleeing to another country, and her children, too, had been contaminated by the same events and people from the past which had so affected her and which, Amanda supposed, was the explanation of Liz's silent battle to possess David and perhaps, as well, explained her own leech-like attachment to Jamie and her readiness to forgive and forget every hurtful thing he said or did. But the bond between her and Jamie was broken now, wasn't it?

Even as the realization dawned on her that Jamie's rejection gave her the perfect opportunity to free herself from her family, she knew she wouldn't leave Vancouver, for to remain in close contact with Hiddie, with Aunt Nanda, with Natasha and David, and, above all, with Jamie and Alice, was the greatest necessity of her life. Regardless of how much Jamie had hurt her she knew she would grasp any gesture of reconciliation he chose to make.

Alice had accused her of snobbishness, which wasn't true because she'd come to admire Alice tremendously, though perhaps she really envied her because she had Jamie. Was that possible? Or maybe she resented Alice having a baby when she herself was unlikely to conceive again because never in a million years would she be able to find a replica of Harry Greene who would desire her and want to give her a child? Maybe she hated watching Paul nursing at Alice's mammoth breasts; maybe she told Alice about childhood diseases because, secretly, she wanted Alice's baby to become ill and die? Oh no. No! She might be catty on occasion, but never vicious; she would never, never wish for any mother to lose her child.

She knew what it was like to carry a baby for nine months — three months of nausea and six months of ever-increasing weight and discomfort ending with the agony of birth pains. To this day, even thinking about the labour pains she'd experienced giving birth to Annabelle and Christopher produced cramps (her period must be due), and then those terrible, interminable nights, rising every three hours to feed the baby. The thought of nursing Annabelle at two in the morning exhausted her even now. Yet it had been so wonderful to feel Annabelle's soft lips closing on her nipples. And her perfect little body! It had been difficult to believe the infant had grown within her. Incredible! She'd never been so proud of herself, or so contented, as during those brief moments when she'd raised her head and looked down at her newborn daughter and, later, her son: That she had produced these two beautiful creatures, that their bodies had developed inside hers was so amazing!

True, she had watched babies sliding from the groaning, exhausted bodies of other women; once she'd watched a surgeon slice open the great belly of an anaesthetized woman, cursing her because he thought that in her determination to bear her child "naturally" she had killed it, having obstinately refused to follow the advice of physicians not to prolong labour any further. Amanda remembered the surgeon bellowing: "Goddamn bitch! Goddamn stupid bitch!" before collapsing and sobbing when they finally got the child out and miraculously resuscitated it. Amanda remembered how the surgeon, a thick-set, red-faced man, had glared at her with his protuberant blue eyes, seemingly angry with her too, for being yet another stupid woman. But she was not stupid. Not stupid at all. She had lots of useful information about babies, and there was no reason in the world why she shouldn't share it with Alice; it wasn't fair that Alice should get angry when all she was trying to do was help. Anyway, the only reason she'd visited the Big House today was because she'd hoped to find Jamie there and to find out how the discussion with David had gone. Yet somehow everything had gone wrong. On impulse, she rang Hilda's number and when Hilda answered gave a rambling, incoherent account of the debacle at Alice's.

"It doesn't surprise me," Hilda pronounced when Amanda's account finally dribbled to a close. "Alice has been aching for an opportunity to get Jamie away from us."

"But it was Jamie who was the most nasty, Hiddie. Not Alice. And it wasn't just what he said, but the way he looked. I could tell that he hates me. I'm still shaken. I could hardly steer the car home."

"It's your own fault, Mandy. You toady to Jamie just like you used to do with Liz."

"Hiddie, that's not true! And I'm not going to allow myself to be beaten down by you, or by anybody else in the family. Everybody uses me as a scapegoat when all I ever do is try to behave decently. I wish I hadn't called you." She hung up the phone and went back to sit at the table, feeling even more depressed. Once — and not so long ago, when Liz was alive — their family had been a cohesive unit where (so she had thought) everyone cared for one another, but now, since Liz's death, a breakup had commenced and everyone acted like swimmers floundering in rough water who, fighting for their own survival, grab hold of and drown those attempting to save them. She heard the phone ring, told herself it was probably Hilda, anxious to make up, and decided not to answer it. It ceased, then five minutes later rang again, and this time Amanda could not resist.

At first, she did not recognize the voice, which seemed to come over a vast distance. "Tashie? Is that you, Tashie?"

"Mandy?"

"Where are you, Tashie?" Amanda waited. When Natasha did not reply Amanda continued, "Tell me where you are and I'll come and get you."

"It doesn't matter."

"Now listen to me, Natasha." Putting her devastating experience with Jamie behind her, Amanda donned the cloak of Reassuring, Capable Registered Nurse. "Tell me where you are."

"Mandy, will you look after the children? I know you'll love them as much as you love Annabelle and Christopher."

"Where are you, Tashie?" She wished someone was with her whom she could send to a neighbour's house to phone the police, who could then trace the call. "Listen to me, Tashie. I won't promise anything unless I'm sitting at a table across from you and looking straight into your eyes. So tell me where you are."

"Nick was right. There are some things a person does which she can't forget."

"Did you hear what I said, Tashie?"

"I can't go back and touch them. I can't put my lips against theirs. I can't, I can't."

"Bullshit!" Amanda snapped. "You think the children give a damn about what you've done? Of course they don't! You could go home and tell them you've murdered someone, and they'd still want to hug and kiss you because they won't care about what you've done as long as they know you love them. Did you hear what I said, Tashie?"

"Yes," Natasha whispered, "but Nick said —"

"Forget Nick. Now, tell me where you are."

"At a telephone booth. On West Broadway."

"All right. You have your car?"

"Yes," Natasha whimpered.

"Here's what you're going to do, Tashie. You're going to meet me at Oakridge, at the food fair. It'll take you about fifteen minutes to get there. All right?"

"Yes."

"Say 'I'll be there, Amanda.' "

"I'll be there, Amanda."

"See you in fifteen minutes," Amanda said into the dead phone. She glanced at the stove clock, which read half past twelve, slammed down the phone, grabbed her car keys and ran from the house.

As always, the mall was filled with people who seemed to be idling time away, and she hurried through the levels to the place where crowds congregated to consume food purchased at food booths. Natasha was alone, and Amanda was shocked to see her looking so worn and untidy, rather like someone who has spent nights in a car, or outside on the sidewalk.

Natasha began speaking the moment Amanda sat on one of the hard chairs at the small table. "I told Mother I was going back. And I told Nick too. I had to, because he wanted us to kill ourselves."

"The guy's crazy," Amanda muttered.

"He made it sound as though it was the only thing left for us to do. He pretended to cut his throat."

"The bastard," Amanda commented.

"I thought he was hurt. I hate myself because I wanted to be with him and do sexual things with him. It was a sort of craziness, because I did the same things with David, but I always felt wonderful doing them with David. I don't understand what's happened to me, why I went back to Nick, why I wanted to be with him in that awful place that smelled of cat. But I just had to. I had to, Mandy. I suppose I needed to find out how far I could go. Nick'd go out in the afternoons, saying he'd bring men back. But he never actually did. And I knew he wouldn't, because he hated the thought of anybody else touching me. That's why he wanted us to die. He couldn't bear to think of me being with David again. I told him we could find a decent place . . . you know, where I could visit him. But he shouted at me. He said he wanted to rip me apart."

"Where is he? Are you still with him?"

"No. I went to Mother's yesterday, and she didn't lecture me or get angry or anything like that. Maybe she understands. I told her I was going home, and I drove there, but couldn't bring myself to go into the house. I couldn't. I couldn't bring myself to face the children. They'd see all the terrible things I'd done, they'd see filth smeared all over me."

"Where have you been?"

"Driving around all night . . . out into the Fraser Valley and up into the mountains."

"You'd better come home with me."

"No. I don't want anybody to see me. I can't bear to have anyone look at me and imagine the things I've been doing."

"For God's sake, Tashie! When you see any pregnant woman in the street you know she's had a man with her, kissing her breasts and all the rest of it. And there's nothing so unusual about discovering you like having a guy that's not your husband fuck you. It's no big deal. You found out for yourself what millions and millions of women already know. It's an awful shock to find out you're no different than any other woman, but it's all over now, so why not come home with me? You don't have to worry about Annabelle and Christopher, they'll be pleased to see you."

"I don't have any clothes."

"So what? You have your credit card? Good. We can pick up a few things in the mall. Come on, let's get going. I thought I'd surprise the kids with dinner at some fancy place where the waiters wear vests and carry linen-covered trays. Know any restaurants like that, Tashie? Come on." They went into a women's clothing store where Natasha used her new platinum American Express card to purchase replacements for the grimy clothes she had on. While a skirt was being shortened, they located a beauty salon where Natasha had a shampoo and an esthetician applied a delicate palette of make-up. "You look more like yourself," Amanda said as Natasha left the chair. "Now let's get your new clothes."

They went back to the dress shop where Natasha entered the change room in stained, wrinkled clothes to emerge ten minutes later, seemingly radiant, in a lemon- and cream-striped suit. "Ta-ta, ta-ta!" Amanda trumpeted. "The return of Gorgeous Tashie!" They nostalgically laughed, collected bags of new and old clothes, called in at a prestigious toy store to purchase gifts for Natasha's and Amanda's children, then, loaded with more bags and boxes, they made their way to Amanda's car.

"There's no need for me to go to your place, Mandy. I can go straight home," Natasha said, as Amanda pulled out of the lot.

"No wavering, no changing your mind?"

"No wavering. I'll get the service station to pick up my car. It needs cleaning anyway."

"Don't forget what I've told you," Amanda said as they drew up to Natasha's house. "It's a little like Alcoholics Anonymous. If you're tempted, you mustn't give in — telephone me instead."

"Thanks." Natasha leaned over and kissed Amanda's cheek. "I think I'll be okay." Amanda watched as Natasha got out of the car and ran up the driveway. When the Powells' house door closed behind her, Amanda sighed and drove off.

Chapter 28

Nanda sat on a couch watching her eldest child drift around the room, touching ornaments and bending over to press her lips against pots of chrysanthemums and vases of fragrant lilies that stood on every table in the room.

"Things going well?" Nanda asked.

"Oh yes." Natasha moved on to another vase. "These lilies are so lovely."

"Take some with you."

"I'll do that. Maybe I'll build a greenhouse like yours and grow flowers. I've never thought of doing it before. You forget how wonderful the scent of flowers is."

"A blessing." Natasha moved to touch more petals.

"Amanda's helped me a lot."

"She's a very sensible person."

"I never realized how forceful she can be."

"It comes from her grandfather. We never noticed it in her before . . . she never had much chance to be assertive when Liz was alive."

"Liz!" Natasha moved on to another table to bury her face in some yellow chrysanthemums. "Liz interfered with everything I've ever done."

"Aren't you exaggerating a bit?"

Natasha flared up. "I'm not! Liz deliberately did things to prevent me from getting something she thought belonged exclusively to her. So please don't defend her, Mother."

"I won't," Nanda said.

"You always excuse people."

"Do I?"

"You've excused what I've done." She moved on to another vase of flowers. "Well, isn't that true?"

"What you did was simply a reaction, dear."

"I wonder." Natasha sat just across from Nanda, leaning forward to watch her mother's face. "I found out a lot about myself," she said.

"No doubt you did."

"I found out there's a lot of the slut in me." Natasha waited a few moments, then said, "Does that surprise you?"

"No."

"Did you ever do anything like I did?"

Nanda slowly shook her head. "I never felt strongly enough. I'm a limited individual."

"My father and Stuart didn't think so."

Nanda smiled. "They saw things in me which weren't there, or maybe it's just that I'm chameleon-like, forever changing myself to please people. Lots of women are like that. Besides, it was necessary for your father and Stuart to believe their women were exceptional. I was plain-faced, had no talents to speak of, nor much in the way of intellectual ability, but I compensated for my limitations by never saying much, just nodding and smiling to people as if I understood everything they said. People — especially men with pronounced ideas on how the world ought to be run — aren't really interested in what others think. Your grandfather, my brother Everest, they never listened to me; neither did your father or Stuart. We think people who agree with us are intelligent, so that's what I did — I simply agreed with everyone. I nodded and smiled, and everyone thought I was an immensely perceptive person."

Natasha laughed, hugged her mother, then drifted around the room again. "Do you think things between David and me will eventually settle down to what they were before?"

"Do you want them to?"

"I guess."

"Then they probably will."

Natasha lifted a small bowl of violets and held them close to her nose. "Every time I look at David I wonder if he's been with another woman."

"I expect he asks himself the same question about you."

"One cancels the other, is that what you're saying?"

"No. Just that, now, such questioning may be unavoidable."

"I'd have killed Liz if I'd known what was going on. She'd come to the house and be so friendly; she was the children's godmother, you know. But all the time she was secretly laughing, thinking of how she'd been acting like a slut with David."

"Why not give Liz the benefit of the doubt, Tashie? Why not try to imagine how David had become a necessity in her life and that perhaps she started drinking to escape the guilt and unhappiness she felt about their arrangement?"

"I don't think Liz felt any guilt."

"Can't you bring yourself to feel a little compassion for her? She probably suffered a lot."

"She wrecked my marriage. I'm surprised you defend her, Mother."

"You're a stronger person than Liz was, Tashie. You — and everybody else too — *thought* Liz was strong because as a child she got away with bossing her sisters and brothers around. You and your cousins carried your childhood image of Liz into adulthood, and not one of you has ever acknowledged that after Muriel's execution Liz had a major breakdown. The doctors thought she might never recover. But she did, because David helped her. As long as David was there she could manage; that's why she panicked when she heard you and David were planning to marry."

"How do you know so much about Liz? Did she tell you?"

"Winnie did. And David's explained how Liz needed him. Well, hasn't he?"

"Yes," Natasha sullenly muttered. "But it doesn't excuse what she did."

"It was a matter of survival, Tashie, so before you go off the deep end condemning Liz, remember you've recently spent several weeks acting the slut — your words — with a petty thief. You believed you had to do that in order to survive. Isn't that what you've just been telling me?"

"Yes, but —"

"No buts, Natasha, no buts."

"Mother, that's not fair. What I did was a reaction to finding out about Liz and David."

"Liz reacted to finding out about you and David."

"But Mother," Natasha cried, "there's a big difference! Can't you see that?"

"All my life I've listened to people tell me there was a qualitative difference between what they did and what I did. When I was a girl, my brother convinced me everything he did was superior to what I did. He was a boy, and I merely a stupid girl. I could jump higher and further and run faster, but that didn't count because I was just a girl. The fact is, Natasha, when it suits us we can always find a qualitative difference between what we do and what other people do."

"Are you trying to get me to admit I've been nothing more than a gullible fool?"

"No. I merely want you to see there is little difference between you and —"

"That's Amanda's line too. And I'm not going to get into an argument with you over what I — or you — or any woman — feels." Natasha made for the door.

"Natasha, come back." Nanda's voice softened. "Please . . . please."

Natasha hesitated, then returned to sit on the couch beside her mother. Natasha had never set herself in defiance against her mother; she deeply loved her and thought she was a wonderful person. To realize, now, she had been on the point of angrily walking away from her gaunt, thin-faced, much-loved aging mother, who'd never once let her down, shamed and frightened her. "I'm sorry, Mother, but I get upset easily these day. I feel uncertain when I think somebody's criticizing me."

"That's understandable. You've been hurt by people you trusted. It's painful, terribly painful. But all I'm trying to say — not very clearly, I'm afraid — is that if you want to be reconciled with David, you must stop blaming others for what you've done."

"But Mother —"

Nanda held up an interrupting hand. "I know what you're about to say, dear. That David and Liz betrayed you, and in a way it's true. But I'm telling you, Tashie, if you can't rid yourself of the hatred you feel for Liz, you'll never be reconciled with David. You can't expect him to forget Liz, any more than it's reasonable for David to think you can forget the weeks you enjoyed taking revenge on him by playing the slut. You did enjoy your revenge, didn't you, Tashie? Well?"

Natasha did not answer. Instead, a heavy blush crept from beneath the neckline of her dress to cover her neck and face. Nanda, a little shocked by the patent evidence of her daughter's sexual memories, watched as the colour climaxed, then, like an ocean tide, slowly receded. Natasha's tongue appeared between her lips to moisten them before she whispered, "Perhaps you're right, Mother. But I still wish it hadn't happened. I wish I could go back to the way it was before."

As she was leaving, Nanda called, "Don't forget the flowers!"

"Another time," Natasha called as she closed the door behind her.

It was unfortunate, Nanda thought, that Natasha couldn't forgive and forget; after all, sexual unfaithfulness is common enough in the animal world. She remembered an incident exemplifying animal infidelity which she'd witnessed as a child: Not far from her home lived a man who bred racing pigeons, and she enjoyed spending time in his loft, watching the sleek birds coo and bill while grooming their feathers. The breeder was particularly proud of one particular pair which he claimed not only won races and produced other champions for him, but also were a perfect example of devotion. "Look at them, m'dear," he'd say to her. "Them two's a lesson fer yer. Them's real sweethearts, ain't yer, m'dearies?" Every evening the birds were released to wheel and dive around the loft, afterwards swooping down to land on the roof where they engaged in confabulations similar to those conducted by human beings, or so it had appeared to her. She would stand beside the breeder observing the pigeons as he pointed out that while most of the birds waddled around on their own, his favourite pair never separated or mingled with other pigeons. "Ain't that somefing ter see, m'dear? That's real love." But one evening as Nanda and the breeder watched, a strange pigeon flew over, circled, then settled on the loft roof. "Bet yer 'e's lost," the breeder said. "See 'is ring?"; and even as he spoke the stranger approached the devoted pair, bowed to them, then flew away, followed by the female. The abandoned male, after bobbing around for a moment, drooped on the loft roof until his body was almost flat. There he stayed motionless, while the upset breeder attempted to explain what had happened: "She dunno wot she's up to, she dunno as 'ow 'e feels so bad 'e wants to peg out." A difficult half-hour passed before the female pigeon returned to the loft as though nothing untoward had occurred.

At the time, Nanda hadn't known what to think, but now as she recalled the incident she realized that the reason she'd never been unfaithful herself was because she'd never experienced the itch of concupiscence, although she knew of women who took masochistic delight in their sluttishness, surrendering themselves to any man who happened by. In fact, there had been such a woman living in Hyndhurst, Margaret Boon by name, though everyone called her Maggie Bloomerless. A terrible story about this woman had circulated around the village: Four men, after telling Maggie about a man who'd gone without a woman for months, took her to a pig sty that housed a boar; there, three of the men pushed her down on her hands and knees and held her, while the fourth aroused the boar until it reared up and the man was able to manipulate its long organ into her body. Nanda remembered she had vomited when she'd heard this story (Resty had told her) and she wondered now if the appalling ugliness of the occurrence and of other similar events she'd seen or heard as a girl and adolescent might not have permanently affected her sexual responses, causing her to neutralize herself, much like a nun drains herself of sexuality upon entering a religious order. Later, when she read novels set in English villages, she became even more confused and puzzled because what she read about village life in the books bore no resemblance to what she'd observed in Hyndhurst. And she must have been quite successful in neutering her sexual responses, she thought, for the two men in her life had envisioned her as the embodiment of everything they desired in a woman: For Cromwell, she had combined visionary perception with sweet virginal sensuality; for Stuart, she had been the quiet-voiced mother and warm, responsive lover — what each had desired, each had found. Neither man had asked for anything more, and by remaining emotionally neutral herself and never demanding anything, she'd supplied them with everything they wanted.

It occurred to Nanda, who pictured herself now as part chameleon, part parasite, that the problem which had arisen in her daughter's life might be due to certain educational and experiential deficiencies in the way she had been raised. As a child and adolescent, she, Nanda, had been aware of almost everything that occurred in the village; she'd seen the worst life had to offer there, and by insinuating herself into relationships with Cromwell and Stuart had found a way of protecting herself, for by remaining inside the unassailable, walled-in keep of their love and financial resources she could be sure no harm would ever come to her. But the opposite was true of Natasha; she had been raised *within* the keep, unaware of the realities beyond its walls until, given the impetus of David's betrayal, she'd flung herself over the ramparts to end, so to speak, in the gutter, ready prey to any man who happened by.

As Nanda resettled herself on the couch, an image of a half-naked woman appeared on the wall opposite her, followed by an image of herself as a child emerging from a copse bordering a field of unmown grass; next, the image of a man appeared: He was buttoning his fly as he walked away from the half-naked woman lying motionless in the grass while at the same time the child backed into the copse, then turned and ran. The images faded, but Nanda continued to stare at the wall as she remembered hearing her father tell her mother one evening at the dinner table that Margaret Boon had been found dead in the field of an estate he managed; she realized, suddenly, that the image on the wall was something she'd actually witnessed as a child — Margaret Boon's murderer as he walked away from her dead body. Was it possible that what she saw in the field that long-ago day explained her determination to protect Natasha as she was growing up, going to such great lengths to keep her from harm's way, yet in the end perhaps doing greater harm because, unknowingly, unintentionally, she had insulated her from any real experience of life?

Nanda closed her eyes and sighed, thinking she'd failed her much-loved first-born child, though why on earth should she feel compelled to explain her daughter's behaviour by sifting through memories of her own life? Why should she upbraid herself in order to excuse the failures of her child? Her parents had not done that on her account. On the contrary. They had always made it abundantly plain that they'd given her life, fed and raised her, and that was the end of it; they'd made it clear that she was in debt to them, not the other way around, an obligation she accepted without question, even after discovering, as each year was added to her life, that her debt to them was being compounded. Even after she had run away to Alderwood House to escape dependence on her parents, she'd continued to "love and honour" them, and the idea that they were accountable in any way for her personal limitations never occurred to her. She had always known her father was a manipulative bully, as she'd always recognized that her brother's pretensions far exceeded his innate abilities; but acceptance of their shortcomings had been expected of her, and whereas those of her father and brother were deemed excusable, her own were not. *Her* shortcomings were confirmation of clearly defined physical and intellectual limitations.

Even now, after so many years had passed and so much experience accumulated, she could still excuse her brother and father. She could set her father's behaviour against his love for her, and say that her brother's childhood and adolescent beliefs had been as real and intense as his later disillusionment and self-condemnation. She could hint at her brother's unfulfillment, at the inevitability of what had happened to him, and imply that those involved with him — herself, David's mother Ruth, Winnie, even Muriel — were merely adjunct players in the very real tragedy of his life. Above all, by resurrecting the past, she could clearly see how certain experiences, coupled with her particular temperament, had resulted in her present inertia. As a young woman she had entered a high-walled bastion, then closed and firmly locked the gates behind her; and now, in old age, she clearly understood that, except for the mound of sterile wealth upon which she sat, she possessed nothing as a person — she was empty, had nothing, was nothing.

Nanda heard the door open and Harjinder Singh's voice informing her that Lord Powell had come to see her. Untidy as always, Jamie pushed past Harjinder Singh and walked over to Nanda. "Hi," he said and slumped into the chair recently occupied by Natasha. "Were you asleep?"

"No. Thinking about the past."

"I expect your past has been more profitable than mine."

"That depends upon how you look at it," Nanda said. The door opened and two servants entered to lay out a tea service. "We can manage, thank you," Nanda said. They bowed and left the room.

"Why do your servants always dash in with pots of tea the minute a visitor arrives?" Jamie stared sullenly at the white cups and teapot, as if accusing them of criminal intent.

"Would you prefer something else? Wine . . . whisky?"

"No." An uneasy silence hovered between them.

"How are Alice and Paul?" He shrugged and raised his hands in a gesture which could have meant anything. "I take it that means they're fine?"

"Yes."

Nanda looked into the teapot, then filled two cups. "Help yourself to cream and sugar," she said.

Jamie ignored the cup of tea. Nanda poured cream into her cup, sipped a little tea, and waited.

After a moment or two Jamie got up and wandered around the room, touching and smelling the flowers as Natasha had done earlier. "I don't know why I came here." He moved on to another table and smelled the flowers. "It won't help. These lilies smell like death. I'm beginning to wonder if I'm going mad . . . crazy." He went to another table. "I can't do anything. I blame Alice . . . the servants . . . our son. I want to avoid acknowledging that I'm the one responsible." He stood in front of a window, his back to Nanda, and she was reminded of the occasion when her brother had stood at a window of another house, soliciting help and being coldly rejected by her. "I go into my room, sit at my desk and all I hear are the two women servants chattering and giggling. I realize I'm magnifying the sound and that I do this to provide myself with an excuse for my inability to work. I imagine what I'll do to the women if they won't shut up — how I'll open my door, drag them into the room and rip off their clothes. I leave my desk, creep over to the door and fling it open, but no one's there. And I know even before I open the door nobody will be there, but planning what I'm going to do to the women when I get hold of them gives me something to think about. It occupies time. You have no idea what I plan . . . the thoughts I have."

He left the window, walked over to stand in front of Nanda, then went back to the window. "Alice tries. She does her best, but she can't prevent Paul from crying." He raised his hands and slapped them against the window pane. "The house is quiet much of the time, but it's the wrong kind of quietness — the quiet of people trying hard not to make any noise." He circulated among the tables, then returned to the window. "Marvellous view. Liz knew what I wanted. Funny that she should know that. But she understood my need for a cocoon of silence, the kind of silence that would isolate me, would expel the external and allow the eternal to approach. It's funny how Liz understood that. At first, I was embarrassed by the way she behaved, like a priestess conducting a primitive rite, but later I came to realize that she saw me as a receptacle into which messages from the galaxy could be dropped. It's not Alice's fault, you understand. She tries and can't be blamed because I sit at my desk and think of the servants' tits and cunts. I'm appalled at my thoughts, because I know they're incredibly modest young women. You've no idea. Anyway . . . it's of no interest to you. I don't know why I'm pestering you with this rot." He made for the door.

"Jamie! Jamie!" He halted with the door partly opened. "Please close the door." He closed the door and stood with his back to it, his hand resting on the door knob. "I have no idea what you require in order to work, but this house has many unused rooms, and it's exceptionally quiet. We could look at some of the rooms if you like. Of course, I appreciate it won't compare with what Liz offered." Nanda left her chair and went across the room to him.

"Well . . ." He hesitated, not wishing to offend Nanda any further. "I suppose I could look. You understand, I'm at my wits' end. I'm like a crazy monk who's convinced himself that the devil has taken over his cell and replaced his familiar icons with images of female devils. Well, I suppose it's not as bad as that — yet. But I can't concentrate. I can't isolate myself. I mean, I was never aware of Liz being in the house. But now! If it keeps up like this . . . And I can't blame Alice, she never wanted to move into Liz's house. I mean, it's my own fault. But I never expected . . ."

"Let's have a look. There may be a suitable room." In silence, they went up to the second floor, past Nanda's room and up another flight of stairs to the third floor. "You probably remember some of these rooms, Jamie. That was Stuart-Hector's . . . Gwenny's . . . Margaret's . . ." She did not indicate that the fourth room was Frances's bedroom. At the end of the hall she opened a door, and they climbed a narrow flight of stairs.

"I'd no idea this place had so many floors," Jamie said.

"Wasted space." She opened a door and they entered a room which projected from the ridge of the main roof and consisted of glass walls on three sides.

"Oh boy! Look at this!" Jamie exclaimed. He stood at the windows looking up and down the Strait of Georgia and the wide Fraser River delta.

"It can be quite cold up here at night, especially in winter. But I'm sure Harjinder Singh can find an electrical heater for you."

"Yes," Jamie negligently said. He was watching clouds drift over the mountains on Vancouver Island to cross the descending sun. "You don't use it?"

"No." The lie was salutary, an offer to surrender a much-favoured spot during the spring and fall bird migrations where on cold days she watched birds dropping down into the Fraser River estuary and marshes. "No one would disturb you here," she said.

Jamie turned away and leaned against the glass, his face hidden by a raised arm. "I've been so afraid," he whispered, and Nanda knew by the timbre of his voice that he was crying. "I haven't known what to do. I haven't wanted to blame Alice. She has enough on her hands with Paul. I expect I've been pretty unbearable these past weeks."

"Of course there's no guarantee," Nanda cautioned.

"It will do. It will do. There's something here. I can feel it already."

"I'll have Harjinder Singh bring up a few things." (Nanda could not bring herself to say anything more about the room and therefore didn't tell Jamie that her lost daughter, Frances, had spent hours in the room, playing.)

"Well, if it's not too much trouble, I'll bring my old portable. Actually it was Liz's, but I commandeered it. I guess, in a way, I commandeered Liz too. But she didn't object." He suddenly turned to look at Nanda. "D'you think Liz might have secretly resented me being there? D'you think that's why . . . ?"

"No, of course not. Liz was glad — proud — that she could help you."

"You really think so?" He prowled around the room, muttering indistinctly. "There's something here. I'm sure there's something here."

"You'll need to go down to the lower floor to use the lavatory."

"That's okay, I'll manage." He continued to walk around the perimeters of the glass-enclosed room. "Liz understood that my need for isolation is the only real necessity in my life. You know, Nanda, as a kid I worshipped Liz. In the nursery, we had all kinds of picture books of princesses and goddesses, but none matched Liz, or so I thought. A couple of times I happened to see her naked when I was working at the house. She was stunning. I believed she was inviolable. Of course, I didn't know about David — the sneaking bastard! — I didn't know he'd been humping her for years." He managed a laugh. "Anyway, that's over. Tashie's had her revengeful fling and the crisis has passed. Remember that old hymn, "The Strife is o'er, the battle done . . ."? There's always a battle, always strife of some kind in those old hymns. You know, Nanda, we ought to sing hymns once in a while. We may have no faith ourselves, but there's no reason we can't appreciate the faith people had in other ages and places. Could you die for your faith, Nanda? Be burned? Impaled? Beheaded? Tortured? Could anyone today have such faith? I can't see myself dying before surrendering my belief in something. Does my lack of faith reduce me, make me less of a man? I don't know. Now, I'm not even sure of my ability to be a poet. And I want to be sure, Nanda. I want to be sure that when I look up at the sky, I will see words dancing among the stars. Maybe things'll change. I can feel something here. Maybe my crisis is over too. I have a new cell here where I can hide away. I'd no idea this room was here." He stopped to peer through the windows. "No street lights. Wonderful."

"Well," Nanda smiled, "it's all yours."

Jamie slipped an arm around her shoulders and hugged her. "Thank you, Nanda. You're quite a guy," he said, then went back to prowling around the small room. "Yes, I can already feel things working in me." He stopped and looked out at the low broken clouds. "Beyond each cloud, beyond each mist-veiled galactic cluster, lies . . . what? The face of God? What do you think, Nanda?"

"I don't know. Though at one time, as a child, I believed someone watched over me."

"Someone who conveniently bound things together, someone who could help you make sense of all the non-sense?"

"Perhaps. But it's easier to have beliefs when you're young." A momentary, shy smile touched Nanda's lips. "I believed I had guardians defending me. I convinced myself I could see them hovering in the darkness around my bed. I suppose it all added up to nothing more than a child's wish to be secure."

"But it's necessary for people to have beliefs. We need to be rich in beliefs, or at least have hope that our present beliefs can be exchanged for tangible assets in the future. To be destitute of belief is to damn oneself." He went back to stare through the windows at a freighter approaching Vancouver. "Do you ever look at other people and wonder what it's like to be inside their bodies and look out on the world through their eyes?"

Nanda laughed. "As a girl, sometimes I thought snakes and bees and rabbits, even trees, were part of me." She sighed. "I regret I can't think like that any more. I remember one afternoon I went into a field of long grass, took off my clothes, lay down and went to sleep. When I awoke a viper was lying on my tummy, sunning itself."

"You hadn't heard the old wives' tale about snakes sliding into women to coil up inside their wombs?"

"In those days I didn't know I even possessed such a thing as a womb. I just lay there and watched the viper until it slid away when the sun went behind a cloud. But while it was there, I thought it was part of me, and I a part of it."

"You were an immature Eve sleeping in sunny Eden. How could you even imagine that your embryo womb was destined to be blamed by generation after generation of humankind for all misfortune and stupidity, for all evil?" Jamie squeezed her narrow shoulders. "How were you to know that one day you too would become victim to the relentless, terrifying necessities of life? How could the child, who peacefully slept with a viper coiled on its smooth-skinned belly, possibly know that one day she would become a woman and accept without question the sullen fury of male penetration? Eh, did you know that then, Nanda?"

"Well, I'd seen what men did with women behind hedges," Nanda dryly commented.

"But did seeing men fucking women in the long grasses make you understand that one day you too would be pinned beneath a man? That you would carry a parasite in your belly for nine months and suffer hell's tortures squeezing it from your womb? Eh, did you know that, Nanda?"

"No. I'd seen a lot, but understood nothing."

"I grasp fragments of a whole I don't understand."

"You underrate yourself, Jamie." Nanda moved towards the door. "I'll arrange for you to have a key to the house."

"That's not essential," Jamie said as he followed her from the room and down flights of stairs. "I mean, it's not imperative for me to have a key. Somebody's bound to be up and around. Besides, I might lose it."

"We'll see."

"It may not work out. I may not have the urge. You know, it comes over me, like an attack of intestinal flu."

"I understand, Jamie." Nanda was becoming impatient.

"Liz left the front door unlocked."

"Perhaps she did, but I'm sure Harjinder Singh wouldn't agree to that. He's very security-conscious." They had descended the stairs and were standing in the central hall.

"Maybe it's too complicated," Jamie said. "Liz made everything so simple." Harjinder Singh came into the hall, crossed to them and politely listened while Nanda explained what was needed. He accepted her instructions and said he would provide Jamie with a key to a side door.

"If you will be so kind as to come with me, Lord Powell," he said.

"This mustn't be any big deal." Jamie explained as he trailed after the servant through various rooms to a door where he was given a key, then shown how to insert it into the lock and give it a double turn in order to open the door.

"The second turn is important, my lord," Harjinder Singh emphasized.

"Yes, yes," Jamie mumbled, now beginning to regret he had accepted Nanda's offer to use the room. "I can see how it works." He felt completely inept, like someone being censured for being unable to carry out the simplest of tasks. Liz had always made everything so easy for him; she'd made sure paper was on his desk; she'd periodically change the typewriter ribbon and clean the worn type; above all, she maintained the cocoon of silence in which he could sit, waiting for the moment when the galactic starborn words appeared in the sky and he could reach out to capture and draw them onto the paper. Of course Liz had often irritated him in spite of her assistance, and he had expended much effort trying to free himself from her influence, but now it seemed her value to him increased in direct proportion to the time elapsed since her death. He refused to speculate about her relationship with David, because to do so would taint his image of her, transforming it into something vile and corrupt. He wanted to keep the special double-image he had of Liz in which she appeared wearing a favourite red dress at the same time she was standing, splendidly naked, in the bathroom drying herself after stepping from the shower. His unacknowledged hatred of David simmered just below the boiling point. How dare his half-brother besmirch the image of a woman whom he, Jamie, had made into his very own icon? Who had given David the right to cup her white, pointed breasts and stroke her egg-shaped belly before opening her thighs with inquisitive hands? And why had Amanda chosen to reveal Liz's secret and inform him Liz had procured the abortion of a fetus begotten in her by David? Surely his imperious Liz would never have permitted some unknown (and perhaps discredited) physician to handle and probe those parts of her body, which Jamie, by combining the innocence of childhood with the idealist ignorance of youth, had deemed sacred and unapproachable. Of course he'd behaved stupidly in refusing to acknowledge there was no difference between Liz and other women, and now as he left Nanda's house and pedalled through pools of pallid light cast by the tall street lamps he mocked himself: Wasn't he the one who had just lectured Nanda on the terrifying necessity that compels women to submit to being impregnated by "sullen males"? Hadn't he pompously talked about the "awful relentlessness of life" and the manner in which it nets the most vain and proudest of individuals? Look how he himself had been trapped. Like a pig in a mud pool, he had wallowed in Alice, then had the trap door slammed by none other than his imperious, glorious Liz, who apparently was determined to enforce with Alice the biological laws which she herself had so coldly ignored. Talk about hypocrisy! Talk about double standards and unending streams of lies, lies, lies! Where did they begin, where did they end? He had no idea where the stream arose, but he knew it had ended with Liz sprawled on her bedroom floor, dead; and with Natasha abandoning her precious passion flowers to shack up with a waiter-cum-petty thief who, as any good journeyman would, had knocked some sense into her pretty little head by alternately fucking her and threatening to kill the both of them. Naturally, things could never be the same again for Natasha: How could they, when she could hardly look at him without blushing, thereby letting him know she thought he was speculating about her escapade? As for David, his face was so stiff it looked as if it had been permanently set in place by an over-conscientious undertaker. He had no alternative but to continue to detest David for the rest of his life because David had taken the irreplaceable from glorious Liz; but it was also true that lately he'd found himself feeling a little sorry for his half-brother when he observed how utterly miserable and defeated he looked. Amanda had told him Natasha and David were more or less back on their old bedroom-footing. (Thank heavens Mandy and he were reconciled. Even Alice had missed Mandy's visits.) But he wondered if Natasha wasn't bluffing, or perhaps indulging in wishful thinking. "Now, now, now," he told himself as he cycled along the street, "you mustn't be too hard on Gorgeous Tashie. After all, she's a very kind-hearted woman who's had the misfortune to marry a lousy SOB. Don't forget that once upon a time, way back when you were ten years old, you were in love with Tashie, and the greatest necessity in your life, then, was getting positioned so you could see her cotton panties when her skirt rose." Oh, those were the days, the unsullied days, when he'd adored Tashie during long summer afternoons, and at night enjoyed yet another lesson on the art of masturbation from ever-dependable Mandy. There was no conflict in him then. He could worship glorious, imperious Liz, adore Tashie's white-clad springy little bottom, hate David because of Liz and Tashie's all-too-obvious preference for him, enjoy snuggling with Amanda, who at eleven proudly exhibited the developing pink-tipped mounds on her chest and the accumulating down on her cloven Venus mound. But the days, months and years of careless childhood had vanished to be replaced by an adolescence which first attacked, then decimated his flimsy defences. One night during his seventeenth year — he'd never forget that moment, no matter how many years he lived — he'd looked out his bedroom window and seen words dancing among the stars. He remembered that at first he thought he was caught up in a mad hallucination, and his immediate reaction was to escape to Amanda's room and bed. But even as he turned to run, another force gripped him and he thrust a sheet of paper into Liz's portable typewriter, which happened to be sitting on his desk (he was a committed borrower of things from his sisters and brother), crouched in the chair and stared up at the words (what a glorious moment it had been!) until he felt the words stream down from the sky, pass through his body and fingers (like an electric shock) and record themselves in geometric forms on the sheets of paper. Afterwards he had awakened Amanda (his confidante in all matters) to show her the papers, but his yawning sister could only manage a comment to the effect that his poems didn't much look like the poetry in her college textbook. He had been furious at her negligent response and had almost throttled her until she realized she should be playing a more supportive role and took another look at the papers, this time saying: "If you can do that, Jamie, you must be a real poet." And that was all there was to it, that was how he'd become a poet. He halted at a street light where Marine Drive intersected a major north-south corridor, crossed the intersection and began the long haul up the hill towards the avenue that stretched east-west along the crest of the great glacial hump of central Vancouver. At the halfway point he turned off and careened down a sharp incline to a gully adjacent to the wide Kitsilano flats. He flew along, remembering the glorious commencement of his poetic career. At eighteen, his first collection of poems had been issued by a publishing company in which Nanda quickly invested a large sum of money; and since no one seemed to understand his geometric concoctions most people more or less echoed what Amanda had said: "If young Powell can do that, he must be a real poet." Only a sceptical few had the courage privately to mutter, "God help us! Not another collection of pretentious crap!" However, when his second volume appeared, people took more notice and began dissecting his poetical efforts, managing to uncover in them all kinds of pertinent observations about life, art and morality. So there he was, at twenty-two, lauded as "one of Canada's major young poets". He loved the recognition (who wouldn't?) and enjoyed the envy he perceived in older writers' eyes and the attention (both soulful and physical) bestowed on him by women of all ages. That so many women expressed willingness to have sex with him struck him as being almost as miraculous as his ability to net star words. He pretended a thorough knowledge of bedroom etiquette, even though his experience at the time was limited to boyhood instruction from Amanda. It was marvellous while it lasted, and he cared not whether the women were pretty or plain, fat or thin, young or aging: All were grist for the unquenchable virility he'd apparently inherited from his father and grandfather. But quite apart from the pleasure he received (and no doubt gave), the women's bodies and behaviour intrigued him, and he would watch them when they believed themselves to be unobserved (as he had once watched Natasha) and afterwards record the manner in which they moved, how they dealt with various parts of their anatomies, and the way they critically eyed themselves before dressing or after removing their clothes. Then that truly frightening thing had occurred: He'd discovered that he was trapping duplicates of poems he'd already published. At first he was simply bewildered, unable to believe that the galaxy would play such a malicious trick on him, but slowly he came to realize that while a poetical flower may be a wonderful sight to behold when it first opens, the wondrous blossoms can rapidly fade, then disintegrate if not carefully tended and guarded. He immediately abandoned the pleasures of flesh and fame to hide in celibate isolation in an east-side basement suite, and there had remained until his meeting with Alice. He did not — could not — regret his relationship with Alice, or the sensual delights he had known with her. No. But the consequences of that relationship were now threatening to extinguish his ability to communicate with the heavens. He did not wish to hurt Alice, nor have her think she had failed him in any way. All he asked was that she understand his periodic need to be isolated in a place of absolute stillness. Was that too much to ask? It was either that, or the cessation of his poetical endeavours, which would be followed by . . . what? He remembered his father's drunken disintegration and violent death and refused to speculate any further on his own future, but he did know that he could not give up the most precious thing in his life; in the silent, glass-enclosed room Nanda offered, he would continue to look up at the stars and once more experience those bursts of ecstasy that "passeth all understanding". Yes, the star words would return. "I know they will return," he told himself. "You'll see, everyone! They *will* appear again," he shouted at the night-wrapped street. "Yahoo!" he screamed, "Yahoo!" as he raced his bicycle diagonally across the corner into the street where he and Alice lived and passed directly into the path of an oncoming car. "No!" he shrieked. "No!" He swerved to the right, the driver of the car frantically swerved left, but Jamie was hit by the car's right fender and thrown headfirst into one of the magnificent elm trees that lined the street. He died on impact, while the driver, a middle-aged woman who lived at the end of the street, was knocked unconscious as her car slammed into a fire hydrant. Five minutes passed before a couple, who were giving their two weimaraners, Buster and Betty, what the couple referred to as their "crap-race", arrived on the scene in a sports car. Because the tree into which Jamie had smashed his head was favoured by dogs, they bounded to it. Buster raised a leg, Betty squatted, and both successfully urinated over Jamie's bloodied head.

"Oh Christ!" the couple said simultaneously. "What the hell's going on? We gotta get hold of those fuckin' dogs. Oh Christ!" They left their little Italian car and ran across the street. "Get the hell out of there," the man shouted while kicking Buster, who then backed off to deposit his evening load of fecal matter, waddling along the sidewalk, whimpering and dropping chunks of excreta as he went. By this time, another car and more people had arrived on the scene, and within minutes two patrol cars and an ambulance drove up.

The driver of the car that had hit Jamie regained consciousness and, sobbing uncontrollably, explained: "He came out of the blue, out of no-where. Oh dear, oh dear. It's Mr. Powell. I've known him for years, since he was a boy. Oh dear, oh dear. He has a new baby. No, no, I don't want to go to the hospital. I want to go home. I recognized him the moment I saw him, but there was nothing I could do. He has a wife and little baby. Oh dear, oh dear. No, no, I don't want to go to the hospital. I don't want to. I won't." But her protests had no effect on the ambulance attendants. They removed the woman from her warped car, placed her on a stretcher, strapped her down, put her into the ambulance and drove away. The couple with the galloping weimaraners waited until a van arrived to gather up Jamie's body before they jumped back into their sports car and drove off. A tow-truck appeared to hoist and drive off with Jamie's bike and the woman's car, the police officers got into their patrol cars and departed, and all that was left as evidence of the fatal accident that had taken place was an askew fire hydrant and the pump off Jamie's bike lying on the grass beyond the sidewalk.

Chapter 29

"He should never have ridden around the streets on that old bike," Hilda categorically said. "It was practically suicidal." The remaining members of the Powell family were sitting uneasily in Alice's living room. Nanda was there too, accompanied by Stuart-Hector to represent the McLeod offshoot of the Powell family. Stuart-Hector loved representing other people; he regarded the process much as missionaries view the conversion of pagan souls.

"That was how Jamie liked to get around," Amanda said.

"Bikes are the coming thing," Stuart-Hector blandly added. "Within thirty years cars'll be banned in cities and people'll be using bikes."

"That'll be discriminatory," Hilda protested.

"Necessity," Stuart-Hector replied. "A world shortage of oil will sky-rocket the price of a barrel to fifty, sixty, seventy-five dollars. Who knows, it could go as high as a hundred."

"That should sweeten Can-Ray's balance sheets," David commented. All present knew that Can-Ray Corporation had invested in Alberta tar-sands and heavy oil extraction in Saskatchewan.

"It might," Stuart-Hector admitted, "though the cost-retail price ratio doesn't augur well for the profit-quotient." Experience had taught Stuart-Hector that hyphenated words muzzled criticism, even among intelligent people like David.

"Do we have to talk as if we're attending a chamber of commerce meeting?" Natasha asked.

Stuart-Hector smiled at her. He thought she looked tired, so unlike the vivacious Natasha he'd known. His mother had given him a carefully ed-ited account of Natasha's little fling and the reasons for it, and although he'd clucked his disapproval, now, looking at Natasha and recalling Liz's beauty, he found himself rather envying the men upon whom his cousin and half-sister had bestowed their sexual favours. Why was there always so much "making do" in relationships, even for people like himself who lived in a world of apparently endless sexual opportunity?

"A passing comment, Tashie," he said.

"We have to talk about something, don't we? We just can't *sit* here." Hilda and her family occupied an entire couch: Hilda in the centre, Jeanette and Louise on her left, Conrad and Max Junior on her right. As always, the children were dressed in clothes Hilda deemed appropriate for the particular social occasion. Today, the girls wore little veiled hats, while Max sported a navy blue blazer and black bow tie. In contrast, Conrad wore a dark grey pinstripe flannel suit and looked shabby and debilitated.

Amanda, sitting in a chair with Annabelle and Christopher leaning against her, wondered if Hilda's domineering ways, along with her sexual demands, had exhausted Conrad. She was waiting for the right moment to smile at what remained of her family, then get up and make her exit. She still couldn't believe Jamie was gone, that his body had been cremated just hours earlier and his ashes thrown onto the surf pounding the rocks surrounding Paradise Island. She had spent the days since his death oozing tears and trying to recall everything that had passed between them during the course of their lives. The more she remembered, the more solidified became her opinion that hers and Jamie's sibling relationship had been an ideal one since their trust in one another had been absolute: She could tell Jamie all the little intimate details about herself and her life and be certain he'd never breathe a single word of it to anyone else. She remembered the warm intimacy of their childhood and pubertal years; what she had taught him, the temptations they'd experienced which later enabled her to understand what happened between Liz and David. In a way, she and Jamie had been lovers, not in the accepted sense, but innocently as two people loving each other. She remembered how jealous she had been when, after the publication of his first book of poems, he had been inundated by people eager to participate in his creative life, how she'd hated the women who inserted themselves into his bed, and how furious she'd been when (in her opinion) Jamie permitted them to exploit him. She recalled the occasion when, being unhappily trapped in nursing school, she'd allowed her resentment to overcome discretion and had told Jamie how she felt. She remembered the way he had flicked her chin with his finger, saying, "Now, now, Mandy, no harsh words." But hadn't it been natural for her to be resentful, because while she waited in a state of moist anticipation for the right man to appear, Jamie had abandoned her and gone to bed with all sorts of women? She forgave him of course, especially after receiving notoriety herself when fellow student nurses wanted to know if *the* Jamie Powell was a relation of hers and really and truly a Lord. Having that small distinction enabled Amanda to get through some bad spells, times when she thought she would never be able to survive the stress of classes, examinations, humiliating criticism from superiors, and the knowledge that compared to other students who laughed their way into dates with young men from the medical school, she held little attraction for them. The one area in which Jamie had always actively supported her was to tell her she was pretty, and for this kindness, she'd been truly grateful. Oh, how she missed him, missed waking up in the late afternoon to find him sitting on her bed, his back against the headboard. Her kids missed him too, although they lacked her backlog of memories among which she could wander, much as one could stroll around a library, opening books and finding memory files on page after page. She knew that of all the family, even including Alice, she herself would be the one most affected by Jamie's death; even though Alice had borne Jamie's son, Amanda believed she had been closer to Jamie and possessed a greater understanding of him than her sister-in-law.

"Can we go, Mom?" Annabelle whispered. She was pale and unhappy.

"Soon," Amanda whispered back. How sensible of Natasha not to have inflicted this sad gathering on her children, but Annabelle had insisted on coming, which meant Christopher had to come too. Tomorrow, perhaps the next day, she would telephone Natasha and they would have a nice long heart-to-heart talk. Poor Tashie. She looked sallow and pinched around the nose. Perhaps she still ached for Nick Parsons: Amanda could understand that because she'd ached for months after leaving Harry. Could Natasha be pregnant? Amanda came close to whistling aloud at *that* thought, but quickly dismissed the possibility. Tashie had been foolish, but she was too knowledgeable to get caught out like a teenager. She smiled at Natasha, then looked at Stuart-Hector, wondering how it was possible for a man as young as he to be so pompous and boring. Poor Nanda. Apart from Natasha, Nanda really hadn't done all that well with her children, except for Frances who'd been a lot like Annabelle, open and candid in her expressions and opinions. Pain stabbed her heart as the possibility of losing Annabelle darted through her mind. She pressed her face against Annabelle's, thinking she would do anything, give anything, to protect her children if ever their lives were threatened. Once, while talking about the relief work she financed, Natasha had whispered that in some Asian countries children no older than theirs were sold into prostitution. They had looked at each other, speechless, unable to believe such a terrible thing could happen. Just to imagine Annabelle . . . No, no, she must not allow such speculations to enter her mind. The funny thing was, she had promised Natasha she'd make a contribution to one of her charities, but hadn't ever done it. How thoughtless of her! What must Tashie think? Although even if she had given money, say, a hundred dollars, would it have made any difference . . . ?

As though aware of her mother's thoughts, Annabelle turned her head and moistly kissed Amanda. "Darling," Amanda whispered. She became aware that Hilda was asking whether she still contemplated moving from Vancouver.

"I've changed my mind," Amanda said. Hilda, as though Amanda had not spoken, went on to say that Conrad knew people who might be interested in purchasing her properties. Amanda briefly nodded, but said no more. She wanted to go home and sit with Annabelle and Christopher. On the whole, she thought, she'd not done too badly with her life when she compared herself to the rest of her family. Hiddie'd made a big mess of her first marriage and looked as if she was heading down the same road with Conrad. Look at him! The poor devil was practically a shell. Women didn't appreciate the advantage they had over men. If a woman set her mind to it, she could wear out a man in no time; ultimately the man would have to cave in if the woman chose to be totally relentless in her sexual demands. She'd remembered how she'd once talked to a prostitute in the hospital after a bungled abortion. Hearing the woman talk so casually about servicing twenty or thirty customers a day fascinated her. The idea of having twenty men lined up outside her door made her knees shake, for at the time she didn't have a single suitor. Worse, she discovered that the prostitute made as much money in an hour as she did in a week. "But you've got your virtue, honey, don't forget that," the prostitute mockingly told her. For a minute or two, Amanda debated whether she should take up the sex trade, since clearly this woman didn't work half as hard as she did for her pitifully meagre wages. But there was a snag: While the prostitute was getting an abundance of what Amanda ached to receive, apparently she didn't enjoy her work. Now, years later, it occurred to Amanda that perhaps lack of enjoyment was inevitable when even the most intense of physical pleasures was turned into an eight-hour working day. What a messy, inescapable problem sex was. It was incorporated into your body at birth, and every time you looked at yourself in the mirror you beheld evidence of it; yet she hadn't ever wanted to be continent, not ever, and she still didn't. Virtue had been thrust upon her just as much as Jamie's poetic vision had been thrust onto him . . .

"Did you hear what I said, Mandy?" Hilda asked. "I said Conrad knows people interested in Kitsilano property."

"I heard you," Amanda snapped. How could Hiddie be so boorish and insistent?

"Perhaps we could defer business matters to another time," Nanda suggested.

"We have to talk about something, don't we? We can't simply sit and stare at each other." The blush on Hilda's cheekbones intensified and she decided for once to defy the restraint Nanda symbolized. "We're stuck here because Jamie was stupid enough to get himself killed by riding an old bike around, instead of driving a car like the rest of us. And I think I know why he did it. He wanted people to see him in the streets, he wanted them to recognize him as Jamie Powell the bike-riding poet."

"That's absolute nonsense, Hiddie," Amanda cried, "and you know it! Jamie rode his bike because it helped him think. I won't allow you to say he rode his bike to have people look at him. Jamie hated publicity. Ask Alice. Alice didn't even know Jamie was a well-known poet until she saw his books in a bookstore. That's true, isn't it, Alice?"

Alice replied by nodding. She hadn't spoken a word, nor moved from the chair where she sat holding Paul, since the family returned to the house. The shock of Jamie's death was so profound her milk had ceased to flow, and the woman who looked after Paul had prepared formula, which had given him chronic diarrhea. Believing the child was ill and she would be blamed for it, the nursemaid telephoned Amanda, who temporarily set aside grieving for Jamie to restore order in Alice's home. She calmed Alice, brought in the Powell family pediatrician and within twenty-four hours the little boy's condition was rectified. But Alice's milk supply did not return. She'd clutched the child she'd once wanted to abort and stared stonily at the physician as he offered advice on feeding and managing Paul, hating him almost as much as she hated the Powell family.

Alice was irrationally convinced that Jamie's family was responsible for his death because, had they left him alone and not interfered in his life, he would never have taken to riding his rattletrap bicycle around the streets of Vancouver at night. She knew that to be true, and remembered Jamie saying, as he lay against her with his head on her stomach, that he was plagued by a family who wouldn't leave him alone and that everything he did, including shacking up in his awful east-side basement suite and riding his old one-speed bike, had been done to defy his family and escape the stifling attention of his sisters. But he was at peace with her. He had told her so. Because she didn't give a hoot what he did. Hadn't he told her she was "quite splendid" when he'd watched her walking from the bed to the bathroom after they'd made love that first night? And wasn't that the first time a man had ever looked upon her as anything except a pair of over-sized tits to be pinched and squeezed? She could look at the men present in this room now and know their reaction to her was of the "pinch and squeeze" variety. Oh, how she hated all of them! Nanda McLeod too. The nerve of that woman! How dare she press a button somewhere and instantly transform a self-made woman, as Alice was, from an employee into a company vice-president! Now she could no longer boast that everything she'd accomplished in her professional life was the outcome of her own determination and hard work. But here they were, Jamie's family: four women, three men; one of them a frozen-faced sister-fucker, one a macho creep, and the other so filled with his own self-importance it was a wonder he didn't swell up with hot air and explode. She'd seen him scan her protuberances and knew exactly what he was thinking, like all other men from her uncle on down. Until Jamie showed up. She and Jamie must have been fated to meet, because from the very first moment when she'd put her backside beside his on the bench in that crap-filled art gallery she'd guessed he was someone special. And the fact they'd met again at English Bay had to be more than coincidence, didn't it? Jamie and she had been destined for each other; that's why she'd been able to work up the nerve to telephone him and ask him for dinner. If only she'd been smarter about his family, she'd have got Jamie to clear out of town with her. Why hadn't she seen the damage they were doing to him? Why? Why? Why? If only she'd been smarter, he'd still be alive. How she hated them! . . .

"Well, I've always maintained that a person has to behave sensibly, not try to be different from other people." The red had not faded from Hilda's cheeks.

"But Jamie *was* different, Hiddie," Amanda said. "He was a poet."

"Well, all I can say is —"

"For God's sake, Hiddie, what does it matter?" Amanda cried. "Jamie's dead. That's what matters. He's dead."

"I know that, Mandy. There's no need to get hysterical."

How much longer, Natasha thought, could she bear to listen to Hilda pick on Amanda? She hadn't realized until this moment how much she disliked Hilda and her crude presumptive mannerisms. Why must she sit and listen to her when all she wanted was to think about the flimsy nature of her restored relationship with David! She and David were trying so hard to carry on as though nothing had happened. But how could she return to David's arms when she saw an image of Liz behind him whenever she looked at him? And when her own arms longed for Nick Parsons? She knew Amanda would soon be telephoning her, once the shock of Jamie's death passed, smiling, probing, trying to gain entrance into the secret areas of her emotions. But she shouldn't condemn Amanda for prying, should she, because in the past she'd always welcomed Amanda's tittle-tattle about the family. She had only herself to blame, just as she was at fault for the mess she was in now. After all, she hadn't been forced to pick up Nick, or go with him to that horrible, degrading motel room. How shameful to be taken in by a man who was nothing more than a petty thief and compulsive liar! Yet Nick had said that although he'd first thought of her as another "hot pants", he'd ended by loving her so much he couldn't go on living without her. But could she believe what he said? When he'd say anything to increase her dependence on him? When he enjoyed shaming her, forcing her to feel she had to do things to please him? There was Amanda looking at her again, probably speculating how things stood between her and David. Suppose she told David every shameful thing, would it help? Would mutual absolution be followed by total reconciliation? That was how things were supposed to work with estranged couples. They talked away their guilt, absolved each other, then came together again. She'd thought of asking David whether he'd tackle the problem with her, but she couldn't bring herself to ask because he was so distant, so reserved, even at night, when he reached out in the bed and placed his hand on her breast to signal his willingness to cross the dividing line should she need him. Oh, if only she could desire David again! Then she could forget Nick Parsons and everything he represented. And forget Liz, too, and the harm she had done to her and David. Amanda once had said there was little difference between men; all were cast in the same mould and none was particularly durable. She'd always denied David was like that. But Liz thought David had special qualities too, which was why she'd shackled him and kept him prisoner. Damn her. Even as children, Liz had imperiously pushed her aside. Maybe if she became pregnant, her passion for David would return . . .

"I'm trying to persuade Mother to fly to Peru with me. Will somebody back me up? I know she'd love Lima. I've suggested trips to Machu Picchu and Cuzco. I'll be there a week on business, so if any of you would care to come along just say so. We'll use the Can-Ray jet." Stuart-Hector's smile embraced everyone, hoping his offer would introduce the sweet wind of relief into the room and drive out the stale air of funereal gloom. "I don't know about you, but I think Mother needs a change. Maybe we all do. We need to lighten up, to remind ourselves there's lots to enjoy in the world."

If Stuart-Hector wasn't so well-meaning, David thought, he'd be unbearable after ten minutes. Still, he was pretty hard to take. His only saving grace was his obvious affection for Nanda, plus the general goodwill he radiated. Which was more than could be said for what remained of the family. Any guy who was prepared to shuttle how many? eight or nine?

self-centred, preoccupied people around South America had to be either nuts, or blissfully philanthropic by nature. Not that he didn't long to get away. God, did he ever! He wanted to pack a bag and skip out, but to where? Anywhere, rather than go back to a house where Natasha tortured herself because of what she'd done and got more and more pinched in the face. Poor Tashie. He hadn't meant to deceive her, had never thought of his relationship with Liz as infidelity, because all he'd ever given her was the support she'd needed to survive. If only Natasha could understand this. After all, *he* was prepared to understand the reasons for her escapade with the bum she'd picked up. Stuart-Hector had hinted that people from Can-Ray had dealt with him. He didn't know what they'd actually done, but he knew Stuart-Hector could be ruthless, which was at odds with his general air of benevolence. Perhaps such dichotomy was possible, even necessary in corporate life: A man might smile happily and think he was acting in the best interests of those he was destroying. Nanda must know, too, what they'd done to the guy, which made it all rather frightening. He could see how they would want to protect Tashie; maybe they just pushed him around a little, slapped a thousand dollars in his hand, then told him to get lost. What would they do if they found out about Anna? Do the same to her? Surely not. After all, Anna was a respected astrophysicist, well known for the formula she'd devised for astronomers to calculate the rotary movement of binary stars. The odd thing was, Anna had approached him, shyly asking if he would be kind enough to check some calculations. He'd agreed, made a few suggestions, and ended by going to her little box of a house on Sixteenth Avenue where she lived alone. She was a tall, heavy-bodied woman, at least ten years older than himself. She told him about her life: how her father, a Hungarian physicist, met her mother, a German-Jewish physician in Paris; how they married and came to Canada in 1940 just before France capitulated to the invading Germans; how her father joined the Los Alamos atomic bomb project while her mother did locums for doctors who had joined the Canadian armed forces. Her mother passion-ately wanted a child, while her father, believing that atomic radiation would make the earth uninhabitable, refused to help bring more children into an overpopulated, polluted world. They finally compromised and Anna was the result. David liked her and recognized she was his intellectual supe-rior, that she possessed, as Jamie did, something he lacked: a touch of intuitive brilliance. It was funny, but going to bed with Anna was his only true infidelity. Not that it happened often. She'd suggested once a month, which suited him. But he enjoyed the relationship (Liz found out and was furious, though there wasn't much she could do except sulk for a couple of weeks) because physically Anna was so different from Natasha and Liz. She was ivory-skinned and her spine and belly mantled with a soft black down. Before going to bed she released her plaited hair, which fascinated him, because it reached her waist and moved over her shoulders like a rippling cloak. There was another aspect to his relationship with Anna: culture. She was a passable pianist, went to concerts, plays, poetry readings, events David seldom attended. She knew of and admired Jamie's work, but did not request an introduction. She had once suggested that the geometric patterns in Jamie's poems might be of greater significance than their content. It was possible, she explained to a polite but sceptical David, that the forms were a runic language being utilized by someone, or something, to send messages, and that Jamie, during periods of mystical insight, upon seeing the forms bouncing among the stars, filled them with words. He must not forget, she solemnly informed David, that the English poet William Blake had conversed with angels. She also liked wine, and sometimes drank too much. By inclination, David was temperate and found her behaviour when tipsy embarrassing. Knowing this, she would first mock, then deride him, contemptuously saying he was a stupid man so abysmally ignorant of the arts he couldn't distinguish between Mahler and Wagner and thought Rainer Maria Rilke was a Nazi general. To David, Anna's bouts of contempt revealed what she truly thought of him, and afterwards he would leave the house determined never to return. His resolution always crumbled when she telephoned the next day to apologize and say (as Liz had) how much she depended upon him. What could he do? It had been the same with Liz when she first invited him to her bed. And Natasha had been the same, too, when she tracked him down in Chalk River. A wave of anger surged through him as he thought of the way these women had pursued him and willfully imposed themselves on him, then pretended he was responsible for what happened afterwards and made it appear he was the one who had pursued them. Of course he couldn't deny he'd been delighted when Natasha showed up in Chalk River. She was so beautiful, so exquisitely put together. He almost laughed aloud when he remembered how he'd worried lest his weight would hurt her breasts. He ought to have known even then that a woman's body has greater resilience than a man's. Lord! How the odour of their prolonged love-making in the dingy room had filled his nostrils. How they had gone at it time after time. He wanted to cross the room and ask her now if she remembered how they had sat in the ghastly old brown-stained bathtub and washed each other, how they bravely said, after Natasha discovered she was pregnant, that they would marry, even if the family disapproved. He wished he could shout across the room and ask her if she remembered all the hours, over all the years, she had spent lying on the couch with her head in his lap, raising her legs so he could admire them and be tempted by the triangular shadow beneath her panties. Remember, Natasha? he wanted to shout. Remember, it's better to forgive than to foster hatred and lose everything of value you've gained. He could not bear to sit any longer in a room with people who knew so much about him and probably felt nothing but contempt for him . . .

"David!" Natasha called as he left his chair and hurried from the room. "David!" She sprang up and followed him.

"If you ask me," Hilda pronounced, "those two are heading for disaster."

"I'll see." Amanda left the room trailed by Annabelle and a sleepy Christopher. She carefully opened the front door and peered out to observe David and Natasha standing by their car. Amanda thought both were crying. As Amanda watched, Natasha reached out to clutch David and he responded by convulsively embracing and kissing her. Then they got into the car and drove away.

Amanda smiled, closed the door and said to her children, "We'll go in a few minutes."

"Can we go to the White Spot for dinner?" Annabelle asked.

"If you want." They returned to the living room.

"Where are Natasha and David?" Hilda asked.

"I think —" Amanda paused to create suspense. "I think — they're rushing home to make up for lost time. And I'm going home too." She gestured at her children."They're exhausted."

"You shouldn't have brought them," Hilda said.

"Yours are here."

Why was it, Hilda thought, that members of her family disagreed with her sensible observations? Couldn't Amanda see that Louise, Jeanette and Max Junior knew how to behave in public? Look at the way Annabelle slouched on the chair with her skirt up so everybody could see her underclothes. Of course it wasn't too surprising. Amanda had always been sloppy, right from the time she was a kid when she used to take off her underpants and run around exposing her bottom to the world. She hasn't changed one bit. She was devious and two-faced too! She'd agree with everything you said, then go behind your back and tell a bunch of lies about you. Amanda wasn't forthright, like herself. She could always be counted on to be straightforward. Her clients knew that. "You're always so practical and forthright," they would say. You had to let people know where you stood, it was only fair. And her clients appreciated her openness. "You're so brutally frank about everything, Hilda," they told her. Oh, at first some might not like her style, but eventually they came to appreciate it, because they knew they could rely on her to speak honestly about their investments. Those who wanted sweet-talk soon left. Just as well, she got along fine without them. But she'd need to smarten Conrad up. Oh, she knew how the family felt about him, but in having him she had more than the others did. Amanda had nobody; Nanda was like a piece of dry kindling that's sat in the basement for ten years; and as for Liz, well, she didn't want to think about what Liz had done. Disgusting. Just to think of what Liz and David did together sickened her. David looked like he'd be on the straight and narrow, like a church minister. You'd think he'd puke at the idea of what he did with Liz. Max looked like butter wouldn't melt in his mouth, but all a woman had to do was stand beside him and he'd start feeling her up. That's how she'd met Max: He was standing behind her in the elevator. She was so mad she chased him along the hall, but all he said was: "I couldn't resist, baby. You're so darn cute." And she fell for it. Mind you, she made sure they were married before she let him into her bed. Amanda thought that she was straight-laced about sex, but she was as much a woman as Amanda was. She just didn't believe in talking about it, but she'd wager she got as much out of a man as Amanda did, though Conrad seemed to be slowing down. Max would have been slowing down too if he'd lived. Funny about some men, always out to prove themselves. That's how Max was. Oh, she knew how he bragged of all the beds he got into, but most of it was just talk. And she didn't care what Amanda thought about Max. She knew that he'd never touched Louise or Jeanette, except to kiss them like any father. He'd adored them from the minute they were born. She had to laugh at Max because he couldn't get over the fact that his baby girls had every part of an adult female's body. Some men are so ignorant about women's bodies! That's why he insisted on transforming his girls into miniature women, dressing them in frilly underwear and expensive dresses. She wished he'd put the money he spent taking them out for champagne lunches into a savings account. The girls miss him. Amanda thinks the girl are hiding something nasty Max did to them, but that's only a concoction of her putrid little mind. She must speak to Stuart-Hector about getting Max Junior into one of the better schools in Ontario. Maybe the girls too. And Nanda should be doing more for Jeanette and Louise. She helped us out when they landed on queer street after Max went. Maybe she should call on Nanda next week and remind her of her family responsibilities. She's getting old and absent-minded and probably needs direction. And she must get onto Amanda about her property. Conrad needs a few commissions . . .

"Mother?" Stuart-Hector said, looking suggestively at the doorway. "Yes, dear." Nanda smiled at him. She wished Stuart-Hector wouldn't try to organize her. And surely he must know she had no intention of going to Peru; the mere thought of being cooped up in an airplane with Hilda was revolting. She had no intention of going anywhere, except home. Poor Alice: She's so withdrawn, so closed off from what's going on around her. She wants us to leave because we interfere with her need to hold onto memories of Jamie. She wants to implant living, warm thoughts of Jamie in her memory so that she can take them out at night and feel him lying beside her. Waking up in the darkness aware of Stuart beside her was almost the best part of her own marriage, so comforting. She wondered if Alice had reached out in the night to touch Jamie. She'd like to tell Alice that such memories never leave a person, but she would probably think she was a prying old woman, sticking her nose where it wasn't wanted. And she'd like to tell Alice that Jamie hadn't stopped believing in himself. Though it was next to impossible to know what people are really thinking and feeling; maybe she didn't care about that. Take Stuart-Hector, was he truly fond of her? Or did he see only her wealth? No, no, that wasn't fair, she mustn't denigrate her son's affection for her. She was sure it was genuine; it was his pompous manner that made what he said seem insincere. She was sure his offer to shuttle everyone off to Peru was well intentioned. She must remember to tell him she appreciated it. She'd like to leave now, but as the oldest member of the Powell family she was obligated to stay. She must speak to Alice before she left. Tell her how hard Dad worked to get the title her baby son now carries. Jamie had contemptuously rejected it, but for Dad, the title was proof he wasn't just one among the ruck of men who lived, died and was promptly forgotten. No, Dad would be remembered. Among all the Toms, Harrys and Jacks who'd ever lived, there'd be only one Hector Powell. There'll never be another Jamie Powell either, though she didn't think there was anything particularly unique about herself. Her kind were a dime a dozen. Her abiding ignorance! Her ignorance of herself, of other people; and, now, in her old age, she seemed to understand less than she had as a child. Perhaps the aging process compounds ignorance. Now, all she had was her protective shell of pretence and the assumptions people made about her. Was it possible that she once had the same capacity to be as intelligent as Annabelle appeared to be? Was it possible she might have developed her intellect more if that had been permitted? As it was, she'd been allowed only to be responsive to the needs of her father and brother, and later to the needs of the men with whom she had cohabited. That word "cohabit": It had always fascinated her and she

knew why, too. She'd been three, maybe four, while walking with her father one afternoon. She'd run ahead to hide behind some gorse bushes,
planning to jump out to surprise him, but when she got to the bushes she'd
seen a man and woman lying on the ground and the woman was wriggling
out of her pink knickers. She rushed back to her father, who walked forward and peered into the bushes, then whispered (she could still hear his
voice): "Shh, sweetheart, they're cohabiting." Until she'd checked the meaning of the word in a dictionary years later, she'd thought "cohabitating"
meant pulling off one's underwear. But why was she now remembering
Dad whispering the word to her? Oh yes. She was recalling the strictures
that had been placed on her; contrasting herself as a child with Annabelle.
Amanda's children think the world of her. They always lie up against her.
Frances liked to do that too: She'd wrap her arms around my neck, put her
nose up against mine, then tell me everything about herself, what she'd
done that day, how she felt, what she'd seen that was interesting or trouble-
some. Even Tashie didn't do that. She mustn't forget to speak to Alice
before she left; she would ask her to visit and bring Paul. She must do
something for Hilda's girls. It's a pity they can't be separated from Hilda
for a while. They're so repressed, without charm. They never seem to enjoy themselves. Does Hilda ever stop to consider what she's doing to them?
What's that Alice is saying . . . ?

Alice stood in the middle of the room, the rest watching her, apparently unable to grasp what she was saying. "I'm going," she said.
"Leaving."

"Going?" Amanda echoed. "Are you going to put Paul to bed?"

"No. I'm getting out of this place." They looked at her, unable to believe the bald statement. "I never wanted to get mixed up with you. I never
wanted to come to this house. I only came here because Jamie asked me
to. He's dead, so I'm leaving."

"But Alice . . ." Amanda jumped up and went towards her.

"Stay away from me. I won't listen to you any more. Stay away." She
flipped a hand towards Amanda as though to fend her off, then left the
room, followed by Amanda, the others trailing. In the hall, Alice placed
the baby on a chair and yelled: "Stay away!" when Amanda moved toward
him. Alice put on a jacket, then picked up a suitcase and handbag.

"Where are you going, Alice?" Amanda asked. "Please. You must tell
us where you're going."

"I don't have to tell you a thing. I don't owe you anything." She looked
at the group assembled by the living room door. "Wait a bit. I *will* tell you
something. The reason I'm getting out of here is to prevent you from getting your hands on my boy."

"But Alice," Amanda pleaded, "no one will touch Paul. This is his home, and yours too."

"It isn't. It's yours."

"But you're Jamie's wife, so it comes to you and Paul."

"Well, I don't want it, and I don't want my son to have it either. Get away," she said to Gurdev who had come forward to take her suitcase and open the door. "I can carry my own stuff." She tucked the baby under her right arm, and clasping her suitcase and handbag, marched from the house to the little red Honda parked under the porte cochère. Amanda, hands extended, followed, while the rest of the family advanced to cluster together on the front steps, children in front, as though poising for a family photograph. When Amanda neared the car she saw the back seat was filled with plastic shopping bags stuffed with Alice's and Paul's clothes. Alice strapped her son into a carrier on the passenger seat, rammed the suitcase into the back, got into the driver's seat and started the motor.

"Alice," Amanda began, "I know you don't think much of me."

"You're right about that," Alice agreed, "though you're no worse than the others."

"But Alice —" The car began to move and Amanda placed a restraining hand on it. "Please, Alice, tell me where you're going. Then I won't have to worry about you and Paul. Alice, please. Please."

"If I told you, you'd be on my doorstep tomorrow."

"I promise, I won't. I promise, Alice." Desperate, Amanda moved until she was standing in front of the car. "Alice, the house and everything in it is yours. Doesn't that mean anything?"

"I don't want it. I just want to be left alone. You get it? I want to be left alone." Alice put the car into gear and nudged Amanda who buckled, then jumped back to avoid falling. "Goddamn it!" Alice shouted. "Goddamn you!" She thrust the car into reverse, backed out, turned the car, bumped into Hilda's Mercedes, straightened the front wheels, then took off down the drive to vanish into passing traffic.

"I tried! I did my best!" Amanda wailed as the others left the steps and hurried over to her. "I said everything I could think of to get her to stay, but she wouldn't. She had all her and Paul's things in the car. Where will she go? What will she do?"

"Now, now." Stuart-Hector patted Amanda's shoulders reassuringly. "We'll find Alice. We're experts at locating resources, including human ones."

"I'll bet you couldn't find a needle in a haystack," Annabelle piped up.

"Want to bet ten dollars on it?" He grinned at Annabelle, tantalizing her.

"I don't believe in gambling. It's obloxious."

"That's just as well, because you'd lose your bet. Haven't you heard of metal detectors?" He raised mocking eyebrows.

Annabelle ignored Stuart-Hector, and once more asked Amanda if they might leave.

"Yes, yes. I'll get our coats." Amanda was very upset. "Stuart-Hector, promise you'll telephone me the minute you find out anything."

"You bet, Mandy. I'll call first thing."

Amanda looked at him with tear-filled eyes. "I never thought Alice'd do that. Never. She must have packed everything in the car before we went to Paradise Island. I can't believe she'd be so underhanded. After all, she has a baby to look after." She pushed past him and followed by Annabelle went into the house to collect their coats.

———

Six months passed, then one morning shortly after Chris and Annabelle had left for school Amanda's phone rang. "I told you we'd find Alice, didn't I, Mandy?" Stuart-Hector's voice was, as usual, cheerful and reassuring.

"Where is she?"

"It proved to be a bit of a problem because she's not in Canada."

"She's in the United States? Where? In Seattle?"

"No. She's in England."

"England!"

"In a small town not far from —"

"Hyndhurst!" Amanda shrieked. "I should have guessed!"

"She's rented a house there. And she's using the name Lady Alice Powell."

"No! Lady Alice and Lord Paul! But how did you find her?"

"I assumed that eventually she'd get in touch with Bill Jeffries — he's handling Jamie's estate. She wants money."

"How clever of you," Amanda breathed into the phone.

"Just logical. She's instructed Jeffries to sell the Vancouver house and Grandfather's house in Hyndhurst."

"Liz's house! Mom's house! Oh no, she mustn't do that."

"They're hers. But not to worry, Mandy." Stuart-Hector liked his plump, sentimental cousin; she let a man know she appreciated what he did. "I've spoken with Mother and she's instructed me to make Jeffries offers on both houses."

"That's wonderful. But listen, Stuart-Hector . . . ask Nanda if I could buy Liz's place. I can manage it if I sell a couple of my Kitsilano properties."

"You bet, if that's what you want. Or you and Mother could split the costs down the middle."

"No. I'd prefer to have Liz's place myself. Everything included."

"Sure thing. Furniture, dishes, everything included."

"You'll see to it right away?"

"I'll give Jeffries a dingle the minute we hang up."

"I mean, if Paul comes back to Vancouver when he's older, then the house'd be there, won't it? And we'll be there too."

Stuart-Hector laughed. "I'm sure you'll be on hand, Mandy. I'll be in touch." Amanda heard the click at the other end, then did a little jig around the kitchen table before dialling Natasha's number. "Tashie, I've got some really exciting news. You'll never guess! Are you ready? Alice is . . . Guess where? No. That's what I said when Stuart-Hector called. No. She's in England. Yes, in Hyndhurst . . . calling herself Lady Alice Powell. And listen, Tashie . . . No, no. It'd be better if I came over to your place. What? You are! Oh, that's wonderful, Tashie. Just wonderful. Listen . . . I have to come over so we can talk and talk. No, I must tell you right now. Alice is selling Liz's house, and Grandfather's too. Your mother's going to buy Grandfather's and I'll buy Liz's. No, no. I'll explain everything. I'll just dash to the bathroom, grab my coat and come straight over."

For the first time since Jamie's death Amanda hummed and smiled to herself. Now she knew exactly what she would do: She would move into Liz's house, and what's more, she would do her best to persuade Natasha to come and live with her. She wouldn't have to worry about what David wanted because Natasha was the boss now and he'd do whatever she decided. Natasha really had him under her thumb. Yes, she and Natasha and David would settle in the Big House with the six children and the baby. There'd be ample room. They'd have marvellous Christmas and birthday parties, just like the Powell family in the past. It would be so wonderful. They'd really settle down. And one day Alice would get tired of England and all its pretensions, and she and Paul would come back to live with them. Oh, she could hardly wait for it all to happen. Everything was going to work out.

Amanda drove the car into the circular driveway, turned off the motor and ran inside the house, calling, "Tashie! Tashie! I have the most wonderful plan! I can hardly wait to tell you. We can get the family together again! And we'll all be so happy!"

L I T E R A T U R E

O n - L i n e

Battle Street Books invites you to download
a selection of Langford's novels, short stories and plays on
the INTERNET in the spirit of *Shareware.*
Here is a sample of what is available:

N o v e l s

The Kingdom of Chombuk

Read the adventures of Crumbthorpe Knottley, funeral director from
Sweet Springs, Saskatchewan, who gets lost in the fog while flying his
plane and discovers *The Kingdom of Chombuk.*

Innocence

Teenager Mary grows up believing if she does what her parents say
she'll have a happy life. But experience destroys her beliefs, and
bitterness replaces hope. She tries to erase painful memories by setting
fire to buildings. When that doesn't help, she travels into the dense bush
of northwest coastal B.C. to make her final escape.

P l a y s

The Perforated Encyclopedia

A lonely woman meets a salesman peddling the ultimate encyclopedia.

The Snake

Guided by his talisman, a bank teller first gains, then loses a fortune.

S h o r t S t o r i e s

The Potlatch and Other Stories

Stories that reveal ways non-aboriginal people interacted with First
Nations people in British Columbia in the 1950s and 1960s.

V I S I T

L I T E R A T U R E O n - L i n e

Our **INTERNET** address is: http://www.netshop.net/BSB/

Book Disk

Order the *Necessities of Life Book Disk* (WordPerfect 5.1/5.2) which can be read on IBM and Macintosh computers. If you are a Macintosh user, you require an Apple Superdrive and the Apple File exchange program. To read the files, use a word processing program such as WordPerfect, Microsoft Word, or Claris Works.

Price: $12.95 plus $2.00 handling charge. (Add 7% sales tax if you are a B.C. resident.)

Send disk to: (please print)

Name:

Address:

City:

Province/State:

Postal/Zip Code:

Please enclose cheque or
money order, payable to:
Langford Publishing Services
175 Battle Street, Kamloops, BC
Canada V2C 2L1

About the Author

Ernest Langford was born in England. He came to Canada as a young man and lived for a while in Ontario before moving to B.C. to earn his living as a full-time writer. He now lives in Kamloops, B.C. with his wife and keeps in close contact with his children and grandchildren in Canada, the United States and South America.

Langford is both novelist and playwright. He has written numerous scripts for stage, radio and television. *The Explorers: Charting the Canadian Wilderness*, a textbook, is used in Canadian classrooms. Five novels, two collections of short stories, and several short dramas have been published on the Internet. The novels include: *Funlandia, The Kingdom of Chombuk, Innocence, Valley of Shadows,* and *The Ten-Bible Secret.*